D0188341

A prolific author of more than one hundred books, **Diana Palmer** got her start as a newspaper reporter. A *New York Times* bestselling author and voted one of the top ten romance writers in America, she has a gift for telling the most sensual tales with charm and humor. Diana lives with her family in Cornelia, Georgia. Visit her website at dianapalmer.com.

USA TODAY bestselling author **Delores Fossen** has sold over seventy novels with millions of copies of her books in print worldwide. She's received the Booksellers' Best Award, the RT Reviewers' Choice Award and was a finalist for the prestigious RITA® Award. In addition, she's had nearly a hundred short stories and articles published in national magazines. You can contact the author through her webpage at deloresfossen.com.

New York Times Bestselling Author

DIANA PALMER

LIONHEARTED

HARLEQUIN
BESTSELLING
AUTHOR
COLLECTION

**HARLEQUIN®
BESTSELLING
AUTHOR
COLLECTION**

Recycling programs
for this product may
not exist in your area.

ISBN-13: 978-1-335-00821-3

Lionhearted
First published as Lionhearted in 2002. This edition published in 2023.
Copyright © 2002 by Diana Palmer

Christmas Guardian
First published in 2009. This edition published in 2023.
Copyright © 2009 by Delores Fossen

Harlequin Enterprises ULC
22 Adelaide St. West, 41st Floor
Toronto, Ontario M5H 4E3, Canada
www.Harlequin.com

Printed in U.S.A.

CONTENTS

Visit her Author Profile page at Harlequin.com,
or dianapalmer.com, for more titles!

LIONHEARTED

Diana Palmer

To the FAO Schwarz gang on Peachtree Road, Atlanta,
and at the Internet Customer Service Department.
Thanks!

PROLOGUE

LEO HART FELT alone in the world. The last of his bachelor brothers, Rey, had gotten married and moved out of the house almost a year ago. That left Leo, alone, with an arthritic housekeeper who came in two days a week and threatened to retire every day. If she did, Leo would be left without a biscuit to his name, or even a hope of getting another one unless he went to a restaurant every morning for breakfast. Considering his work schedule, that was impractical.

He leaned back in the swivel chair at his desk in the office he now shared with no one. He was happy for his brothers. Most of them had families now, except newly married Rey. Simon and Tira had two little boys. Cag and Tess had a boy. Corrigan and Dorie had a boy and a baby girl. When he looked back, Leo realized that women had been a missing commodity in his life of late. It was late September. Roundup was just over, and there had been so much going on at the ranch, with business, that he'd hardly had time for a night out. He was feeling it.

Even as he considered his loneliness, the phone rang.

"Why don't you come over for supper?" Rey asked when he picked up the receiver.

"Listen," Leo drawled, grinning, "you don't invite your brother over to dinner on your honeymoon."

"We got married after Christmas last year," Rey pointed out.

"Like I said, you're still on your honeymoon," came the amused reply. "Thanks. But I've got too much to do."

"Work doesn't make up for a love life."

"You'd know," Leo chuckled.

"Okay. But the invitation's open, whenever you want to accept it."

"Thanks. I mean it."

"Sure."

The line went dead. Leo put the receiver down and stretched hugely, bunching the hard muscles in his upper arms. He was the boss as much as his brothers on their five ranch properties, but he did a lot of the daily physical labor that went with cattle raising, and his tall, powerful body was evidence of it. He wondered sometimes if he didn't work that hard to keep deep-buried needs at bay. In his younger days, women had flocked around him, and he hadn't been slow to accept sensual invitations. But he was in his thirties now, and casual interludes were no longer satisfying.

He'd planned to have a quiet weekend at home, but Marilee Morgan, a close friend of Janie Brewster's, had cajoled him into taking her up to Houston for dinner and to see a ballet she had tickets for. He was partial to ballet, and Marilee explained that she couldn't drive herself because her car was in the shop. She was easy on the eyes, and she was sophisticated. Not that Leo was tempted to let himself be finagled into any sort of intimacy with her. He didn't want her carrying tales of his private life to Janie, who had an obvious and uncomfortable crush on him.

He knew that Marilee would never have asked him to take her any place in Jacobsville, Texas, because it was a small town and news of the date would inevitably get back to Janie. It might help show the girl that Leo was a free agent, but it wouldn't help his friendship with Fred Brewster to know that Leo was playing fast and loose with Janie's best friend. Some best friend, he thought privately.

But taking Marilee out would have one really good consequence—it would get him out of a dinner date at the Brewsters' house. He and Fred Brewster were friends and business associates, and he enjoyed the time he spent with the older man. Well, except for two members of his family, he amended darkly. He didn't like Fred's sister, Lydia. She was a busybody who had highfalutin ideas. Fortunately, she was hardly ever around and she didn't live with Fred. He had mixed feelings about Fred's daughter, Janie, who was twenty-one and bristling with psychology advice after her graduation from a junior college in that subject. She'd made Cag furious with her analyses of his food preferences, and Leo was becoming adept at avoiding invitations that would put him in her line of fire.

Not that she was bad looking. She had long, thick light brown hair and a neat little figure. But she also had a crush on Leo, which was very visible. He considered her totally unacceptable as a playmate for a man his age, and he knocked back her attempts at flirting with lazy skill. He'd known her since she was ten and wearing braces on her teeth. It was hard to get that image out of his mind.

Besides, she couldn't cook. Her rubber chicken dinners were infamous locally, and her biscuits could be classified as lethal weapons.

Thinking about those biscuits made him pick up the phone and dial Marilee.

She was curt when she picked up the phone, but the minute he spoke, her voice softened.

"Well, hello, Leo," she said huskily.

"What time do you want me to pick you up Saturday night?"

There was a faint hesitation. "You won't, uh, mention this to Janie?"

"I have as little contact with Janie as I can. You know that," he said impatiently.

"Just checking," she teased, but she sounded worried. "I'll be ready to leave about six."

"Suppose I pick you up at five and we'll have supper in Houston before the ballet?"

"Wonderful! I'll look forward to it. See you then."

"See you."

He hung up, but picked up the receiver again and dialed the Brewsters' number.

As luck would have it, Janie answered.

"Hi, Janie," he said pleasantly.

"Hi, Leo," she replied breathlessly. "Want to talk to Dad?"

"You'll do," he replied. "I have to cancel for dinner Saturday. I've got a date."

There was the faintest pause. It was almost imperceptible. "I see."

"Sorry, but it's a long-standing one," he lied. "I can't get out of it. I forgot when I accepted your dad's invitation. Can you give him my apologies?"

"Of course," she told him. "Have a good time."

She sounded strange. He hesitated. "Something wrong?" he asked.

"Nothing at all! Nice talking to you, Leo. Bye."

Janie Brewster hung up and closed her eyes, sick with disappointment. She'd planned a perfect menu. She'd practiced all week on a special chicken dish that was tender and succulent. She'd practiced an exquisite crème brûlée as well, which was Leo's favorite dessert. She could even use the little tool to caramelize the sugar topping, which had taken a while to perfect. All that work, and for nothing. She'd have been willing to bet that Leo hadn't had a date for that night already. He'd made one deliberately, to get out of the engagement.

She sat down beside the hall table, her apron almost stiff with flour, her face white with dustings of it, her hair disheveled. She was anything but the picture of a perfect date. And wasn't it just her luck? For the past year, she'd mounted a real campaign to get Leo to notice her. She'd flirted with him shamelessly at Micah Steele's wedding to Callie Kirby, until a stabbing scowl had turned her shy. It had angered him that she'd caught the bouquet Callie had thrown. It had embarrassed her that he glared so angrily at her. Months later, she'd tried, shyly, every wile she had on him, with no success. She couldn't cook and she was not much more than a fashion plate, according to her best friend, Marilee, who was trying to help her catch Leo. Marilee had plenty of advice, things Leo had mentioned that he didn't like about Janie, and Janie was trying her best to improve in the areas he'd mentioned. She was even out on the ranch for the first time in her life, trying to get used to horses and cattle and dust and dirt. But if she couldn't get Leo to the house to show him her new skills, she didn't have a lot of hope.

"Who was that on the phone?" Hettie, their house-keeper, called from the staircase. "Was it Mr. Fred?"

"No. It was Leo. He can't come Saturday night. He's got a date."

"Oh." Hettie smiled sympathetically. "There will be other dinners, darlin'."

"Of course there will," Janie said and smiled back. She got out of the chair. "Well, I'll just make it for you and me and Dad," she said, with disappointment plain in her voice.

"It isn't as if Leo has any obligation to spend his weekends with us, just because he does a lot of business with Mr. Fred," Hettie reminded her gently. "He's a good man. A little old for you, though," she added hesitantly.

Janie didn't answer her. She just smiled and walked back into the kitchen.

LEO SHOWERED, SHAVED, dressed to the hilt and got into the new black Lincoln sports car he'd just bought. Next year's model, and fast as lightning. He was due for a night on the town. And missing Janie's famous rubber chicken wasn't going to disappoint him one bit.

His conscience did nag him, though, oddly. Maybe it was just hearing Janie's friend, Marilee, harp on the girl all the time. In the past week, she'd started telling him some disturbing things that Janie had said about him.

He was going to have to be more careful around Janie. He didn't want her to get the wrong idea. He had no interest in her at all. She was just a kid.

He glanced in the lighted mirror over the steering wheel before he left the sprawling Hart Ranch. He had thick blond-streaked brown hair, a broad forehead, a slightly crooked nose and high cheekbones. But his teeth were good and strong, and he had a square jaw and a nice wide mouth. He wasn't all that handsome, but compared to most of his brothers, he was a hunk. He chuckled at that rare conceit and closed the mirror. He was rich enough that his looks didn't matter.

He didn't fool himself that Marilee would have found him all that attractive without his bankroll. But she was pretty and he didn't mind taking her to Houston and showing her off, like the fishing trophies he displayed on the walls of his study. A man had to have his little vanities, he told himself. But he thought about Janie's disappointment when he didn't show up for supper, her pain if she ever found out her best friend was stabbing her in the back, and he hated the guilt he felt.

He put on his seat belt, put the car in gear, and took off down the long driveway. He didn't have any reason to feel guilty, he told himself firmly. He was a bachelor, and he'd never done one single thing to give Janie Brewster the impression that he wanted to be the man in her life. Besides, he'd been on his own too long. A cultural evening in Houston was just the thing to cure the blues.

CHAPTER ONE

LEO HART WAS half out of humor. It had been a long week as it was, and now he was faced with trying to comfort his neighbor, Fred Brewster, who'd just lost the prize young Salers bull that Leo had wanted to buy. The bull was the offspring of a grand champion whose purchase had figured largely in Leo's improved cross-breeding program. He felt as sad as Fred seemed to.

"He was fine yesterday," Fred said heavily, wiping sweat off his narrow brow as the two men surveyed the bull in the pasture. The huge creature was lying dead on its side, not a mark on it. "I'm not the only rancher who's ever lost a prize bull, but these are damned suspicious circumstances."

"They are," Leo agreed grimly, his dark eyes surveying the bull. "It's just a thought, but you haven't had a problem with an employee, have you? Christabel Gaines said they just had a bull die of unknown causes. This happened after they fired a man named Jack Clark a couple of weeks ago. He's working for Duke Wright now, driving a cattle truck."

"Judd Dunn said it wasn't unknown causes that killed the bull, it was bloat. Judd's a Texas Ranger," Fred reminded him. "If there was sabotage on the ranch he co-owns with Christabel, I think he'd know it. No,

Christabel had that young bull in a pasture with a lot of clover and she hadn't primed him on hay or tannin-containing forage beforehand. She won't use antibiotics, either, which would have helped prevent trouble. Even so, you can treat bloat if you catch it in time. It was bad luck that they didn't check that pasture, but Christabel's shorthanded and she's back at the vocational school full-time, too. Not much time to check on livestock."

"They had four other bulls that were still alive," Leo pointed out, scowling.

Fred shrugged. "Maybe they didn't like clover, or weren't in the same pasture." He shook his head. "I'm fairly sure their bull died of bloat. That's what Judd thinks, anyway. He says Christabel's unsettled by having those movie people coming next month to work out a shooting schedule on the ranch and she's the only one who thinks there was foul play." Fred rubbed a hand through his silver hair. "But to answer your question—yes, I did wonder about a disgruntled ex-employee, but I haven't fired anybody in over two years. So you can count out vengeance. And it wasn't bloat. My stock gets antibiotics."

"Don't say that out loud," Leo chuckled. "If the Tremaynes hear you, there'll be a fight."

"It's my ranch. I run it my way." Fred looked sadly toward the bull again. He was having financial woes the likes of which he'd never faced. He was too proud to tell Leo the extent of it. "This bull is a hell of a loss right now, too, with my breeding program under way. He wasn't insured, so I can't afford to replace him. Well, not just yet," he amended, because he didn't want Leo to think he was nearly broke.

"That's one problem we can solve," Leo replied. "I've got that beautiful Salers bull I bought two years ago, but it's time I replaced him. I'd have loved to have had yours, but while I'm looking for a replacement, you can borrow mine for your breeding season."

"Leo, I can't let you do that," Fred began, overwhelmed by the offer. He knew very well what that bull's services cost.

Leo held up a big hand and grinned. "Sure you can. I've got an angle. I get first pick of your young bulls next spring."

"You devil, you," Fred said, chuckling. "All right, all right. On that condition, I'll take him and be much obliged. But I'd feel better if there was a man sitting up with him at night to guard him."

Leo stretched sore muscles, pushing his Stetson back over his blond-streaked brown hair. It was late September, but still very hot in Jacobsville, which was in southeastern Texas. He'd been helping move bulls all morning, and he was tired. "We can take care of security for him," Leo said easily. "I've got two cowboys banged up in accidents who can't work cattle. They're still on my payroll, so they can sit over here and guard my bull while they recuperate."

"And we'll feed them," Fred said.

Leo chuckled. "Now that's what I call a real nice solution. One of them," he confided, "eats for three men."

"I won't mind." His eyes went back to the still bull one more time. "He was the best bull, Leo. I had so many hopes for him."

"I know. But there are other champion-sired Salers bulls," Leo said.

"Sure. But not one like that one." He gestured toward the animal. "He had such beautiful conformation—" He broke off as a movement to one side caught his attention. He turned, leaned forward and then gaped at his approaching daughter. "Janie?" he asked, as if he wasn't sure of her identity.

Janie Brewster had light brown hair and green eyes. She'd tried going blond once, but these days her hair was its natural color. Straight, thick and sleek, it hung to her waist. She had a nice figure, a little on the slender side, and pretty little pert breasts. She even had nice legs. But anyone looking at her right now could be forgiven for mistaking her for a young bull rider.

She was covered with mud from head to toe. Even her hair was caked with it. She had a saddle over one thin shoulder, leaning forward to take its weight. The separation between her boots and jeans was imperceptible. Her blouse and arms were likewise. Only her eyes were visible, her eyebrows streaked where the mud had been haphazardly wiped away.

"Hi, Daddy," she muttered as she walked past them with a forced smile. "Hi, Leo. Nice day."

Leo's dark eyes were wide-open, like Fred's. He couldn't even manage words. He nodded, and kept gaping at the mud doll walking past.

"What have you been doing?" Fred shouted after his only child.

"Just riding around," she said gaily.

"Riding around," Fred murmured to himself as she trailed mud onto the porch and stopped there, calling for their housekeeper. "I can't remember the last time I saw her on a horse," he added.

"Neither can I," Leo was forced to admit.

Fred shook his head. "She has these spells lately," he said absently. "First it was baling hay. She went out with four of the hands and came home covered in dust and thorns. Then she took up dipping cattle." He cleared his throat. "Better to forget that altogether. Now it's riding. I don't know what the hell's got into her. She was all geared up to transfer to a four-year college and get on with her psychology degree. Then all of a sudden, she announces that she's going to learn ranching." He threw up his hands. "I'll never understand children. Will you?" he asked Leo.

Leo chuckled. "Don't ask me. Fatherhood is one role in life I have no desire to play. Listen, about my bull," he continued. "I'll have him trucked right over, and the men will come with him. If you have any more problems, you just let me know."

Fred was relieved. The Harts owned five ranches. Nobody had more clout than they did, politically and financially. The loan of that bull would help him recoup his losses and get back on his feet. Leo was a gentleman. "I'm damned grateful, Leo. We've been having hard times lately."

Leo only smiled. He knew that the Brewsters were having a bad time financially. He and Fred had swapped and traded bulls for years—although less expensive ones than Fred's dead Salers bull—and they frequently did business together. He was glad he could help.

He did wonder about Janie's odd behavior. She'd spent weeks trying to vamp him with low-cut blouses and dresses. She was always around when he came to see Fred on business, waiting in the living room in a seductive pose. Not that Janie even knew how to be seductive, he told himself amusedly. She was twenty-one, but hardly in the class with her friend Marilee Morgan, who was only four years older than Janie but could give Mata Hari lessons in seduction.

He wondered if Marilee had been coaching her in tomboyish antics. That would be amusing, because lately Marilee had been using Janie's tactics on him. The former tomboy-turned-debutante had even finagled him into taking her out to eat in Houston. He wondered if Janie knew. Sometimes friends could become your worst enemy, he thought. Luckily Janie only had a crush on him, which would wear itself out all the faster once she knew he had gone out with her best friend. Janie was far too young for him, and not only in age. The sooner she realized it, the better. Besides, he didn't like her new competitive spirit. Why was she trying to compete with her father in ranch management all of a sudden? Was it a liberation thing? She'd never shown any such inclination before, and her new appearance was appalling. The one thing Leo had admired about her was the elegance and sophistication with which she dressed. Janie in muddy jeans was a complete turnoff.

He left Fred at the pasture and drove back to the ranch, his mind already on ways and means to find out what had caused that healthy bull's sudden demise.

JANIE WAS LISTENING to their housekeeper's tirade through the bathroom door.

"I'll clean it all up, Hettie," she promised. "It's just dirt. It will come out."

"It's red mud! It will never come out!" Hettie was

grumbling. "You'll be red from head to toe forever! People will mistake you for that nineteenth-century Kiowa, Satanta, who painted everything he owned red, even his horse!"

Janie laughed as she stripped off the rest of her clothes and stepped into the shower. Besides being a keen student of Western history, Hettie was all fire and wind, and she'd blow out soon. She was such a sweetheart. Janie's mother had died years ago, leaving behind Janie and her father and Hettie—and Aunt Lydia who lived in Jacobsville. Fortunately, Aunt Lydia only visited infrequently. She was so very house-proud, so clothes-conscious, so debutante! She was just like Janie's late mother, in fact, who had raised Janie to be a little flower blossom in a world of independent, strong women. She spared a thought for her mother's horror if she could have lived long enough to see what her daughter had worn at college. There, where she could be herself, Janie didn't wear designer dresses and hang out with the right social group. Janie studied anthropology, as well as the psychology her aunt Lydia had insisted on—and felt free to insist, since she helped pay Janie's tuition. But Janie spent most of her weekends and afternoons buried in mud, learning how to dig out fragile pieces of ancient pottery and projectile points.

But she'd gone on with the pretense when she was home—when Aunt Lydia was visiting, of course—proving her worth at psychology. Sadly, it had gone awry when she psychoanalyzed Leo's brother Callaghan last year over the asparagus. She'd gone to her room howling with laughter after Aunt Lydia had hung on every word approvingly. She was sorry she'd embarrassed Cag, but the impulse had been irresistible. Her aunt was *so* gullible. She'd felt guilty afterward, though, for not telling Aunt Lydia her true interests.

She finished her shower, dried off, and changed into new clothes so that she could start cleaning up the floors where she'd tracked mud. Despite her complaints, Hettie would help. She didn't really mind housework. Neither did Janie, although her late mother would be horrified if she could see her only child on the floor with a scrub brush alongside Hettie's ample figure.

Janie helped with everything, except cooking. Her expertise in the kitchen was, to put it mildly, nonexistent. But, she thought, brightening, that was the next thing on her list of projects. She was undergoing a major self-improvement. First she was going to learn ranching—even if it killed her—and then she was going to learn to cook.

She wished this transformation had been her idea, but actually, it had been Marilee's. The other girl had told her, in confidence, that she'd been talking to Leo and Leo had told her flatly that the reason he didn't notice Janie was that she didn't know anything about ranching. She was too well-dressed, too chic, too sophisticated. And the worst thing was that she didn't know anything about cooking, either, Marilee claimed. So if Janie wanted to land that big, hunky fish, she was going to have to make some major changes.

It sounded like a good plan, and Marilee had been her friend since grammar school, when the Morgan family had moved next door. So Janie accepted Marilee's advice with great pleasure, knowing that her best friend would never steer her wrong. She was going to stay home—

not go back to college—and she was going to show Leo Hart that she could be the sort of woman who appealed to him. She'd work so hard at it, she'd have to succeed!

Not that her attempts at riding a horse were anything to write home about, she had to admit as she mopped her way down the long wooden floor of the hall. But she was a rancher's daughter. She'd get better with practice.

SHE DID KEEP TRYING. A week later, she was making biscuits in the kitchen—or trying to learn how—when she dropped the paper flour bag hard on the counter and was dusted from head to toe with the white substance.

It would have to be just that minute that her father came in the back door with Leo in tow.

"Janie?" her father exclaimed, wide-eyed.

"Hi, Dad!" she said with a big grin. "Hi, Leo."

"What in blazes are you doing?" her father demanded.

"Putting the flour in a canister," she lied, still smiling.

"Where's Hettie?" he asked.

Their housekeeper was hiding in the bedroom, supposedly making beds, and trying not to howl at Janie's pitiful efforts. "Cleaning, I believe," she said.

"Aunt Lydia not around?"

"Playing bridge with the Harrisons," she said.

"Bridge!" her father scoffed. "If it isn't bridge, it's golf. If it isn't golf, it's tennis… Is she coming over today to go over those stocks with me or not?" he persisted, because they jointly owned some of his late wife's shares and couldn't sell them without Lydia's permission. If he could ever find the blasted woman!

"She said she wasn't coming over until Saturday, Dad," Janie reminded him.

He let out an angry sigh. "Well, come on, Leo, I'll show you the ones I want to sell and let you advise me. They're in my desk...damn bridge! I can't do a thing until Lydia makes up her mind."

Leo gave Janie a curious glance but he kept walking and didn't say another word to her. Minutes later, he left—out the front door, not the back.

JANIE'S SELF-IMPROVEMENT CAMPAIGN continued into the following week with calf roping, which old John was teaching her out in the corral. Since she could now loop the rope around a practice wooden cow with horns, she was progressing to livestock.

She followed John's careful instruction and tossed her loop over the head of the calf, but she'd forgotten to dig her heels in. The calf hadn't. He jerked her off her feet and proceeded to run around the ring like a wild thing, trying to get away from the human slithering after him at a breakneck pace.

Of course, Leo would drive up next to the corral in time to see John catch and throw the calf, leaving Janie covered in mud. She looked like a road disaster.

This time Leo didn't speak. He was too busy laughing. Janie couldn't speak, either, her mouth was full of mud. She gave both men a glare and stomped off toward the back door of the house, trailing mud and unspeakable stuff, fuming the whole while.

A bath and change of clothes improved her looks and her smell. She was resigned to finding Leo gone when she got out, so she didn't bother to dress up or put on makeup. She wandered out to the kitchen in jeans and a loose long-sleeved denim shirt, with her hair in a lop-sided ponytail and her feet bare.

"You'll step on something sharp and cripple yourself," Hettie warned, turning from the counter where she was making rolls, her ample arms up to the elbows in flour.

"I have tough feet," Janie protested with a warm smile. She went up and hugged Hettie hard from behind, loving the familiar smells of freshly washed cotton and flour that seemed to cling to her. Hettie had been around since Janie was six. She couldn't imagine life without the gray-haired, blue-eyed treasure with her constantly disheveled hair and worried expression. "Oh, Hettie, what would we do without you?" she asked on a sigh, and closed her eyes.

"Get away, you pest," Hettie muttered, "I know what you're up to... Janie Brewster, I'll whack you!"

But Janie was already out of reach, dangling Hettie's apron from one hand, her green eyes dancing with mischief.

"You put that back on me or you'll get no rolls tonight!" Hettie raged at her.

"All right, all right, I was only kidding," Janie chuckled. She replaced the apron around Hettie's girth and was fastening it when she heard the door open behind her.

"You stop teaching her these tricks!" Hettie growled at the newcomer.

"Who, me?" Leo exclaimed with total innocence.

Janie's hands fumbled with the apron. Her heart ran wild. He hadn't left. She'd thought he was gone, and she hadn't bothered with her appearance. He was still here, and she looked like last year's roast!

"You'll drop that apron, Janie," Leo scolded playfully.

Janie glanced at him as she retied the apron. "You can talk," she chided. "I hear your housekeepers keep quitting because you untie aprons constantly! One kept a broom handle!"

"She broke it on my hard head," he said smugly. "What are you making, Hettie?"

"Rolls," she said. She glanced warily at Leo. "I can't make biscuits. Sorry."

He gave her a hard glare. "Just because I did something a little offbeat…"

"Carried that little chef right out of his restaurant, with him kicking and screaming all the way, I heard," Hettie mused, eyes twinkling.

"He said he could bake biscuits. I was only taking him home with me to let him prove it," Leo said belligerently.

"That's not what he thought," Hettie chuckled. "I hear he dropped the charges…?"

"Nervous little guy," Leo said, shaking his head. "He'd never have worked out, anyway." He gave her a long look. "You sure you can't bake a biscuit? Have you ever tried?"

"No, and I won't. I like working here," she said firmly.

He sighed. "Just checking." He peered over her shoulder fondly. "Rolls, huh? I can't remember when I've had a homemade roll."

"Tell Fred to invite you to supper," Hettie suggested.

He glanced at Janie. "Why can't she do it?"

Janie was tongue-tied. She couldn't think at all.

The lack of response from her dumbfounded Leo. To have Janie hesitate about inviting him for a meal was shocking. Leo scowled and just stared at her openly, which only made her more nervous and uncertain. She knew she looked terrible. Leo wanted a woman who could do ranch work and cook, but surely he wanted one who looked pretty, too. Right now, Janie could have qualified for the Frump of the Year award.

She bit her lower lip, hard, and looked as if she were about to cry.

"Hey," he said softly, in a tone he'd never used with her before, "what's wrong?"

"Have to let this rise," Hettie was murmuring after she'd covered the dough and washed her hands, oblivious to what was happening behind her. "Meanwhile I'm going to put another load of clothes in the washer, darlin'," she called to Janie over her shoulder.

The door into the dining room closed, but they didn't notice.

Leo moved closer to Janie, and suddenly his big, lean hands were on her thin shoulders, resting heavily over the soft denim. They were warm and very strong.

Her breath caught in the back of her throat while she looked up into black eyes that weren't teasing or playful. They were intent, narrow, faintly glittering. There was no expression on his handsome face at all. He looked into her eyes as if he'd never seen them, or her, before—and she looked terrible!

"Come on," he coaxed. "Tell me what's wrong. If it's something I can fix, I will."

Her lips trembled. Surely, she could make up something, quick, before he moved away!

"I got hurt," she whispered in a shameful lie. "When the calf dragged me around the corral."

"Did you?" He was only half listening. His eyes were

on her mouth. It was the prettiest little mouth, like a pink
bow, full and soft, just barely parted over perfect, white
teeth. He wondered if she'd been kissed, and how often.
She never seemed to date, or at least, he didn't know
about her boyfriends. He shouldn't be curious, either,
but Marilee had hinted that Janie had more boyfriends
than other local girls, that she was a real rounder.

Janie was melting. Her knees were weak. Any minute, she was going to be a little puddle of love looking
up at his knees.

He felt her quiver under his hands, and his scowl
grew darker. If she was as sophisticated as Marilee said
she was, why was she trembling now? An experienced
woman would be winding her arms around his neck already, offering her mouth, curving her body into his...

His fingers tightened involuntarily on her soft arms.
"Come here," he said huskily, and tugged her right up
against his tall, muscular body. Of all the Harts, he was
the tallest, and the most powerfully built. Janie's breasts
pressed into his diaphragm. She felt him tauten at the
contact, felt his curiosity as he looked down into her
wide, soft, dazed eyes. Her hands lightly touched his
shirtfront, but hesitantly, as if it embarrassed her to touch
him at all.

He let out a soft breath. His head was spinning with
forbidden longings. Janie was barely twenty-one. She
was the daughter of a man he did business with. She
was off-limits. So why was he looking at her mouth and
feeling his body swell sensuously at just the brush of her
small breasts against him?

"Don't pick at my shirt," he said quietly. His voice

was unusually deep and soft, its tone unfamiliar. "Flatten your hands on my chest."

She did that, slowly, as if she were just learning how to walk. Her hands were cold and nervous, but they warmed on his body. She stood very still, hoping against hope that he wasn't going to regain the senses she was certain he'd momentarily lost. She didn't even want to breathe, to do anything that would distract him. He seemed to be in a trance, and she was feeling dreams come true in the most unexpected and delightful way.

He smiled quizzically. "Don't you know how?"

Her lips were dry. She moistened them with just the tip of her tongue. He seemed to find that little movement fascinating. He watched her mouth almost hungrily. "How…to…do what?" she choked.

His hand went to her cheek and his thumb suddenly ran roughly over her lips, parting them in a whip of urgent, shocking emotion. "How to do this," he murmured as his head bent.

She saw the faint smile on his hard mouth as his lips parted. They brushed against hers in tiny little whispers of contact that weren't nearly enough to feed the hunger he was coaxing out of her.

Her nails curled into his shirt and he tensed. She felt thick hair over the warm, hard muscles of his chest. Closer, she felt the hard, heavy thunder of his pulse there, under her searching hands.

"Nice," he whispered. His voice was taut now, like his body against her.

She felt his big hands slide down her waist to her hips while he was playing with her mouth in the most arousing way. She couldn't breathe. Did he know? Could he tell that she was shaking with desire?

Her lips parted more with every sensuous brush of his mouth against them. At the same time, his hands moved to her narrow hips and teased against her lower spine. She'd never felt such strange sensations. She felt her body swell, as if it had been stung all over by bees, but the sensation produced pleasure instead of pain.

He nibbled at her upper lip, feeling it quiver tentatively as his tongue slid under it and began to explore. One lean hand slid around to the base of her hips and slowly gathered them into his, in a lazy movement that made her suddenly aware of the changing contours of his body.

She gasped and pulled against his hand.

He lifted his head and searched her wide, shocked green eyes. "Plenty of boyfriends, hmm?" he murmured sarcastically, almost to himself.

"Boy…friends?" Her voice sounded as if she were being strangled.

His hand moved back to her waist, the other one moved to her round chin and his thumb tugged gently at her lower lip. "Leave it like this," he whispered. His mouth hovered over hers just as it parted, and she found herself going on tiptoe, leaning toward him, almost begging for his mouth to come down and cover hers.

But he was still nibbling at her upper lip, gently toying with it, until he tilted her chin and his teeth tugged softly at the lower lip. His mouth brushed roughly over hers, teaching it to follow, to plead, then to demand something more urgent, more thorough than this slow torment.

Her nails bit into his chest and she moaned.

As if he'd been waiting patiently for that tiny little sound, his arms swallowed her up whole and his eyes, when they met hers, glittered like candlelight from deep in a cave.

His hand was in her ponytail, ripping away the rubber band so that he could catch strands of it in his strong fingers and angle her face just where he wanted it.

"Maybe you are old enough…" he breathed just before his mouth plunged deeply into hers.

She tautened all over with heated pleasure. Her body arched against him, no longer protesting the sudden hardness of him against her. She reached up to hold him, to keep that tormenting, hungry mouth against her lips. It was every dream she'd ever dreamed, coming true. She could hardly believe it was happening here, in broad daylight, in the kitchen where she'd been trying so hard to learn to make things that would please him. But he seemed to be pleased, just the same. He groaned against her lips, and his arms were bruising now, as if he wasn't quite in control. That was exciting. She threw caution to the winds and opened her mouth deliberately under the crush of his, inviting him in.

She felt his tongue go deep into the soft darkness, and she shivered as his mouth devoured hers.

Only the sound of a door slamming penetrated the thick sensual fog that held them both in thrall.

Leo lifted his head, slowly, and looked down into a face he didn't recognize. Janie's green eyes were like wet emeralds in her flushed face. Her lips were swollen, soft, sensual. Her body was clinging to his. He had her off the floor in his hungry embrace, and his body was throbbing with desire.

He knew that she could feel him, that she knew he was aroused. It was a secret thing, that only the two of them knew. It had to stay that way. He had to stop. This was wrong...!

He let go of her slowly, easing her back, while he sucked in a long, hard breath and shivered with a hunger he couldn't satisfy. He became aware of the rough grip he had on her upper arms and he relaxed it at once. He'd never meant to hurt her.

He fought for control, reciting multiplication tables silently in his mind until he felt his body unclench and relax.

It troubled him that he'd lost control so abruptly, and with a woman he should never have touched. He hadn't meant to touch her in the first place. He couldn't understand why he'd gone headfirst at her like that. He was usually cool with women, especially with Janie.

The way she was looking at him was disturbing. He was going to have a lot of explaining to do, and he didn't know how to begin. Janie was years too young for him, only his body didn't think so. Now he had to make his mind get himself out of this predicament.

"That shouldn't have happened," he said through his teeth.

She was hanging on every word, deaf to meanings, deaf to denials. Her body throbbed. "It's like the flu," she said, dazed, staring up at him. "It makes you...ache."

He shook her gently. "You're too young to have aches," he said flatly. "And I'm old enough to know better than to do something this stupid. Are you listening to me? This shouldn't have happened. I'm sorry."

Belatedly, she realized that he was backtracking. Of course he hadn't meant to kiss her. He'd made his opinion of her clear for years, and even if he liked kissing her, it didn't mean that he was ready to rush out and buy a ring. Quite the opposite.

She stepped away from him, her face still flushed, her eyes full of dreams she had to hide from him.

"I... I'm sorry, too," she stammered.

"Hell," he growled, ramming his hands into his pockets. "It was my fault. I started it."

She moved one shoulder. "No harm done." She cleared her throat and fought for inspiration. It came unexpectedly. Her eyes began to twinkle wickedly. "I have to take lessons when they're offered."

His eyebrows shot up. Had he heard her say that, or was he delusional?

"I'm not the prom queen," she pointed out. "Men aren't thick on the ground around here, except old bachelors who chew tobacco and don't bathe."

"I call that prejudice," he said, relaxing into humor.

"I'll bet you don't hang out with women who smell like dirty horses," she said.

He pursed his lips. Like hers, they were faintly swollen. "I don't know about that. The last time I saw you, I recall, you were neck-deep in mud and sh—"

"You can stop right there!" she interrupted, flushing.

His dark eyes studied her long hair, liking its thick waves and its light brown color. "Pity your name isn't Jeanie," he murmured. "Stephen Foster wrote a song about her hair."

She smiled. He liked her hair, at least. Maybe he liked her a little, too.

She was pretty when she smiled like that, he thought, observing her. "Do I get invited to supper?" he drawled, lost in that soft, hungry look she was giving him. "If you say yes, I might consider giving you a few more lessons. Beginner class only, of course," he added with a grin.

CHAPTER TWO

JANIE WAS SURE she hadn't heard him say that, but he was still smiling. She smiled back. She felt pretty. No makeup, no shoes, disheveled—and Leo had kissed her anyway. She beamed. At least, she beamed until she remembered the Hart bread mania. Any of them would do anything for a biscuit. Did that extend to homemade rolls?

"You're looking suspicious," he pointed out.

"A man who would kidnap a poor little pastry chef might do anything for a homemade roll," she reminded him.

He sighed. "Hettie makes wonderful rolls," he had to admit.

"Oh, you!" She hit him gently and then laughed. He was impossible. "Okay, you can come to supper."

He beamed. "You're a nice girl."

Nice. Well, at least he liked her. It was a start. It didn't occur to her, then, that a man who was seriously interested in her wouldn't think of her as just "nice."

Hettie came back into the room, still oblivious to the undercurrents, and got out a plastic bowl. She filled it with English peas from the crisper. "All right, my girl, sit down here and shell these. You staying?" she asked Leo.

"She said I could," he told Hettie.

"Then you can go away while we get it cooked."

"I'll visit my bull. Fred's got him in the pasture."

Leo didn't say another word. But the look he gave Janie before he left the kitchen was positively wicked.

But if she thought the little interlude had made any permanent difference in her relationship with Leo, Janie was doomed to disappointment. He came to supper, but he spent the whole time talking genetic breeding with Fred, and although he was polite to Janie, she might as well have been on the moon.

He didn't stay long after supper, either, making his excuses and praising Hettie for her wonderful cooking. He smiled at Janie, but not the way he had when they were alone in the kitchen. It was as if he'd put the kisses out of his mind forever, and expected her to act as if he'd never touched her. It was disheartening. It was heartbreaking. It was just like old times, except that now Leo had kissed her and she wanted him to do it again. Judging by his attitude over supper, she had a better chance of landing a movie role.

SHE SPENT THE next few weeks remembering Leo's hungry kisses and aching for more of them. When she wasn't daydreaming, she was practicing biscuit-making. Hettie muttered about the amount of flour she was going through.

"Janie, you're going to bankrupt us in the kitchen!" the older woman moaned when Janie's fifth batch of biscuits came out looking like skeet pigeons. "That's your second bag of flour today!"

Janie was glowering at her latest effort on the baking sheet. "Something's wrong, and I can't decide what.

I mean, I put in salt and baking powder, just like the recipe said…"

Hettie picked up the empty flour bag and read the label. Her eyes twinkled. "Janie, darlin', you bought self-rising flour."

"Yes. So?" she asked obliviously.

"If it's self-rising, it already has the salt and baking powder in it, doesn't it?"

Janie burst out laughing. "So that's what I'm doing wrong! Hand me another bag of flour, could you?"

"This is the last one," Hettie said mournfully.

"No problem. I'll just drive to the store and get some more. Need anything?"

"Milk and eggs," Hettie said at once.

"We've got four chickens," Janie exclaimed, turning, "and you have to buy eggs?"

"The chickens are molting."

Janie smiled. "And when they molt, they don't lay. Sorry. I forgot. I'll be back in a jiffy," she added, peeling off her apron.

She paused just long enough to brush her hair out, leaving it long, and put on a little makeup. She thrust her arms into her nice fringed leather jacket, because it was seasonally cool outside as well as raining, and popped into her red sports car. You never could tell when you might run into Leo, because he frequently dashed into the supermarket for frozen biscuits and butter when he was between cooks.

SURE ENOUGH, AS SHE started for the checkout counter with her milk, eggs and flour, she spotted Leo, head and shoulders above most of the men present. He was wearing that long brown Australian drover's coat he favored in wet weather, and he was smiling in a funny sort of way.

That was when Janie noticed his companion. He was bending down toward a pretty little brunette who was chattering away at his side. Janie frowned, because that dark wavy hair was familiar. And then she realized who it was. Leo was talking to Marilee Morgan!

She relaxed. Marilee was her friend. Surely, she was talking her up to Leo. She almost rushed forward to say hello, but what if she interrupted at a crucial moment? There was, after all, the annual Jacobsville Cattleman's Ball in two weeks, the Saturday before Thanksgiving. It was very likely that Marilee was dropping hints right and left that Janie would love Leo to escort her.

She chuckled to herself. She was lucky to have a friend like Marilee.

IF JANIE HAD known what Marilee was actually saying to Leo, she might have changed her mind about the other woman's friendship and a lot of other things.

"It was so nice of you to drive me to the store, Leo," Marilee was cooing at Leo as they walked out. "My wrist is really sore from that fall I took."

"No problem," he murmured with a smile.

"The Cattleman's Ball is week after next," Marilee added coyly. "I would really love to go, but nobody's asked me. I won't be able to drive by then, either, I'm sure. It was a bad sprain. They take almost as long as a broken bone to heal." She glanced up at him, weighing her chances. "Of course, Janie's told everybody that you're taking her. She said you're over there all the time now, that it's just a matter of time before you buy her a ring. Everybody knows."

He scowled fiercely. He'd only kissed Janie, he hadn't proposed marriage, for God's sake! Surely the girl wasn't going to get possessive because of a kiss? He hated gossip, especially about himself. Well, Janie could forget any invitations of that sort. He didn't like aggressive women who told lies around town. Not one bit!

"You can go with me," he told Marilee nonchalantly. "Despite what Janie told you, I am no woman's property, and I'm damned sure not booked for the dance!"

Marilee beamed. "Thanks, Leo!"

He shrugged. She was pretty and he liked her company. She wasn't one of those women who felt the need to constantly compete with men. He'd made his opinion about that pretty clear to Marilee in recent weeks. It occurred to him that Janie was suddenly trying to do just that, what with calf roping and ranch work and hard riding. Odd, when she'd never shown any such inclination before. But her self-assured talk about being his date for the ball set him off and stopped his mind from further reasoning about her sudden change of attitude.

He smiled down at Marilee. "Thanks for telling me about the gossip," he added. "Best way to curb it is to disprove it publicly."

"Of course it is. You mustn't blame Janie too much," she added with just the right amount of affection. "She's very young. Compared to me, I mean. If we hadn't been neighbors, we probably wouldn't be friends at all. She seems so…well, so juvenile at times, doesn't she?"

Leo frowned. He'd forgotten that Marilee was older than Janie. He thought back to those hard, hungry kisses he'd shared with Janie and could have cursed himself for his weakness. She was immature. She was building a whole affair on a kiss or two. Then he remembered something unexpectedly.

He glanced down at Marilee. "You said she had more boyfriends than anybody else in town."

Marilee cleared her throat. "Well, yes, *boy*friends. Not men friends, though," she added, covering her bases. It was hard to make Janie look juvenile if she was also a heartbreaking rounder.

Leo felt placated, God knew why. "There's a difference."

Marilee agreed. A tiny voice in her mind chided her for being so mean to her best friend, but Leo was a real hunk, and she was as infatuated with him as Janie was. All was fair in love and war, didn't they say? Besides, it was highly unlikely that Leo would ever ask Janie out—but, just in case, Marilee had planted a nice little suspicion in his mind to prevent that. She smiled as she walked beside him to his truck, dreaming of the first of many dances and being in Leo's arms. One day, she thought ecstatically, he might even want to marry her!

JANIE WENT THROUGH two more bags of flour with attempts at biscuits that became better with each failed try. Finally, after several days' work, she had produced an edible batch that impressed even Hettie.

In between cooking, she was getting much better on horseback. Now, mounted on her black-and-white quarter horse, Blackie, she could cut out a calf and drive it into the makeshift corral used for doctoring sick animals. She could throw a calf, too, with something like professionalism, despite sore muscles and frequent bruises. She could rope, after a fashion, and she was riding better all the time. At least the chafing of her thighs against the saddle had stopped, and the muscles had acclimatized to the new stress being placed on them.

Saturday night loomed. It was only four days until the Cattleman's Ball, and she had a beautiful spaghetti-strapped lacy oyster-white dress to wear. It came to her ankles and was low-cut in front, leaving the creamy skin of her shoulders bare. There was a side-slit that went up her thigh, exposing her beautiful long legs. She paired the dress with white spiked high heels sporting ankle straps which she thought were extremely sexy, and she had a black velvet coat with a white silk lining to defend against the cold evening air. Now all she lacked was a date.

She'd expected Leo to ask her to the ball after those hungry kisses, despite his coolness later that day. But he hadn't been near the ranch since he'd had supper with her and her father. What made it even more peculiar was that he'd talked with her father out on the ranch several times. He just didn't come to the house. Janie assumed that he was regretting those hard kisses, and was afraid that she was taking him too seriously. He was avoiding her. He couldn't have made it plainer.

That made it a pretty good bet that he wasn't planning to take her to any Cattleman's Ball. She phoned Marilee in desperation.

The other woman sounded uneasy when she heard Janie's voice, and she was quick to ask why Janie had phoned.

"I saw you with Leo in the grocery store the week before last," Janie began, "and I didn't interfere, because I was sure you were trying to talk him into taking me to the ball. But he didn't want to, did he?" she added sadly.

There was a sound like someone swallowing, on the other end of the phone. "Well, actually, no. I'm sorry." Marilee sounded as if she were strangling on the words.

"Don't feel bad," Janie said gently. "It's not your fault. You're my best friend in the whole world. I know you tried."

"Janie…"

"I had this beautiful white dress that I bought specially," Janie added on a sigh. "Well, that's that. Are you going?"

There was a tense pause. "Yes."

"Good! Anybody I know?"

"N…no," Marilee stammered.

"You have fun," Janie said.

"You…uh…aren't going, are you?" Marilee added.

Her friend certainly was acting funny, Janie thought. "No, I don't have a date," Janie chuckled. "There'll be other dances, I guess. Maybe Leo will ask me another time." After he's got over being afraid of me, she added silently. "If you see him," she said quickly, "you might mention that I can now cut out cattle and throw a calf. And I can make a biscuit that doesn't go through the floor when dropped!"

She was laughing, but Marilee didn't.

"I have to get to the hairdresser, Janie," Marilee said. "I'm really sorry…about the ball."

"Not your fault," Janie repeated. "Just have enough fun for both of us, okay?"

"Okay. See you."

The line went dead and Janie frowned. Something must be very wrong with Marilee. She wished she'd been more persistent and asked what was the matter. Well, she'd go over to Marilee's house after the dance to pump her for all the latest gossip, and then she could find out what was troubling her friend.

She put the ball to the back of her mind, despite the disappointment, and went out to greet her father as he rode in from the pasture with two of his men.

He swung out of the saddle at the barn and grinned at her. "Just the girl I wanted to see," he said at once. He pulled out his wallet. "I've got to have some more work gloves, just tore the last pair I had apart on barbed wire. How about going by the hardware store and getting me another pair of those suede-palmed ones, extra large?"

"My pleasure," Janie said at once. Leo often went to the hardware store, and she might accidentally run into him there. "Be back in a jiffy!"

"Don't speed!" her father called to her.

She only chuckled, diving into her sports car. She remembered belatedly that she didn't have either purse or car keys, or her face fixed, and jumped right back out again to rectify those omissions.

Ten minutes later, she was parking her car in front of the Jacobsville Hardware Store. With a wildly beating heart, she noticed one of the black double-cabbed Hart Ranch trucks parked nearby. Leo! She was certain it was Leo!

With her heart pounding, she checked her makeup in the rearview mirror and tugged her hair gently away from her cheeks. She'd left it down today deliberately, remembering that Leo had something of a weakness for long hair. It was thick and clean, shining like a soft brown curtain. She was wearing a long beige skirt with riding boots, and a gold satin blouse. She looked pretty good, even if she did say so herself! Now if Leo would just notice her...

She walked into the hardware store with her breath catching in her throat as she anticipated Leo's big smile at her approach. He was the handsomest of the Hart brothers, and really, the most personable. He was kindness itself. She remembered his soft voice in her kitchen, asking what was wrong. Oh, to have that soft voice in her ear forever!

There was nobody at the counter. That wasn't unusual, the clerks were probably waiting on customers. She walked back to where the gloves were kept and suddenly heard Leo's deep voice on the other side of the high aisle, unseen.

"Don't forget to add that roll of hog wire to the order," he was telling one of the clerks.

"I won't forget," Joe Howland's pleasant voice replied. "Are you going to the Cattleman's Ball?" Joe added just as Janie was about to raise her voice and call to Leo over the aisle.

"I guess I am," Leo replied. "I didn't plan to, but a pretty friend needed a ride and I'm obliging."

Janie's heart skipped and fell flat. Leo already had a date? Who? She moved around the aisle and in sight of Leo and Joe. Leo had his back to her, but Joe noticed her and smiled.

"That friend wouldn't be Janie Brewster, by any chance?" Joe teased loudly.

The question made Leo unreasonably angry. "Listen,

just because she caught the bouquet at Micah Steele's wedding is no reason to start linking her with me," he said shortly. "She may have a good family background, she may be easy on the eyes, she may even learn to cook someday—miracles still happen. But no matter what she does, or how well, she is never going to appeal to me as a woman!" he added. "Having her spreading ludicrous gossip about our relationship all over town isn't making her any more attractive to me, either. It's a dead turnoff!"

Janie felt a shock like an electric jolt go through her. She couldn't even move for the pain.

Joe, horrified, opened his mouth to speak.

Leo made a rough gesture with one lean hand, burning with pent-up anger. "She looks like the rough side of a corncob lately, anyway," Leo continued, warming to his subject. "The only thing she ever had going for her were her looks, and she's spent the last few weeks covered in mud or dust or bread flour. She's out all hours proving she can compete with any man on the place and she can't stop bragging about what a great catch she's made with me. She's already told half the town that I'm a kiss short of buying her an engagement ring. That is, when she isn't putting it around that I'm taking her to the Cattleman's Ball, when I haven't even damned well asked her! Well, she's got her eye on the wrong man. I don't want some half-baked kid with a figure like a boy and an ego the size of my boots! I wouldn't have Janie Brewster for a wife if she came complete with a stable of purebred Salers bulls, and that's saying something. She makes me sick to my stomach!"

Joe had gone pale and he was grimacing. Curious, Leo turned…and there was Janie Brewster, staring at him down the aisle with a face as tragic as if he'd just taken a whittling knife to her heart.

"Janie," he said slowly.

She took a deep, steadying breath and managed to drag her eyes away from his face. "Hi, Joe," she said with a wan little smile. Her voice sounded choked. She couldn't possibly look for gloves, she had to get away! "Just wanted to check and see if you'd gotten in that tack Dad ordered last week," she improvised.

"Not just yet, Janie," Joe told her in a gentle tone. "I'm real sorry."

"No problem. No problem at all. Thanks, Joe. Hello, Mr. Hart," she said, without really meeting Leo's eyes, and she even managed a smile through her tattered dignity. "Nice day out, isn't it? Looks like we might even get that rain we need so badly. See you."

She went out the door with her head high, as proudly as a conquering army, leaving Leo sick to his stomach for real.

"Why the hell didn't you say something?" Leo asked Joe furiously.

"Didn't know how," Joe replied miserably.

"How long had she been standing there?" Leo persisted.

"The whole time, Leo," came the dreaded reply. "She heard every word."

As if to punctuate the statement, from outside came the sudden raucous squeal of tires on pavement as Janie took off toward the highway in a burst of speed. She was driving her little sports car, and Leo's heart stopped as he realized how upset she was.

He jerked his cell phone out of his pocket and dialed

the police department. "Is that Grier?" he said at once when the call was answered, recognizing Jacobsville's new assistant police chief's deep voice. "Listen, Janie Brewster just lit out of town like a scalded cat in her sports car. She's upset and it's my fault, but she could kill herself. Have you got somebody out on the Victoria road who could pull her over and give her a warning? Yeah. Thanks, Grier. I owe you one."

He hung up, cursing harshly under his breath. "She'll be spitting fire if anybody tells her I sent the police after her, but I can't let her get hurt."

"Thought she looked just a mite too calm when she walked out the door," Joe admitted. He glanced at Leo and grimaced. "No secret around town that she's been sweet on you for the past year or so."

"If she was, I've just cured her," Leo said, and felt his heart sink. "Call me when that order comes in, will you?"

"Sure thing."

Leo climbed into his truck and just sat there for a minute, getting his bearings. He could only imagine how Janie felt right now. What he'd said was cruel. He'd let his other irritations burst out as if Janie were to blame for them all. What Marilee had been telling him about Janie had finally bubbled over, that was all. She'd never done anything to hurt him before. Her only crime, if there was one, was thinking the moon rose and set on Leo Hart and taking too much for granted on the basis of one long kiss.

He laughed hollowly. Chances were good that she wouldn't be thinking it after this. Part of him couldn't help blaming her, because she'd gone around bragging about how he was going to marry her, and how lucky he was to have a girl like her in his life. Not to mention telling everybody he was taking her to the Cattleman's Ball.

But Janie had never been one to brag about her accomplishments, or chase men. The only time she'd tried to vamp Leo, in fact, had been in her own home, when her father was present. She'd never come on to him when they were alone, or away from her home. She'd been old-fashioned in her attitudes, probably due to the strict way she'd been raised. So why should she suddenly depart from a lifetime's habits and start spreading gossip about Leo all over Jacobsville? He remembered at least once when she'd stopped another woman from talking about a girl in trouble, adding that she hated gossip because it was like spreading poison.

He wiped his sweaty brow with the sleeve of his shirt and put his hat on the seat beside him. He hated what he'd said. Maybe he didn't want Janie to get any ideas about him in a serious way, but there would have been kinder methods of accomplishing it. He didn't think he was ever going to forget the look on her face when she heard what he was saying to Joe. It would haunt him forever.

MEANWHILE, JANIE WAS setting new speed records out on the Victoria road. She'd already missed the turnoff that led back toward Jacobsville and her father's ranch. She was seething, hurting, miserable and confused. How could Leo think such things about her? She'd never told anybody how she felt about him, except Marilee, and she hadn't been spreading gossip. She hated gossip. Why did he know so little about her, when they'd known each other for years? What hurt the most was that he obviously believed those lies about her.

She wondered who could have told him such a thing. Her thoughts went at once to Marilee, but she chided herself for thinking ill of her only friend, her best friend. Certainly it had to be an enemy who'd been filling Leo's head full of lies. But…she didn't have any enemies that she knew of.

Tears were blurring her eyes. She knew she was going too fast. She should slow down before she wrecked the car or ran it into a fence. She was just thinking about that when she heard sirens and saw blue lights in her rearview mirror.

Great, she thought. Just what I need. I'm going to be arrested and I'll spend the night in the local jail.…

She stopped and rolled down her window, trying unobtrusively to wipe away the tears while waiting for the uniformed officer to bend down and speak to her.

He came as a surprise. It wasn't a patrolman she knew, and she knew most of them by sight at least. This one had black eyes and thick black hair, which he wore in a ponytail. He had a no-nonsense look about him, and he was wearing a badge that denoted him as the assistant chief.

"Miss Brewster?" he asked quietly.

"Y…yes."

"I'm Cash Grier," he introduced himself. "I'm the new assistant police chief here."

"Nice to meet you," she said with a watery smile. "Sorry it has to be under these circumstances." She held out both wrists with a sigh. "Want to handcuff me?"

He pursed his lips and his black eyes twinkled unexpectedly. He didn't look like a man who knew what humor was. "Isn't that a little kinky for a conversation? What sort of men *are* you used to?"

She hesitated for just a second before she burst out laughing. He wasn't at all the man he appeared to be. She put her hands down.

"I was speeding," she reminded him.

"Yes, you were. But since you don't have a rap sheet, you can have a warning, just this once," he added firmly. "The speed limit is posted. It's fifty on all county roads."

She peered up at him. "This is a *county* road?" she emphasized, which meant that he was out of his enforcement area.

Nodding, he grinned. "And you're right, I don't have any jurisdiction out here, so that's why you're getting a warning and a smile." The smile faded. "In town, you'll get a ticket and a heavy scowl. Remember that."

"I will. Honest." She wiped at her eyes again. "I got a little upset, but I shouldn't have taken it out on the road. I'm sorry. I won't do it again."

"See that you don't." His dark eyes narrowed as if in memory. "Accidents are messy. Very messy."

"Thanks for being so nice."

He shrugged. "Everybody slips once in a while."

"That's exactly what I did…"

"I didn't mean you," he interrupted. His lean face took on a faintly dangerous cast. "I'm not nice. Not ever."

She was intimidated by that expression. "Oh."

He wagged a finger at her nose. "Don't speed."

She put a hand over her heart. "Never again. I promise."

He nodded, walked elegantly to his squad car and

drove toward town. Janie sat quietly for a minute, getting herself back together. Then she started the car and went home, making up an apology for her father about his gloves without telling him the real reason she'd come home without them. He said he'd get a new pair the next day himself, no problem.

Janie cried herself to sleep in a miserable cocoon of shattered dreams.

As LUCK WOULD have it, Harley Fowler, Cy Parks's foreman, came by in one of the ranch pickup trucks the very next morning and pulled up to the back door when he saw Janie walk out dressed for riding and wearing a broad-brimmed hat. Harley's boss, Cy did business with Fred Brewster, and Harley was a frequent visitor to the ranch. He and Janie were friendly. They teased and played like two kids when they were together.

"I've been looking for you," Harley said with a grin as he paused just in front of her. "The Cattleman's Ball is Saturday night and I want to go, but I don't have a date. I know it's late to be asking, but how about going with me? Unless you've got a date or you're going with your dad…?" he added.

She grinned back. "I haven't got a date, and Dad's away on business and has to miss the ball this year. But I do have a pretty new dress that I'm dying to wear! I'd love to go with you, Harley!"

"Really?" His lean face lit up. He knew Janie was sweet on Leo Hart, but it was rumored that he was avoiding her like measles these days. Harley wasn't in love with Janie, but he genuinely liked her.

"Really," Janie replied. "What time will you pick me up?"

"About six-thirty," he said. "It doesn't start until seven, but I like to be on time."

"That makes two of us. I'll be ready. Thanks, Harley!"

"Thank you!" he said. "See you Saturday."

He was off in a cloud of dust, waving his hand out the window as he pulled out of the yard. Janie sighed with relief. She wanted nothing more in the world than to go to that dance and show Leo Hart how wrong he was about her chasing him. Harley was young and nice looking. She liked him. She would go and have a good time. Leo would be able to see for himself that he was off the endangered list, and he could make a safe bet that Janie would never go near him again without a weapon! As she considered it, she smiled coldly. Revenge was petty, but after the hurt she'd endured at Leo's hands, she felt entitled to a little of it. He was never going to forget this party. Never, as long as he lived.

CHAPTER THREE

THE ANNUAL JACOBSVILLE Cattleman's Ball was one of
the newer social events of the year. It took place the
Saturday before Thanksgiving like clockwork. Every
cattleman for miles around made it a point to attend,
even if he avoided all other social events for the year.
The Ballenger brothers, Calhoun and Justin, had just
added another facility to their growing feedlot enter-
prise, and they looked prosperous with their wives in
gala attire beside them. The Tremayne brothers, Connal,
Evan, Harden and Donald, and their wives were also in
attendance, as were the Hart boys; well, Corrigan, Callaghan, Rey and Leo at least, and their wives. Simon and
Tira didn't attend many local events except the brothers'
annual Christmas party on the ranch.

Also at the ball were Micah Steele, Eb Scott, J. D.
Langley, Emmett Deverell, Luke Craig, Guy Fenton,
Ted Regan, Jobe Dodd, Tom Walker and their wives.
The guest list read like a who's who of Jacobsville, and
there were so many people that the organizers had rented
the community center for it. There was a live country-
western band, a buffet table that could have fed a pla-
toon of starving men, and enough liquor to drown a
herd of horses.

Leo had a highball. Since he hadn't done much drinking in recent years, his four brothers were giving him strange looks. He didn't notice. He was feeling so miserable that even a hangover would have been an improvement.

Beside him, Marilee was staring around the room with wide, wary eyes.

"Looking for somebody?" Leo asked absently.

"Yes," she replied. "Janie said she wasn't coming, but that isn't what your sister-in-law Tess just told me."

"What did she say?"

Marilee looked worried. "Harley Fowler told her he was bringing Janie."

"Harley?" Leo scowled. Harley Fowler was a courageous young man who'd actually backed up the town's infamous mercenaries—Eb Scott, Cy Parks and Micah Steele—when they helped law enforcement face down a gang of drug dealers the year before. Harley's name hadn't been coupled with any of the local belles, and he was only a working-class cowboy. Janie's father might be financially pressed at the moment, but his was a founding family of Jacobsville, and the family had plenty of prestige. Fred and his sister-in-law Lydia would be picky about who Janie married. Not, he thought firmly, that Janie was going to be marrying Harley....

"Harley's nice," Marilee murmured. "He's Cy Parks's head foreman now, and everybody says he's got what it takes to run a business of his own." What Marilee didn't add was that Harley had asked her out several times before his raid on the drug lord with the local mercenaries, and she'd turned him down flat. She'd thought he bragged and strutted a little too much, that he was too immature for her. She'd even told him so. It had made her a bitter enemy of his.

Now she was rather sorry that she hadn't given him a chance. He really was different these days, much more mature and very attractive. Not that Leo wasn't a dish. But she felt so guilty about Janie that she couldn't even enjoy his company, much less the party. If Janie showed up and saw her with Leo, she was going to know everything. It wasn't conducive to a happy evening at all.

"What's wrong?" Leo asked when he saw her expression.

"Janie's never going to get over it if she shows up and sees me with you," she replied honestly. "I didn't think how it would look..."

"I don't belong to anybody," Leo said angrily. "It's just as well to let Janie know that. So what if she does show up? Who cares?"

"I do," Marilee sighed.

Just as she spoke, Janie came in the door with a tall, good-looking, dark-haired man in a dark suit with a ruffled white shirt and black bow tie. Janie had just taken off her black velvet coat and hung it on the rack near the door. Under it, she was wearing a sexy white silk gown that fell softly down her slender figure to her shapely ankles. The spaghetti straps left her soft shoulders almost completely bare, and dipped low enough to draw any man's eyes. She was wearing her thick, light brown hair down. It reached almost to her waist in back in a beautiful, glossy display. She wore just enough makeup to enhance her face, and she was clinging to Harley's arm with obvious pleasure as they greeted the Ballengers and their wives.

Leo had forgotten how pretty Janie could look when she worked at it. Lately, he'd only seen her covered in mud and flour. Tonight, her figure drew eyes in that dress. He remembered the feel of her in his arms, the eager innocence of her mouth under his, and he suddenly felt uneasy at the way she was clinging to Harley's arm.

If he was uncomfortable, Marilee was even more so. She stood beside Leo and looked as if she hated herself. He took another long sip of his drink before he guided her toward Harley and Janie.

"No sense hiding, is there?" he asked belligerently.

Marilee sighed miserably. "No sense at all, I guess."

They moved forward together. Janie noticed them and her eyes widened and darkened with pain for an instant. Leo's harsh monologue at the hardware store had been enough to wound her, but now she was seeing that she'd been shafted by her best friend, as well. Marilee said Janie didn't know her date, but all along, apparently, she'd planned to come with Leo. No wonder she'd been so curious about whether or not Janie was going to show up.

Everything suddenly made perfect sense. Marilee had filled Leo up with lies about Janie gossiping about him, so that she could get him herself. Janie felt like an utter fool. Her chin lifted, but she didn't smile. Her green eyes were like emerald shards as they met Marilee's.

"H-hi, Janie," Marilee stammered, forcing a smile. "You said you weren't coming tonight."

"I wasn't," Janie replied curtly. "But Harley was at a loose end and didn't have a date, so he asked me." She looked up at the tall, lean man beside her, who was some years younger than Leo, and she smiled at him with genuine affection even through her misery. "I haven't danced in years."

"You'll dance tonight, darlin'," Harley drawled, smiling warmly as he gripped her long fingers in his. He looked elegant in his dinner jacket, and there was a faint arrogance in his manner now that hadn't been apparent before. He glanced at Marilee and there was barely veiled contempt in the look.

Marilee swallowed hard and avoided his piercing gaze.

"I didn't know you could dance, Harley," Marilee murmured, embarrassed.

He actually ignored her, his narrow gaze going to Leo. "Nice turnout, isn't it?" he asked the older man.

"Nice," Leo said, but he didn't smile. "I haven't seen your boss tonight."

"The baby had a cold," Harley said. "He and Lisa don't leave him when he's sick." He looked down at Janie deliberately. "Considering how happy the two of them are, I guess marriage isn't such a bad vocation after all," he mused.

"For some, maybe," Leo said coldly. He was openly glaring at Harley.

"Let's get on the dance floor," Harley told Janie with a grin. "I'm anxious to try out that waltz pattern I've been learning."

"You'll excuse us, I'm sure," Janie told the woman who was supposed to be her best friend. Her eyes were icy as she realized how she'd been betrayed by Marilee's supposed "help" with Leo.

Marilee grimaced. "Oh, Janie," she groaned. "Let me explain...."

But Janie wasn't staying to listen to any halfhearted explanations. "Nice to see you, Marilee. You, too, Mr. Hart," she added with coldly formal emphasis, not quite meeting Leo's eyes. But she noted the quick firming of his chiseled lips with some satisfaction at the way she'd addressed him.

"Why do you call him Mr. Hart?" Harley asked as they moved away.

"He's much older than we are, Harley," she replied, just loudly enough for Leo to hear her and stiffen with irritation. "Almost another generation."

"I guess he is."

Leo took a big swallow of his drink and glared after them.

"She'll never speak to me again," Marilee said in a subdued tone.

He glared at her. "I'm not her personal property," he said flatly. "I never was. It isn't your fault that she's been gossiping and spreading lies all over town."

Marilee winced.

He turned his attention back to Janie, who was headed onto the dance floor with damned Harley. "I don't want her. What the hell do I care if she likes Harley?"

The music changed to a quick, throbbing Latin beat. Matt Caldwell and his wife, Leslie, were out on the dance floor already, making everybody else look like rank beginners. Everybody clapped to the rhythm until the very end, when the couple left the dance floor. Leo thought nobody could top that display until Harley walked to the bandleader, and the band suddenly broke into a Strauss waltz. That was when Harley and Janie took the floor. Then, even Matt and Leslie stood watching with admiration.

Leo stared at the couple as if he didn't recognize them. Involuntarily, he moved closer to the dance floor to watch. He'd never seen two people move like that to music besides Matt and Leslie.

The rhythm was sweet, and the music had a sweeping beauty that Janie mirrored with such grace that it was like watching ballet. Harley turned and Janie followed every nuance of movement, her steps matching his exactly. Her eyes were laughing, like her pretty mouth, as they whirled around the dance floor in perfect unison.

Harley was laughing, too, enjoying her skill as much as she enjoyed his. They looked breathless, happy—young.

Leo finished his drink, wishing he'd added more whiskey and less soda. His dark eyes narrowed as they followed the couple around the dance floor as they kept time to the music.

"Aren't they wonderful?" Marilee asked wistfully. "I don't guess you dance?"

He did. But he wasn't getting on that floor and making a fool of himself with Marilee, who had two left feet and the sense of rhythm of a possum.

"I don't dance much," Leo replied tersely.

She sighed. "It's just as well, I suppose. That would be a hard act to follow."

"Yes."

The music wound to a peak and suddenly ended, with Janie draped down Harley's side like a bolt of satin. His mouth was almost touching hers, and Leo had to fight not to go onto the floor and throw a punch at the younger man.

He blinked, surprised by his unexpected reaction. Janie was nothing to him. Why should he care what she did? Hadn't she bragged to everyone that he was taking her to this very dance? Hadn't she made it sound as if they were involved?

Janie and Harley left the dance floor to furious, genuine applause. Even Matt Caldwell and Leslie congratulated them on the exquisite piece of dancing. Apparently, Harley had been taking lessons, but Janie seemed to be a natural.

But the evening was still young, as the Latin music started up again and another unexpected couple took the floor. It was Cash Grier, the new assistant police chief, with young Christabel Gaines in his arms. Only a few people knew that Christabel had been married to Texas Ranger Judd Dunn since she was sixteen—a marriage on paper, only, to keep herself and her invalid mother from losing their family ranch. But she was twenty-one now, and the marriage must have been annulled, because there she was with Cash Grier, like a blond flame in his arms as he spun her around to the throbbing rhythm and she matched her steps to his expert ones.

Unexpectedly, as the crowd clapped and kept time for them, handsome dark-eyed Judd Dunn himself turned up in evening dress with a spectacular redhead on his arm. Men's heads turned. The woman was a supermodel, internationally famous, who was involved in a film shoot out at Judd and Christabel's ranch. Gossip flew. Judd watched Christabel with Grier and glowered. The redhead said something to him, but he didn't appear to be listening. He watched the two dancers with a rigid posture and an expression more appropriate for a duel than a dance. Christabel ignored him.

"Who is that man with Christabel Gaines?" Marilee asked Leo.

"Cash Grier. He used to be a Texas Ranger some years ago. They say he was in government service as well."

Leo recalled that Grier had been working in San Antonio with the district attorney's office before he took the position of assistant police chief in Jacobsville. There was a lot of talk about Grier's mysterious past. The man was an enigma, and people walked wide around him in Jacobsville.

"He's dishy, isn't he? He dances a *paso doble* even better than Matt, imagine that!" Marilee said aloud. "Of course, Harley does a magnificent waltz. Who would ever have thought he'd turn out to be such a sexy, mature man…"

Leo turned on his heel and left Marilee standing by herself, stunned. He walked back to the drinks table with eyes that didn't really see. The dance floor had filled up again, this time with a slow dance. Harley was holding Janie far too close, and she was letting him. Leo remembered what he'd said about her in the hardware store, and her wounded expression, and he filled another glass with whiskey. This time he didn't add soda. He shouldn't have felt bad, of course. Janie shouldn't have been so possessive. She shouldn't have gossiped about him…

"Hi, Leo," his sister-in-law Tess said with a smile as she joined him, reaching for a clear soft drink.

"No booze, huh?" he asked with a grin, noting her choice.

"I don't want to set a bad example for my son," she teased, because she and Cag had a little boy now. "Actually, I can't hold liquor. But don't tell anybody," she added. "I'm the wife of a tough ex-Special Forces guy. I'm supposed to be a real hell-raiser."

He smiled genuinely. "You are," he teased. "A lesser woman could never have managed my big brother and an albino python all at once."

"Herman the python's living with his own mate these days," she reminded him with a grin, "and just between us, I don't really miss him!" She glanced toward her husband and sighed. "I'm one lucky woman."

"He's one lucky man." He took a sip of his drink and she frowned.

"Didn't you bring Marilee?" she asked.

He nodded. "Her wrist was still bothering her too much to drive, so I let her come with me. I've been chauffeuring her around ever since she sprained it."

Boy, men were dense, Tess was thinking. As if a woman couldn't drive with only one hand. She glanced past him at Marilee, who was standing by herself watching as a new rhythm began and Janie moved onto the floor with Harley Fowler. "I thought she was Janie's best friend," she mentioned absently. "You can never tell about people."

"What do you mean?"

She shrugged. "I overheard her telling someone that Janie had been spreading gossip about you and her all over town." She shook her head. "That's not true. Janie's so shy, it's hard for her to even talk to most men. I've never heard her gossip about anyone, even people she dislikes. I can't imagine why Marilee would tell lies about her."

"Janie told everybody I was bringing her to the ball," he insisted with a scowl.

"Marilee told people that Janie said that," Tess corrected. "You really don't know, do you? Marilee's crazy about you. She had to cut Janie out of the picture before she could get close to you. I guess she found the perfect way to do it."

Leo started to speak, but he hesitated. That couldn't be true.

Tess read his disbelief and just smiled. "You don't believe me, do you? It doesn't matter. You'll find out the truth sooner or later, whether you want to or not. I've got to find Cag. See you later!"

Leo watched her walk away with conflicting emotions. He didn't want to believe—he *wouldn't* believe—that he'd been played for a sucker. He'd seen Janie trying to become a cattleman with his own eyes, trying to compete with him. He knew that she wanted him because she'd tried continually to tempt him when he went to visit her father. She flirted shamelessly with him. She'd melted in his arms, melted under the heat of his kisses. She hadn't made a single protest at the intimate way he'd held her. She felt possessive of him, and he couldn't really blame her, because it was his own lapse of self-control that had given her the idea that he wanted her. Maybe he did, physically, but Janie was a novice and he didn't seduce innocents. Her father was a business associate. It certainly wouldn't be good business to cut his own throat with Fred by making a casual lover of Janie.

He finished the whiskey and put the glass down. He felt light-headed. That was what came of drinking when he hadn't done it in a long time. This was stupid. He had to stop behaving like an idiot just because Fred Brewster's little girl had cut him dead in the receiving line and treated him like an old man. He forced himself to walk normally, but he almost tripped over Cag on the way.

His brother caught him by the shoulders. "Whoa, there," he said with a grin. "You're wobbling."

Leo pulled himself up. "That whiskey must be 200 proof," he said defensively.

"No. You're just not used to it. Leave your car here when it's time to go," he added firmly. "Tess and I will drop Marilee off and take you home. You're in no fit state to drive."

Leo sighed heavily. "I guess not. Stupid thing to do."

"What, drinking or helping Marilee stab Janie in the back?"

Leo's eyes narrowed on his older brother's lean, hard face. "Does Tess tell you everything?"

He shrugged. "We're married."

"If I ever get married," Leo told him, "my wife isn't going to tell anybody anything. She's going to keep her mouth shut."

"Not much danger of your getting married, with that attitude," Cag mused.

Leo squared his shoulders. "Marilee looks really great tonight," he pointed out.

"She looks pretty sick to me," Cag countered, eyeing the object of their conversation, who was standing alone against the opposite wall, trying to look invisible.

"She should, too, after spreading that gossip around town about Janie chasing you."

"Janie did that, not Marilee," Leo said belligerently. "She didn't have any reason to make it sound like we were engaged, just because I kissed her."

Cag's eyebrows lifted. "You kissed her?"

"It wasn't much of a kiss," Leo muttered gruffly. "She's so green, it's pathetic!"

"She won't stay that way long around Harley," Cag chuckled. "He's no playboy, but women love him since he helped our local mercs take on that drug lord Manuel Lopez and won. I imagine he'll educate Janie."

Leo's dark eyes narrowed angrily. He hated the thought of Harley kissing her. He really should do something about that. He blinked, trying to focus his mind on the problem.

"Don't trip over the punch bowl," Cag cautioned dryly. "And for God's sake, don't try to dance. The gossips would have a field day for sure!"

"I could dance if I wanted to," Leo informed him.

Cag leaned down close to his brother's ear. "Don't 'want to.' Trust me." He turned and went back to Tess, smiling as he led her onto the dance floor.

Leo joined Marilee against the wall.

She glanced at him and grimaced. "I've just become the Bubonic Plague," she said with a miserable sigh. "Joe Howland from the hardware store is here with his wife," she added uncomfortably. "He's telling people what you said to Janie and that I was responsible for her getting the rough side of your tongue."

He glanced down at her. "How is it your fault?"

She looked at her shoes instead of at him. She felt

guilty and hurt and ashamed. "I sort of told Janie that you said you'd like her better if she could ride and rope and make biscuits, and stop dressing up all the time."

He stiffened. He felt the jolt all the way to his toes. "You told her that?"

"I did." She folded her arms over her breasts and stared toward Janie, who was dancing with Harley and apparently having a great time. "There's more," she added, steeling herself to admit it. "It wasn't exactly true that she was telling people you were taking her to this dance."

"Marilee, for God's sake! Why did you lie?" he demanded.

"She's just a kid, Leo," she murmured uneasily. "She doesn't know beans about men or real life, she's been protected and pampered, she's got money, she's pretty...." She moved restlessly. "I like you a lot. I'm older, more mature. I thought, if she was just out of the picture for a little bit, you...you might start to like me."

Now he understood the look on Janie's face when he'd made those accusations. Tess was right. Marilee had lied. She'd stabbed her best friend in the back, and he'd helped her do it. He felt terrible.

"You don't have to tell me what a rat I am," she continued, without looking up at him. "I must have been crazy to think Janie wouldn't eventually find out that I was lying about her." She managed to meet his angry eyes. "She never gossiped about you, Leo. She wanted you to take her to this party so much that it was all she talked about for weeks. But she never told anybody you were going to. She thought I was helping her by hinting that she'd like you to ask her." She laughed coldly. "She was the best friend I ever had, and I've stabbed her in the back. She'll never speak to me again after tonight, and I deserve whatever I get. For what it's worth, I'm really sorry."

Leo was still trying to adjust to the truth. He could talk himself blue in the face, but Janie would never listen to him now. He was going to be about as welcome as a fly at her house from now on, especially if Fred found out what Leo had said to and about her. It would damage their friendship. It had already killed whatever feeling Janie had for him. He knew that without the wounded, angry glances she sent his way from time to time.

"You said you didn't want her chasing you," Marilee reminded him weakly, trying to find one good thing to say.

"No danger of that from now on, is there?" he agreed, biting off the words.

"None at all. So a little good came out of it."

He looked down at her with barely contained anger. "How could you do that to her?"

"I don't even know." She sighed raggedly. "I must have been temporarily out of my mind." She moved away from the wall. "I wonder if you'd mind driving me home? I… I really don't want to stay any longer."

"I can't drive. Cag's taking us home."

"You can't drive? Why?" she exclaimed.

"I think the polite way of saying it is that I'm stinking drunk," he said with glittery eyes blazing down at her.

She grimaced. No need to ask why he'd gotten that way. "Sorry," she said inadequately.

"You're sorry. I'm sorry. It doesn't change anything." He looked toward Janie, conscious of new and painful regrets. It all made sense now, her self-improvement campaign. She'd been dragged through mud, thrown from horses, bruised and battered in a valiant effort to become what she thought Leo wanted her to be.

He winced. "She could have killed herself," he said huskily. "She hadn't been on a horse in ages or worked around cattle." He looked down at Marilee with a black scowl. "Didn't you realize that?"

"I wasn't thinking at the time," Marilee replied. "I've always worked around the ranch, because I had to. I never thought of Janie being in any danger. But I guess she was, at that. At least she didn't get hurt."

"That's what you think," Leo muttered, remembering how she'd looked at the hardware store.

Marilee shrugged and suddenly burst into tears. She dashed toward the ladies' room to hide them.

At the same time, Harley left Janie at the buffet table and went toward the rest rooms himself.

Leo didn't even think. He walked straight up to Janie and caught her by the hand, pulling her along with him.

"What do you think you're doing?" she raged. "Let go of me!"

He ignored her. He led her right out the side door and onto the stone patio surrounded by towering plants that, in spring, were glorious in blossom. He pulled the glass door closed behind him and moved Janie off behind one of the plants.

"I want to talk to you," he began, trying to get his muddled mind to work.

She pulled against his hands. "I don't want to talk to you!" she snapped. "You go right back in there to your date, Leo Hart! You brought Marilee, not me!"

"I want to tell you…" he tried again.

She aimed a kick at his shin that almost connected.

He sidestepped, overbalancing her so that she fell heavily against him. She felt good in his arms, warm, delicate and sweetly scented. His breath caught at the feel of her soft skin under his hands where the dress was low-cut in back.

"Harley will…be missing me!" she choked.

"Damn Harley," he murmured huskily and the words went into her mouth as he bent and took it hungrily.

His arms swallowed her, warm under the dark evening suit, where her hands rested just at his rib cage. His mouth was ardent, insistent, on her parted lips.

He forced them apart, nipping the upper one with his teeth while his hands explored the softness of her skin. He was getting drunk on her perfume. He felt himself going taut as he registered the hunger he was feeling to get her even closer. It wasn't enough.…

His hands went to her hips and jerked them hard into the thrust of his big body, so that she could feel how aroused he was.

She stiffened and then tried to twist away, frantic at the weakness he was making her feel. He couldn't do this. She couldn't let him do it. He was only making a point, showing her that she couldn't resist him. He didn't even like her anymore. He'd brought her best friend to the most talked-about event in town!

"You…let me go!" she sobbed, tearing her mouth from his. "I hate you, Leo Hart!"

He was barely able to breathe, much less think, but he wasn't letting go. His eyes glittered down at her. "You don't hate me," he denied. "You want me. You tremble

every time I get within a foot of you. It's so noticeable
a blind man couldn't mistake it." He pulled her close,
watching her face as her thighs touched his. "A woman's
passion arouses a man's," he whispered roughly. "You
made me want you."

"You said I made you sick," she replied, her voice
choking on the word.

"You do." His lips touched her ear. "When a man is
this aroused, and can't satisfy the hunger, it makes him
sick," he said huskily, with faint insolence. He dragged
her hips against his roughly. "Feel that? You've got me
so hot I can't even think…!" Leo broke off abruptly as
Janie stomped on his foot.

"Does that help?" she asked while he was hobbling
on the foot her spiked heel hadn't gone into.

She moved back from him, shaking with desire and
anger, while he cursed roundly and without inhibition.

"That's what you get for making nasty remarks to
women!" she said furiously. "You don't want me! You
said so! You want Marilee. That's why you're taking her
around with you. Remember me? I'm that gossiping pest
who runs after you everywhere. Except that I'll never do
it again, you can bet your life on that! I wouldn't have
you on ice cream!"

He stood uneasily on both feet, glaring at her. "Sure
you would," he said with a venomous smile. His eyes
glittered like a diamondback uncoiling. "Just now, I
could have had you in the rosebushes. You'd have done
anything I wanted."

He was right. That was what hurt the most. She
pushed back her disheveled hair with a trembling hand.

"Not anymore," she said, feeling sick. "Not when I know what you really think of me."

"Harley brought you," he said coldly. "He's a boy playing at being a man."

"He's closer to my age than you are, Mr. Hart!" she shot back.

His face hardened and he took a quick step toward her.

"That's what you've said from the start," she reminded him, near tears. "I'm just a kid, you said. I'm just a kid with a crush, just your business associate's pesky daughter."

He'd said that. He must have been out of his mind. Looking at her now, with that painful maturity in her face, he couldn't believe he'd said any such thing. She was all woman. And she was with Harley. Damn Harley!

"Don't worry, I won't tell Dad that you tried to seduce me on the patio with your new girlfriend standing right inside the room," she assured him. "But if you ever touch me again, I'll cripple you, so help me God!"

She whirled and jerked open the patio door, slamming it behind her as she moved through the crowd toward the buffet table.

Leo stood alone in the cold darkness with a sore foot, wondering why he hadn't kept his mouth shut. If a bad situation could get worse, it just had.

CHAPTER FOUR

JANIE AND HARLEY were back on the dance floor by the time Leo made his way inside, favoring his sore foot.

Marilee was standing at the buffet table, looking as miserable as he felt.

"Harley just gave me hell," she murmured tightly as he joined her. "He said I was lower than a snake's belly, and it would serve me right if Janie never spoke to me again." She looked up at him with red-rimmed eyes. "Do you think your brother would mind dropping us off now? He could come right back...."

"I'll ask him," Leo said, sounding absolutely fed up.

He found Cag talking to Corrigan and Rey at the buffet table. Their wives were in another circle, talking to each other.

"Could you run Marilee home now and drop me off on the way back?" he asked Cag in a subdued tone.

Corrigan gaped at him. "You've never left a dance until the band packed up."

Leo sighed. "There's a first time for everything."

The women joined them. Cag tugged Tess close. "I have to run Leo and Marilee home."

Tess's eyebrows went up. "Now? Why so early?"

Leo glared. His brothers cleared their throats.

"Never mind," Cag said quickly. "I won't be a minute…"

"Rey and I would be glad to do it…" Meredith volunteered, with a nod from her husband.

"No need," Dorie said with a smile, cuddling close to her husband. "Corrigan can run Leo and Marilee home and come right back. Can't you, sweetheart?" she added.

"Sure I can," he agreed, lost in her pretty eyes.

"But you two don't usually leave until the band does, either," Leo pointed out. "You'll miss most of the rest of the dance if you drive us."

Corrigan pursed his lips. "Oh, we've done our dancing for the night. Haven't we, sweetheart?" he prompted.

Dorie's eyes twinkled. She nodded. "Indeed we have! I'll just catch up on talk until he comes back. We can have the last dance together. Don't give it a thought, Leo."

Leo was feeling the liquor more with every passing minute, but he was feeling all sorts of undercurrents. The women looked positively gleeful. His brothers were exchanging strange looks.

Corrigan looked past Leo to Cag and Rey. "You can all come by our house after the dance," he promised.

"What for?" Leo wanted to know, frowning suspiciously.

Corrigan hesitated and Cag scowled.

Rey cleared his throat. "Bull problems," he said finally, with a straight face. "Corrigan's advising me."

"He's advising me, too," Cag said with a grin. "He's advising both of us."

All three of them looked guilty as hell. "I know more

about bulls than Corrigan does," Leo pointed out. "Why don't you ask me?"

"Because you're in a hurry to go home," Corrigan improvised. "Let's go."

Leo went to get Marilee. She said a subdued, hurried goodbye to Cag and Rey and then their wives. Leo waited patiently, vaguely aware that Cag and Rey were standing apart, talking in hushed whispers. They were both staring at Leo.

As Marilee joined him, Leo began to get the idea. Corrigan had sacrificed dancing so that he could pump Leo for gossip and report back to the others. They knew he was drinking, which he never did, and they'd probably seen him hobble back into the room. Then he'd wanted to leave early. It didn't take a mind reader to put all that together. Something had happened, and his brothers—not to mention their wives—couldn't wait to find out what. He glared at Corrigan, but his brother only grinned.

"Let's go, Marilee," Leo said, catching her by the arm.

She gave one last, hopeful glance at Janie, but was pointedly ignored. She followed along with Leo until the music muted to a whisper behind them.

WHEN MARILEE HAD been dropped off, and they were alone in the car, Corrigan glanced toward his brother with mischievous silvery eyes and pursed his lips.

"You're limping."

Leo huffed. "You try walking normally when some crazy woman's tried to put her heel through your damned boot!"

"Marilee stepped on you?" Corrigan said much too carelessly.

"Janie stepped on me, on purpose!"

"What were you doing to her at the time?"

Leo actually flushed. It was visible in the streetlight they stopped under waiting for a red light to change on the highway.

"Well!" Corrigan exclaimed with a knowing expression.

"She started it," he defended himself angrily. "All these months, she's been dressing to the hilt and waylaying me every time I went to see her father. She damned near seduced me on the cooking table in her kitchen last month, and then she goes and gets on her high horse because I said a few little things I shouldn't have when she was eavesdropping!"

"You said a lot of little things," his brother corrected. "And from what I hear, she left town in a dangerous rush and had to be slowed down by our new assistant chief. In fact, you called and asked him to do it. Good thinking."

"Who told you that?" Leo demanded.

Corrigan grinned. "Our new assistant chief."

"Grier can keep his nose out of my business or I'll punch it for him!"

"He's got problems of his own, or didn't you notice him step outside with Judd Dunn just before we left?" Corrigan whistled softly. "Christabel may think she's her own woman, but Judd doesn't act like any disinterested husband I ever saw."

"He's got a world famous model on his arm," Leo pointed out.

"It didn't make a speck of difference once he saw

Christabel on that dance floor with Grier. He was ready to make a scene right there." He glanced at Leo. "And *he* wasn't drinking," he emphasized.

"I am not jealous of Janie Brewster," Leo told him firmly.

"Tell that to Harley. He had to be persuaded not to go after you when Janie came back inside in tears," Corrigan added, letting slip what he'd overheard.

That made it worse. "Harley can mind his own damned business, too!"

"He is. He likes Janie."

"Janie's not going to fall for some wet-behind-the-ears would-be world-saver," Leo raged.

"He's kind to her. He teases her and picks at her. He treats her like a princess." He gave his brother a wry glance. "I'll bet he wouldn't try to seduce her in the rosebushes."

"I didn't! Anyway, there weren't any damned rosebushes out there."

"How do you know that?"

Leo sighed heavily. "Because if there had been, I'd be wearing them."

Corrigan chuckled. Having had his own problems with the course of true love, he could sympathize with his brother. Sadly, Leo had never been in love. He'd had crushes, he'd had brief liaisons, but there had never been a woman who could stand him on his ear. Corrigan was as fascinated as their brothers with the sudden turn of events. Leo had tolerated Janie Brewster, been amused by her, but he'd never been involved enough to start a fight with her, much less sink two large whiskeys when he hardly even touched beer.

"She's got a temper, fancy that?" Corrigan drawled.

Leo sighed. "Marilee was telling lies," he murmured. "She said Janie had started all sorts of gossip about us. I'd kissed her, and liked it, and I was feeling trapped. I thought the kiss gave her ideas. And all the time... Damn!" he ground out. "Tess knew. She told me that Marilee had made up the stories, and I wouldn't listen."

"Tess is sharp as a tack," his older brother remarked.

"I'm as dull as a used nail," Leo replied. "I don't even know when a woman is chasing me. I thought Janie was. And all the time, it was her best friend Marilee." He shook his head. "Janie said I was the most conceited man she ever met. Maybe I am." He glanced out the window at the silhouettes of buildings they passed in the dark. "She likes Harley. That would have been funny a few months ago, but he keeps impressive company these days."

"Harley's matured. Janie has, too. I thought she handled herself with dignity tonight, when she saw you with Marilee." He chuckled. "Tira would have emptied the punch bowl over her head," he mused, remembering his redheaded sister-in-law's temper.

"Simon would have been outraged," he added. "He hates scenes. You're a lot like him," he said unexpectedly, glancing at the younger man. "You can cut up, but you're as somber as a judge when you're not around us. Especially since we've all married."

"I'm lonely," Leo said simply. "I've had the house to myself since Rey married Meredith and moved out, almost a year ago. Mrs. Lewis retired. I've got no biscuits, no company..."

"You've got Marilee," he was reminded.

"Marilee sprained her wrist. She's needed me to drive her places," Leo said drowsily.

"Marilee could drive with one hand. I drove with a broken arm once."

Leo didn't respond. They were driving up to the main ranch house, into the driveway that made a semicircle around the front steps. The security lights were on, so was the porch light. But even with lights on in the front rooms of the sprawling brick house, it looked empty.

"You could come and stay with any of us, whenever you wanted to," Corrigan reminded him. "We only live a few miles apart."

"You've all got families. Children. Well, except Meredith and Rey."

"They're not in a hurry. Rey's the youngest. The rest of us are feeling our ages a bit more."

"Hell," Leo growled, "you're only two years older than me."

"You're thirty-five," he was reminded. "I'll be thirty-eight in a couple of months."

"You don't look it."

"Dorie and the babies keep me young," Corrigan admitted with a warm smile. "Marriage isn't as bad as you think it is. You have someone to cook for you, a companion to share your sorrows when the world hits you in the head, and your triumphs when you punch back. Not to mention having a warm bed at night."

Leo opened the door but hesitated. "I don't want to get married."

Corrigan's pale eyes narrowed. "Dorie was just a little younger than Janie when I said the same thing to her. I mistook her for an experienced woman, made a very heavy pass, and then said some insulting things to her when she pulled back at the last minute. I sent her running for the nearest bus, and my pride stopped me from carrying her right back off it again. She went away. It was eight long years before she came home, before I was able to start over with her." His face hardened. "You know what those years were like for me."

Leo did. It was painful even to recall them. "You never told me why she left."

Corrigan rested his arm over the steering wheel. "She left because I behaved like an idiot." He glanced at his brother. "I don't give a damn what Marilee's told you about Janie, she isn't any more experienced than Dorie was. Don't follow in my footsteps."

Leo wouldn't meet the older man's eyes. "Janie's a kid."

"She'll grow up. She's making a nice start, already."

Leo brushed back his thick, unruly hair. "I was way out of line with her tonight. She said she never wanted to see me again."

"Give her time."

"I don't care if she doesn't want to see me," Leo said belligerently. "What the hell do I want with a mud-covered little tomboy, anyway? She can't even cook!"

"Neither can Tira," Corrigan pointed out. "But she's a knockout in an evening gown. So is our Janie, even if she isn't as pretty as Marilee."

Leo shrugged. "Marilee's lost a good friend."

"She has. Janie won't ever trust her again, even if she can forgive her someday."

Leo glanced back at his older brother. "Isn't it amazing how easy it is to screw up your whole life in a few unguarded minutes?"

"That's life, *compadre*. I've got to go. You going to be okay?"

Leo nodded. "Thanks for the ride." He glowered at Corrigan. "I guess you're in a hurry to get back, right?"

Corrigan's eyes twinkled. "I don't want to miss the last dance!"

Or the chance to tell his brothers everything that had happened. But, what the hell, they were family.

"Drive safely," Leo told Corrigan as he closed the car door.

"I always do." Corrigan threw up his hand and drove away.

Leo disarmed the alarm system and unlocked the front door, pausing to relock it and rearm the system. He'd been the victim of a mugging last October in Houston, and it had been Rey's new wife, Meredith, who had saved him from no worse than a concussion. But now he knew what it was to be a victim of violent crime, and he was much more cautious than he'd ever been before.

He tossed his keys on his chest of drawers and took off his jacket and shoes. Before he could manage the rest, he passed out on his own bed.

JANIE BREWSTER WAS very quiet on the way home. Harley understood why. He and Janie weren't an item, but he hated seeing a woman cry. He'd wanted, very badly, to punch Leo Hart for that.

"You should have let me hit him, Janie," he remarked thoughtfully.

She gave him a sad little smile. "There's been enough gossip already, although I appreciate the thought."

"He was drinking pretty heavily," Harley added. "I noticed that one of his brothers took him and Marilee home early. Nice of him to find a designated driver, in that condition. He looked as if he was barely able to walk without staggering."

Janie had seen them leave, with mixed emotions. She turned her small evening bag in her lap. "I didn't know he drank hard liquor at all."

"He doesn't," Harley replied. "Eb Scott said that he'd never known Leo to take anything harder than a beer in company." He glanced at her. "That must have been some mixer you had with him."

"He'd been drinking before we argued," she replied. She looked out the darkened window. "Odd that Marilee left with him."

"You didn't see the women snub her, I guess," he murmured. "Served her right, I thought." His eyes narrowed angrily as he made the turn that led to her father's ranch. "It's low to stab a friend in the back like that. Whatever her feelings for Hart, she should have put your feelings first."

"I thought you liked her, Harley."

He stiffened. "I asked her out once, and she laughed."

"What?"

He stared straight ahead at the road, the center of which was lit by the powerful headlights of the truck he was driving. "She thought it was hilarious that I had the nerve to ask her to go on a date. She said I was too immature."

Ouch, she thought. A man like Harley would have

too much pride to ever go near a woman who'd dented his ego that badly.

He let out a breath. "The hell of it is, she was right," he conceded with a wry smile. "I had my head in the clouds, bragging about my mercenary training. Then I went up against Lopez with Eb and Cy and Micah." He grimaced. "I didn't have a clue."

"We heard that it was a firefight."

He nodded. His eyes were haunted. "My only experience of combat was movies and television." His lean hands gripped the wheel hard. "The real thing is less... comfortable. And that's all I'll say."

"Thank you for taking me to the ball," she said, changing the subject because he looked so tormented.

His face relaxing, he glanced at her. "It was my pleasure. I'm not ready to settle down, but I like you. Anytime you're at a loose end, we can see a movie or get a burger."

She chuckled. "I feel the same way. Thanks."

He pursed his lips and gave her a teasing glance. "We could even go dancing."

"I liked waltzing."

"I want to learn those Latin dances, like Caldwell and Grier." He whistled. "Imagine Grier doing Latin dances! Even Caldwell stood back and stared."

"Mr. Grier is a conundrum," she murmured. "Not the man he seems, on the surface."

"How would you know?" he asked.

She cleared her throat. "He stopped me for speeding out on the Victoria road."

"Good for him. You drive too fast."

"Don't you start!"

He frowned. "What was he doing out there? He doesn't have jurisdiction outside Jacobsville."

"I don't know. But he's very pleasant."

He hesitated. "There's some, shall we say, unsavory gossip about him around town," he told her.

"Unsavory, how?" she asked, curious.

"It's probably just talk."

"Harley!"

He slowed for a turn. "They say he was a government assassin at one point in his life."

She whistled softly. "You're kidding!"

He glanced at her. "When I was in the Rangers, I flew overseas with a guy who was dressed all in black, armed to the teeth. He didn't say a word to the rest of us. I learned later that he was brought over for a very select assignment with the British commandos."

"What has that got to do with Grier?"

"That's just the thing. I think it *was* Grier."

She felt cold chills running up her arms.

"It was several years ago," he reiterated, "and I didn't get a close look, but sometimes you can tell a man just by the way he walks, the way he carries himself."

"You shouldn't tell anybody," she murmured, uneasy, because she liked Grier.

"I never would," Harley assured her. "I told my boss, but nobody else. Grier isn't the sort of man you'd ever gossip about, even if half the things they tell are true."

"There's more?" she exclaimed.

He chuckled. "He was in the Middle East helping pinpoint the laser-guided bombs, he broke up a spy ring in Manhattan as a company agent, he fought with the freedom fighters in Afghanistan, he foiled an assassination attempt against one of our own leaders under the nose of the agency assigned to protect them...you name it, he's done it. Including a stint with the Texas Rangers and a long career in law enforcement between overseas work."

"A very interesting man," she mused.

"And intimidating to our local law enforcement guys. Interesting that Judd Dunn isn't afraid of him."

"He's protective of Christabel," Janie told him. "She's sweet. She was in my high school graduating class."

"Judd's too old for her," Harley drawled. "He's about Leo Hart's age, isn't he, and she's just a few months older than you."

He was insinuating that Leo was too old for her. He was probably right, but it hurt to hear someone say it. Nor was she going to admit something else she knew about Christabel, that Judd had married the girl when she was just sixteen so that she wouldn't lose her home. Christabel was twenty-one and Judd had become her worst enemy.

"Sorry," Harley said when he noticed her brooding expression.

"About what?" she asked, diverted.

"I guess you think I meant Leo Hart's too old for you."

"He is," she said flatly.

He looked as if he meant to say more, but the sad expression on her face stopped him. He pulled into her driveway and didn't say another word until he stopped the truck at her front door.

"I know how you feel about the guy, Janie," he said then. "But you can want something too much. Hart isn't a marrying man, even if his brothers were. He's a bad risk."

She turned to face him, her eyes wide and eloquent. "I've told myself that a hundred times. Maybe it will sink in."

He grimaced. He traced a pattern on her cheek with a lean forefinger. "For what it's worth, I'm no stranger to unreturned feelings." He grimaced. "Maybe some of us just don't have the knack for romance."

"Speak for yourself," she said haughtily. "I have the makings of a Don Juanette, as Leo Hart is about to discover!"

He tapped her cheek gently. "Stop that. Running wild won't change anything, except to make you more miserable than you are."

She drew in a long breath. "You're right, of course. Oh, Harley, why can't we make people love us back?"

"Wish I knew," he said. He leaned forward and kissed her lightly on the lips. "I had fun. I'm sorry you didn't."

She smiled. "I did have fun. At least I didn't end up at the ball by myself, or with Dad, to face Leo and Marilee."

He nodded, understanding. "Where is your dad?"

"Denver," she replied on a sigh. "He's trying to interest a combine in investing in the ranch, but you can't tell anybody."

He scowled. "I didn't realize things were that bad."

She nodded. "They're pretty bad. Losing his prize bull was a huge financial blow. If Leo hadn't loaned him that breeding bull, I don't know what we'd have done. At least he likes Dad," she added softly.

It was Harley's opinion that he liked Fred Brewster's

daughter, too, or he wouldn't have been putting away whiskey like that tonight. But he didn't say it.

"Can I help?" he asked instead.

She smiled at him. "You're so sweet, Harley. Thanks. But there's not much we can do without a huge grub-stake. So," she added heavily, "I'm going to give up school and get a job."

"Janie!"

"College is expensive," she said simply. "Dad can't really afford it right now, and I'm not going to ask him to try. There's a job going at Shea's…"

"You can't work at Shea's!" Harley exclaimed. "Janie, it's a roadhouse! They serve liquor, and most nights there's a fight."

"They serve pizza and sandwiches, as well, and that's what the job entails," she replied. "I can handle it."

It disturbed Harley to think of an innocent, sweet girl like Janie in that environment. "There are openings at fast-food joints in town," he said.

"You don't get good tips at fast-food joints. Stop while you're ahead, Harley, you won't change my mind," she said gently.

"If you take the job, I'll stop in and check on you from time to time," he promised.

"You're a sweetheart, Harley," she said, and meant it. She kissed him on the cheek, smiled, and got out of the cab. "Thanks for taking me to the ball!"

"No sweat, Cinderella," he said with a grin. "I enjoyed it, too. Good night!"

"Good night," she called back.

She went inside slowly, locking the door behind her. Her steps dragging, she felt ten years older. It had been a real bust of an evening all around. She thought about Leo Hart and she hoped he had the king of hangovers the next morning!

THE NEXT DAY, Janie approached the manager of Shea's, a nice, personable man named Jed Duncan, about the job.

He read over her résumé while she sat in a leather chair across from his desk and bit her fingernails.

"Two years of college," he mused. "Impressive." His dark eyes met hers over the pages. "And you want to work in a bar?"

"Let me level with you," she said earnestly. "We're in financial trouble. My father can't afford to send me back to school, and I won't stand by and let him sink without trying to help. This job doesn't pay much, but the tips are great, from what Debbie Connor told me."

Debbie was her predecessor, and had told her about the job in the first place. Be honest with Jed, she'd advised, and lay it on the line about money. So Janie did.

He nodded slowly, studying her. "The tips are great," he agreed. "But the customers can get rowdy. Forgive me for being blunt, Miss Brewster, but you've had a sheltered upbringing. I have to keep a bouncer here now, ever since Calhoun Ballenger had it out with a customer over his ward—now his wife—and busted up the place. Not that Calhoun wasn't in the right," he added quickly. "But it became obvious that hot tempers and liquor don't mix, and you can't run a roadhouse on good intentions."

She swallowed. "I can get used to anything, Mr. Duncan. I would really like this job."

"Can you cook?"

She grinned. "Two months ago, I couldn't. But I can now. I can even make biscuits!"

He chuckled. "Okay, then, you should be able to make a pizza. We'll agree that you can work for two weeks and we'll see how it goes. You'll waitress and do some cooking. If you can cope, I'll let you stay. If not, or if you don't like the work, we'll call it quits. That suit you?"

She nodded. "It suits me very well. Thank you!"

"Does your father know about this?" he added.

She flushed. "He will, when he gets home from Denver. I don't hide things from him."

"It's not likely that you'll be able to hide this job from him," he mused with a chuckle. "A lot of our patrons do business with him. I wouldn't like to make more enemies than I already have."

"He won't mind," she assured him with a smile. She crossed her fingers silently.

"Then come along and I'll acquaint you with the job," Jed said, moving around the desk. "Welcome aboard, Miss Brewster."

She smiled. "Thanks!"

CHAPTER FIVE

FRED BREWSTER CAME home from Denver discouraged. "I couldn't get anybody interested," he told Janie as he flopped down in his favorite easy chair in the living room. "Everybody's got money problems, and the market is down. It's a bad time to fish for partners."

Janie sat down on the sofa across from him. "I got a job."

He just stared at her for a minute, as if he didn't hear her. "You what?"

"I got a job," she said, and smiled at him. "I'll make good money in tips. I start tonight."

"Where?" he asked.

"A restaurant," she lied. "You can even come and eat there, and I'll serve you. You won't have to tip me, either!"

"Janie," he groaned. "I wanted you to go back and finish your degree."

She leaned forward. "Dad, let's be honest. You can't afford college right now, and if I went, it would have to be on work-study. Let me do this," she implored. "I'm young and strong and I don't mind working. You'll pull out of this, Dad, I know you will!" she added gently. "Everybody has bad times. This is ours."

He scowled. "It hurts my pride..."

She knelt at his feet and leaned her arms over his thin, bony knees. "You're my dad," she said. "I love you. Your problems are my problems. You'll come up with an angle that will get us out of this. I don't have a single doubt."

Those beautiful eyes that were so like his late wife's weakened his resolve. He smiled and touched her hair gently. "You're like your mother."

"Thanks!"

He chuckled. "Okay. Do your waitress bit for a few weeks and I'll double my efforts on getting us out of hock. But no late hours," he emphasized. "I want you home by midnight, period."

That might be a problem. But why bother him with complications right now?

"We'll see how it goes," she said easily, getting to her feet. She planted a kiss on his forehead. "I'd better get you some lunch!"

She dashed into the kitchen before he could ask any more questions about her new employment.

But she wasn't so lucky with Hettie. "I don't like the idea of you working in a bar," she told Janie firmly.

"Shhhh!" Janie cautioned, glancing toward the open kitchen door. "Don't let Dad hear you!"

Hettie grimaced. "Child, you'll end up in a brawl, sure as God made little green apples!"

"I will not. I'm going to waitress and make pizzas and sandwiches, not get in fights."

Hettie wasn't convinced. "Put men and liquor together, and you get a fight every time."

"Mr. Duncan has a bouncer," she confided. "I'll be fine."

"Mr. Hart won't like it," she replied.

"Nothing I do is any of Leo Hart's business anymore," Janie said with a glare. "After the things he's said about me, his opinion wouldn't get him a cup of coffee around here!"

"What sort of things?" Hettie wanted to know.

She rubbed her hands over the sudden chill of her arms. "That I'm a lying, gossiping, man-chaser who can't leave him alone," she said miserably. "He was talking about me to Joe Howland in the hardware store last week. I heard every horrible word."

Hettie winced. She knew how Janie felt about the last of the unmarried Hart brothers. "Oh, baby. I'm so sorry!"

"Marilee lied," she added sadly. "My best friend! She was telling me what to do to make Leo notice me, and all the time she was finding ways to cut me out of his life. She was actually at the ball with Leo. He took her…" She swallowed hard and turned to the task at hand. Brooding was not going to help her situation. "Want a sandwich, Hettie?"

"No, darlin', I'm fine," the older woman told her. She hugged Janie warmly. "Life's tangles work themselves out if you just give them enough time," she said, and went away to let that bit of homespun philosophy sink in.

Janie was unconvinced. Her tangles were bad ones. Maybe her new job would keep Leo out of her thoughts. At least she'd never have to worry about running into him at Shea's, she told herself. After Saturday night, he was probably off hard liquor for life.

BY SATURDAY NIGHT, Janie had four days of work under her belt and she was getting used to the routine. Shea's opened at lunchtime and closed at eleven. Shea's served pizza and sandwiches and chips, as well as any sort of liquor a customer could ask for. Janie often had to serve drinks in between cooking chores. She got to recognize some of the customers on sight, but she didn't make a habit of speaking to them. She didn't want any trouble.

Her father had, inevitably, found out about her nocturnal activities. Saturday morning, he'd been raging at her for lying to him.

"I do work in a restaurant," she'd defended herself. "It's just sort of in a bar."

"You work in a bar, period!" he returned, furious. "I want you to quit, right now!"

It was now or never, she told herself, as she faced him bravely. "No," she replied quietly. "I'm not giving notice. Mr. Duncan said I could work two weeks and see if I could handle it, and that's just what I'm going to do. And don't you dare talk to him behind my back, Dad," she told him.

He looked tormented. "Girl, this isn't necessary!"

"It is, and not only because we need the money," she'd replied. "I need to feel independent."

He hadn't considered that angle. She was determined, and Duncan did have a good bouncer, a huge man called, predictably, Tiny. "We'll see," he'd said finally.

Janie had won her first adult argument with her parent. She felt good about it.

HARLEY SHOWED UP two of her five nights on the job, just to check things out. He was back again tonight. She grinned at him as she served him pizza and beer.

"How's it going?" he asked.

She looked around at the bare wood floors, the no-frills surroundings, the simple wooden tables and chairs and the long counter at which most of the customers—male customers—sat. There were two game machines and a jukebox. There were ceiling fans to circulate the heat, and to cool the place in summer. There was a huge dance floor, where people could dance to live music on Friday and Saturday night. The band was playing now, lazy Western tunes, and a couple was circling the dance floor alone.

"I really like it here," she told Harley with a smile. "I feel as if I'm standing on my own two feet for the first time in my life." She leaned closer. "And the tips are really nice!"

He chuckled. "Okay. No more arguments from me." He glanced toward Tiny, a huge man with tattoos on both arms and a bald head, who'd taken an immediate liking to Janie. He was reassuringly close whenever she spoke to customers or served food and drinks.

"Isn't he a doll?" Janie asked, smiling toward Tiny, who smiled back a little hesitantly, as if he were afraid his face might crack.

"That's not a question you should ask a man, Janie," he teased.

Grinning, she flipped her bar cloth at him, and went back to work.

LEO WENT LOOKING for Fred Brewster after lunch on Monday. He'd been out of town at a convention, and he'd lost touch with his friend.

Fred was in his study, balancing figures that didn't want to be balanced. He looked up as Hettie showed Leo in.

"Hello, stranger," Fred said with a grin. "Sit down. Want some coffee? Hettie, how about…!"

"No need to shout, Mr. Fred, it's already dripping," she interrupted him with a chuckle. "I'll bring it in when it's done."

"Cake, too!" he called.

There was a grumble.

"She thinks I eat too many sweets," Fred told Leo. "Maybe I do. How was the convention?"

"It was pretty good," Leo told him. "There's a lot of talk about beef exports to Japan and improved labeling of beef to show country of origin. Some discussion of artificial additives," he confided with a chuckle. "You can guess where that came from."

"J. D. Langley and the Tremayne brothers."

"Got it in one guess." Leo tossed his white Stetson into a nearby chair and sat down in the one beside it. He ran a hand through his thick gold-streaked brown hair and his dark eyes pinned Fred. "But aside from the convention, I've heard some rumors that bother me," he said, feeling his way.

"Oh?" Fred put aside his keyboard mouse and sat back. He'd heard about Janie's job, he thought, groaning inwardly. He drew in a long breath. "What rumors?" he asked innocently.

Leo leaned forward, his crossed arms on his knees. "That you're looking for partners here."

"Oh. That." Fred cleared his throat and looked past Leo. "Just a few little setbacks…"

"Why didn't you come to me?" Leo persisted, scowling. "I'd loan you anything you needed on the strength of your signature. You know that."

Fred swallowed. "I do...know that. But I wouldn't dare. Under the circumstances." He avoided Leo's piercing stare.

"What circumstances?" Leo asked with resignation, when he realized that he was going to have to pry every scrap of information out of his friend.

"Janie."

Leo's breath expelled in a rush. He'd wondered if Fred knew about the friction between the two of them. It was apparent that he did. "I see."

Fred glanced at him and winced. "She won't hear your name mentioned," he said apologetically. "I couldn't go to you behind her back, and she'd find out anyway, sooner or later. Jacobsville is a small town."

"She wouldn't be likely to find out when she's away at college," Leo assured him. "She has gone back, hasn't she?"

There was going to be an explosion. Fred knew it without saying a word. "Uh, Leo, she hasn't gone back, exactly."

His eyebrows lifted. "She's not here. I asked Hettie. She flushed and almost dragged me in here without saying anything except Janie wasn't around. I assumed she'd gone back to school."

"No. She's, uh, got a job, Leo. A good job," he added, trying to reassure himself. "She likes it very much."

"Doing what, for God's sake?" Leo demanded. "She has no skills to speak of!"

"She's cooking. At a restaurant."

Leo felt his forehead. "No fever," he murmured to himself. It was a well-known fact that Janie could burn water in a pan. He pinned Fred with his eyes. "Would you like to repeat that?"

"She's cooking. She can cook," he added belligerently at Leo's frank astonishment. "Hettie spent two months with her in the kitchen. She can even make—" he started to say "biscuits" and thought better of it "—pizza."

Leo whistled softly. "Fred, I didn't know things were that bad. I'm sorry."

"The bull dying was nobody's fault," Fred said heavily. "But I used money I hoped to recoup to buy him, and there was no insurance. Very few small ranchers could take a loss like that and remain standing. He was a champion's offspring."

"I know that. I'd help, if you'd let me," Leo said earnestly.

"I appreciate it. But I can't."

There was a long, pregnant pause. "Janie told you about what happened at the ball, I suppose," Leo added curtly.

"No. She hasn't said a single word about that," Fred replied. He frowned. "Why?" He understood, belatedly, Leo's concerned stare. "She did tell me about what happened in the hardware store," he added slowly. "There's more?"

Leo glanced away. "There was some unpleasantness at the ball, as well. We had a major fight." He studied his big hands. "I've made some serious mistakes lately. I believed some gossip about Janie that I should never have credited. I know better now, but it's too late. She won't let me close enough to apologize."

That was news. "When did you see her?" Fred asked, playing for time.

"In town at the bank Friday," he said. "She snubbed me." He smiled faintly. It had actually hurt when she'd given him a harsh glare, followed by complete oblivion to his presence. "First time that's happened to me in my life."

"Janie isn't usually rude," Fred tried to justify her behavior. "Maybe it's just the new job…"

"It's what I said to her, Fred," the younger man replied heavily. "I really hurt her. Looking back, I don't know why I ever believed what I was told."

Fred was reading between the lines. "Marilee can be very convincing, Janie said. And she had a case on you."

"It wasn't mutual," Leo said surprisingly. "I didn't realize what was going on. Then she told me all these things Janie was telling people…" He stopped and cursed harshly. "I thought I could see through lies. I guess I'm more naive than I thought I was."

"Any man can be taken in," Fred reassured him. "It was just bad luck. Janie never said a word about you in public. She's shy, although you might not realize it. She'd never throw herself at a man. Well, not for real," he amended with a faint smile. "She did dress up and flirt with you. She told Hettie it was the hardest thing she'd ever done in her life, and she agonized over it for days afterward. Not the mark of a sophisticated woman, is it?"

Leo understood then how far he'd fallen. No wonder she'd been so upset when she overheard him running down her aggressive behavior. "No," he replied. "I wish I'd seen through it." He smiled wryly. "I don't like aggressive, sophisticated women," he confessed. "Call it a fatal flaw. I liked Janie the way she was."

"Harmless?" Fred mused.

Leo flushed. "I wouldn't say that."

"Wouldn't you?" Fred leaned back in his chair, smiling at the younger man's confusion. "I've sheltered Janie too much. I wanted her to have a smooth, easy path through life. But I did her no favors. She's not a dress-up doll, Leo, she's a woman. She needs to learn independence, self-sufficiency. She has a temper, and she's learning to use that, too. Last week, she stood up to me for the first time and told me what she was going to do." He chuckled. "I must confess, it was pretty shocking to realize that my daughter was a woman."

"She's going around with Harley," Leo said curtly.

"Why shouldn't she? Harley's a good man—young, but steady and dependable. He, uh, did go up against armed men and held his own, you know."

Leo did know. It made him furious to know. He didn't hang out with professional soldiers. He'd been in the service, and briefly in combat, but he'd never fought drug dealers and been written up in newspapers as a local hero.

Fred deduced all that from the look on Leo's lean face. "It's not like you think," he added. "She and Harley are friends. Just friends."

"Do I care?" came the impassioned reply. He grabbed up his Stetson and got to his feet. He hesitated, turning back to Fred. "I won't insist, but Janie would never have to know if I took an interest in the ranch," he added firmly.

Fred was tempted. He sighed and stood up, too. "I've worked double shifts for years, trying to keep it solvent. I've survived bad markets, drought, unseasonable cold.

But this is the worst it's ever been. I could lose the property so easily."

"Then don't take the risk," Leo insisted. "I can loan you what it takes to get you back in the black. And I promise you, Janie will never know. It will be between the two of us. Don't lose the ranch out of pride, Fred. It's been in your family for generations."

Fred grimaced. "Leo…"

The younger man leaned both hands on the desk and impaled Fred with dark eyes. "Let me help!"

Fred studied the determination, the genuine concern in that piercing stare. "It would have to be a secret," he said, weakening.

Leo's eyes softened. "It will be. You have my word. Blake Kemp's our family attorney. I'll make an appointment. We can sit down with him and work out the details."

Fred had to bite down hard on his lower lip to keep the brightness in his eyes in check. "You can't possibly know how much…" He choked.

Leo held up a hand, embarrassed by his friend's emotion. "I'm filthy rich," he said curtly. "What good is money if you can't use it to help out friends? You'd do the same for me in a heartbeat if our positions were reversed."

Fred swallowed noticeably. "That goes without saying." He drew in a shaky breath. "Thanks," he bit off.

"You're welcome." Leo slanted his hat across his eyes. "I'll phone you. By the way, which restaurant is Janie working at?" he added. "I might stop by for lunch one day."

"That wouldn't be a good idea just yet," Fred said,

feeling guilty because Leo still didn't know what was going on.

Leo considered that. "You could be right," he had to agree. "I'll let it ride for a few days, then. Until she cools down a little, at least." He grinned. "She's got a hell of a temper, Fred. Who'd have guessed?"

Fred chuckled. "She's full of surprises lately."

"That she is. I'll be in touch."

Leo was gone and Fred let the emotion out. He hadn't realized how much his family ranch meant to him until he was faced with the horrible prospect of losing it. Now, it would pass to Janie and her family, her children. God bless Leo Hart for being a friend when he needed one so desperately. He grabbed at a tissue and wiped his eyes. Life was good. Life was very good!

FRED WAS STILL up when Janie got home from work. She was tired. It had been a long night. She stopped in the kitchen to say good-night to Hettie before she joined her father in his study.

"Hettie said Leo came by," she said without her usual greeting. She looked worried. "Why?"

"He wanted to check on his bull," he lied without meeting her eyes.

She hesitated. "Did he…ask about me?"

"Yes," he said. "I told him you had a job working in a restaurant."

She stared at her feet. "Did you tell him which one?"

He looked anxious. "No."

She met his eyes. "You don't have to worry, Dad. It's none of Leo Hart's business where I work, or whatever else I do."

"You're still angry," he noted. "I understand. But he wants to make peace."

She swallowed, hearing all over again his voice taunting her, baiting her. She clenched both hands at her sides. "He wants to bury the hatchet? Good. I know exactly where to bury it."

"Now, daughter, he's not a bad man."

"Of course he's not. He just doesn't like me," she bit off. "You can't blame him, not when he's got Marilee."

He winced. "I didn't think. You lost your only friend."

"Some friend," she scoffed. "She's gone to spend the holidays in Colorado," she added smugly. "A rushed trip, I heard."

"I imagine she's too ashamed to walk down the main street right now," her father replied. "People have been talking about her, and that's no lie. But she's not really a bad woman, Janie. She just made a mistake. People do."

"You don't," she said unexpectedly, and smiled at him. "You're the only person in the world who wouldn't stab me in the back."

He flushed. Guilt overwhelmed him. What would she say when she knew that he was going to let Leo Hart buy into the ranch, and behind her back? It was for a good cause, so that she could eventually inherit her birthright, but he felt suddenly like a traitor. He could only imagine how she'd look at him if she ever found out....

"Why are you brooding?" she teased. "You need to put away those books and go to bed."

He stared at the columns that wouldn't balance and thought about having enough money to fix fences, repair the barn, buy extra feed for the winter, buy replacement heifers, afford medicine for his sick cattle and veterinarian's fees. The temptation was just too much for him. He couldn't let the ranch go to strangers.

"Do you ever think about down the road," Fred murmured, "when your children grow up and take over the ranch?"

She blinked. "Well, yes, sometimes," she confessed. "It's a wonderful legacy," she added with a soft smile. "We go back such a long way in Jacobsville. It was one of your great-uncles who was the first foreman of the Jacobs ranch properties when the founder of our town came here and bought cattle, after the Civil War. This ranch was really an offshoot of that one," she added. "There's so much history here!"

Fred swallowed. "Too much to let the ranch go down the tube, or end up in the hands of strangers, like the Jacobs place did." He shook his head. "That was sad, to see Shelby and Ty thrown off their own property. That ranch had been in their family over a hundred years."

"It wasn't much of a ranch anymore," she reminded him. "More of a horse farm. But I understand what you mean. I'm glad we'll have the ranch to hand down to our descendants." She gave him a long look. "You aren't thinking of giving it up without a fight?"

"Heavens, no!"

She relaxed. "Sorry. But the way you were talking…"

"I'd do almost anything to keep it in the family," Fred assured her. "You, uh, wouldn't have a problem with me taking on a partner or an investor?"

"Of course not," she assured him. "So you found someone in Colorado after all?" she added excitedly. "Somebody who's willing to back us?"

"Yes," he lied, "but I didn't hear until today."

"That's just great!" she exclaimed.

He gave her a narrow look. "I'm glad you think so. Then you can give up that job and go back to college..."

"No."

His eyebrows went up. "But, Janie..."

"Dad, even with an investor, we still have the day-to-day operation of the ranch to maintain," she reminded him gently. "How about groceries? Utilities? How about cattle feed and horse feed and salt blocks and fencing?"

He sighed. "You're right, of course. I'll need the investment for the big things."

"I like my job," she added. "I really do."

"It's a bad place on the weekends," he worried.

"Tiny likes me," she assured him. "And Harley comes in at least two or three times a week, mostly on Fridays and Saturdays, to make sure I'm doing all right. I feel as safe at Shea's as I do right here with you."

"It's not that I mind you working," he said, trying to explain.

"I know that. You're just worried that I might get in over my head. Tiny doesn't let anybody have too much to drink before he makes them leave. Mr. Duncan is emphatic about not having drunks in the place."

Fred sighed. "I know when I'm licked. I may show up for pizza one Saturday night, though."

She grinned. "You'd be welcome! I could show you off to my customers."

"Leo wanted to know where you were working," he said abruptly. "He wanted to come by and see you."

Her face tautened. "I don't want to see him."

"So I heard. He was, uh, pretty vocal about the way you snubbed him."

She tossed back her hair. "He deserved it. I'm nobody's doormat. He isn't going to walk all over me and get away with it!"

"He won't like you working at Shea's, no matter what you think."

"Why do you care?" she asked suspiciously.

He couldn't tell her that Leo might renege on the loan if he knew Fred was letting her work in such a dive. He felt guilty as sin for not coming clean. But he was so afraid of losing the ranch. It was Janie's inheritance. He had to do everything he could to keep it solvent.

"He's my friend," he said finally.

"I used to think he was mine, too," she replied. "But friends don't talk about each other the way he was talking about me. As if I'd ever gossip about him!"

"I think he knows that now, Janie."

She forced the anger to the back of her mind. "I guess if he knew what I was doing, he'd faint. He doesn't think I can cook at all."

"I did tell him you had a cooking job," he confided.

Her eyes lit up. "You did? What did he say?"

"He was...surprised."

"He was astonished," she translated.

"It bothered him that you snubbed him. He said he felt really bad about the things he said, that you overheard. He, uh, told me about the fight you had at the ball, too."

Her face colored. "What did he tell you?"

"That you'd had a bad argument. Seemed to tickle him that you had a temper," he added with a chuckle.

"He'll find out I have a temper if he comes near me again." She turned. "I'm going to bed, Dad. You sleep good."

"You, too, sweetheart. Good night."

He watched her walk away with a silent sigh of relief. So far, he thought, so good.

CHAPTER SIX

THE FOLLOWING WEDNESDAY, Leo met with Blake Kemp and Fred Brewster in Kemp's office, to draw up the instrument of partnership.

"I'll never be able to thank you enough for this, Leo," Fred said as they finished a rough draft of the agreement.

"You'd have done it for me," Leo said simply. "How long will it take until those papers are ready to sign?" he asked Kemp.

"We'll have them by Monday," Kemp assured him.

"I'll make an appointment with your receptionist on the way out," Leo said, rising. "Thanks, Blake."

The attorney shook his outstretched hand, and then Fred's. "All in a day's work. I wish most of my business was concluded this easily, and amiably," he added wryly.

Leo checked his watch. "Why don't we go out to Shea's and have a beer and some pizza, Fred?" he asked the other man, who, curiously, seemed paler.

Fred was scrambling for a reason that Leo couldn't go to Shea's. "Well, because, uh, because Hettie made chili!" he remembered suddenly. "So why don't you come home and eat with me? We've got Mexican corn bread to go with it!"

Leo hesitated. "That does sound pretty good," he had to admit. Then he remembered. Janie would be there. He

was uncomfortable with the idea of rushing in on her un-
expectedly, especially in light of recent circumstances.
He was still a little embarrassed about his own behavior.
He searched for a reason to refuse, and found one. "Oh,
for Pete's sake, I almost forgot!" he added, slapping his
forehead. "I'm supposed to have supper with Cag and
Tess tonight. We're going in together on two new Santa
Gertrudis bulls. How could I have forgotten...got to run,
Fred, or I'll never make it on time!"

"Sure, of course," Fred said, and looked relieved.
"Have a good time!"

Leo chuckled. "I get to play with my nephew. That's
fun, all right. I like kids."

"You never seemed the type," Fred had to admit.

"I'm not talking about having any of my own right
away," Leo assured him. "I don't want to get married.
But I like all my nephews, not to mention my niece."

Fred only smiled.

"Thanks for the offer of supper, anyway," he told the
older man with a smile. "Sorry I can't come."

Fred relaxed. "That's okay, Leo. More for me," he
teased. "Well, I'll go home and have my chili. Thanks
again. If I can ever do anything for you, anything at all,
you only have to ask."

Leo smiled. "I know that, Fred. See you."

They parted in the parking lot. Leo got in his double-
cabbed pickup and gunned the engine.

Fred got into his own truck and relaxed. At least, he
thought, he didn't have to face Leo's indignation today.
With luck, Leo might never realize what was going on.

Leo, honest to the core, phoned Cag and caged an invitation to supper to discuss the two new bulls the broth-

ers were buying. But he had some time before he was due at his brother's house. He brooded over Fred's dead bull, and Christabel's, and he began to wonder. He had a bull from that same lot, a new lineage of Salers bulls that came from a Victoria breeder. Two related bulls dying in a month's time seemed just a bit too much for coincidence. He picked up the phone and called information.

CAG AND TESS were still like newlyweds, Leo noted as he carried their toddler around the living room after supper, grinning from ear to ear as the little boy, barely a year old, smiled up at him and tried to grab his nose. They sat close together on the sofa and seemed to radiate love. They were watching him with equal interest.

"You do that like a natural," Cag teased.

Leo shifted the little boy. "Lots of practice," he chuckled. "Simon's two boys, then Corrigan's boy and their new girl, and now your son." He lifted an eyebrow. "Rey and Meredith are finally expecting, too, I hear."

"They are," Cag said with a sigh. He eyed his brother mischievously. "When are you planning to throw in the towel and join up?"

"Me? Never," Leo said confidently. "I've got a big house to myself, all the women I can attract, no responsibilities and plenty of little kids to spoil as they grow." He gave them an innocent glance. "Why should I want to tie myself down?"

"Just a thought," Cag replied. "You'll soon get tired of going all the way to town every morning for a fresh biscuit." Cag handed the baby back to Tess.

"I'm thinking of taking a cooking course," Leo remarked.

Cag roared.

"I could cook if I wanted to!" Leo said indignantly.

Tess didn't speak, but her eyes did.

Leo stuffed his hands in his pockets. "Well, I don't really want to," he conceded. "And it is a long way to town. But I can manage." He sprawled in an easy chair. "There's something I want to talk to you about—besides our new bulls."

"What?" Cag asked, sensing concern.

"Fred's big Salers bull that died mysteriously," Leo said. "Christabel and Judd Dunn lost one, too, a young bull."

"Judd says it died of bloat."

"I saw the carcass, he didn't. He thinks Christabel made it up, God knows why. He wouldn't even come down from Victoria to take a look at it. It wasn't bloat. But she didn't call a vet out, and they didn't find any marks on Fred's bull." He sighed. "Cag, I've done a little checking. The bulls are related. The young herd sire of these bulls died recently as well, and the only champion Salers bull left that's still walking is our two-year-old bull that I loaned to Fred, although it's not related to the dead ones."

Cag sat up straight, scowling. "You're kidding."

Leo shook his head. "It's suspicious, isn't it?"

"You might talk to Jack Handley in Victoria, the rancher we bought our bull from."

"I did." He leaned forward intently. "Handley said he fired two men earlier this year for stealing from him. They're brothers, John and Jack Clark. One of them is a thief, the other has a reputation for vengeance that boggles the mind. When one former employer fired Jack

Clark, he lost his prize bull and all four young bulls he'd got from it. No apparent cause of death. Handley checked and found a pattern of theft and retribution with those brothers going back two years. At least four employers reported similar problems with theft and firing. There's a pattern of bull deaths, too. The brothers were suspects in a recent case in Victoria, but there was never enough evidence to convict anyone. Until now, I don't imagine anyone's connected the dots."

"How the hell do they keep getting away with it?" Cag wanted to know.

"There's no proof. And they're brawlers," Leo said. "They intimidate people."

"They wouldn't intimidate us," Cag remarked.

"They wouldn't. But do you see the common thread here? Handley crossed the brothers. He had a new, expensive Salers bull that he bred to some heifers, and he sold all the young bulls this year, except for his seed bull. His seed bull, and all its offspring, which isn't many, have died. Christabel Gaines's young bull was one of Handley's, like Fred's. And Jack Clark was fired by Judd Dunn for stealing, too."

Cag was scowling. "Where are the brothers now?"

"I asked Handley. He says John Clark is working on a ranch near Victoria. We know that Jack, the one with a reputation for getting even, is right here in Jacobsville, driving a cattle truck for Duke Wright," Leo said. "I called Wright and told him what I know. He's going to keep an eye on the man. I called Judd Dunn, too, but he was too preoccupied to listen. He's smitten with that redheaded supermodel who's in the movie they're making on Christabel's ranch—Tippy Moore, the 'Georgia Firefly.'"

"He'll land hard, if I make my guess," Cag said. "She's playing. He isn't."

"He's married, too," Leo said curtly. "Something he doesn't seem to remember."

"He only married Christabel because she was going to lose the ranch after her father beat her nearly to death in a drunken rage. Her mother was an invalid. No way could the two of them have kept it solvent," Cag added. "That's not a real marriage. I'm sure he's already looked into annulling it when she turns twenty-one."

"She was twenty-one this month," Leo said. "Poor kid. She's got a real case on him, and she's fairly plain except for those soulful brown eyes and a nice figure. She couldn't compete with the Georgia Firefly."

"So ask yourself what does a supermodel worth millions want with a little bitty Texas Ranger?" Cag grinned.

Tess gave him a speaking look. "As a happily married woman, I can tell you that if I wasn't hung up on you, Judd Dunn would make my mouth water."

Cag whistled.

Leo shrugged. "Whatever. But I think we should keep a close eye on our Salers bull, as well as Wright's new cattle-truck driver. Handley says Clark likes to drink, so it wouldn't hurt to keep an eye out at Shea's, as well."

Cag frowned thoughtfully. "You might have a word with Janie…"

"Janie?"

"Janie Brewster," his brother said impatiently. "Tell

her what the man looks like and have her watch him if he ever shows up out there."

Leo stared at his brother. "Will you make sense? Why would Janie be at Shea's roadhouse in the first place?"

Realization dawned. Cag looked stunned, and then uncomfortable.

Tess grimaced. "He doesn't know. I guess you'd better tell him."

"Tell me what?" Leo grumbled.

"Well, it's like this," Cag said. "Janie's been working at Shea's for a couple of weeks..."

"She's working in a bar?" Leo exploded violently.

Cag winced. "Now, Leo, she's a grown woman," he began calmly.

"She's barely twenty-one!" he continued, unabashed. "She's got no business working around drunks! What the hell is Fred thinking, to let her get a job in a place like that?"

Cag sighed. "Talk is that Fred's in the hole and can hardly make ends meet," he told Leo. "I guess Janie insisted on helping out."

Leo got to his feet and grabbed up his white Stetson, his lips in a thin line, his dark eyes sparking.

"Don't go over there and start trouble," Cag warned. "Don't embarrass the girl with her boss!"

Leo didn't answer him. He kept walking. His footsteps, quick and hard, described the temper he was in. He even slammed the door on the way out, without realizing he had.

Cag looked at Tess worriedly as Leo's car careened down the driveway. "Should I warn her?" he asked Tess.

She nodded. "At least she'll be prepared."

Cag thought privately that it was unlikely that any-body could prepare for Leo in a temper, but he picked up the phone just the same.

SHEA'S WASN'T CROWDED when Leo jerked to a stop in the parking lot. He walked into the roadhouse with blood in his eye. Three men at a table near the door stopped talking when they saw him enter. Apparently they thought he looked dangerous.

Janie was thinking the same thing. She'd assured Cag that she wasn't afraid of Leo, but it was a little different when the man was walking toward her with his eyes narrow and his lips compressed like that.

He stopped at the counter. He noted her long apron, her hands with a dusting of flour, a pencil behind her ear. She looked busy. There were three cowboys at the counter drinking beers and apparently waiting for piz-zas. A teenage boy was pulling a pizza on a long paddle out of a big oven behind her.

"Get your things," he told Janie in a tone he hadn't used with her since she was ten and had gotten into a truck with a cowboy who offered her a trip to the vis-iting carnival. He'd busted up that cowboy pretty bad, and for reasons Janie only learned later. She'd had a very close call. Leo had saved her. But she didn't need saving right now.

She lifted her chin and glared at him. The night of the ball came back to her vividly. "How's your foot?" she asked with sarcasm.

"My foot is fine. Get your things," he repeated curtly.

"I work here."

"Not anymore."

She crossed her arms. "You planning to carry me out kicking and screaming? Because that's the only way I'm leaving."

"Suits me." He started around the counter.

She picked up a pitcher of beer and dumped the contents on him. "Now you listen to me… Leo!"

The beer didn't even slow him down. He had her up in his arms and he turned, carrying her toward the door. She was kicking and screaming for all she was worth.

That attracted Tiny, the bouncer. He was usually on the job by six, but he'd arrived late today. To give him credit, the minute he saw Janie, he turned and went toward the big man bullying her.

He stepped in front of Leo. "Put her down, Leo," he drawled.

"You tell him, Tiny!" Janie sputtered.

"I'm taking her home where she'll be safe," Leo replied. He knew Tiny. The man was sweet-natured, but about a beer short of a six-pack on intelligence. He was also as big as a house. It didn't hurt to be polite. "She shouldn't be working in a bar."

"It isn't a bar," Tiny said reasonably. "It's a roadhouse. It's a nice roadhouse. Mr. Duncan don't allow no drunks. You put Miss Janie down, Leo, or I'll have to hit you."

"He'll do it," Janie warned. "I've seen him do it. He's hit men even bigger than you. Haven't you, Tiny?" she encouraged.

"I sure have, Miss Janie."

Leo wasn't backing down. He glared at Tiny. "I said," he replied, his voice dangerously soft, "I'm taking her home."

"I don't think she wants to go, Mr. Hart," came a new source of interference from the doorway behind him.

He swung around with Janie in his big arms. It was Harley Fowler, leaning against the doorjamb, looking intimidating. It would have been a joke a year ago. The new Harley made it look good.

"You tell him, Harley!" Janie said enthusiastically.

"You keep still," Leo told her angrily. "You've got no business working in a rough joint like this!"

"You have no right to tell me where I can work," Janie shot right back, red-faced and furious. "Won't Marilee mind that you're here pestering me?" she added viciously.

His cheeks went red. "I haven't seen Marilee in two weeks. I don't give a damn if I never see her again, either."

That was news. Janie looked as interested as Harley seemed to.

Tiny was still hovering. "I said, put her down," he persisted.

"Do you really think you can take on Tiny and me both?" Harley asked softly.

Leo was getting mad. His face tautened. "I don't know about Tiny," he said honestly, putting Janie back on her feet without taking his eyes off Harley. "But you're a piece of cake, son."

As he said it, he stepped forward and threw a quick punch that Harley wasn't expecting. With his mouth open, Harley tumbled backward over a table. Leo glared at Janie.

"You want this job, keep it," he said, ice-cold except for the glitter in those dark eyes. "But if you get slugged during a brawl or hassled by amorous drunks, don't come crying to me!"

"As…as if I ever…would!" she stammered, shocked by his behavior.

He turned around and stalked out the door without giving Harley a single glance.

Janie rushed to Harley and helped him back to his feet. "Oh, Harley, are you hurt?" she asked miserably.

He rubbed his jaw. "Only my pride, darlin'," he murmured with a rough chuckle. "Damn, that man can throw a punch! I wasn't really expecting him to do it." His eyes twinkled. "I guess you're a little more important to him than any of us realized."

She flushed. "He's just trying to run my life."

Tiny came over and inspected Harley's jaw. "Gonna have a bruise, Mr. Fowler," he said politely.

Harley grinned. He was a good sport, and he knew a jealous man when he saw one. Leo had wanted to deck him at the ball over Janie, but he'd restrained himself. Now, maybe, he felt vindicated. But Harley wished there had been a gentler way of doing it. His jaw was really sore.

"The beast," Janie muttered. "Come on, Harley, I'll clean you up in the bathroom before it gets crowded. Okay, guys, fun's over. Drink your beer and eat your pizzas."

"Yes, mother," one of the men drawled.

She gave him a wicked grin and led Harley to the back. She was not going to admit the thrill it had given her that Leo was worried about her job, or that people thought he was jealous of Harley. But she felt it all the way to her bones.

Leo was lucky not to get arrested for speeding on his way to Fred's house. He had the sports car flat-out on the four lane that turned onto the Victoria road, and he burned rubber when he left the tarmac and turned into Fred's graveled driveway.

Fred heard him coming and knew without a doubt what was wrong.

He stood on the porch with his hands in his jean pockets as he studied the darkening sky behind Leo, who was already out of the car and headed for the porch. His Stetson was pulled down right over his eyes, cocked as they said in cowboy vernacular, and Fred had never seen Leo look so much like a Hart. The brothers had a reputation for being tough customers. Leo looked it right now.

"I want her out of that damned bar," Leo told Fred flatly, without even a conventional greeting. "You can consider it a term of the loan, if you like, but you get her home."

Fred grimaced. "I did try to talk her out of it, when I found out where she was working," he said in his own defense. "Leo, she stood right up to me and said she was old enough to make her own decisions. What do I say to that? She's twenty-one and she told me she wasn't giving up her job."

Leo cursed furiously.

"What happened to your shirt?" Fred asked suddenly. He leaned closer and made a face. "Man, you reek of beer!"

"Of course I do! Your daughter baptized me in front of a crowd of cowboys with a whole pitcher of the damned stuff!" Leo said indignantly.

Fred's eyes opened wide. "Janie? My Janie?"

Leo looked disgusted. "She flung the pitcher at me. And then she set the bouncer on me and appealed to Harley Fowler for aid."

"Why did she need aid?" Fred asked hesitantly.

"Oh, she was kicking and screaming, and they thought she was in trouble, I guess."

"Kicking…?"

Leo's lips compressed. "All right, if you have to know, I tried to carry her out of the bar and bring her home. She resisted."

Fred whistled. "I'd say she resisted." He was trying very hard not to laugh. He looked at Leo's clenched fists. One, the right one, was bleeding. "Hit somebody, did you?"

"Harley," he returned uncomfortably. "Well, he shouldn't have interfered! He doesn't own Janie, she's not his private stock. If he were any sort of a man, he'd have insisted that she go home right then. Instead, he stands there calmly ordering me to put her down. Ordering me. Hell! He's lucky it was only one punch!"

"Oh, boy," Fred said, burying his face in his hand. Gossip was going to run for a month on this mixer.

"It wasn't my fault," Leo argued, waving his hands. "I went in there to save her from being insulted and harassed by drunk men, and look at the thanks I get? Drenched in beer, threatened by ogres, giggled at…"

"Who giggled?"

Leo shifted. "This little brunette who was sitting with one of the Tremayne brothers' cowboys."

Fred cleared his throat. He didn't dare laugh. "I guess it was a sight to see."

Grimacing, Leo flexed his hand. "Damned near broke

my fingers on Harley's jaw. He needs to learn to keep his mouth shut. Just because he's not afraid of drug lords, he shouldn't think he can take me on and win."

"I'm sure he knows that now, Leo."

Leo took a deep breath. "You tell her I said she's going to give up that job, one way or the other!"

"I'll tell her." It won't matter, though, he thought privately. Janie was more than likely to dig her heels in big time after Leo's visit to Shea's.

Leo gave him a long, hard stare. "I'm not mean with money, I don't begrudge you that loan. But I'm not kidding around with you, Fred. Janie's got no business in Shea's, even with a bouncer on duty. It's a rough place. I've been there on nights when the bouncer didn't have time for a cup of coffee, and there's been at least one shooting. It's dangerous. Even more dangerous right now."

Something in the younger man's tone made Fred uneasy. "Why?"

"Fred, you don't breathe a word of this, even to Janie, understand?"

Fred nodded, curious.

Leo told him what he'd learned from Handley about the Clark brothers, and the loss of the related Salers bulls.

Fred's jaw flew open. "You think my bull was killed deliberately?"

"Yes, I do," Leo admitted solemnly. "I'm sorry to tell you that, because I can't prove it and neither can you. Clark is shrewd. He's never been caught in the act. If you can't prove it, you can't prosecute."

Fred let out an angry breath. "Of all the damned mean, low things to do!"

"I agree, and it's why I'm putting two men over here to watch my bull," he added firmly. "No sorry cattle-killer is going to murder my bull and get away with it. I'm having video cameras installed, too. If he comes near that bull, I'll have his hide in jail!"

Fred chuckled. "Don't I wish he'd try," he said thoughtfully.

"So do I, but I don't hold out a lot of hope," Leo returned. He moved his shoulders restlessly. The muscles were stretched, probably from Janie's violent squirming. He remembered without wanting to the feel of her soft breasts pressed hard against his chest, and he ached.

"Uh, about Janie," Fred continued worriedly.

Leo stared at him without speaking.

"Okay," the older man said wearily. "I'll try to talk some sense into her." He pursed his lips and peered up at Leo. "Of course, she could be a lot of help where she is right now," he murmured thoughtfully. "With the Clark man roaming around loose, that is. She could keep an eye on him if he comes into Shea's. If he's a drinking man, that's the only joint around that sells liquor by the drink."

"She doesn't know what he looks like," Leo said.

"Can't you find out and tell her?"

Leo sighed. "I don't like her being in the line of fire."

"Neither do I." Fred gave the other man a curious scrutiny. "You and Harley and I could arrange to drop in from time to time, just to keep an eye on her."

"She'll have to ask Harley. I won't."

"You're thinking about it, aren't you?" Fred persisted.

Leo was. His eyes narrowed. "My brothers could drop in occasionally, and so could our ranch hands. The Tremaynes would help us out. I know Harden. I'll talk to him. And most of our cowhands go into Shea's on the weekend. I'll talk to our cattle foreman."

"I know Cy Parks and Eb Scott," Fred told him. "They'd help, too."

Leo perked up. With so many willing spies, Janie would be looked after constantly, and she'd never know it. He smiled.

"It's a good idea, isn't it?"

Leo glared at him. "You just don't want to have to make Janie quit that job. You're scared of her, aren't you? What's the matter, think she'd try to drown you in cheap beer, too?"

Fred burst out laughing. "You have to admit, it's a shock to think of Janie throwing beer at anybody."

"I guess it is, at that," Leo seconded, remembering how shy Janie had been. It was only after Marilee had caused so much trouble with her lies that Leo had considered Janie's lack of aggression.

In the past, that was, he amended, because he'd never seen such aggression as he'd encountered in little Janie Brewster just an hour ago.

He shook his head. "It was all I could do not to get thrown on the floor. She's a handful when she's mad. I don't think I've ever seen her lose her temper before."

"There's a lot about her you don't know," Fred said enigmatically.

"Okay, she can stay," Leo said at once. "But I'll find out what Clark looks like. I'll get a picture if I can manage it. Maybe Grier at the police station would have an idea. He's sweet on Christabel Gaines, and she lost a bull to this dude, so he might be willing to assist."

"Don't get Judd Dunn mad," Fred warned.

Leo shrugged. "He's too stuck on his pretty model to care much about Christabel right now, or Grier, either. I don't want any more bulls killed, and I want that man out of the way before he really hurts somebody."

"Have you talked to his boss?"

"Duke Wright didn't have a clue that his new truck driver was such an unsavory character," Leo said, "and he was keen to fire him on the spot. I persuaded him not to. He needs to be where we can watch him. If he puts a foot wrong, we can put him away. I love animals," Leo said in an uncharacteristically tender mood. "Especially bulls. The kind we keep are gentle creatures. They follow us around like big dogs and eat out of our hands." His face hardened visibly. "A man who could cold-bloodedly kill an animal like that could kill a man just as easily. I want Clark out of here. Whatever it takes. But Janie's going to be watched, all the time she's working," Leo added firmly. "Nobody's going to hurt her."

Fred looked at the other man, sensing emotions under the surface that Leo might not even realize were there.

"Thanks, Leo," he said.

The younger man squared his shoulders and shrugged. "I've got to go home and change my shirt." He looked down at himself and smiled ruefully. "Damn. I may never drink another beer."

"It tastes better than it wears," Fred said, deadpan.

Leo gave him a haughty look and went home.

CHAPTER SEVEN

LEO STOPPED BY Cash Grier's office at the police station in Jacobsville, catching the new assistant chief of police on his lunch hour.

"Come on in," Grier invited. He indicated his big desk, which contained a scattering of white boxes with metal handles. "Like Chinese food? That's moo goo gai pan, that's sweet-and-sour pork, and that's fried rice. Help yourself to a plate."

"Thanks, but I had barbecue at Barbara's Café," Leo replied, sitting down. He noted with little surprise that the man was adept with chopsticks. "I saw Toshiro Mifune catch flies with those things in one of the 'Samurai Trilogy' films," he commented.

Grier chuckled. "Don't believe everything you see, and only half of what you hear," he replied. He gave Leo a dark-eyed appraisal over his paper plate. "You're here about Clark, I guess."

Leo's eyebrows jumped.

"Oh, I'm psychic," Grier told him straight-faced. "I learned that when I was in the CIA knocking off enemy government agents from black helicopters with a sniper kit."

Leo didn't say a word.

Grier just shook his head. "You wouldn't believe the stuff I've done, to hear people talk."

"You're mysterious," Leo commented. "You keep to yourself."

Grier shrugged. "I have to. I don't want people to notice the aliens spying on me." He leaned forward confidentially. "You see them, too, don't you?" he asked in a hushed tone.

Leo began to get it. He started laughing and was secretly relieved when Grier joined him. The other man leaned back in his chair, with his booted feet propped on his desk. He was as fit as Leo, probably in even better condition, if the muscles outlined under that uniform shirt were any indication. Grier was said to move like lightning, although Leo had never seen him fight. The man was an enigma, with his black hair in a rawhide ponytail and his scarred face giving away nothing—unless he wanted it to.

"That's more like it," Grier said as he finished his lunch. "I thought I'd move to a small town and fit in." He smiled wryly. "But people are all the same. Only the scenery changes."

"It was the same for Cy Parks when he first moved here," Leo commented.

Grier gave him a narrow look. "Are you asking a question?"

"Making a comment," Leo told him. "One of our local guys was in the military during a conflict a few years back, in a special forces unit," he added deliberately, recounting something Cy Parks had told him about Harley Fowler. "He saw you on a plane, out of uniform and armed to the teeth."

Grier began to nod. "It's a small world, isn't it?" he asked pleasantly. He put down his plate and the chopsticks with deliberate preciseness. "I did a stint with military intelligence. And with a few…government agencies." He met Leo's curious eyes. "How far has that gossip traveled?"

"It got to Cy Parks and stopped abruptly," Leo replied, recalling what Cy had said to Harley about loose lips. "Jacobsville is a small town. We consider people who live here family, whether or not we're related to them. Gossip isn't encouraged."

Grier was surprised. He actually smiled. "If you asked Parks, or Steele, or Scott why they moved here," he said after a minute, "I imagine you'd learn that what they wanted most was an end to sitting with their backs to the wall and sleeping armed."

"Isn't that why you're here?" Leo wanted to know.

Grier met his eyes levelly. "I don't really know why I'm here, or if I can stay here," he said honestly. "I think I might eventually fit in. I'm going to give it a good try for six months," he added, "no matter how many rubbernecked yahoos stand outside my office trying to hear every damned word I say!" he raised his voice.

There were sudden, sharp footfalls and the sound of scurrying.

Leo chuckled. Grier hadn't even looked at the door when he raised his voice. He shrugged and smiled sheepishly. "I don't have eyes in the back of my head, but I love to keep people guessing about what I know."

"I think that may be part of the problem," Leo advised.

"Well, it doesn't hurt to keep your senses honed. Now. What do you want to know about Clark?"

"I'd like some way to get a photo of him," Leo confessed. "A friend of mine is working at Shea's. I'm going to ask her if she'll keep an eye on who he talks to, what he does, if he comes in there. She'll need to know what he looks like."

Grier sobered at once. "That's dangerous," he said. "Clark's brother almost killed a man he suspected of spying on him, up in Victoria. He made some threats, too."

Leo frowned. "Why are guys like that on the streets?"

"You can't shoot people or even lock them up without due process here in the States," Grier said with a wistful smile. "Pity."

"Listen, do they give you real bullets to go with that gun?" Leo asked, indicating the .45 caliber automatic in a shoulder holster that the man was wearing.

"I haven't shot anybody in months," Grier assured him. "I was a cyber crime specialist in the D.A.'s office San Antonio. I didn't really beat up that guy I was accused of harassing, I just told him I'd keep flies off him if he didn't level with me about his boss's illegal money laundering. I had access to his computerized financial records," he added with a twinkle in his dark eyes.

"I heard about that," Leo chuckled. "Apparently you used some access codes that weren't in the book."

"They let me off with a warning. When they checked my ID, I still had my old 'company' card."

Leo just shook his head. He couldn't imagine Grier being in trouble for very long. He knew too much. "All that specialized background, and you're handing out speeding tickets in Jacobsville, Texas."

"Don't knock it. Nobody's shot at me since I've been here." He got up and opened his filing cabinet with a key. "I have to keep it locked," he explained. "I have copies of documents about alien technology in here." He glanced at Leo to see if he was buying it and grinned. "Did you read that book by the Air Force guy who discovered night vision at a flying saucer crash?" He turned back to the files. "Hell, I should write a book. With what I know, governments might topple." He hesitated, frowned, with a file folder in his hand. "Our government might topple!"

"Clark?" Leo prompted.

"Clark. Right." He took a paper from the file, replaced it, closed the cabinet and locked it again. "Here. You don't have a clue where this photo came from, and I never saw you."

Leo was looking at a photograph of two men, obviously brothers, in, of all things, a newspaper clipping. Incredibly, they'd been honored with a good citizen award in another Texas town for getting a herd of escaped cattle out of the path of traffic and back into a fenced pasture with broken electric fencing.

"Neat trick," Grier said. "They cut the wire to steal the cattle, and then were seen rounding them up. Everybody thought they were saving the cattle. They had a tractor trailer truck just down the road and told people they were truck drivers who saw the cattle out and stopped to help." He laughed wholeheartedly. "Can you believe it?"

"Can you copy this for me?"

"That's a copy of the original. You can have it," Grier told him. "I've got two more."

"You were expecting trouble, I gather," Leo continued.

"Two expensive bulls in less than a month, both from the same herd sire, is a little too much coincidence even for me," Grier said as he sat back down. "When I heard Clark was working for Duke Wright, I put two and two together."

"There's no proof," Leo said.

"Not yet. We'll give him a little time and see if he'll oblige us by hanging himself." He laced his lean, strong hands together on the desk in front of him. "But you warn your friend not to be obvious. These are dangerous men."

"I'll tell her."

"And stop knocking men over tables in Shea's. It's outside the city limits, so I can't arrest you. But I can have the sheriff pick you up for brawling," Grier said abruptly, and he was serious. "You can't abduct women in plain sight of the public."

"I wasn't abducting her, I was trying to save her!"

"From what?"

"Fistfights!"

Grier lost it. He got up from his desk. "Get out," he invited through helpless laughter. "I have real work to do here."

"If Harley Fowler said I hit him without provocation, he's lying," Leo continued doggedly. "He never should have ordered me to put her down, and leave my hands free to hit him!"

"You should just tell the woman how you feel," Grier advised. "It's simpler." He glanced at Leo's swollen hand. "And less painful."

Leo didn't really know how he felt. That was the problem. He gave Grier a sardonic look and left.

HE WORRIED ABOUT letting Janie get involved, even from the sidelines, with Clark. Of course, the man might not even come near Shea's. He might buy a bottle and drink on the ranch, in the bunkhouse. But it wasn't a long shot to think he might frequent Shea's if he wanted company while he drank.

He disliked anything that might threaten Janie, and he didn't understand why he hated Harley all of a sudden. But she was in a great position to notice a man without being obvious, and for everyone's sake, Clark had to be watched. A man who would kill helpless animals was capable of worse.

He went looking for her Sunday afternoon, in a misting rain. She wasn't at home. Fred said that she was out, in the cold rain no less, wandering around the pecan trees in her raincoat. Brooding, was how Fred put it. Leo climbed back into his pickup and went after her.

Janie was oblivious to the sound of an approaching truck. She had her hands in her pockets, her eyes on the ground ahead of her, lost in thought.

It had been a revelation that Leo was concerned about her working at Shea's, and it had secretly thrilled her that he tried to make her quit. But he'd washed his hands of her when she wouldn't leave willingly, and he'd hurt her feelings with his comment that she shouldn't complain if she got in trouble. She didn't know what to make of his odd behavior. He'd given her a hard time, thanks to Marilee. But she hadn't been chasing him lately, so she couldn't understand why he was so bossy about her life. And she did feel guilty that he'd slugged poor Harley, who was only trying to help her.

The truck was almost on top of her before she finally heard the engine and jumped to the side of the ranch trail.

Leo pulled up and leaned over to open the passenger door. "Get in before you drown out there," he said.

She hesitated. She wasn't sure if it was safe to get that close to him.

He grimaced. "I'm not armed and dangerous," he drawled. "I just want to talk."

She moved closer to the open door. "You're in a very strange mood lately," she commented. "Maybe the lack of biscuits in your life has affected your mind."

Both eyebrows went up under his hat.

She flushed, thinking she'd been too forward. But she got into the truck and closed the door, removing the hood of her raincoat from her long, damp hair.

"You'll catch cold," he murmured, turning up the heat.

"It's not that wet, and I've got a lined raincoat."

He drove down the road without speaking, made a turn, and ended up in a field on the Hart ranch, a place where they could be completely alone. He put the truck in Park, cut off the engine, and leaned back against his door to study her from under the wide brim of his Stetson. "Your father says you won't give up the job."

"He's right," she replied, ready to do battle.

His fingers tapped rhythmically on the steering wheel. "I've been talking to Grier," he began.

"Now listen here, you can't have me arrested because I won't quit my job!" she interrupted.

He held up a big, lean hand. "Not about that," he corrected. "We've got a man in town who may be involved in some cattle losses. I want you to look at this picture and tell me if you've ever seen him in Shea's."

He took the newspaper clipping out of his shirt pocket, unfolded it, and handed it to her.

She took it gingerly and studied the two faces surrounded by columns of newsprint. "I don't know the man on the left," she replied. "But the one on the right comes in Saturday nights and drinks straight whiskey," she said uneasily. "He's loud and foul-mouthed, and Tiny had to ask him to leave last night."

Leo's face tightened. "He's vindictive," he told her.

"I'll say he is," she agreed at once. "When Tiny went out to get into his car, all his tires were slashed."

That was disturbing. "Did he report it to the sheriff?"

"He did," she replied. "They're going to look into it, but I don't know how they'll prove anything."

Leo traced an absent pattern on the seat behind her head. They were silent while the rain slowly increased, the sound of it loud on the hood and cab of the truck. "The man we're watching is Jack Clark," he told her, "the man you recognize in that photo." He took it back from her, refolded it, and replaced it in his pocket. "If he comes back in, we'd like you to see who he talks to. Don't be obvious about it. Tell Tiny to let it slide about his tires, I'll see that they're replaced."

"That's nice of you," she replied.

He shrugged. "He's protective of you. I like that."

His eyes were narrow and dark and very intent on her face. She felt nervous with him all at once and folded her hands in her lap to try and keep him from noticing. It was like another world, closed up with him in a truck in a rainstorm. It outmatched her most fervent dreams of close contact.

"What sort of cattle deaths do you suspect him of?" she asked curiously.

"Your father's bull, for one."

Her intake of breath was audible. "Why would he kill Dad's bull?" she wanted to know.

"It was one of the offspring of a bull he killed in Victoria. He worked for the owner, who fired him. Apparently his idea of proper revenge is far-reaching."

"He's nuts!" she exclaimed.

He nodded. "That's why you have to be careful if he comes back in. Don't antagonize him. Don't stare at him. Don't be obvious when you look at him." He sighed angrily. "I hate the whole idea of having you that close to a lunatic. I should have decked Tiny as well as Fowler and carried you out of there anyway."

His level, penetrating gaze made her heart race. "I'm not your responsibility," she challenged.

"Aren't you?" His dark eyes slid over her from head to toe. His head tilted back at a faintly arrogant angle.

She swallowed. He looked much more formidable now than he had at Shea's. "I should go," she began.

He leaned forward abruptly, caught her under the arms, and pulled her on top of him. He was sprawled over the front seat, with one long, powerful leg braced against the passenger floorboard and the other on the seat. Janie landed squarely between his denim-clad legs, pressed intimately to him.

"Leo!" she exclaimed, horribly embarrassed at the intimate proximity and trying to get up.

He looped an arm around her waist and held her there,

studying her flushed face with almost clinical scrutiny. "If you keep moving like that, you're going to discover the major difference between men and women in a vivid way, any minute."

She stilled at once. She knew what he meant. She'd felt that difference with appalling starkness at the ball. In fact, she was already feeling it again. She looked at him and her face colored violently.

"I told you," he replied, pursing his lips as he surveyed the damage. "My, my, didn't we know that men are easily aroused when we're lying full length on top of them?" he drawled. "We do now, don't we?"

She hit his shoulder, trying to hold on to her dignity as well as her temper. "You let go of me!"

"Spoilsport," he chided. He shifted her so that her head fell onto his shoulder and he could look down into her wide, startled eyes. "Relax," he coaxed. "What are you so afraid of?"

She swallowed. The closeness was like a drug. She felt swollen. Her legs trembled inside the powerful cage his legs made for them. Her breasts were hard against his chest, and they felt uncomfortably tight as well.

He looked down at them with keen insight, even moving her back slightly so that he could see the hard tips pressing against his shirt.

"You stop…looking at that!" she exclaimed without thinking.

He lifted an eyebrow and his smile was worldly. "A man likes to know that he's making an impression," he said outrageously.

She bit her lower lip, still blushing. "You're making too much of an impression already," she choked.

He leaned close and brushed his mouth lazily over her parted lips. "My body likes you," he whispered huskily. "It's making very emphatic statements about what it wants to do."

"You need...to speak...firmly to it," she said. She was trying to sound adult and firm, but her voice shook. It was hard to think, with his mouth hovering like that.

"It doesn't listen to reason," he murmured. He nibbled tenderly at her upper lip, parting it insistently from its companion. His free hand came up to tease around the corners of her mouth and down her chin to the opening her v-necked blouse made inside her raincoat.

His mouth worked on her lips while his hands freed her from the raincoat and slowly, absently, from her blouse as well. She was hardly aware of it. His mouth was doing impossibly erotic things to her lips, and one of his lean, strong hands was inside her blouse, teasing around the lacy edges of her brassiere.

The whole time, one long, powerful leg was sliding against the inside of her thigh, in a way so arousing that she didn't care what he did to her, as long as he didn't try to get up.

Her hands had worked their way into his thick, soft hair, and she was lifting up, trying to get closer to those slow, maddening fingers that were brushing against the soft flesh inside her bra. She'd never dreamed that a man could arouse her so quickly with nothing more invasive than a light brushing stroke of his hand. But she was on fire with hunger, need, aching need, to have him thrust those fingers down inside her frilly bra and close on her breast. It was torture to have him tease her like this. He was watching her face, too, watching the hunger grow with a dark arrogance that was going to make her squirm later in memory.

Right now, of course, she didn't care how he looked at her. If he would just slide that hand…down a…couple of…inches!

She was squirming in another way now, twisting her body ardently, pushing up against his stroking fingers while his mouth nibbled and nipped at her parted lips and his warm breath went into her mouth.

The rain was falling harder. It banged on the hood, and on top of the cab, with tempestuous fury. Inside, Janie could hear the tormented sound of her own breathing, feel her heartbeat shaking her madly, while Leo's practiced caresses grew slower and lazier on her taut body.

"Will you…please…!" she sputtered, gripping his arms.

"Will I please, what?" he whispered into her mouth.

"T-t-touch me!" she cried.

He nipped her upper lip ardently. "Touch you where?" he tormented.

Tears of frustration stung her eyes as they opened, meeting his. "You…know…where!"

He lifted his head. His face was taut, his eyes dark and glittery. He watched her eyes as his hand slowly moved down to where she ached to have it. She ground her teeth together to keep from crying out when she felt that big, warm, strong hand curl around her breast.

She actually shuddered, hiding her face in his throat as the tiny culmination racked her slender body and made it helpless.

"You are," he breathed, "the most surprising little treasure…"

His mouth searched for hers and suddenly ravished it while his hand moved on her soft flesh, molding it, tracing it, exploring it, in a hot, explosive silence. He kissed her until her mouth felt bruised and then she felt his hand move again, lifting free of her blouse, around to her back, unhooking the bra.

She didn't mind. She lifted up to help him free the catch. She looked up at him with wild, unsatisfied longing, shivering with reaction to the force of the desire he was teaching her.

"It will change everything," he whispered as he began to move the fabric away from her body. "You know that."

"Yes." She shivered.

Both hands slid against her rib cage, carrying the fabric up with them until he uncovered her firm, tip-tilted little breasts. He looked at them with pure pleasure and delight. His thumbs edged out and traced the wide, soft nipples until they drew into hard, dusky peaks. His mouth ached to taste them.

She shifted urgently in his arms, feeling him turn toward her, feeling his leg insinuate itself even more intimately against her. He looked into her dazed eyes as his hand pressed hard against the lowest part of her spine and moved her right in against the fierce arousal she'd only sensed before.

She gasped, but he didn't relent. If anything, he brought her even closer, so that he was pressed intimately to her and the sensations exploded like sensual fire in her limbs.

"Leo!" she cried out, shivering.

"You turn me on so hard that I can't even think," he ground out as he bent to her open mouth. "I didn't mean for this to happen, Janie," he groaned into her mouth as he turned her under him on the seat and pressed his hips down roughly against hers. "Feel me," he whispered. "Feel me wanting you!"

She was lost, helpless, utterly without hope. She clung to him with no thought for her virtue or the future. She was drowning in the most delicious erotic pleasure she'd ever dreamed of experiencing. She could feel him, feel the rough, thrusting rhythm of his big body as he buffeted her against the seat. Something hit her arm. She was twisted in his embrace, and one leg was almost bent backward as he crushed her under him. Any minute, limbs were going to start breaking, she thought, and even that didn't matter. She wanted him...! She didn't realize she'd said it aloud until she heard his voice, deep and strained.

"I want you, too," he whispered back.

She felt his hand between them, working at her jeans. His hand was unfastening them. She felt it, warm and strong, against her belly. It was sliding down. She moved to make it easier for him, her mouth savage under the devouring pressure of his lips...

Leo heard the loud roar of an approaching engine in his last lucid second before he went in over his head. He froze against Janie's warm, welcoming body. His head lifted. He could barely breathe.

He looked down into her wide, misty eyes. It only then occurred to him that they were cramped together on the seat, his body completely covering hers, her bra and blouse crumpled at her collarbone, her jeans half-way down over her hips.

"What the hell are we doing?!" he burst out, shocked.

"You mean you don't know?" she gasped with unconscious humor.

He looked at the windows, so fogged up that nothing was visible outside them. He looked down at Janie, lying drowsy and submissive under the heavy crush of him.

He drew his hand away from her jeans and whipped onto his back so that he could help her sit up. He slid back into his own seat, watching her fumble her clothes back on while he listened, shell-shocked, to the loud tone of a horn from the other vehicle.

Janie was a mess. Her lips were swollen. Her cheeks were flushed. Her clothes were wrinkled beyond belief. Her hair stood out all around from the pressure of his hands in it.

He was rumpled, too, his hair as much as hers. His hat was on the floorboard somewhere, streaked with water from her raincoat and dirt from the floor mats. His shirt had obvious finger marks and lipstick stains on it.

He just stared at her for a long moment while the other vehicle came to a stop beside his truck. He couldn't see anything. All the windows were thickly fogged. Absently, he dug in the side pocket of the door for the red rag he always carried. He wiped the fog from the driver's window and scowled as he saw his brother Cag sitting in another ranch truck, with Tess beside him. They were trying not to stare and failing miserably!

CHAPTER EIGHT

BELATEDLY, LEO ROLLED the window down and glared at his brother and sister-in-law. "Well?" he asked belligerently.

"We just wondered if you were all right," Cag said, clearing his throat and trying very hard not to look at Janie. "The truck was sitting out here in the middle of nowhere, but we didn't see anybody inside."

"That's right," Tess said at once. "We didn't see anybody. At all. Or anything."

"Not anything." Cag nodded vigorously.

"I was showing Janie a photo of the Clark man," Leo said curtly. He pulled it out of his pocket. It was crumpled and slightly torn. He glared at it, trying to straighten it. "See?"

Cag cleared his throat and averted his eyes. "You, uh, should have taken it out of your pocket before you showed it to her... I'm going!"

Cag powered his window up with a knowing grin and gunned the engine, taking off in a spray of mud. Leo let his own window back up with flattened lips.

Janie was turned away from him, her shoulders shaking. Odd little noises that she was trying to smother kept slipping out. She was about to burst trying not to laugh.

He leaned back against the seat and threw the clipping at her.

"It's not my fault," she protested. "I was sitting here minding my own business when you got amorous."

He pursed his swollen lips and gave her a look that would have melted butter. "Amorous. That's a good word for it."

She was coming down from the heights and feeling self-conscious. She picked up the clipping and handed it back to him, belatedly noticing his white Stetson at her feet. She picked it up, too, and grimaced. "Your poor hat."

He took it from her and tossed it into the small back seat of the double cab. "It will clean," he said impatiently.

She folded her hands in her lap, toying with the streaked raincoat that she'd propped over her legs.

"Marilee caused a lot of trouble between us," he said after a minute, surprising her into meeting his somber gaze. "I'm sorry about that."

"You mean I don't really make you sick?" she asked in a thin voice.

He winced. "I was furious about what I thought you'd done," he confessed. "It was a lie, Janie, like all the other terrible things I said. I'm sorry for every one of them, if it does any good."

She toyed with a button on her raincoat and stared out the window at the rain. It did help, but she couldn't stop wondering if he hadn't meant it. Maybe guilt brought the apology out of him, rather than any real remorse. She knew he didn't like hurting people.

A long sigh came from the other side of the pickup.

"I'll drive you back home," he said after a minute, and put the truck in gear. "Fasten your seat belt, honey."

The endearment made her feel warm all over, but she didn't let it show. She didn't really trust Leo Hart.

He turned back onto the main road. "Fred and I are going to mob you with company at Shea's," he said conversationally. "Between us, we know most of the ranchers around Jacobsville. You can ask Harley to keep dropping in from time to time, and Fred and I will talk to the others."

She gave him a quick glance. "Harley's jaw was really bruised."

His eyes darkened. "He had no business interfering. You don't belong to damned Harley!"

She didn't know what to say. That sounded very much like jealousy. It couldn't be, of course.

His dark eyes glanced off hers. "Do you sit around in parked trucks with him and let him take your blouse off?" he asked suddenly, furiously.

"I do *not!*" she exploded.

He calmed down at once. He shifted in the seat, still uncomfortable from the keen hunger she'd kindled in his powerful body. "Okay."

Her long fingers clenched on the fabric of the coat. "You have no right to be jealous of me!" she accused angrily.

"After what we just did?" he asked pleasantly. "In your dreams, Janie."

"I don't belong to you, either," she persisted.

"You almost did," he replied, chuckling softly. "You have no idea what a close call that was. Cag and Tess saved you."

"Excuse me?"

He gave her a rueful glance. "Janie, I had your jeans half off, or have you forgotten already?"

"Leo!"

"I'm not sure I could have stopped," he continued, slowing to make a turn. "And you were no damned help at all," he added with affectionate irony, "twisting your hips against me and begging me not to stop."

She gasped. Her face went scarlet. "Of all the blatant…!"

"That's how it was, all right," he agreed. "Blatant. For the record, when a man gets that hard, it's time to call a halt any way you can, before you get in over your head. I can tell you haven't had much practice at it, but now is a good time to listen to advice."

"I don't need advice!"

"Like hell you don't. Once I got my mouth on your soft belly, you'd never have been able to make me stop."

She stared at him with slowly dawning realization. She remembered the hot, exquisite pleasure of his mouth on her breasts. She could only imagine how it would feel to let him kiss her there, on her hips, on her long legs….

"You know far too much about women," she gritted.

"You know absolutely nothing about men," he countered. He smiled helplessly. "I love it. You were in over your head the minute I touched you with intent. You'd have let me do anything I wanted." He whistled softly. "You can't imagine how I felt, knowing that. You were the sweetest candy I've ever had."

He was confounding her. She didn't know what to make of the remarks. He'd been standoffish, insulting, offensive and furious with her. Now he'd done a complete about-face. He was acting more like a lover than a big brother.

His dark eyes cut around sideways and sized up her expression. "Do you think things can just go back to the way they were before?" he asked softly. "I remember telling you that it was going to change everything."

She swallowed. "I remember."

"It already has. I look at you and get aroused, all over again," he said bluntly. "It will only get worse."

Her face flamed. "I will not have an affair with you."

"Great. I'm glad to know you have that much self-control. You can teach it to me."

"I won't get in a truck with you again," she muttered.

"I'll bring the car next time," he said agreeably. "Of course, we'll have to open both doors. I'll never be able to stretch out in the front seat the way I did in the cab of this truck."

Her fingers clenched on the raincoat. "That won't happen again."

"It will if I touch you."

She glared at him. "You listen here…!"

He pulled the truck onto a dirt road that led through one of Fred's pastures, threw it out of gear, switched off the engine and reached for Janie with an economy of motion that left her gasping.

He had her over his lap, and his mouth hit hers with the force of a gust of wind. He burrowed into her parted lips while one lean hand went to her spine, grinding her into the fierce arousal that just the touch of her had provoked.

"Feel that?" he muttered against her lips. "Now try to stop me."

She went under in a daze of pleasure. She couldn't even pretend to protest, not even when his big hand found her breast and caressed it hungrily right through the cloth of her blouse.

Her arms went around his neck. She lifted closer, shivering, as she felt the aching hunger of his body echo in her own. She moaned helplessly.

"Of all the stupid things I've done lately..." He groaned, too, his big arms wrapping her up tight as the kiss went on and on and on.

He moved out from under the steering wheel and shifted her until she was straddling his hips, her belly lying against his aroused body so blatantly that she should have been shocked. She wasn't. He felt familiar to her, beloved to her. She wanted him. Her body yielded submissively to the insistent pressure of both his hands on her hips, dragging them against his in a fever of desire.

The approaching roar of a truck engine for the second time in less than an hour brought his head up. He looked down into Janie's heated face, at the position they were in. His dazed eyes went out the windshield in time to see Fred's old pickup coming down the long pasture road about a quarter mile ahead of them.

He let out a word Janie had only heard Tiny use during heated arguments with patrons, and abruptly put her back in her own seat, pausing to forcefully strap her into her seat belt.

She felt shaky all over. Her eyes met his and then went involuntarily to what she'd felt so starkly against her hungry body. She flushed.

"Next time you'll get a better look," he said harshly. "I wish I could explain to you how it feels."

She wrapped her arms around her body. "I know... how it feels," she whispered unsteadily. "I ache all over."

The bad temper left him at once. He scowled as he watched her, half-oblivious to Fred's rapid approach. He couldn't take his eyes off her. She was delicious.

She managed to meet his wide, shocked eyes. "I'm sorry."

"For what?" he asked huskily. "You went in head-first, just like I did."

She searched his eyes hungrily. Her body was on fire for him. "If you used something..." she said absently.

He actually flushed. He got back under the steering wheel and avoided looking at her. He couldn't believe what she was saying.

Fred roared up beside them and pulled onto the hard ground to let his window down.

"Rain's stopped," he told Leo. "I thought I'd run over to Eb Scott's place and have a talk with him about getting his cowboys to frequent Shea's at night."

"Good idea," Leo said, still flushed and disheveled.

Fred wisely didn't look too closely at either of them, but he had a pretty good idea of what he'd interrupted. "I won't be long, sweetheart," he told Janie.

"Okay, Dad. Be careful," she said in a husky voice.

He nodded, grinned and took off.

Leo started the engine. He was still trying to get his breath. He stared at the dirt path ahead instead of at Janie. "I could use something," he said after a minute. "But lovemaking is addictive, Janie. One time would be a beginning, not a cure, do you understand?"

She shook her head, embarrassed now that her blood was cooling.

He reached out and caught one of her cold hands in his, intertwining their fingers. "You can't imagine how flattered I am," he said quietly. "You're a virgin, and you'd give yourself to me…"

She swallowed hard. "Please. Don't."

His hand contracted. "I'll drive you home. If you weren't working next Saturday, we could take in a movie and have dinner somewhere."

Her heart jumped up into her throat. "M-me?"

He looked down at her with the beginnings of possession. "You could wear that lacy white thing you wore to the ball," he added softly. "I like your shoulders bare. You have beautiful skin." His eyes fell to her bodice and darkened. "Beautiful breasts, too, with nice nipples…"

"Leo Hart!" she exclaimed, horrified.

He leaned over and kissed her hungrily. "I'll let you look at me next time," he whispered passionately. "Then you won't be so embarrassed when we compare notes."

She thought of seeing him without clothes and her whole face colored.

"I know what I said, but…" she protested.

He stopped the truck, bent, and kissed her again with breathless tenderness. "You've known me half your life, Janie," he said, and he was serious. He searched her worried eyes. "Am I the kind of man who takes advantage of a green girl?"

She was worried, too. "No," she had to admit.

His breathing was uneven as he studied her flushed face. "I never would," he agreed. "You were special to me even before I kissed you the first time, in your own kitchen." His head bent again. His mouth trailed across hers in soft, biting little kisses that made her moan. "But now, after the taste of you I've just had, I'm going to be your shadow. You don't even realize what's happened, do you?"

"You want me," she said huskily.

His teeth nibbled her upper lip. "It's a little more complicated than sex." He kissed her again, hard, and lifted his head with flattering reluctance. "Look up addiction in the dictionary," he mused. "It's an eye-opener."

"Addiction?"

His nose brushed hers. "Do you remember how you moaned when I put my hands inside your blouse?"

She swallowed. "Yes."

"Now think how it would feel if I'd put my mouth on your breast, right over the nipple."

She shivered.

He nodded slowly. "Next time," he promised, his voice taut and hungry. "You have that to look forward to. Meanwhile, you keep your eyes and ears open, and don't do anything at work that gives Clark a hint that you're watching him," he added firmly.

"I'll be careful," she promised unsteadily.

His eyes were possessive on her soft face. "If he touches you, I'll kill him."

It sounded like a joke. It wasn't. She'd never seen that look in a man's eyes before. In fact, the way he was watching her was a little scary.

His big hand slid under her nape and brought her mouth just under his. "You belong to me, Janie," he whispered as his head moved down. "Your first man is going to be me. Believe it!"

The kiss was as arousing as it was tender, but it didn't last long. He forced himself to let her go, to move away. He started the truck again, put it in gear, and went back down the farm road. But his hand reached for hers involuntarily, his fingers curling into hers, as if he couldn't bear to lose contact with her. She didn't know it, but he'd reached a decision in those few seconds. There was no going back now.

JACK CLARK DID show up in the bar on the following Friday night.

Janie hadn't told any of the people she worked with about him, feeling that any mention of what she knew about him might jeopardize her safety.

But she did keep a close eye on him. The man was rangy and uncouth. He sat alone at a corner table, looking around as if he expected trouble and was impatient for it to arrive.

A cowboy from Cy Parks's spread, one of Harley Fowler's men, walked to the counter and sat down, ordering a beer and a pizza.

"Hey, Miss Janie," he said with a grin that showed a missing front tooth. "Harley said to tell you he'd be in soon to see you."

"That's sweet of him," she said with a grin. "I'll just put your order in, Ned."

She scribbled the order on a slip of green paper and put it up on the long string for Nick, the teenage cook, with a clothespin.

"Where's my damned whiskey?" Clark shouted. "I been sitting here five minutes waiting for it!"

Janie winced as Nick glanced at her and shrugged,

indicating the pizza list he was far behind on. He'd taken the order and got busy all of a sudden. Tiny was nowhere in sight. He was probably out back having a cigarette. Nick was up to his elbows in dough and pizza sauce. Janie had to get Clark's order, there was nobody else to do it.

She got down a shot glass, poured whiskey into it, and put it on one of the small serving trays.

She took it to Clark's table and forced a smile to her lips. "Here you are, sir," she said, placing the shot glass in front of him. "I'm sorry it took so long."

Clark glared up at her from watery blue eyes. "Don't let that happen again. I don't like to be kept waiting."

"Yes, sir," she agreed.

She turned away, but he caught her apron strings and jerked her back. She caught her breath as his hand slid to the ones tied at her waist.

"You're kind of cute. Why don't you sit on my lap and help me drink this?" he drawled.

He was already half-lit, she surmised. She would have refused him the whiskey, if Tiny had been close by, despite the trouble he'd already caused. But now she was caught and she didn't know how to get away. All her worst fears were coming to haunt her.

"I have to get that man's drink," she pointed to Harley's cowboy. "I'll come right back, okay?"

"That boy can get his drink."

"He's making pizza," she protested. "Please."

That was a mistake. He liked it when women begged. He smiled at her. It wasn't a pleasant smile. "I said, come here!"

He jerked her down on his thin, bony legs and she screamed.

In a flash, two cowboys were on their feet and heading toward Clark, both of them dangerous looking.

"Well, looky, looky, you've got guardian angels in cowboy boots!" Clark chuckled. He stood up, dragging Janie with him. "Stay back," he warned, catching her hair in its braid. "Or else." He slapped her, hard, across the face, making her cry out, and his hand went into his pocket and came out with a knife. He flicked it and a blade appeared. He caught her around the shoulders from behind and brandished the knife. "Stay back, boys," he said again. "Or I'll cut her!"

The knife pressed against her throat. She was shaking. She remembered all the nice self-defense moves she'd ever learned in her life from watching television or listening to her father talk. Now, she knew how useless they were. Clark would cut her throat if those men tried to help her. She had visions of him dragging her outside and assaulting her. He could do anything. There was nobody around to stop him. These cowboys weren't going to rush him and risk her life. If only Leo were here!

She was vaguely aware of Nick sliding out of sight toward the telephones. If he could just call the sheriff, the police, anybody!

Her hands went to Clark's wrist, trying to get him to release the press of the blade.

"You're hurting," she choked.

"Really?" He pressed harder.

Janie felt his arm cutting off the blood to her head. Then she remembered something she'd heard of a female victim doing during an attack. If she fainted, he might turn her loose.

"Can't…breathe…" she gasped, and closed her eyes. He might drop her if she sagged, he might cut her throat. She could die. But they'd get him. That would almost be worth it.…

She let her body sag just as she heard a shout from the doorway. She pretended to lose consciousness. In the next few hectic seconds, Clark threw her to the floor so hard that she hit right on her elbow and her head, and groaned aloud with the pain of impact.

At the same moment, Leo Hart and Harley Fowler exploded into the room from the front door and went right for Clark, knife and all. They'd been in the parking lot, talking about Janie's situation, and had come running when they heard the commotion.

Harley aimed a kick at the knife and knocked it out of Clark's hands, but Clark was good with his feet, too. He landed a roundhouse kick in Harley's stomach and put him over a table. Leo slugged him, but he twisted around, got Leo's arm behind him and sent him over a table, too.

The two cowboys held back, aware of Leo's size and Harley's capability, and the fact that Clark had easily put both of them down.

There was a sudden silence. Janie dragged herself into a sitting position in time to watch Cash Grier come through the doorway and approach Clark.

Clark dived for the knife, rolled, and got to his feet. He lunged at Grier with the blade. The assistant police chief waited patiently for the attack, and he smiled. It was the coldest, most dangerous smile Janie had ever seen in her life.

Clark lunged confidently. Grier moved so fast that he was like a blur.

Seconds later, the knife was in Grier's hand. He threw it, slamming it into the wall next to the counter so deep that it would take Tiny quite some time, after the brawl, to pull it out again. He turned back to Clark even as the knife hit, fell into a relaxed stance, and waited.

Clark rushed him, tipsy and furious at the way the older man had taken his knife away. Grier easily side-stepped the intended punch, did a spinning heel kick that would have made Chuck Norris proud, and proceeded to beat the living hell out of the man with lightning punches and kicks that quickly put him on the floor, breathless and drained of will. It was over in less than three minutes. Clark held his ribs and groaned. Grier stood over him, not even breathing hard, his hand going to the handcuffs on his belt. He didn't even look winded.

Leo had picked himself up and rushed to Janie, propping her against his chest while she nursed her elbow.

"Is it broken?" he asked worriedly.

She shook her head. "Just bruised. Is my mouth bleeding?" she asked, still dazed from the confrontation.

He nodded. His face was white. He cursed his own helplessness. Between them, he and Harley should have been able to wipe the floor with Clark. He pulled out a white linen handkerchief and mopped up the bleeding lip and the cut on her cheek from Clark's nails. A big, bad bruise was already coming out on the left side of her face.

By now, Grier had Clark against a wall with a minimum of fuss. He spread the man's legs with a quick movement of his booted feet and nimbly cuffed him.

"I'll need a willing volunteer to see the magistrate and file a complaint," Grier asked.

"Right here," Harley said, wiping his mouth with a handkerchief. "I expect Mr. Hart will do the same."

"You bet," Leo agreed. "But I've got to get Janie home first."

"No rush," Grier said, with Clark by the neck. "Harley, you know where magistrate Burr Wiley lives, don't you? I'm taking Clark by there now."

"Yes, sir, I do, I'll drive right over there and swear out a complaint so you can hold that...gentleman," Harley agreed, substituting for the word he really meant to use. "Janie, you going to be okay?" he added worriedly.

She was wobbly, but she got to her feet, with Leo's support. "Sure," she said. She managed a smile. "I'll be fine."

"I'll get you!" Clark raged at Janie and Leo. "I'll get both of you!"

"Not right away," Grier said comfortably. "I'll have the judge set bail as high as it's possible to put it, and we'll see how many assault charges we can press."

"Count on me for two of them!" Janie volunteered fearlessly, wincing as her jaw protested.

"But not tonight," Leo said, curling his arm around her. "Come on, honey," he said gently. "I'll take you home."

They followed Grier with his prisoner and Harley out the door and over to Leo's big double-cabbed pickup truck.

He put her inside gently and moved around to the

driver's seat. She noticed then, for the first time, that he was in working clothes.

"You must have come right from work," she commented.

"We were moving livestock to a new pasture," he replied. "One of the bulls got out and we had to chase him through the brush. Doesn't it show?" he added with a nod toward his scarred batwing chaps and his muddy boots. "I meant to be here an hour ago. Harley and I arrived together. Just in the nick of time, too."

"Two of Cy Parks's guys were at the counter," she said, "but when Clark threatened to cut me, they were afraid to rush him."

He caught her hand in his and held it tight, his eyes going to the blood on her face, her blouse, her forearm. She was going to have a bruise on her pretty face. The sight of those marks made him furious.

"I'll be all right, thanks to all of you," she managed to say.

"We weren't a hell of a lot of help," he said with a rueful smile. "Even Harley didn't fare well. Clark must have a military background of some sort. But he was no match for Grier." He shook his head. "It was like watching a martial arts movie. I never even saw Grier move."

She studied him while he started the truck and put their seat belts on. "Did he hurt you?"

"Hurt my pride," he replied, smiling gently. "I've never been put across a table so fast."

"At least you tried," she pointed out. "Thank you."

"I should never have let you stay in there," he said. "It's my fault."

"It was my choice."

He kissed her eyelids shut. "My poor baby," he said softly. "I'm not taking you to your father in this condition," he added firmly, noting the blood on her blouse and face. "I'll take you home with me and clean you up, first. We'll phone him and tell him there was a little trouble and you'll be late."

"Okay," she said. "But he's no wimp."

"I know that." He put the truck in gear. "Humor me. I want to make sure you're all right."

"I'm fine," she argued, but then she smiled. "You can clean me up, anyway."

He pursed his lips and smiled wickedly. "Best offer I've had all night," he replied as he pulled out of the parking lot.

CHAPTER NINE

THE HOUSE WAS QUIET, deserted. The only light was the one in the living room. Leo led Janie down the hall to his own big bedroom, closed the door firmly, and led her into his spacious blue-tiled bathroom.

The towels were luxurious, sea-blue-and-white-striped blue towels, facecloths and hand towels. There were soaps of all sorts, a huge heated towel rack, and a whirlpool bath.

He tugged her to the medicine cabinet and turned her so that he could see her face. "You've got a bad scratch here," he remarked. He tilted her chin up, and found another smaller cut on the side of her throat, thankfully not close enough to an artery to have done much damage.

His hands went to her blouse. She caught them.

"It's all right," he said gently.

She let go.

He unfastened the blouse and tossed it onto the floor, looking her over for other marks. He found a nasty bruise on her shoulder that was just coming out. He unfastened the bra and let it fall, too, ignoring her efforts to catch it. There was a bruise right on her breast, where Clark had held her in front of him.

"The bastard," he exclaimed, furious, as he touched the bruise.

"He got a few bruises, too, from Grier," she said, trying to comfort him. He looked devastated.

"He'd have gotten more from me, if I hadn't walked right into that punch," he said with self-contempt. "I can't remember the last time I took a stupid hit like that."

She reached up and touched his lean face gently. "It's all right, Leo."

He looked down at her bare breasts and his eyes narrowed hotly. "I don't like that bruise."

"I got a worse one when my horse threw me last month," she told him. "It will heal."

"It's in a bad place."

She smiled. "So was the other one."

He unzipped her jeans and she panicked.

He didn't take any notice. He bent and removed her shoes and socks and then stripped the jeans off her. She was wearing little lacy white briefs and his hands lingered on them.

"Leo!" she screeched.

He grimaced. "I knew it was going to be a fight all the way, and you're in no condition for another one." He unbraided her hair and let it tangle down her shoulders. He turned and started the shower.

"I can do this!" she began.

His hands were already stripping off the briefs. He stopped with his hands on her waist and looked at her with barely contained passion. "I thought you'd be in a class of your own," he said huskily. "You're a knockout, baby." He lifted her and stood her up in the shower, putting a washcloth in her hand before he closed the sliding glass door. "I'll get your things in the wash."

She was too shell-shocked to ask if he knew how to

use a washing machine. *Well, you fool,* she told herself, *you stood there like a statue and let him take your clothes off and stare at you! What are you complaining about?*

She bathed and used the shampoo on the shelf in the shower stall, scrubbing until she felt less tainted by Clark's filthy touch.

She turned off the shower and climbed out, wrapping herself in one of the sea-blue towels. It was soft and huge, big enough for Leo, who was a giant of a man. It swallowed her up whole.

Before she could wonder what she was going to do about something to wear, he opened the door and walked right in with a black velvet robe.

"Here," he said, jerking the towel away from her and holding out the robe.

She scurried into it, red-faced and embarrassed.

He drew her back against him and she realized that she wasn't the only one who'd just had a shower. He was wearing a robe, too. But his was open, and the only thing under it was a pair of black silk boxer shorts that left his powerful legs bare. His chest was broad and covered with thick, curling hair. He turned her until she was facing him, and his eyes were slow and curious.

"You'll have bruises. Right now, I want to treat those cuts with antibiotic cream. Then we'll dry your hair and brush it out." He smiled. "It's long and thick and glossy. I love your hair."

She smiled shyly. "It takes a lot of drying."

"I'm not in a hurry. Neither are you. I phoned your dad and told him as little as I could get away with."

"Was he worried?"

He lifted an eyebrow as he dug in the cabinet for the

antibiotic cream. "About your virtue, maybe," he teased. "He thinks I've got you here so I can make love to you."

She felt breathless. "Have you?" she asked daringly.

He turned back to her with the cream in one big hand. His eyes went over her like hands. "If you want it, yes. But it's up to you."

That was a little surprising. She stood docilely while he applied the cream to her cuts and then put it away. He hooked a hair dryer to a plug on the wall and linked his fingers through her thick light brown hair while he blew it dry. There was something very intimate about standing so close to him while he dried her hair. She thought she'd never get over the delight of it, as long as she lived. Every time she washed her hair from now on, she'd feel Leo's big hands against her scalp. She smiled, her head back, her eyes closed blissfully.

"Don't go to sleep," he teased as he put the hair dryer down.

"I'm not."

She felt his lips in her hair at the same moment she felt his hands go down over her shoulders and into the gap left by the robe.

If she'd been able to protest, that would have been the time to do it. But she hesitated, entranced by the feel of his hands so blatantly invading the robe, smoothing down over her high, taut breasts as if he had every right to touch her intimately whenever he felt like it.

Seconds later, the robe was gone, she was turned against him, his robe was on the floor, and she was experiencing her first adult embrace without clothing.

She whimpered at the fierce pleasure of feeling his bare, hair-roughened chest against her naked breasts.

Her nails bit into the huge muscles of his upper arms as she sucked in a harsh breath and tried to stay on her feet.

"You like that, do you?" he whispered at her lips. "I know something that's even more exciting."

He picked her up in his arms and started kissing her hungrily. She responded with no thought of denying him whatever he wanted.

He carried her to the bed, paused to whip the covers and the pillows out of the way, and placed her at the center of it. His hands went to the waistband of his boxer shorts, but he hesitated, grinding his teeth together as he looked at her nudity with aching need.

He managed to control his first impulse, which was to strip and bury himself in her. He eased onto the bed beside her, his chest pressing her down into the mattress while his mouth opened on her soft lips and pressed them wide apart.

"I've ached for this," he ground out, moving his hands from her breasts down her hips to the soft inside of her thighs. "I've never wanted anything so much!"

She tried to speak, but one of his hands invaded her in the most intimate touch she'd ever experienced. Her eyes flew open and she gaped up at him.

"You're old enough, Janie," he whispered, moving his hand just enough to make her tense.

As he spoke, he touched her delicately and when she protested, he eased down to cover her mouth with his. His fingers traced her, probed, explored her until she began to whimper and move with him. It was incredible. She was lying here, naked, in his bed, letting him explore her body as if it belonged to him. And she was…enjoying it. Glorying in it. Her back arched and she moaned as he found a pressure and a rhythm that lifted her off the bed on a wave of pleasure.

One of his long, powerful legs hooked over one of hers. She felt him at her hip, aroused and not hiding it. Through the thin silk, she was as aware of him as if he'd been naked.

"Touch me," he groaned. "Don't make me do it all. Help me."

She didn't understand what he wanted. Her hands went to his chest and began to draw through the thick hair there.

"No, baby," he whispered into her mouth. He caught one of her hands and tugged it down to the shorts he was wearing. "Don't be afraid. It's all right."

He coaxed her hand onto that part of him that was blatantly male. She gasped. He lifted his head and looked into her eyes, but he wouldn't let her hand withdraw. He spread her fingers against him, grimacing as the waves of pleasure hit him and closed his eyes on a shudder.

His reaction fascinated her. She knew so little. "Does it…hurt?"

"What?" he asked huskily. "Your hand, or what it's doing?"

"Both. Either."

He pressed her hand closer, looking down. "Look," he whispered, coaxing her eyes to follow his. It was intimate. But not intimate enough for him.

"Don't panic, baby," he whispered, levering onto his back. He ripped off the shorts and tossed them onto the carpet. He rolled onto his side and caught one of her hands, insistent now, drawing it to him.

She made a sound as she looked, for the first time,

at an aroused male without a thing to conceal him except her hand.

"Don't be embarrassed," he whispered roughly. "I wouldn't want any other woman to see me like this."

"You wouldn't?"

He shook his head. It was difficult not to lose control. But he eased her fingers back to him and held them there. "I'm vulnerable."

Her eyes brightened. "Oh." She hadn't considered that he was as helpless as she was to resist the pleasure of what they were doing.

His own hand went back to her body. He touched her, as she was touching him, and he smiled at her fascination.

She couldn't believe it was happening at all. She stared up at him with all her untried longings in her eyes, on her rapt face. She belonged to him. He belonged to her. It was incredible.

"Are you going to?" she whispered.

He kissed her eyelids lazily. "Going to what?"

"Take me," she whispered back.

He chuckled, deep in his throat. "What a primitive description. It's a mutual thing, you know. Wouldn't you take me, as well?"

Her eyes widened. "I suppose I would," she conceded. She stiffened and shivered. "Oh!"

His eyes darkened. There was no more humor on his face as his touch became slowly invasive. "Will you let me satisfy you?" he asked.

"I don't…understand."

"I know. That's what makes it so delicious." He bent slowly, but not to her mouth. His lips hovered just above her wide nipple. "This is the most beautiful thing I've ever done with a woman," he whispered. His lips parted. "I want nothing, except to please you."

His mouth went down over the taut nipple in a slow, exquisite motion that eventually all but swallowed her breast. She felt his tongue moving against the nipple, felt the faint suction of his mouth. All the while, his hand was becoming more insistent, and far more intimate, on her body. He felt her acceptance, even as she opened her legs for him and began to moan rhythmically with every movement of his hands.

"Yes," he whispered against her breast when he felt the pulsing of her body. "Let me, baby." He lifted his head and looked down into her eyes as she moaned piteously.

She was pulsating. She felt her body clench. She was slowly drifting up into a glorious, rhythmic heat that filled her veins, her arteries, the very cells of her body with exquisite pleasure. She'd never dreamed there was such pleasure.

"Janie, touch me, here," he whispered unsteadily.

She felt his hand curling around her fingers, teaching her, insistent, his breath jerky and violent as he twisted against her.

"Baby," he choked, kissing her hungrily. "Baby, baby!"

He moved, his big body levering slowly between her long legs. He knelt over her, his eyes wild, his body shuddering, powerfully male, and she looked up at him with total submission, still shivering from the taste of pleasure he'd already given her. It would be explosive, ecstatic. She could barely breathe for the anticipation.

She was lost. He was going to have her now. She loved him. She was going to give herself. There was nothing that could stop them, nothing in all the world!

"Mr. Hart! Oh, Mr. Hart! Are you in here?"

Leo stiffened, his body kneeling between her thighs, his powerful hands clenching on them. He looked blindly down into her wide, dazed eyes. He shuddered violently and his eyes closed on a harsh muffled curse.

He threw himself onto the bed beside her, on his belly. He couldn't stop shaking. He gasped at a jerky breath and clutched the sheet beside his head as he fought for control.

"Mr. Hart!" the voice came again.

He suddenly remembered that he hadn't locked the bedroom door, and the cowboy didn't know that he wasn't alone. Even as he thought it, he heard the doorknob turn. "Open that door…and you're fired!" he shouted hoarsely. Beside him, Janie actually gasped as she belatedly realized what was about to happen.

The doorknob was released at once. "Sorry, sir, but I need you to come out here and look at this bull. I think there's something wrong with him, Mr. Hart! We got him loaded into one of the trailers and put him in the barn, but…"

"Call the vet!" he shouted. "I'll be there directly!"

"Yes, sir!"

Footsteps went back down the carpeted hall. Leo lifted his head. Beside him, Janie looked as shattered as he felt. Tears were swimming in her eyes.

He groaned softly, and pulled her to him, gently. "It's all right," he whispered, kissing her eyelids shut. "Don't cry, baby. Nothing happened."

"Nothing!" she choked.

His hands smoothed down the long line of her back. "Almost nothing," he murmured dryly.

She was horrified, not only at her own behavior, but at what had almost happened. "If he hadn't called to you," she began in a high-pitched whisper.

His hands tangled in her long hair and he brought her mouth under his, tenderly. He nibbled her upper lip. "Yes, I know," he replied gently. "But he did." He pulled away from her and got to his feet, stretching hugely, facing her. He watched her try not to look at him with amused indulgence. But eventually, she couldn't resist it. Her eyes were huge, shocked...delighted.

"Now, when we compare notes, you'll have ammunition," he teased.

She flushed and averted her eyes, belatedly noticing that she wasn't wearing clothes, either. She tugged the sheet up over her breasts, but it was difficult to feel regrets when she looked at him.

He was smiling. His eyes were soft, tender. He looked down at what he could see of her body above the sheet with pride, loving the faint love marks on her breasts that his mouth had made.

"Greenhorn," he chided at her scarlet blush. "Well, you know a lot more about men now than you did this morning, don't you?"

She swallowed hard. Her eyes slid down him. She didn't look away, but she was very flushed, and not only because of what she was seeing. Her body throbbed in the most delicious way.

"I think I'd better take you home. Now," he added with a rueful chuckle. "From this point on, it only gets worse."

He was still passionately aroused. He wondered if she realized what it meant. He chuckled at her lack of comprehension. "I could have you three times and I'd still be like this," he said huskily. "I'm not easily satisfied."

She shivered as she looked at him, her body yielded, submissive.

"You want to, don't you?" he asked quietly, reading her expression. "So do I. More than you know. But we're not going that far together tonight. You've had enough trauma for a Friday night."

He caught her hand and pulled her up, free of the sheet and open to his eyes as he led her back into the bathroom. He turned on the shower and climbed in with her, bathing both of them quickly and efficiently, to her raging embarrassment.

He dried her and then himself before he put his shorts back on and left her to get her things. He'd washed them while she was in the shower the first time and put them in the dryer. They were clean and sweet-smelling, and the bloodstains were gone.

But when she went to take them from him, he shook his head. "One of the perks," he said softly. "I get to dress you."

And he did, completely. Then he led her to the dresser, and ran his own brush through her long, soft hair, easing it back from her face. The look in his eyes was new, fascinating, incomprehensible. She looked back at him with awe.

"Now you know something about what sex feels like, even though you're still very much a virgin," he said matter-of-factly. "And you won't be afraid of the real thing anymore, when it happens, will you?"

She shook her head, dazed.

He put the brush down and framed her face in his big, lean hands. He wasn't smiling. "You belong to me now," he said huskily. "I belong to you. Don't agonize over what you let me do to you tonight. It's as natural as breathing. Don't lie awake feeling shame or embarrassment. You saw me as helpless as I saw you. There won't be any jokes about it, any gossiping about it. I'll never tell another living soul what you let me do."

She relaxed. She hadn't really known what to expect. But he sounded more solemn than he'd ever been. He was looking at her with a strange expression.

"Are you sorry?" she asked in a hushed whisper.

"No," he replied quietly. "It was unavoidable. I was afraid for you tonight. I couldn't stop Clark. Neither could Harley. Until Grier walked in, I thought you'd had it. What happened in here was a symptom of the fear, that's all. I wanted to hold you, make you part of me." He drew in a shaky breath and actually shivered. "I wanted to go right inside you, Janie," he whispered bluntly. "But we'll save that pleasure for the right time and place. This isn't it."

She colored and averted her eyes.

He turned her face back to his. "Meanwhile," he said slowly, searching her eyes, "we'll have no more secrets, of any kind, between us."

She stood quietly against him, watching his face. "Nobody's seen me without my clothes since I was a little kid," she whispered, as if it was a fearful secret.

"Not that many women have seen me without mine," he replied unexpectedly. He smiled tenderly.

Her eyebrows arched.

"Shocked?" he mused, moving away to pull clothes out of his closet and socks out of his drawers. He sat down to pull on the socks, glancing at her wryly. "I'm not a playboy. I'm not without experience, but there was always a limit I wouldn't cross with women I only knew slightly. It gives people power over you when they know intimate things about you."

"Yes," she said, moving to sit beside him on the bed, with her hands folded in her lap. "Thanks."

"For what?"

She smiled. "For making it feel all right. That I…let you touch me that way, I mean."

He finished pulling on his socks and tilted her face up to his. He kissed her softly. "I won't ever touch another woman like that," he whispered into her mouth. "It would be like committing adultery, after what we did on this bed."

Her heart flew up into the clouds. Her wide, fascinated eyes searched his. "Really?"

He chuckled. "Are you anxious to rush out and experiment with another man?"

She shook her head.

"Why?"

She smiled shyly. "It would be like committing adultery," she repeated what he'd said.

He stood up and looked down at her with possession. "It was a near thing," he murmured. "I don't know whether to punch that cowboy or give him a raise for interrupting us. I lost it, in those last few seconds. I couldn't have stopped."

"Neither could I." She lifted her mouth for his soft kiss. She searched his eyes, remembering what he'd told her. "But the books say a man can only do it once," she blurted out, "and then he has to rest."

He laughed softly. "I know. But a handful of men can go all night. I'm one of them."

"Oh!"

He pulled up his slacks and fastened them before he shouldered into a knit shirt. He turned back to her, smoothing his disheveled hair. "I was contemplating even much more explosive pleasures when someone started shouting my name."

This was interesting. "More explosive pleasures?" she prompted.

He drew her up against him and held her close. "What we did and what we didn't do, is the difference between licking an ice-cream cone and eating a banana split," he teased. "What you had was only a small taste of what we can have together."

"Wow," she said softly.

"Wow," he echoed, bending to kiss her hungrily. He sighed into her mouth. "I was almost willing to risk getting you pregnant, I was so far gone." He lifted his head and looked at her. "How do you feel about kids, Janie?"

"I love children," she said honestly. "How about you?"

"Me too. I'm beginning to rethink my position on having them." His lean hand touched her belly. "You've got nice wide hips," he commented, testing them.

She felt odd. Her body seemed to contract. She searched his eyes because she didn't understand what was happening to her.

"You can tell Shea's you're through," he said abruptly. "I'm not risking you again. If we can't keep Clark in jail for the foreseeable future, we have to make plans to keep you safe."

Her lips parted. She'd all but forgotten her horrible experience. She touched her throat and felt again the prick of the knife. "You said he was vindictive."

"He'll have to get through me," he said. "And with a gun, I'm every bit his equal," he added.

She reached up and touched his hard mouth. "I don't want you to get hurt."

"I don't want you to get hurt," he seconded. His face twisted. "Baby, you are the very breath in my body," he whispered, and reached for her.

She felt boneless as he kissed her with such passion and fire that she trembled.

"I wish I didn't have to take you home," he groaned at her lips. "I want to make love to you completely. I want to lie against you and over you, and inside you!"

She moaned at his mouth as it became deep and insistent, devouring her parted lips.

He was shivering. He had to drag his mouth away from hers. He looked shattered. He touched her long hair with a hand that had a faint tremor. "Amazing," he whispered gruffly. "That I couldn't see it, before it happened."

"See what?" she asked drowsily.

His eyes fell to her swollen, parted lips. "Never mind," he whispered. He bent and kissed her with breathless tenderness. "I'm taking you home. Then I'll see about my bull. Tomorrow morning, I'll come and get you and we'll see about swearing out more warrants against Clark."

"You don't think Clark will get out on bond?" she asked worriedly.

"Not if Grier can prevent it." He reached for his truck

keys and took her by the arm. "We'll go out the back," he said. "I don't want anyone to know you were here with me tonight. It wouldn't look good, even under the circumstances."

"Don't worry, nobody will know," she assured him.

THE NEXT MORNING, Fred Brewster came into the dining room looking like a thunderstorm.

"What were you doing in Leo Hart's bedroom last night when you were supposed to be working, Janie?" he asked bluntly.

She gaped at him with her mouth open. He was furious.

"How in the world...?" she exclaimed.

"One of the Harts' cowboys went to get him about a sick bull. He saw Leo sneaking you out the back door!" He scowled and leaned closer. "And what the hell happened to your face? Leo said you had a troublesome customer and he was bringing you home! What the hell's going on, Janie?"

She was scrambling for an answer that wouldn't get her in even more trouble when they heard a pickup truck roar up the driveway and stop at the back door. A minute later there was a hard rap, and the door opened by itself.

Leo came in, wearing dressy boots and slacks, a white shirt with a tie, and a sports coat. His white Stetson had been cleaned and looked as if it had never been introduced to a muddy truck mat. He took off the hat and tossed it onto the counter, moving past Fred to look at Janie's face.

"Damn!" he muttered, turning her cheek so that the

violet bruise was very noticeable. "I didn't realize he hit you that hard, baby!"

"Hit her?!" Fred burst out. "Who hit her, and what was she doing in your bedroom last night?!"

Leo turned toward him, his face contemplative, his dark eyes quiet and somber. "Did she tell you?" he asked.

"I never!" Janie burst out, flushing.

"One of your cowboys mentioned it to one of my cowboys," Fred began.

Leo's eyes flashed fire. "He'll be drawing his pay at the end of the day. Nobody, but nobody, tells tales about Janie!"

Father and daughter exchanged puzzled glances.

"Why are you so shocked?" he asked her, when he saw her face. "Do you think I take women to my house, ever?"

She hadn't considered that. Her lips parted on a shocked breath.

He glanced at Fred, who was still unconvinced. "All right, you might as well know it all. Jack Clark made a pass at her in Shea's and when she protested, he pulled a knife on her." He waited for that to sink in, and for Fred to sit down, hard, before he continued. "Harley and I got there about the same time and heard yelling. We went inside to find Janie with a knife at her throat. We rushed Clark, but he put both of us over a table. Janie's co-worker had phoned the sheriff, but none of the deputies were within quick reach, so they radioed Grier and he took Clark down and put him in jail." He grimaced, looking at Janie's face. "She was covered with blood and so upset that she could hardly stand. I couldn't bring myself to take her home in that condition, so I took her home with me and cleaned her up and calmed her down first."

Fred caught Janie's hand in his and held it hard. "Oh, daughter, I'm sorry!"

"It's okay. We were trying to spare you, that's all," she faltered.

Leo pulled a cell phone from his pocket, dialed a number, and got his foreman. "You tell Carl Turley that he's fired. You get him the hell out of there before I get home, or he'll need first aid to get off the ranch. Yes. Yes." His face was frightening. "It was true. Clark's in jail now, on assault charges. Of course nothing was going on, and you can repeat that, with my blessing! Just get Turley out of there! Right."

He hung up and put the phone away. He was vibrating with suppressed fury, that one of his own men would gossip about him and Janie, under the circumstances. "So much for gossip," he gritted.

"Thanks, Leo," Fred said tersely. "And I'm sorry I jumped to the wrong conclusion. It's just that, normally, a man wouldn't take a woman home with him late at night unless he was…well…"

"…planning to seduce her?" Leo said for him. He looked at Janie and his eyes darkened.

She flushed.

"Yes," Fred admitted uncomfortably.

Leo's dark eyes began to twinkle as they wandered over Janie like loving hands. "Would this be a bad time to tell you that I have every intention of seducing her at some future time?"

CHAPTER TEN

FRED LOOKED AS if he'd swallowed a chicken, whole. He flushed, trying to forget that Leo had loaned him the money to save his ranch, thinking only of his daughter's welfare. "Now, look here, Leo…" he began.

Leo chuckled. "I was teasing. She's perfectly safe with me, Fred," he replied. He caught Janie's hand and tugged her to her feet. "We have to go see the magistrate about warrants," he said, sobering. "I want him to see these bruises on her face," he added coldly. "I don't think we'll have any problem with assault charges."

Janie moved closer to Leo. He made her feel safe, protected. He bent toward her, his whole expression one of utter tenderness. Belatedly, Fred began to understand what he was seeing. Leo's face, to him, was an open book. He was shocked. At the same time, he realized that Janie didn't understand what was going on. Probably she thought he was being brotherly.

"Don't you want breakfast first?" Fred offered, trying to get his bearings again.

For the first time, Leo seemed to notice the table. His hand, holding Janie's, contracted involuntarily. Bacon, scrambled eggs, and…biscuits? Biscuits! He scowled, letting go of Janie's fingers to approach the bread basket. He reached down, expecting a concretelike substance, remembering that he and Rey had secretly sailed some of Janie's earlier efforts at biscuit-making over the target range for each other and used them for skeet targets. But these weren't hard. They were flaky, delicate. He opened one. It was soft inside. It smelled delicious.

He was barely aware of sitting down, dragging Janie's plate under his hands. He buttered a biscuit and put strawberry jam on it. He bit into it and sighed with pure ecstasy.

"I forgot about the biscuits," Janie told her father worriedly.

Fred glanced at their guest and grimaced. "Maybe we should have saved it for a surprise."

Leo was sighing, his eyes closed as he chewed.

"We'll never get to the magistrate's now," Janie thought aloud.

"He'll run out of biscuits in about ten minutes, at that rate," Fred said with a grin.

"I'll get another plate. We can split the eggs and bacon," Janie told her father, inwardly beaming with pride at Leo's obvious enjoyment of her efforts. Now, finally, the difficulty of learning to cook seemed worth every minute.

Leo went right on chewing, oblivious to movement around him.

The last biscuit was gone with a wistful sigh when he became aware of his two companions again.

"Who made the biscuits?" Leo asked Janie.

She grimaced. "I did."

"But you can't cook, honey," he said gently, trying to soften the accusation.

"Marilee said you didn't like me because I couldn't make biscuits or cook anything edible," she confessed without looking at him. "So I learned how."

He caught her fingers tightly in his. "She lied. But those were wonderful biscuits," he said. "Flaky and soft inside, delicately browned. Absolutely delicious."

She smiled shyly. "I can make them anytime you like."

He was looking at her with pure possession. "Every morning," he coaxed. "I'll stop by for coffee. If Fred doesn't mind," he added belatedly.

Fred chuckled. "Fred doesn't mind," he murmured dryly.

Leo scowled. "You look like a cat with a mouse."

Fred shrugged. "Just a stray thought. Nothing to worry about."

Leo held the older man's reluctant gaze and understood the odd statement. He nodded slowly. He smiled sheepishly as he realized that Fred wasn't blind at all.

Fred got up. "Well, I've got cattle to move. How's your bull, by the way?" he added abruptly, worried.

"Colic," Leo said with a cool smile. "Easily treated and nothing to get upset over."

"I'm glad. I had visions of you losing yours to Clark as well."

"He isn't from the same herd as yours was, Fred," Leo told him. "But even so, I think we'll manage to keep Clark penned up for a while. Which reminds me," he added, glancing at Janie. "We'd better get going."

"Okay. I'll just get the breakfast things cleared away first."

Leo sat and watched her work with a smitten expression on his face. Fred didn't linger. He knew a hooked fish when he saw one.

THEY SWORE OUT warrants and presented them to the sheriff. Clark had already been transferred to the county lockup, after a trip to the hospital emergency room the night before, and Leo and Janie stopped in to see Grier at the police station.

Grier had just finished talking to the mayor, a pleasant older man named Tarleton Connor, newly elected to his position. Connor and Grier had a mutual cousin, as did Grier and Chet Blake, the police chief. Chet was out of town on police business, so Grier was nominally in charge of things.

"Have a seat," Grier invited, his eyes narrow and angry on Janie's bruised face. "If it's any consolation, Miss Brewster, Clark's got bruised ribs and a black eye."

She smiled. It was uncomfortable, because it irritated the bruise. "Thanks, Mr. Grier," she said with genuine appreciation.

"That goes double for me," Leo told him. "He put Harley and me over a table so fast it's embarrassing to admit it."

"Why?" Grier asked, sitting down behind his desk. "The man was a martial artist," he elaborated. "He had a studio up in Victoria for a while, until the authorities realized that he was teaching killing techniques to ex-cons."

Leo's jaw fell.

Grier shrugged. "He was the equivalent of a black belt, too. Harley's not bad, but he needs a lot more training from Eb Scott before he could take on Clark." He pursed his lips and his eyes twinkled as he studied Leo's expression. "Feel better now?"

Leo chuckled. "Yes. Thanks."

Grier glanced at Janie's curious expression. "Men don't like to be overpowered by other men. It's a guy thing," he explained.

"Anybody ever overpower you?" Leo asked curiously.

"Judd Dunn almost did, once. But then, I taught him everything he knows."

"You know a lot," Janie said. "I never saw anybody move that fast."

"I was taught by a guy up in Tarrant County," Grier told her with a smile. "He's on television every week. Plays a Texas Ranger."

Janie gasped.

"Nice guy," Grier added. "And a hell of a martial artist."

Leo was watching him with a twinkle in his own eyes. "I did think the spinning heel kick looked familiar."

Grier smiled. He sat up. "About Clark," he added. "His brother came to see him at the county lockup this morning and got the bad news. With only one charge so far, Harley's, he's only got a misdemeanor..."

"We took out a warrant for aggravated assault and battery," Leo interrupted. "Janie had a knife at her throat just before you walked in."

"So I was told." Grier's dark eyes narrowed on Janie's throat. The nick was red and noticeable this morning. "An inch deeper and we'd be visiting you at the funeral home this morning."

"I know," Janie replied.

"You kept your head," he said with a smile. "It probably saved your life."

"Can you keep Clark in jail?" she asked worriedly.

"I'll ask Judge Barnett to set bail as high as he can. But Clark's brother isn't going to settle for a public defender. He said he'd get Jack the best attorney he could find, and he'd pay for it." He shrugged. "God knows what he'll pay for it with," he added coldly. "John Clark owes everybody, up to and including his boss. So does our local Clark brother."

"He may have to have a public defender."

"We'll see. But meanwhile, he's out of everybody's way, and he'll stay put."

"What about his brother?" Leo wanted to know. "Is Janie in any danger?"

Grier shook his head. "John Clark went back to Victoria after he saw his brother. I had him followed, by one of my off-duty guys, just to make sure he really left. But I'd keep my eyes open, if I were you, just the same. These boys are bad news."

"We'll do that," Leo said.

HE DROVE JANIE back to his own ranch and took her around with him while he checked on the various projects he'd initiated. He pulled up at the barn and told her to stay in the truck.

She was curious until she remembered that he'd fired the man who'd interrupted them the night before. She was glad about the interruption, in retrospect, but uneasy about the gossip that man had started about her and Leo.

He was back in less than five minutes, his face hard,

his eyes blazing. He got into the truck and glanced at her, forcibly wiping the anger out of his expression.

"He's gone," he told her gently. "Quit without his check," he added with a rueful smile. "I guess Charles told him what I said." He shrugged. "He wasn't much of a cowboy, at that, if he couldn't tell colic from bloat."

She reached out and put her nervous fingers over his big hand on the steering wheel. He flinched and she jerked her hand back.

"No!" He caught her fingers in his and held them tight. "I'm sorry," he said at once, scowling. "You've never touched me voluntarily before. It surprised me. I like it," he added, smiling.

She was flushed and nervous. "Oh. Okay." She smiled shyly.

He searched her eyes with his for so long that her heart began to race. His face tautened. "This won't do," he said in a husky, deep tone. He started the truck with a violent motion and drove back the way they'd come, turning onto a rutted path that led into the woods and, far beyond, to a pasture. But he stopped the truck halfway to the pasture, threw it out of gear, and cut off the engine.

He had Janie out of her seat belt and into his big arms in seconds, and his hungry mouth was on her lips before she could react.

She didn't have any instincts for self-preservation left. She melted into his aroused body, not even protesting the intimate way he was pressing her hips against his. Her arms curled around his neck and she kissed him back with enthusiasm.

She felt his hands going under her blouse, against her

breasts. That felt wonderful. It was perfectly all right, because she belonged to him.

He lifted his mouth from hers, breathing hard, and watched her eyes while his hands caressed her. She winced and he caught his breath.

"I'm sorry!" he said at once, soothing the bruise he'd forgotten about. "I didn't mean to hurt you," he whispered.

She reached up to kiss his eyelids shut, feeling the shock that ran through him at the soft caress. His hands moved to her waist and rested there while he held his breath, waiting. She felt the hunger in him, like a living thing. Delighted by his unexpected submission to her mouth, she kissed his face softly, tenderly, drawing her lips over his thick eyebrows, his eyelids, his cheeks and nose and chin. They moved to his strong throat and lingered in the pulsating hollow.

One lean hand went between them to the buttons of his cotton shirt. He unfastened them quickly, jerking the fabric out of her way, inviting her mouth inside.

Her hands spread on the thick mat of hair that covered the warm, strong muscles of his chest. Her mouth touched it, lightly, and then not lightly. She moved to where his heart beat roughly, and then over the flat male nipple that was a counterpart to her own. But the reaction she got when she put her mouth over it was shocking.

He groaned so harshly that she was sure she'd hurt him. She drew back, surprising a look of anguish on his lean face.

"Leo?" she whispered uneasily.

"It arouses me," he ground out, then he shivered.

She didn't know what to do next. He looked as if he ached to have her repeat the caress, but his body was as taut as a rope against her.

"You'll have to tell me what to do," she faltered. "I don't want to make it worse."

"Whatever I do is going to shock you speechless," he choked out. "But, what the hell…!"

He dragged her face back to his nipple and pressed it there, hard. "You know what I want."

She did, at some level. Her mouth eased down against him with a soft, gentle suction that lifted him back against the seat with a harsh little cry of pleasure. His hands at the back of her head were rough and insistent. She gave in and did what he was silently asking her for. She felt him shudder and gasp, his body vibrating as if it was overwhelmed by pleasure. He bit off a harsh word and trembled violently for a few seconds before he turned her mouth away from him and pressed her unblemished cheek against his chest. His hands in her hair trembled as they caressed her scalp. His heartbeat was raging under her mouth.

He fought to breathe normally. "Wow," he whispered unsteadily.

Her fingers tangled in the thick hair under them. "Did you really like it?" she whispered back.

He actually laughed, a little unsteadily. "Didn't you feel what was happening to me?"

"You were shaking."

"Yes. I was, wasn't I? Just the way you were shaking last night when I touched you…"

Her cheek slid back onto his shoulder so that she

could look up into his soft eyes. "I didn't know a man would be sensitive, there, like a woman is."

He bent and drew his lips over her eyelids. "I'm sensitive, all right." His lips moved over her mouth and pressed there hungrily. "It isn't enough, Janie. I've got to have you. All the way."

"Right now?" she stammered.

He lifted his head and looked down at her in his arms. He was solemn, unsmiling, as he met her wide eyes. His body was still vibrating with unsatisfied desire. Deliberately, he drew her hips closer against his and let her feel him there.

She didn't protest. If anything, her body melted even closer.

One lean hand went to her belly and rested there, between them, while he searched her eyes. "I want…to make you pregnant," he said in a rough whisper.

Her lips fell open. She stared at him, not knowing what to say.

He looked worried. "I've never wanted that with a woman," he continued, as if he was discussing the weather. His fingers moved lightly on her body. "Not with anyone."

He was saying something profound. She hadn't believed it at first, but the expression on his face was hard to explain away.

"My father would shoot you," she managed to say weakly.

"My brothers would shoot me, too," he agreed, nodding.

She was frowning. She didn't understand.

He bent and kissed her, with an odd tenderness. He

laughed to himself. "Just my luck," he breathed against her lips, "to get mixed up with a virgin who can cook."

"We aren't mixed up," she began.

His hand contracted against the base of her spine, grinding her into him, and one eyebrow went up over a worldly smile as she blushed.

She cleared her throat. "We aren't very mixed up," she corrected.

He nibbled at her upper lip. "I look at you and get turned on so hard I can hardly walk around without bending over double. I touch you and I hurt all over. I dream of you every single night of my life and wake up vibrating." He lifted his head and looked down into her misty eyes. He wasn't smiling. He wasn't kidding. "Never like this, Janie. Either we have each other, or we stop it, right now."

Her fingers touched his face lovingly. "You can do whatever you like to me," she whispered unsteadily.

His jaw tautened. "Anything?"

She nodded. She loved him with all her heart.

His eyes closed. His arms brought her gently against him, and his mouth buried itself in her throat, pressing there hot and hard for a few aching seconds. Then he dragged in a harsh breath and sat up, putting her back in her seat and fastening her seat belt.

He didn't look at her as he fastened his own belt and started the truck. She sat beside him as he pulled out onto the highway, a little surprised that he didn't turn into the road that led to his house. She'd expected him to take her there. She swallowed hard, remembering the way they'd pleasured each other on his big bed the night before, remembering the look of his powerful body without clothes. She flushed with anticipated delight. She was out of her mind. Her father was going to kill her. She looked at Leo with an ache that curled her toes up inside her shoes, and didn't care if he did. Some things were worth dying for.

Leo drove right into town and pulled into a parking spot in front of the drugstore. Right, she thought nervously, he was going inside to buy...protection...for what they were going to do. He wanted a child, though, he'd said. She flushed as he got out of the truck and came around to open her door.

He had to unfasten her seat belt first. She didn't even have the presence of mind to accomplish that.

He helped her out of the truck and looked down at her with an expression she couldn't decipher. He touched her cheek gently, and then her hair, and her soft mouth. His eyes were full of turmoil.

He tugged her away from the truck and closed her door, leading her to the sidewalk with one small hand tightly held in his fingers.

She started toward the drugstore.

"Wrong way, sweetheart," he said tenderly, and led her right into a jewelry store.

The clerk was talking to another clerk, but he came forward, smiling, when they entered the shop.

"May I help you find something?" he asked Leo.

"Yes," Leo said somberly. "We want to look at wedding bands."

Janie felt all the blood draining out of her face. It felt numb. She hoped she wasn't going to pass out.

Leo's hand tightened around her fingers, and slowly

linked them together as he positioned her in front of the case that held engagement rings and wedding rings.

The clerk took out the tray that Leo indicated. Leo looked down at Janie with quiet, tender eyes.

"You can have anything you want," he said huskily, and he wasn't talking solely of rings.

She met his searching gaze with tears glistening on her lashes. He bent and kissed the wetness away.

The clerk averted his eyes. It was like peering through a private window. He couldn't remember ever seeing such an expression on a man's face before.

"Look at the rings, Janie," Leo said gently.

She managed to focus on them belatedly. She didn't care about flashy things, like huge diamonds. She was a country girl, for all her sophistication. Her eyes kept coming back to a set of rings that had a grape leaf pattern. The wedding band was wide, yellow gold with a white gold rim, the pattern embossed on the gold surface. The matching engagement ring had a diamond, but not a flashy one, and it contained the same grape leaf pattern on its circumference.

"I like this one," she said finally, touching it.

There was a matching masculine-looking wedding band. She looked up at Leo.

He smiled. "Do you want me to wear one, too?" he teased.

Her eyes were breathless with love. She couldn't manage words. She only nodded.

He turned his attention back to the clerk. "We'll take all three," he said.

"They'll need to be sized. Let me get my measuring rod," the clerk said with a big grin. The rings were expensive, fourteen karat, and that diamond was the highest quality the store sold. The commission was going to be tasty.

"It isn't too expensive?" Janie worried.

Leo bent and kissed the tip of her nose. "They're going to last a long time," he told her. "They're not too expensive."

She couldn't believe what was happening. She wanted to tell him so, but the clerk came back and they were immediately involved in having their fingers sized and the paperwork filled out.

Leo produced a gold card and paid for them while Janie looked on, still shell-shocked.

Leo held her hand tight when they went back to the truck. "Next stop, city hall," he murmured dryly. "Rather, the fire station—they take the license applications when city hall is closed. I forgot it was Saturday." He lifted both eyebrows at her stunned expression. "Might as well get it all done in one day. Which reminds me." He pulled out his cell phone after he'd put her in the truck and phoned the office of the doctors Coltrain. While Janie listened, spellbound, he made an appointment for blood tests for that afternoon. The doctors Coltrain had a Saturday clinic.

He hung up and slipped the phone back into his pocket with a grin. "Marriage license next, blood tests later, and about next Wednesday, we'll have a nice and quiet small wedding followed by," he added huskily, "one hell of a long passionate wedding night."

She caught her breath at the passion in his eyes. "Leo, are you sure?" she wanted to know.

He dragged her into his arms and kissed her so hungrily that a familiar couple walking past the truck actually stared amusedly at them for a few seconds before hurrying on past.

"I'm sorry, baby. I can't…wait…any longer," he ground out into her eager mouth. "It's marriage or I'm leaving the state!" He lifted his head, and his eyes were tortured. He could barely breathe. "Oh, God, I want you, Janie!"

She felt the tremor in his big body. She understood what he felt, because it was the same with her. She drew in a slow breath. It was desire. She thought, maybe, there was some affection as well, but he was dying to have her, and that was what prompted marriage plans. He'd said often enough that he was never going to get married.

He saw all those thoughts in her eyes, even through the most painful desire he'd ever known. "I'll make you glad you said yes," he told her gruffly. "I won't ever cheat on you, or hurt you. I'll take care of you all my life. All of yours."

It was enough, she thought, to take a chance on. "All right," she said tenderly. She reached up and touched his hard, swollen mouth. "I'll marry you."

It was profound, to hear her say it. He caught his breath at the raging arousal the words produced in his already-tortured body. He groaned as he pressed his mouth hard into the palm of her hand.

She wasn't confident enough to tease him about his desire for her. But it pleased her that he was, at least, fiercely hungry for her in that way, if no other.

He caught her close and fought for control. "We'd better go and get a marriage license," he bit off. "We've already given Evan and Anna Tremayne an eyeful."

"What?" she asked drowsily.

"They were walking past when I kissed you," he said with a rueful smile.

"They've been married for years," she pointed out.

He rubbed his nose against hers. "Wait until we've been married for years," he whispered. "We'll still be fogging up windows in parked trucks."

"Think so?" she asked, smiling.

"Wait and see."

He let go of her, with obvious reluctance, and moved back under the steering wheel. "Here we go."

THEY APPLIED FOR the marriage license, had the blood tests, and then went to round up their families to tell them the news.

Janie's aunt Lydia had gone to Europe over the holidays on an impromptu sightseeing trip, Fred Brewster told them when they gave him the news. "She'll be livid if she misses the wedding," he said worriedly.

"She can be here for the first christening," Leo said with a grin at Janie's blush. "You can bring Hettie with you, and come over to the ranch for supper tomorrow night," he added, amused at Fred's lack of surprise at the announcement. "I've invited my brothers to supper and phoned Barbara to have it catered. I wanted to break the news to all of them at once."

"Hettie won't be surprised," Fred told them, tongue-in-cheek. "But she'll enjoy a night out. We'll be along about six."

"Fine," Leo said, and didn't offer to leave Janie at home. He waited until she changed into a royal-blue pantsuit with a beige top, and carried her with him to the ranch.

He did chores and paperwork with Janie right beside him, although he didn't touch her.

"A man only has so much self-control," he told her with a wistful sigh. "So we'll keep our hands off each other, until the wedding. Fair enough?"

She grinned at him. "Fair enough!"

He took her home after they had supper at a local restaurant. "I'd love to have taken you up to Houston for a night on the town," he said when he walked her to her door. "But not with your face like that." He touched it somberly. "Here in Jacobsville, everybody already knows what happened out at Shea's last night. In Houston, people might think I did this, or allowed it to happen." He bent and kissed the painful bruise. "Nobody will ever hurt you again as long as I live," he swore huskily.

She closed her eyes, savoring the soft touch of his mouth. "Are you sure you want to marry me?" she asked.

"I'm sure. I'll be along about ten-thirty," he added.

She looked up at him, puzzled. "Ten-thirty?"

He nodded. "Church," he said with a wicked grin. "We have to set a good example for the kids."

She laughed, delighted. "Okay."

"See you in the morning, pretty girl," he said, and brushed his mouth lightly over hers before he bounded back down the steps to his car and drove off with a wave of his hand.

FRED WAS AMAZED that Leo did take her to church, and then came back to the house with her for a lunch of

cold cuts. He and Fred talked cattle while Janie lounged
at Leo's side, still astounded at the unexpected turn of
events. Fred couldn't be happier about the upcoming
nuptials. He was amused that Hettie had the weekend
off and didn't know what had happened. She had a shock
coming when she arrived later in the day.

Leo took Janie with him when he went home, approv-
ing her choice of a silky beige dress and matching high
heels, pearls in her ears and around her throat, and her
hair long and luxurious down her back.

"Your brothers will be surprised," Janie said worriedly on the way there.

Leo lifted an eyebrow. "After the Cattleman's Ball?
Probably not," he said. Then he told her about Corrigan
offering to drive him home so that he could pump him
for information to report back to the others.

"You were very intoxicated," she recalled, embarrassed when she recalled the fierce argument they'd had.

"I'd just found out that Marilee had lied about you,"
he confided. "And seeing you with damned Harley didn't
help."

"You were jealous," she realized.

"Murderously jealous," he confessed at once. "That
only got worse, when you took the job at Shea's." He
glanced at her. "I'm not having you work there any longer. I don't care what compromises I have to make to
get you to agree."

She smiled to herself. "Oh, I don't mind quitting,"
she confessed. "I'll have enough to do at the ranch, after
we're married, getting settled in."

"Let's try not to talk about that right now, okay?"

She stared at him, worriedly. "Are you getting cold feet?" she asked.

"I'll tell you what I'm getting," he said, turning dark eyes to hers. And he did tell her, bluntly, and starkly. He nodded curtly at her scarlet flush and directed his attention back at the road. "Just for the record, the word 'marriage' reminds me of the words 'wedding night,' and I go nuts."

She whistled softly.

"So let's think about food and coffee and my brothers and try not to start something noticeable," he added in a deep tone. "Because all three of them are going to be looking for obvious signs and they'll laugh the place down if they see any."

"We can recite multiplication tables together," she agreed.

He glanced at her with narrow eyes. "Great idea," he replied sarcastically. "That reminds me of rabbits, and guess what rabbits remind me of?"

"I know the Gettysburg Address by heart," she countered. "I'll teach it to you."

"That will put me to sleep."

"I'll make biscuits for supper."

He sat up straight. "Biscuits? For supper? To go with Barbara's nice barbecue, potato salad and apple pie. Now that's an idea that just makes my mouth water! And here I am poking along!" He pushed down on the accelerator. "Honey, you just said the magic word!"

She chuckled to herself. Marriage, she thought, was going to be a real adventure.

CHAPTER ELEVEN

NOT ONLY DID CORRIGAN, Rey and Cag show up for supper with their wives, Dorie, Meredith and Tess, but Simon and Tira came all the way from Austin on a chartered jet. Janie had just taken off her apron after producing a large pan of biscuits, adding them to the deliciously spread table that Barbara and her assistant had arranged before they left.

All four couples arrived together, the others having picked up Simon and Tira at the Jacobsville airport on the way.

Leo and Janie met them at the door. Leo looked unprepared.

"All of you?" he exclaimed.

Simon shrugged. "I didn't believe them," he said, pointing at the other three brothers. "I had to come see for myself."

"We didn't believe him, either," Rey agreed, pointing at Leo.

They all looked at Janie, who moved closer to Leo and blushed.

"If she's pregnant, you're dead," Cag told Leo pointedly when he saw the look on Janie's face. He leaned closer before Leo could recover enough to protest. "Have you been beating her?"

"She is most certainly not pregnant!" Leo said, offended. "And you four ought to know that I have never hit a woman in my life!"

"But he hit the guy who did this to me," Janie said with pride, smiling up at him as she curled her fingers into his big ones.

"Not very effectively, I'm afraid," Leo confessed.

"That's just because the guy had a black belt," Janie said, defending Leo. "Nobody but our assistant police chief had the experience to bring him down."

"Yes, I know Grier," Simon said solemnly. "He's something of a legend in law enforcement circles, even in Austin."

"He has alien artifacts in his filing cabinet, and he was a government assassin," Janie volunteered with a straight face.

Everybody stared at her.

"He was kidding!" Leo chuckled.

She grinned at him. He wrinkled his nose at her. They exchanged looks that made the others suddenly observant. All at once, they became serious.

"We can do wedding invitations if we e-mail them tonight," Cag said offhand. He pulled a list from his pocket. "This is a list of the people we need to invite."

"I can get the symphony orchestra to play," Rey said, nodding. "I've got their conductor's home phone number in my pocket computer." He pulled it out.

"We can buy the gown online and have it overnighted here from Neiman-Marcus in Dallas," Corrigan volunteered. "All we need is her dress size. What are you, a size ten?"

Janie balked visibly, but nodded. "Here comes her father," Dorie said enthusiastically, noting the new arrival.

"I'll e-mail the announcement to the newspaper," Tess said. "They have a Tuesday edition, we can just make it. We'll need a photo."

There was a flash. Tira changed the setting on her digital camera. "How's this?" she asked, showing it to Tess and Meredith.

"Great!" Meredith said. "We can use Leo's computer to download it and e-mail it straight to the paper, so they'll have it first thing tomorrow. We can e-mail it to the local television station as well. Come on!"

"Wait for me! I'll write the announcement," Dorie called to Corrigan, following along behind the women.

"Hey!" Janie exclaimed.

"What?" Tira asked, hesitating. "Oh, yes, the reception. It can be held here. But the cake! We need a caterer!"

"Cag can call the caterer," Simon volunteered his brother.

"It's my wedding!" Janie protested.

"Of course it is, dear," Tira said soothingly. "Let's go, girls."

The women vanished into Leo's study. The men went into a huddle. Janie's father and Hettie came in the open door, looking shell-shocked.

"Never mind them," Leo said, drawing Janie to meet her parent and her housekeeper. "They're taking care of the arrangements," he added, waving his hand in the general direction of his brothers and sisters-in-law. "Apparently, it's going to be a big wedding, with a formal gown and caterers and newspaper coverage." He grinned. "You can come, of course."

Janie hit him. "We were going to have a nice, quiet little wedding!"

"You go tell them what you want, honey," he told Janie. "Just don't expect them to listen."

Hettie started giggling. Janie glared at her.

"You don't remember, do you?" the housekeeper asked Janie. "Leo helped them do the same thing to Dorie, and Tira, and Tess, and even Meredith. It's payback time. They're getting even."

"I'm afraid so," Leo told Janie with a smug grin. "But look at the bright side, you can just sit back and relax and not have to worry about a single detail."

"But, my dress…" she protested.

He patted her on the shoulder. "They have wonderful taste," he assured her.

Fred was grinning from ear to ear. He never would have believed one man could move so fast, but he'd seen the way Leo looked at Janie just the morning before. It was no surprise to him that a wedding was forthcoming. He knew a man who was head over heels when he saw one.

BY THE END of the evening, Janie had approved the wedding gown, provided the statistics and details of her family background and education, and climbed into the car with Leo to let him take her home.

"The rings will be ready Tuesday, they promised," he told her at her father's door. He smiled tenderly. "You'll be a beautiful bride."

"I can't believe it," she said softly, searching his lean face.

He drew her close. "Wednesday night, you'll believe it," he said huskily, and bent to kiss her with obvious restraint. "Now, good night!"

He walked to the car. She drifted inside, wrapped in dreams.

IT WAS A honey of a society wedding. For something so hastily concocted, especially with Christmas approaching, it went off perfectly. Even the rings were ready on time, the dress arrived by special overnight delivery, the blood tests and marriage license were promptly produced, the minister engaged, press coverage assured, the caterer on time—nothing, absolutely nothing, went wrong.

Janie stood beside Leo at the Hart ranch at a makeshift arch latticed with pink and white roses while they spoke their vows. Janie had a veil, because Leo had insisted. And after the last words of the marriage ceremony were spoken, he lifted the veil from Janie's soft eyes and looked at her with smoldering possession. He bent and kissed her tenderly, his lips barely brushing hers. She had a yellowing bruise on one cheek and she was careful to keep that side away from the camera, but Leo didn't seem to notice the blemish.

"You are the most beautiful bride who ever spoke her vows," he whispered as he kissed her. "And I will cherish you until they lay me down in the dark!"

She reached up and kissed him back, triggering a burst of enthusiastic ardor that he was only able to curb belatedly. He drew away from her, smiling sheepishly at their audience, caught her hand, and led her back to the house through a shower of rice.

The brothers were on the job even then. The press was delicately prompted to leave after the cake and punch were consumed, the symphony orchestra was coaxed to load their instruments. The guests were delicately led to the door and thanked. Then the brothers carried their wives away in a flurry of good wishes and, at last, the newlyweds were alone, in their own home.

Leo looked at Janie with eyes that made her heart race. "Alone," he whispered, approaching her slowly, "at last."

He bent and lifted her, tenderly, and carried her down the hall to the bedroom. He locked the door. He took the phone off the hook. He closed the curtains. He came back to her, where she stood, a little apprehensive, just inside the closed door.

"I'm not going to hurt you," he said softly. "You're a priceless treasure. I'm going to be slow, and tender, and I'm going to give you all the time you need. Don't be afraid of me."

"I'm not, really," she said huskily, watching him divest her of the veil and the hairpins that held her elaborate coiffure in place with sprigs of lily of the valley. "But you want me so much," she tried to explain. "What if I can't satisfy you?"

He laughed. "You underestimate yourself."

"Are you sure?"

He turned her around so that he could undo the delicate hooks and snaps of her gown. "I'm sure."

She let him strip her down to her lacy camisole, white

stockings and lacy white garter belt, her eyes feeding on the delighted expression that claimed his lean face.

"Beautiful," he said huskily. "I love you in white lace."

"You're not bad in a morning coat," she teased, liking the vested gray ceremonial rig he was wearing.

"How am I without it?" he teased.

"Let's find out." She unbuttoned his coat and then the vest under it. He obligingly stripped them off for her, along with his tie, and left the shirt buttons to her hands. "You've got cuff links," she murmured, trying to release them.

"I'll do it." He moved to the chest of drawers and put his cuff links in a small box, along with his pocket change and keys. He paused to remove his shirt and slacks, shoes and socks before he came back to her, in silky gray boxer shorts like the ones he'd worn the night they were almost intimate.

"You are…magnificent," she whispered, running her hands over his chest.

"You have no idea how magnificent, yet." He unsnapped the shorts and let them fall, coaxing her eyes to him. He shivered at the expression on her face, because he was far more potent than he'd been the one time she'd looked at him like this.

While she was gaping, he unfastened the camisole with a delicate flick of his fingers and unhooked the garter belt. He stripped the whole of it down her slender body and tipped her back onto the bed while he pulled the stockings off with the remainder of her clothing.

He pulled back the cover and tossed the pillows off to the side before he arranged her on the crisp white sheets and stood over her, vibrating with desire, his eyes eating her nude body, from her taut nipples to the visible trembling of her long, parted legs.

She watched him come down to her with faint apprehension that suddenly vanished when he pressed his open mouth down, hard, right on her soft belly.

He'd never touched her like that, and in the next few feverish minutes, she went from shock to greater shock as he displayed his knowledge of women.

"No, you can't, you can't!" she sobbed, but he was, he did, he had!

She arched up toward his mouth with tears of tortured ecstasy raining down her cheeks in a firestorm of sensation, sobbing as the pleasure stretched her tight as a rope under the warm, expert motions of his lips.

She gasped as the wave began to hit her. Her eyes opened, and his face was there, his body suddenly right over hers, his hips thrusting down. She felt him, and then looked and saw him, even as she felt the small stabbing pain of his invasion. The sight of what was happening numbed the pain, and then it was gone altogether as he shifted roughly, dragging his hips against hers as he enforced his possession of her innocence.

Her nails bit into his long back as he moved on her, insisting, demanding. His face, above her, was strained, intent.

"Am I hurting you?" he ground out.

"N-no!" she gasped, lifting toward him, her eyes wide, shocked, fascinated.

He looked down, lifting himself so that he could watch her body absorb him. "Look," he coaxed through his teeth. "Look, Janie. Look at us."

She glanced down and her breath caught at the intimate sight that met her eyes. She gasped.

"And we've barely begun," he breathed, shifting suddenly, fiercely, against her.

She sobbed, shivering.

He did it again, watching her face, assessing her reaction. "I can feel you, all around me, like a soft, warm glove," he whispered, his lips compressing as pleasure shot through him with every deepening motion of his hips. "Take me, baby. Take me inside you. Take all of me. Make me scream, baby," he murmured.

She was out of her mind with the pleasure he was giving her. She writhed under him, arching her hips, pushing against him, watching his face. She shifted and he groaned harshly. She laughed, through her own torment, and suddenly cried out as the pleasure became more and more unbearable. Her hands went between them, in a fever of desire.

"Yes," he moaned as he felt her trembling touch. "Yes. Oh… God…baby…do it, do it! Do it!"

She was going to die. She opened her eyes and looked at him, feeling her body pulse as he shortened and deepened his movements, watching her with his mouth compressed, his eyes feverish.

"Do it…harder," she choked.

He groaned in anguish and his hips ground into hers suddenly, his hands catching her wrists and slamming them over her head as he moved fiercely above her, his eyes holding hers prisoner as his body enforced its possession violently.

She felt her body strain to accommodate him and in

the last few mad seconds, she wondered if she would be able to...

He blurred in her sight. She was shaking. Her whole body rippled in a shuddering parody of convulsions, whipping against his while her mouth opened, gasping at air, and her voice uttered sounds she'd never heard from it in her entire life.

"Get it," he groaned. "Yes. Get it...!"

He cried out and then his body, too, began to shudder rhythmically. A sound like a harsh sob tore from his throat. He groaned endlessly as his body shivered into completion. Seconds, minutes, hours, an eternity of pleasure later, he collapsed on her.

They both shivered in the aftermath. She felt tears on her face, in her mouth. She couldn't breathe. Her body ached, even inside, and when she moved, she felt pleasure stab her in the most secret places, where she could still feel him.

She sobbed, her nails biting into the hands pinning her wrists.

He lifted his head. "Look at me," he whispered, and when she did, he began to move again.

She sobbed harder, her legs parting, her hips lifting for him, her whole body shivering in a maelstrom of unbelievable delight.

"I can go again, right now," he whispered huskily, holding her eyes. "Can you? Or will it hurt?"

"I can't...feel pain," she whimpered. Her eyes closed on a shiver and then opened again, right into his. "Oh, please," she whispered brokenly. "Please, please...!"

He began to move, very slowly. "I love watching you," he whispered breathlessly. "Your face is beautiful, like this. Your body…" He looked down at it, watching its sensuous movements in response to his own. "I could eat you with a spoon right now, Mrs. Hart," he added shakily. "You are every dream of perfection that I've ever had."

"And you…are mine," she whispered. She lifted up to him, initiating the rhythm, whimpering softly as the pleasure began to climb all over again. "I love you…so much," she sobbed.

His body clenched. He groaned, arched, his face going into her throat as his body took over from his mind and buffeted her violently.

She went over the edge almost at once, holding on for dear life while he took what he wanted from her. It was feverish, ardent, overwhelming. She thought she might faint from the ecstasy when it throbbed into endless satiation. He went with her, every second of the way. She felt him when his body gave up the pleasure he sought, felt the rigor, heard the helpless throb of his voice at her ear when he shuddered and then relaxed completely.

She held him close, drinking in the intimate sound and feel and scent of his big body over hers in the damp bed. It had been a long, wild loving. She'd never imagined, even in their most passionate encounters, that love-making would be like this.

She told him so, in shy whispers.

He didn't answer her. He was still, and quiet, for such a long time that she became worried.

"Are you all right?" she whispered at his ear. Over her, she could hear and feel the beat of his heart as it slowly calmed.

His head lifted, very slowly. He looked into her wide

eyes. "I lost consciousness for a few seconds," he said quietly. He touched her lower lip, swollen from the fierce pressure of his mouth just at the last. "I thought… I might die, trying to get deep enough to satisfy us both."

She flushed.

He put his finger over her lips. He wasn't smiling. He moved deliberately, letting her feel him. "You aren't on the Pill," he said. "And I was too hot to even think of any sort of birth control. Janie," he added, hesitantly, "I think I made you pregnant."

Her eyes searched his. "You said you wanted to," she reminded him in a whisper.

"I do. But it should have been your choice, too," he continued, sounding worried.

She traced his long, elegant nose and smiled with delicious exhaustion. "Did you hear me shouting, Leo, stop and run to the pharmacy to buy protection!"

He laughed despite the gravity of the situation. "Was that about the time I was yelling, 'get it, baby'?"

She hit his chest, flushed, and then laughed.

"You did, too, didn't you?" he asked with a smug grin. "So did I. Repeatedly." He groaned as he moved slowly away from her and flopped onto his back, stretching his sore muscles. "Damn, I'm sore! And I told you I could go all night, didn't I?"

She sat up, torn between shock and amusement as she met his playful eyes. "Sore? Men get sore?"

"When they go at it like that, they do," he replied sardonically. "What a wedding night," he said, whistling through his lips as he studied her nude body appreciatively. "If they gave medals, you could have two."

Her eyebrows arched. "Really? I was… I was all right?"

He tugged her down to him. "Women have egos, too, don't they?" he asked tenderly. He pushed her damp hair away from her cheeks and mouth. "You were delicious. I've never enjoyed a woman so much."

"I didn't know anything at all."

He brought her head down and kissed her eyelids. "It isn't a matter of knowledge."

She searched his eyes. "You had enough of that for both of us," she murmured.

"Bodies in the dark," he said, making it sound unimportant. "I wanted to have you in the light, Janie," he said solemnly. "I wanted to look at you while I was taking you."

"That's a sexist remark," she teased.

"You took me as well," he conceded. He touched her mouth with a long forefinger. "I've never seen anything so beautiful," he whispered, and sounded breathless. "Your face, your body…" His face clenched. "And the pleasure." His eyes closed and he shivered. "I've never known anything like it." His eyes opened again. "It was love," he whispered to her, scowling. "Making love. Really making love."

Her breath caught in her throat. She traced his sideburn to his ear. "Yes."

"Do you know what I'm trying to tell you?" he asked quietly.

She looked down into his eyes and saw it there. Her heart jumped into her throat. "You're telling me that you love me," she said.

He nodded. "I love you. I knew it when Clark assaulted you, and I went at him. It hurt my pride that I couldn't make him beg for forgiveness. I cleaned you up and dried your hair, and knew that I loved you, all at once. It was a very small step from there to a wedding ring." He brought hers to his lips and kissed it tenderly. "I couldn't bear the thought of losing you. Not after that."

She smiled dreamily. "I loved you two years ago, when you brought me a wilted old daisy you'd picked out in the meadow, and teased me about it being a bouquet. You didn't know it, but to me, it was."

"I've given you a hard time," he told her, with obvious regret. "I'm sorry."

She leaned down and kissed him tenderly. "You made up for it." She moved her breasts gently against his chest. "I really can go all night," she whispered. "When you've recovered, I'll show you."

He chuckled under the soft press of her mouth, and his big arms swallowed her. "When *you're* recovered, I'll let you. I love you, Mrs. Hart. I love you with all my heart."

"I love you with all mine." She kissed him again, and thought how dreams did, sometimes, actually come true.

A WEEK LATER, they celebrated their first Christmas together at a family party, to which Janie's father, Aunt Lydia and Hettie were also invited. After kissing her with exquisite tenderness beneath the mistletoe, Leo gave Janie an emerald necklace, to match her eyes, he said, and she gave him an expensive pocket watch, with his name and hers engraved inside the case.

ON NEW YEAR'S Eve, the family gathered with other families at the Jacobsville Civic Center for the first annual celebration. A live band played favorites and couples danced on the polished wood floor. Calhoun Ballenger had mused aloud that since Jacobsville's economy was based on cattle and agriculture, they should drop a pair of horns instead of a ball to mark the new year. He was red-faced at the celebration, when the city fathers took him seriously and did that very thing.

While Leo and Janie stood close together on the patio of the second floor ballroom to watch the neon set of longhorns go down to the count, a surprising flurry of snow came tumbling from the sky to dust the heads of the crowd.

"It's snowing!" Janie exclaimed, holding out a hand to catch the fluffy precipitation. "But it never snows in Jacobsville! Well, almost never."

Leo caught her close as the horns went to the bottom of the courthouse tower across the street and bent to her mouth, smiling. "One more wish come true," he teased, because he knew how much she loved snow. "Happy New Year, my darling," he whispered.

"Happy New Year," she whispered back, and met his kiss with loving enthusiasm, to the amused glances of the other guests. They were, after all, newlyweds.

The new year came and soon brought with it unexpected tragedy. John Clark went back to Victoria to get his jailed brother a famous attorney, but he didn't have any money. So he tried to rob a bank to get the money. He was caught in the act by a security guard and a Texas Ranger who was working on a case locally. Judd Dunn was one of the two men who exchanged shots with Clark in front of the Victoria Bank and Trust. Clark missed.

Judd and the security guard didn't. Ballistics tests were required to pinpoint who fired the fatal bullet.

Jack Clark, still in jail in Victoria, was let out long enough to attend his brother's funeral in Victoria. He escaped from the kindly sheriff's deputy who was bringing him back in only handcuffs instead of handcuffs and leg chains. After all, Jack Clark had been so docile and polite, and even cried at his brother's grave. The deputy was rewarded for his compassion by being knocked over the head twice with the butt of his own .38 caliber service revolver and left for dead in a driving rain in the grass next to the Victoria road. Later that day, his squad car was found deserted a few miles outside Victoria.

It was the talk of the town for several days, and Leo and Janie stayed close to home, because they knew Clark had scores to settle all around Jacobsville. They were in their own little world, filled with love. They barely heard all the buzz and gossip. But what they did hear was about Tippy Moore and Cash Grier.

"Tippy's not Grier's sort," Janie murmured sleepily. They didn't do a lot of sleeping at night, even now. She cuddled up in her husband's lap and nuzzled close. "He needs someone who is gentle and sweet. Not a harpy."

He wrapped her up close and kissed the top of her head. "What would you know about harpies?" he teased. "You're the single sweetest human being I've ever known."

She smiled.

"Well, except for me, of course," he added.

"Leo Hart!" she exclaimed, drawing back.

"You said I was sweet," he murmured, bending his head. "You said it at least six times. You were clawing my back raw at the time, and swearing that you were never going to live through what I was doing to you..."

She tugged his head down and kissed him hungrily. "You're sweet, all right," she whispered raggedly. "Do it again...!"

He groaned. They were never going to make it to the bed. But the doors were locked...what the hell.

An hour later, he carried her down the hall to their bedroom and tucked her up next to him, exhausted and still smiling.

"At least," he said wearily, "hopefully Clark will go to prison for a long, long time when he's caught. He won't be in a position to threaten you again."

"Or you." She curled closer. "Did I tell you that Marilee phoned me yesterday?"

He stiffened. "No."

She smiled. "It's okay. She only wanted to apologize. She's going to Europe to visit her grandmother in London. I told her to have a nice trip."

"London's almost far enough away."

She sighed, wrapping her arms around him. "Be generous. She'll never know what it is to be as happy as we are."

"Who will?" he teased, but the look he gave her was serious. He touched her hair, watching her succumb to sleep.

He lay awake for a long time, his eyes intent on her slender, sleeping body. She made wonderful biscuits, she could shoot a shotgun, she made love like a fairy. He wondered what he'd ever done in his life to deserve her.

"Dreams," she whispered, shocking him.

"What, honey?"

She nuzzled her face into his throat and melted into him. "Dreams come true," she whispered, falling asleep again.

He touched her lips with his and smoothed back her long hair. "Yes, my darling," he whispered with a long, sweet smile. "Dreams come true."

* * * * *

Also by Delores Fossen

HQN

Visit her Author Profile page at Harlequin.com,
or deloresfossen.com, for more titles!

CHRISTMAS GUARDIAN

Delores Fossen

To Dakota and Danielle

PROLOGUE

San Antonio, Texas

JORDAN TAYLOR HEARD the pounding, but it took him a moment to realize it wasn't part of the nightmare he'd been having. Someone was banging on his door.

He checked the clock on the nightstand. Three in the morning. He cursed, threw back the covers and grabbed his Sig Sauer, because visits at this time of morning were never good.

"Jordan, open up!" a woman said. Not a shout, exactly, but close.

He recognized that voice and cursed again. Shelly Mackey, his ex, both as a business associate and a girlfriend. He wouldn't need the Sig Sauer. Well, probably not. Since he hadn't seen or heard from Shelly in months and since her voice sounded a couple of steps beyond frantic, Jordan decided to bring the gun with him anyway.

"You have to help me!" Shelly insisted. She continued to pound on the door. "Please. Hurry."

That got him moving faster. Shelly wasn't the drama queen type. Jordan didn't bother to dress. He pulled on only his boxers and raced out of his bedroom.

Her voice wasn't coming from the front of the house,

he realized, but from the door off his kitchen. Jordan sprinted that way.

But the pounding stopped.

He stopped, too, just short of the door. He waited a moment. Listened.

And heard nothing.

"Shelly?" he called out.

Still nothing. That gave him another jolt of adrenaline. Shelly was likely in big trouble.

Jordan lifted his gun as he reached for the doorknob. Then, he heard it. The sound of a car engine.

Someone was driving away. Not fast. More like easing away, the tires barely whispering on the brick driveway that encircled his house. Jordan unlocked the door, jerked it open, but he caught only a flash of the bloodred taillights before the car disappeared into the darkness.

With his gun aimed, he shot glances around his heavily landscaped yard. He didn't see anyone, but the soft grunt he heard had him aiming his attention lower. To the porch.

There was a basket with a blanket draped over it.

"What the hell?" he mumbled.

Jordan kept his attention on the yard, just in case the someone or something that had caused Shelly to run was still out there. He stooped down and lifted the corner of the blanket.

A baby stared back at him.

Jordan had never remembered being speechless before, but he sure was now. He looked beneath the blanket again, certain he was mistaken.

No mistake.

The tiny baby was still there. Still staring at him with eyes that seemed to ask who are you and why am I here?

Jordan wanted to know the same thing.

He grabbed the basket, brought it inside so he could set it on the floor and shut the door. He also reached for his phone and jabbed in Shelly's number. Each ring felt like a week-long wait.

"Jordan," she finally answered. He didn't know who sounded more frantic—him or her.

"Talk to me," he snarled.

"Someone's trying to kill me."

Despite the baby-in-the-basket bombshell, he wasn't immune to the fear he heard in her voice. "Where are you? I'll send help, and then you can come back for the little delivery you left on my porch."

"I'm sorry. I didn't want to do things this way, but I had no choice. They're after me, because of the baby. He's in danger, Jordan. The worst kind. And I need you to protect him."

Him. A boy.

Then it hit Jordan. He threw back the blanket and had a better look at that little face. Dark brown hair. Dark brown eyes. About two months old at the most. He quickly did the math. He'd last slept with Shelly nine or ten months ago. Break-up sex. And he hadn't seen her since.

Jordan groaned, and because he had no choice, he sank down on the floor next to the basket.

"I've sanitized my office," Shelly continued, her words rushing together. "Actually, I burned it to the ground. They won't find anything there, but I don't want them tracing the baby to you. Don't let anyone know you have him. Please. There can be no chain of custody when it comes to him, understand?"

No. He didn't. But he focused on Shelly and her safety. "Tell me where you are so I can help you."

"You can help me by taking care of the baby. There are no records and no paperwork to connect me to that child. It has to stay that way. I've created a phony trail for us, too. If anyone digs into our connection, they'll find proof you fired me because I was embezzling from your company. The documentation will imply that we're enemies and that you're the last person on earth that I'd ask for help."

This conversation was getting more and more confusing. "Is this baby mine?" Jordan demanded.

Silence. He knew she was still on the line because he could hear her breathing. "Just protect him, please," she said moments later. "A person might come looking for him. If she uses the code words, red ruby, then you can trust her."

"Red ruby? You gotta be kidding me. A code word? For what? Why?"

"I have to disappear for a while," Shelly said, obviously ignoring him. "But when I can, I'll explain everything."

With that, she hung up.

Jordan didn't waste a second, not even to curse. He redialed Shelly's number. But she didn't answer. The call went straight to voice mail.

Time for plan B. He phoned one of his agents, Cody Guillory, his right-hand man at Sentron, the private security agency that Jordan owned. Since Cody was pulling duty at headquarters, he answered on the first ring.

"I'm guessing whatever's wrong got you out of bed?" Cody greeted.

"Yeah, it did. I have a situation," Jordan replied. "Shelly could be in danger. She still has the same cell number and possibly the same phone she used when she worked for Sentron so try to track that. Discreetly. Let me know where she is."

"Will do. Give me a couple of minutes. Anything else?"

Jordan looked at the baby and debated what he should say. *Don't let anyone know you have him,* Shelly had warned. She'd even used another rare *please.* For now, he'd take the plea and warning to heart. "Just find her and send someone in case she needs help," Jordan said, and he ended the call.

The only illumination came from the moonlight seeping in through the windows, but it was enough for him to see the basket. Jordan stared at the baby, whose eyes were drifting down to sleep, and because he didn't know what else to do, he groaned and considered the most obvious scenario. Had Shelly given birth to his child without telling him? And if so, why wouldn't he have heard rumors that he was a daddy? There'd been no signs, no hints, nothing to indicate that this child was his.

Except for the dark brown hair, dark brown eyes.

Like Jordan's own.

Still, that didn't mean he'd fathered this baby.

He needed to talk with Shelly, and even though it was clear she was in the middle of a personal crisis, he tried her number again. Again, it went straight to voice mail. This time he decided to leave a message.

"Shelly, we need to talk." He wanted to say more,

much more, but a cell conversation wasn't secure. His number wouldn't show up on her caller ID or phone records because all calls from his house and business were routed through a scrambler, but someone could get her phone and listen to any message he might leave.

Someone's trying to kill me, she'd said. Even with the shock of finding the baby, Jordan hadn't forgotten that. Like him, Shelly now owned a security agency. Even though she'd been in business less than a year, her start-up agency provided services as bodyguards, personal protection, P.I.s.

And probably more.

That *more* had nearly gotten him killed a few times. *Was that what was happening to Shelly now? Had a case gone wrong, and was someone trying to use the baby to get to her?* Maybe she'd had no choice but to bring the child to him, but it damn well had been her choice not to tell him before now.

If the child was his, that is.

The phone rang, slicing through the silence and waking the baby. He started to fuss. Jordan had no idea how to deal with that, so he lightly rocked the basket. Thankfully, the little guy hushed, and Jordan took the call.

"It's Cody. I tracked Shelly's phone, no problem, but while I was doing that, I heard her name on the police scanner, and I zoomed in on the conversation with our equipment." He paused. "About five minutes ago, a traffic cop responded to a failed carjacking just about a half mile from your place. It's Shelly's car."

Oh, God. "How bad?"

"Bad." And that was all Cody said for several long moments. "Shelly's dead."

That hit Jordan like a punch to the gut. He squeezed his eyes shut. "You're sure it's her?"

"Yes, I've tapped into the camera at the traffic light, and I can see her face. It's Shelly, all right. Looks like a gunshot to the head."

Jordan forced away the grief and pain and grabbed the basket so he could take the baby with him to his home office. He turned on his secure laptop. "Send me the feed from that traffic camera. Audio, too. And get one of our agents over there."

"I've already dispatched Desmond—" Cody paused, and in the background Jordan could hear the chatter from the laser listening device that Cody was using to zoom in on the scene. "An eyewitness is talking to the traffic cop right now."

The images popped onto his computer screen. Jordan saw Shelly's car. The driver's door was wide open. Her body was sprawled out in the middle of the street, limp and lifeless. *Hell.* If he'd just gotten to the door sooner, if he could have stopped her from leaving his place, then maybe she'd still be alive.

Another patrol car arrived, but Jordan zoomed in on the conversation between the traffic cop and a twenty-something woman dressed in a fast-food restaurant uniform. An eyewitness. Her body language and nearly hysterical tone told Jordan she probably hadn't been involved in this as anything more than a spectator to a horrific crime.

"The man didn't want her car," Jordan heard the woman say, and he cranked up the volume.

"What do you mean?" the cop asked.

Tears streamed down the eyewitness's face. "That

man dragged her from her car and tried to force her into his black SUV. He was trying to kidnap her or something."

Or something. Jordan was afraid he knew what that something was. This man wanted information about the baby. But why?

The eyewitness broke down, sobbing while she frantically shook her head. "The woman fought him," she finally said, her trembling fingers held close to her mouth. "She tried to get away. But he shot her and then drove off."

There it was. The brutal end of one nightmare and the start of another.

This wasn't a botched carjacking. Shelly had been murdered. And Jordan instinctively knew the man in the SUV wasn't finished.

The killer would come after the baby next.

CHAPTER ONE

Fourteen months later
December 22nd

KINLEY FORD WAS after two things: Jordan Taylor and the truth. Tonight, she might finally get both.

If she didn't get killed first, that is.

Because if he did indeed know what was going on, he might take extreme measures to stop anyone from finding out.

Swallowing hard, she stepped inside the reception area of the Sentron Security Agency to find the Christmas party in full swing. The place sparkled, not just with some of the guests in their glittery dresses. There was also an angel ice sculpture on a center table, and it was flanked on each side with white roses in crystal vases and bottles of champagne angled into gleaming, silver ice buckets.

Kinley dismissed all of that and looked around. There he was, on the far side of the room next to the massive Christmas tree.

Jordan Taylor.

He looked lethal. And was. She'd studied every bit of information she could learn about him. Over the years, he'd killed three people. All in the line of duty, of course.

But that still gave him a dangerous edge that she would be a fool to dismiss.

Kinley hated to think of him as her last resort, but she had exhausted her list of persons of interest. She'd exhausted her bank account. And herself. She wouldn't give up if she failed tonight—she would never give up— but she literally had no idea where to go next.

Beside her, her "date," Cody Guillory, took her coat, then her arm and led her not in Jordan's direction but toward a tall blond-haired man by the ten-foot-long table filled from corner to corner with party food.

"Anna," Cody said using the alias she'd given him, "this is Burke Dennison." Cody checked his watch. "In about three hours, he'll be my new boss."

Burke flashed a thousand-watt smile. With that sun-blond hair, blue eyes and tan, he looked every bit the golden boy he was. At thirty-one he was a self-made millionaire and about to take the reins of one of the most successful security agencies in the state.

Burke used his champagne glass to make a sweeping motion around the reception area at Sentron headquarters. "I bought the place," Burke let her know. "Isn't that a hoot? I'm a ranch hand's son from Dime Box, Texas, for Christ's sake. Who would have thought it?"

Jordan Taylor obviously had, since he was the present owner and about to relinquish control a mere three days before Christmas.

Kinley wanted to know why.

For fourteen months, she'd examined the lives of more than a hundred people and had looked for any changes in their lifestyles. This was a major change for Jordan.

But the question was, did it have anything to do with Shelly's murder?

"Well, if I'd had the cash, I certainly would have bought the place," Cody remarked. He, too, looked around. Almost lovingly. "My life is here." He shrugged, then smiled. "And usually my body. Burke, don't you expect me to give you eighty hours a week the way I gave Jordan."

Both men laughed, but she didn't think it was her imagination that there was some tension beneath. Maybe Cody wasn't thrilled with gaining a new owner, or losing the old one.

When a tuxed waiter moved closer, Cody snagged two fluted glasses of champagne and handed her one so they could toast Burke. Kinley thanked him and pretended to have a sip while she pretended to be interested in the conversation Burke started about some changes he wanted to make.

She'd gotten good at pretending.

In fact, everything about her was a facade, starting with the red party dress she'd bought from a secondhand store. The symbolic necklace that she wore twenty-four/seven. Her dyed-blond hair. Her name. She was using the alias Anna Carlyle tonight, but she had three other IDs in her apartment. She'd lived a lie for so long. Too long.

"Excuse me a moment," Kinley said to Cody and Burke.

She stepped away and tried to be subtle. She mingled, introducing herself. She even sampled a spicy bacon-wrapped shrimp from the table, all the while making her way to Jordan.

There was an auburn-haired woman talking with him,

but as if he'd known all along that Kinley was coming his way, he slid his gaze in her direction. He whispered something to the redhead and she stepped away, but not before giving Kinley a bit of the evil eye. Probably because she thought Kinley was her romantic competition. That couldn't be further from the truth.

"Nice party," she said, extending her hand. "I'm Anna Carlyle."

He kept his attention fastened to her face. Studying her with those intense brown eyes that were as dark and rich as espresso.

This was the first time she'd seen him up close, the first time she'd gotten a good look at him, and sadly, Kinley realized she wasn't immune to a hot guy. Funny, after what she'd been through she was surprised to feel any emotions other than grief and fear, but Jordan Taylor had an old-fashioned way of reminding her that beneath the facade, she was still a woman.

Simply put, he was the most physically attractive man she'd ever met.

He wasn't slick and golden like his Sentron successor, Burke. Jordan had a sinister edge that extended from his classically chiseled face to the casual way he wore his tux. The tie was loose. His left hand was crammed in his pocket. The other held not a glass of champagne but whiskey straight up.

It smelled as expensive and high-end as he did.

His hair was loose, a bit long, brushing against the bottom of his collar. It was also fashionably unstyled, as if he didn't have to spend much time to make it look as if he could have been posing on the cover of some rock magazine.

"Anna Carlyle, huh?" he asked. And it was definitely a question.

That pulled her from her female fantasy induced by his good looks and smell. "Yes. Cody was kind enough to invite me to the party. And you're…?"

The corner of his mouth lifted. Not a smile of humor, though. It made Kinley want to take a step back. She didn't. She held her ground.

"Jordan Taylor," he finally said. "But you already know that, don't you?"

She was in the process of bringing the champagne glass to her mouth for a fake sip, but Kinley froze. Nearly panicked. Then he tamped down the fear that she was about to be exposed. She didn't mind being revealed as a liar, but exposure could be deadly.

"Yes, I did know you were Jordan Taylor," she admitted. "You're the host of this party. I must have seen your picture in the paper or something."

He eased his hand from his pocket. In his palm was a slim platinum-colored PDA. He held up the tiny screen for her to see.

She saw a picture of herself.

Specifically, a picture of her in the coffee shop across the street. Her worried eyes were fixed on the Sentron building. He flicked a button, and another photo appeared. Also of her. This time she was parked in a car on the street just up from his San Antonio estate.

Oh, God.

Kinley glanced over her shoulder, looking for the quickest way out. There wasn't one. To get to the doors, she'd have to make her way through at least three dozen people, including twenty or so security specialists who among other things were trained to apprehend suspects. But Jordan likely wouldn't even let her get that far, because he was the most qualified security specialist in the room and was only a few inches from her.

She couldn't read his expression. He didn't seem angry. Or even curious. He just stood there, calmly, while he apparently waited for her to make the next move.

"I was thinking about hiring a bodyguard," she lied. "I wanted to check out Sentron first."

He made a *hmm* sound, slipped the PDA into his pocket, set both their drinks aside and grabbed her arm. "Let's take a walk, have a little chat."

Once again she held her ground. Fear shot through her, but Kinley couldn't go with him. She had to get out of there. "I should get back to my date. Cody will be wondering where I am."

"No, he won't."

Because Jordan said it so confidently, Kinley glanced over her shoulder again. Cody and Jordan exchanged a subtle glance, and Jordan's grip tightened on her arm.

"When I realized you were following me, I sent Cody to the coffee shop. His orders were to strike up a conversation with you and then to invite you to tonight's party—an invitation I figured you'd jump at." He paused, met her gaze. "Cody's very good at his job, isn't he?"

He was. Kinley hadn't suspected a thing. Maybe because she'd been so excited about the possibility of learning the truth of what'd happened fourteen months ago?

"I'm leaving," Kinley insisted.

"Yes. After we have that chat." Jordan didn't give her a choice. He practically dragged her in the direction of a hall.

"I have a gun," she warned.

"No, you don't. Before you stepped foot in this building, I scanned you—thoroughly." He tipped his head to a small camera-like device positioned over the front doors. "If you'd been carrying concealed, I would have already disarmed you."

That caused her heart to drop even further. What had she gotten herself into? And better yet, how could she get herself out of it?

He opened a door and maneuvered her inside. Even though she didn't stand a chance of overpowering him, Kinley got ready to fight back. She gripped her purse so she could use it to hit him.

But Jordan didn't attack her. He turned on the lights and shut the door. The room was filled with wall monitors, desks, computers and other equipment. No people, though. She was very much alone with a man who might kill her.

"This is Sentron's command center," he explained. "Soundproof and secure. We won't be overheard here."

Which meant there'd be no one to hear her if she screamed.

He took out the PDA again and began to flick through more pictures. There was one from her college yearbook. Another of her in an airport terminal. Her passport photo. But the bulk was from newspaper articles when she'd been reported missing and presumed dead two years ago.

"There's about three million dollars' worth of equipment in this room, including facial recognition software. When I realized you had me under surveillance, I pulled up every image in every available databank." Jordan turned, aimed those eyes at her again. "I know who you are, Kinley Ford."

Since she didn't know how to respond to that, she didn't say anything.

"You're twenty-eight. Not a natural blonde. You have a Ph.D. in Chemical Engineering from University of Texas. Two years ago the research lab where you worked exploded, and everyone thought you were dead. You obviously weren't. You surfaced again fourteen months ago, only to disappear again. Now you're here." He out-stretched his hands. "Why?"

Kinley chose her words carefully. "I knew Shelly."

He drew his arms back in, clicked off his PDA. "Did you have something to do with her murder?"

"No." But Kinley knew she didn't sound very convincing. "Did you?"

For the first time, she saw some emotion. For just a second, there was something in his eyes. Not pain, exactly. But some sentiment that he quickly reined in. "No." He didn't sound any more convincing than she had.

They stared at each other.

"You knew Shelly," Kinley accused.

He nodded. "She was a former business associate. I fired her because she was embezzling from me."

Yes. She'd read all about that. "And she was your lover. I saw a picture of you two in the newspaper." In the photo, Shelly hadn't been able to conceal the attraction she was feeling. It'd come through even in a grainy black-and-white image. Not for Jordan, though. In that photo, he was wearing the same poker face he had now.

"What do you want?" he asked.

"The truth. Among other things, I want to know who killed Shelly and why."

For just a second, his mouth froze around the syllable he'd been about to say. Then, he obviously rethought his response. "What other things?"

Kinley blinked, because that'd been a slip of the tongue. "I was her client. And her friend." She had to pause and take a deep breath. "I left something important with her."

Mercy, had she stuttered on the word *important?*

Her nerves were so raw now that she didn't know. "I tried to retrieve the item," she continued, "but then I learned her office was destroyed and that she was dead."

She didn't think for a minute that Jordan was just going to accept her explanation. No. The question came immediately. "What kind of item?"

"That's personal." And she'd had more than enough of this intimidation. Kinley straightened her shoulders, tucked her purse beneath her arm and started for the door.

She didn't make it far.

Jordan stepped in front of her, blocking her path and sending her straight into him. He was solid. She learned that the hard way when her breasts landed against his chest. If he had any reaction to the contact, he didn't show it. He merely stepped back so that he was right in front of the door.

"Who sent you here?" he demanded.

"No one." That was the first real truth she'd told tonight. "And I'm leaving."

"Not now, you're not." He blocked her again when she tried to go around him. When Kinley tried again, he caught her, whirled her around and pinned her against the door. "Who knows you're here?"

It wasn't a question she'd anticipated, and now it was her turn to study his eyes to see what had prompted him to bring up one of her biggest concerns. "Obviously your people know."

"Just Cody. And he doesn't know your real name. He thinks you came because I wanted to have sex with you. So, who knows you're here?"

"No one. I've been careful."

He gave a slight eye roll and tipped his head toward the PDA where he had pictures of her. "If I saw you, someone else could have, too."

True. And that terrified her. It had terrified her from day one, but even that wasn't enough to make her stop this search. She had to know if Jordan had the answers she needed.

Well, one answer in particular.

"What's this really all about?" she asked, hating that her voice was shaky. Heck, she was shaking. And the full-body contact he was giving her wasn't helping. She felt trapped. Threatened.

"I want to know the same thing," he countered. "What *item* did you leave with Shelly?"

She shook her head. "I can't say."

"You mean you won't."

"Can't," she insisted. She met his gaze. "What do you know about this?"

He stayed quiet a moment. "I figure if you take what I know and what you know, we'll have a complete picture. So, you show me yours, and I'll show you mine. You first."

Kinley considered that and then considered the alternative. She couldn't afford a stalemate. Nor could she afford the consequences of what would happen if she spilled all. So, she took it slowly. "I honestly don't know who killed Shelly."

"But you know who was after her and why," he snapped.

"Maybe." She groaned. "Look, I can't think like this. Just back up."

To her surprise, he did, and then made an impatient circular motion with his right index finger to signal her to keep talking.

Best to start at the beginning, she thought. That was the easy part. Too bad she didn't know if she could trust him with the ending.

"Shelly's death could be linked to what happened at the Bassfield Research Facility where I worked," Kinley explained. "Secrets went missing. Illegal deals were made. The authorities have caught some people responsible, but since there might have been others involved in the illegal activity, they thought it best that I be placed in witness protection in another state."

"Yet you're here," he pointed out. "Not in witness protection but at my company's Christmas party."

Kinley was certain she couldn't keep the emotion or the heartbreak out of her expression. "Finding the item I left with Shelly is critical. It's worth the risk of leaving witness protection."

"And you think I know where this…'item' is?"

She closed her eyes a moment, shook her head. "I don't know. But I made a list of all of Shelly's friends, family members and enemies. I've made it through that entire list—"

He put her right back against the wall. It happened so fast that it robbed her of her breath. "You asked these people questions?"

That urgency and his stark concern didn't help her breathing. "No. I didn't want to raise any suspicions so I followed them the way I followed you. I watched them, looking for any signs that they might know something."

His eyes turned even darker. "Because if someone got this *item,* they'd be able to draw you out of hiding. Why? What do they want?"

"Information about the last project I was working on." It was a guess. But a good one, since she hadn't been able to think of another reason. She hadn't been privy to all top-secret data used in the project, however.

"You were working on antidotes for chemical weapons." Again, it wasn't a question.

She nodded, not surprised that he knew about the project that'd nearly gotten her killed and had cost her everything. "The formula for the primary antidote went missing. Someone may think I know where it is. I don't," she quickly added. "That's the truth."

"For a change." He turned on his PDA again, scrolled through some pages and stopped on one. Not a picture. This one had some kind of code in it. "That's your DNA. Day before yesterday, I had Cody collect your cup from the coffee shop, and I ran the test myself. No one but me has seen the results. Or compared it to anyone else's."

Oh, mercy.

Her breath shuttered, and there was no way to hold back the flood of emotion or what she had to say. She touched her fingers to her necklace and waited until Jordan's attention went to the stone. "It's a red ruby."

She saw it. The recognition in his eyes. Just a split second. It was all she needed to continue.

"My son would be sixteen months old by now. Brown hair. Brown eyes." Kinley swallowed hard. "You have him, don't you? Shelly left him with you?"

Jordan calmly placed the PDA back into his jacket pocket. "Yes." A muscle flickered in his jaw. "I have him. Your DNA matches his."

A helpless sound left her mouth. She lost it. Her legs turned limp. Her breath vanished. And if it hadn't been for Jordan catching her, she would have fallen to the floor. "Thank God." And even though she knew she sounded hysterical, Kinley just kept repeating it.

"Don't thank God just yet. The child was safe. Now he's not. By coming here, you've placed him, you and me in grave danger."

She fought to regain her breath so she could speak. "I never meant to do that, I swear."

"The road to hell is paved with good intentions," he mumbled. Then cursed. "We have to sanitize this situation and do some damage control."

She shook her head. "How?"

But before he could answer, the doorknob turned. Kinley tried to brace herself for anyone and anything. It was almost second nature since she'd been living in fear for months.

"This is damage control," Jordan whispered to her.

He shoved his left hand around the back of her neck, dragged her to him and kissed her.

CHAPTER TWO

WHILE HE KISSED HER, Jordan drew his gun and used their bodies to hide the Sig Sauer.

He wanted the gun ready in case the pretense didn't work. And in case they were about to be met by someone who'd followed Kinley.

The door opened and from the corner of his eye, Jordan saw their visitors.

Cody and Burke.

Despite his instant relief at seeing nonenemy faces, Jordan didn't break the kiss. In fact, he took it up a notch and made it look as if he was groping Kinley's breasts when he reholstered his gun.

"Sorry for the interruption," Cody drawled.

Only then did Jordan jerk away from her. He tried to look surprised, which wasn't very difficult since that damage-control kiss had sent a coil of blazing heat through his entire body.

Hell.

Nothing like reacting like a red-blooded male instead of a security specialist in the middle of a potentially dangerous situation.

"Something wrong?" Jordan asked the men. Beside him, Kinley was breathing hard. Hopefully from the danger and not the blasted kiss.

Jordan made a mental note to figure a different form of damage control. Something that didn't involve her mouth or her breasts.

"Nothing's wrong," Burke assured him. He smiled. Cody didn't. He had a puzzled look on his face. "It's just that some folks have to leave to go to other parties, and I want to make a toast to celebrate your new semi-retired status."

"Of course." It couldn't have come at a better time, because a toast and then an exit was the fastest way to get Kinley out of there.

Kinley smiled and fixed her lipstick. Her mouth was trembling a bit, and she looked as if she'd been popped with a stun gun. Again, he hoped that was from the fear. He took her by the arm, and they followed Burke and Cody.

"I give you a week," Cody said, looking over his shoulder at Jordan. "And you'll be so bored you'll be begging Burke to sell you back the company."

"I doubt that." There wasn't a chance of boredom now that Kinley had arrived with her dangerous baggage. Not a chance, either, of his wanting to buy back Sentron. He didn't intend to go back to working an eighty-hour week.

Well, maybe not.

He'd made that plan when he thought he would have to devote more time to protecting the child that'd been left on his doorstep. Now that Kinley was here, though, his life was in major limbo.

And so were his emotions.

Jordan slowed his pace and hated that ache in the pit of his stomach. But from the moment he'd run that first DNA test, he had known the child wasn't his. Biologically, anyway. He'd also known that perhaps one day someone would show up and want the baby back.

He just hadn't counted on it being tonight.

Part of him had hoped it would never happen. He wasn't one to wish a person harm, but after fourteen months, he had adjusted to the idea that the baby's biological parents weren't coming for him. Or that they were dead, killed by the same people who'd murdered Shelly. And then he'd seen Kinley Ford's DNA he'd pulled from the coffee cup.

She was the biological mother, all right.

Now the question was, what was he going to do about it?

All eyes shifted in their direction when the four returned to the party. To speed things up, Jordan grabbed two glasses of champagne from the waiter, handed one to Kinley and then slid his arm back around her waist. He even gave her a lusty, long look that he figured everyone could interpret.

Burke lifted his glass into the air. "Ten years ago Jordan Taylor created this company from scratch. He trained every agent in this room. Now Jordan's company and mine, Burke Securities, will be merged to form not just the best, but the biggest personal security agency in the state. I only hope I'll earn the same loyalty and support that you've shown him over the years." The glass went higher. "To Jordan. Thanks for creating the benchmark of security services. And thanks even more for selling it all to me."

That brought a few chuckles, and the room echoed with "Hear! Hear!" and applause as others joined the toast.

Jordan took one last look around the room. "I'll miss this place and all of you." He shrugged. "Well, maybe not when I'm tossing back shots of Glen Garioch on a private beach somewhere in the Pacific, but I'm sure there'll be moments when I'll miss you…a little."

Jordan forced a smile, took the master keycard from his jacket and handed it to Burke. A symbolic gesture, but one that tugged at his heart. "Don't run the place into the ground, all right?"

"I won't," Burke assured him.

They shook hands, embraced briefly, while some photos were snapped. But Jordan had no intentions of lingering. He'd already said goodbye to his key agents, including Cody, Desmond Parisi and Alonzo Mateo, and he nodded farewell to two of his newer employees, Chris Sutton and Wally Arceneaux. Then, he took a final sip of the champagne, and he set Kinley's and his glasses aside so they could head for the door.

Cody stepped out of the gathering to hand Kinley her coat. "You might need this," he added. Still no smile, not even a phony one. He was obviously riled that Jordan had sold the company. One day Jordan might be able to explain to him why he'd done it. "Enjoy your evening."

Jordan seriously doubted there'd be anything enjoyable about it. He only hoped it didn't turn deadly.

He helped Kinley with her coat and tried not to rush to the door. Jordan got them out of there and headed to the adjacent parking lot. It was cold, near freezing, and the wind barreled out of the north right at them. He kept her close, snuggled intimately into the crook of his arm, and he kissed her. This time it was on the corner of her mouth in the hopes that it wouldn't carry the punch of a full-mouth kiss.

It did anyway.

She was attractive. There was no denying that. But he reminded himself that everything about her was a facade. Well, except for the fear. She was trembling, but he was almost certain it wasn't from the cold.

Kinley looked up at him. "Where's my—"

Jordan pressed his lips to hers so she couldn't finish the question. Still walking, he kept his mouth over hers a second and then drew back slightly. "Lip readers," he mumbled.

Her smoke-gray eyes widened, and she gave a shaky nod, understanding that if someone were filming them, a lip reader would be able to determine anything they said.

Including a question about the child.

They reached his silver Porsche and got inside, behind the bulletproof custom-tinted glass and into a space that would not only conceal them, but was also soundproof. They could see out, but no one could see in. And an alarm would beep if anyone tried to scan the vehicle with thermal or sound detectors. Since Jordan heard no beep, it was safe to talk.

But not necessarily smart to tell her everything he knew.

For now, he couldn't trust her. Yes, Kinley was the birth mother, and she also knew the code word, but that didn't mean her maternal instincts had been the reason she'd come to him. He needed more answers about her motives, and while he was finding those answers, he had to continue with more damage control.

"Now can I ask my question?" she wanted to know.

He settled for saying, "It's safe."

She didn't waste any time. "Where's my son?"

Jordan didn't waste time, either. "You had to have known the risks of coming to me. So why did you?"

She didn't get defensive. Thanks to the security lights in the parking lot, Jordan could see her clearly. The light bathed her troubled face and danced off the red crystals on her dress.

"I just needed to know he was alive," she whispered. "That he was okay. I couldn't live not knowing." She scraped her thumbnail over the red polish on her right index finger and flaked it off. "I knew there were risks, but I thought I'd minimized them."

"Obviously not, if I figured out who you were and what you wanted."

She shook her head. "I didn't think you had him. I only thought you'd have information. Or rather I hoped you would. I wasn't very optimistic because I'd read that Shelly and you were enemies, that she embezzled from you."

Jordan sighed. "That was Shelly's version of damage control. She didn't want anyone to be able to link me to the child."

Still, that hadn't stopped SAPD and even a federal investigator from questioning him. It also hadn't stopped three different P.I.s, who'd been hired by God knows who to find out what'd happened in the last minutes of Shelly's life. Jordan figured all three P.I.s had probably worked for the same person, but he'd never been able to dig through the layers of security and paperwork to come up with a name. Or a reason why the baby was so important.

But that was something Kinley could perhaps tell him.

He used the car's mirrors to glance around the parking lot. "You're a cautious woman," he remarked. "Would you know if someone had followed you?"

"I thought I would. But I was obviously wrong."

"Other than me, would you know if someone had followed you?" He wasn't being cocky. He was just better than most at that sort of thing.

"People have followed me in the past, but after I left witness protection this last time, I haven't noticed anyone."

That didn't mean someone wasn't there. Jordan had another look at those mirrors.

"You gave up your company for my son," she said. Not a question, nor an accusation. Her voice was heavy with emotion.

He glanced at her and decided to change the subject. "I'm going with two possible theories here. First, that the child's father is behind all of this danger."

She was shaking her head before he even finished. "No. He's dead. He died trying to murder me and my brother."

Okay. That was a story he knew a little about but wanted to hear more of later. "Second theory. Someone wants the baby for leverage. The people after you want information, and they believe if they have your child, they'll be able to manipulate you into giving them what they want."

Kinley stared at him so long he wasn't sure she would jump on to this subject change, but she finally looked away and returned to chipping off her nail polish. "The research facility where I was employed was working on several projects. One was the chemical weapon antidote that I told you about. Several researchers were working on it, and occasionally, I assisted them."

"Assisted?" He latched right on to that and mentally cursed when he spotted something he didn't like in the mirror.

Hell.

"Usually I was just a consult for a particular facet of a project," she explained. "For instance, I only worked on a portion of the formula for the primary antidote. I never got to see the finished results. None of us did. That was the way the facility maintained security."

Jordan calmly started the car, put on his seat belt and kept his eyes on the mirror. "But even though you don't have the big picture, you have pieces. Others have pieces. And you have the names of those others."

"Yes." That was all she said for several moments. "Brenna Martel was one of the top lab assistants at the research facility. She's in a federal prison serving a life sentence. But there are others who disappeared after the facility was destroyed and the federal investigation started." Another pause. "I've written notes about the research, and I've gone over them a thousand times, but I just don't know why someone would still be after me."

"Notes?" he questioned.

"They're encrypted," she huffed, obviously noting his concern. "I wouldn't just leave information like that lying around for anyone to see."

But someone would look hard for info like that. "And these notes are where exactly?"

"Hidden in my apartment."

Jordan didn't even have to think about this. "I want to see them." In fact, he wanted to study them and then interrogate Kinley and put anyone in those notes under surveillance until all of this finally made some sense.

"I can show you what I have," she answered. "But I want to see Maddox."

He glanced at her, frowned. "Who the hell is Maddox?"

"My son," she said as if the answer were obvious. "That's what I named him. You didn't know?"

"No. Shelly didn't get around to that when she left him on my doorstep." Jordan had been calling him Gus. "And I couldn't exactly go digging for his name or paternity, now could I?"

"No." Despite the fear and the seriousness of their situation, she smiled softly. "Do you have a picture of him?"

"Not a chance. And as for you seeing him, that's not gonna happen until you can convince me that you're here as a mother and not as someone who wants to use him as a pawn in some sick game."

The smile vanished, and her mouth opened in outrage. "I wouldn't do that. God, what do you think I am?"

"You're a woman who left her baby with a bodyguard because it was too dangerous to keep him with you. The danger's still there." He glanced in the mirror again.

"I know that," she snapped. "Shelly had been my friend since high school. I trusted her. And she died protecting my son. If I could change that I would. But I can't. And I've searched and searched, and I can't make the danger go away." The minitirade seemed to drain her, and she groaned and rested her head against the back of the seat.

Jordan huffed, glanced in the mirror again and tried not to let her emotion get to him. He didn't want sympathy or pity playing into this. "This isn't convincing me that you should be mother of the year."

That brought her head off the seat. "I don't want to be mother of the year. I simply want my son."

"And then what?" he challenged.

"I take him and I find someplace safe." Her voice grew softer. "If necessary, we'll live our lives in hiding, but we'll do that together."

Not anytime soon, she wouldn't. Maybe not ever. Jordan didn't intend to hand over Gus until he was damn sure that it was safe to do so, and Kinley hadn't done anything to convince him of that.

"So, what do we do now?" she asked.

"Soon, we'll go to your apartment and get those notes." However, he also had a more pressing problem. "But for now we'll just drive, and we'll see if that guy parked up the street plans to follow us."

She snapped toward the side mirror and stared into the glass. "What guy?"

"Black sedan near the intersection."

Her breath suddenly went uneven. "How long has he been there?"

"He arrived not long after we got in the car. It could be nothing," he admitted. But Jordan didn't believe that.

It was likely a huge *something*.

"Put on your seat belt," he instructed. As he eased out of the parking lot, Jordan kept his attention fastened to his rearview mirror so he could watch the other vehicle.

CHAPTER THREE

KINLEY'S HEART DROPPED.

This couldn't be happening. She'd been so careful and so sure that no one had followed her. Yet, the black car was there and made the same turn Jordan did when he drove away from the Sentron building.

She felt sick to her stomach. And she was terrified. She had to do something to stop this.

But what?

What she couldn't do was call the police. That would likely alert the wrong people, and it'd be impossible to explain everything that had happened. That kind of explanation could get her son hurt.

"Let me out," she insisted. "Maybe he'll follow me and won't connect any of this to my son."

"Too late. We're already connected. I'm just hoping this person is curious, that's all, and we can convince him that we're together because we're would-be lovers."

Maybe. But she hated to risk that much on a *maybe*. She stared in the side mirror. The car stayed steady behind them. "Any idea who is back there?"

"Nope. But I hope to change that." Placing his gun on his lap, Jordan took out his cell phone, and he pressed in some numbers.

"Cody," Jordan said when the man apparently answered. "I'm traveling north on San Pedro, and I have a shadow. Can you slip away from the party and run a visual?" A moment later, Jordan ended the call. "Cody will get back to me when he has something."

Kinley latched on to that hope but still had her doubts. "He'll be able to see the person following us? How?" she wanted to know.

"Traffic cameras. We might know soon who's after us. And knowing who might tell us why. We might get lucky. This could be someone from witness protection. It might not have anything to do with Gus."

"Gus?"

Jordan huffed. "That's what I call your son."

She repeated it under her breath. It was hard to pin that name to her baby. She'd always thought of him as Maddox. But then, she hadn't seen him in fourteen months. He wouldn't even know her.

But her son obviously knew Jordan.

Where had Jordan kept him all this time? What kind of a caregiver had he been? Kinley wanted to know every precious detail of what she'd missed, but first, they had to deal with the person in that black car.

She checked the mirror again, as did Jordan. The car was still there—at a distance but menacing. "Will you try to lose the guy?"

"Not just yet. I want to give Cody some time to get a photo so he can use the facial recognition program."

"Good," she mumbled.

"Well, maybe not good. Remember, I've identified others who've followed me, and I've never been able to link it back to the person who hired them." He glanced at her. "That's where you can help. Think hard. Who could have known that you left Gus with Shelly?"

She pulled in a long breath. "I've already thought hard, and I don't believe anyone knew. After all, Shelly had him for nearly a month before the trouble started."

"Okay. Then what started the trouble?"

Kinley had thought hard about this as well. "A lot of bad things happened around that time. I was drawn out of hiding because someone was trying to kill my brother, Lucky. He's a P.I., and he started looking for the head researcher, Dexter Sheppard, because Lucky believed Dexter had murdered me. He obviously hadn't, but Dexter *had* convinced me and his lab assistant, Brenna Martel, to fake our deaths and his in that explosion."

"Why do that?" Jordan wanted to know.

"Because Dexter said it was the only way for us to stay alive. He had taken money from the wrong people, and he'd promised to deliver a chemical weapon that we couldn't deliver. He convinced me that all of us would die if I went to the authorities."

"And you believed him?"

"Yes," she said with regret. "I guess Dexter did a good job faking my death because my brother thought I was indeed dead. But he didn't think the same of Dexter. He thought Dexter was in hiding but couldn't find him. So, Lucky followed Dexter's sister, Marin, to Fall Creek, a small town not too far from here. And when the attempts to kill both Marin and my brother started all over again, I knew I had to do something to try to save them."

"So you went to Fall Creek, too," Jordan commented.

"I did, and while I was trying to save my brother and Marin, Brenna Martel showed up there. Someone had been trying to kill her, too, and Brenna was desperate. She mistakenly thought if she kidnapped me, then she could force my brother to tell her where Dexter was. But my brother didn't even have proof that Dexter was alive, much less where he might be hiding out. We soon got proof, of course…when Dexter tried to kill us. He died during that last attempt."

Jordan stayed quiet a moment, obviously processing all that. "Brenna Martel knew you'd had a baby?"

"Of course. But she didn't know where he was."

Jordan cursed under his breath. "This Brenna Martel could have figured out that you and Shelly were old friends. She could have sent someone to get Gus, and Shelly was murdered in the process."

"I doubt it. Brenna was on the run like me, and she didn't have the money to hire anyone." She checked the car behind them again. "I don't suppose the danger could have stemmed from Shelly? I mean, what if someone was after her for some reason, and they saw Maddox with her and decided to use him to get to her?"

He shook his head. "I dug deep for that connection. Didn't find it." Jordan didn't add more because his phone rang. The call was brief, just a couple of seconds. "Cody has a photo of our snoop in the black car and is looking for a match. Hold on."

That was the only warning she got before Jordan gunned the engine of the powerful sports car. They bolted forward, and then he took an immediate left turn. Even with her seat belt on, she went sliding against him. She righted herself, looked in the mirror.

The black car was still behind them.

"He's definitely following us," Kinley mumbled.

"Yeah." And that was all Jordan said for several moments. He kept his speed right at sixty, which wasn't too far over the limit. He also kept watch in the mirror and one hand on his gun when he made another turn.

Toward her apartment, she realized.

Of course he knew where she lived. He'd probably learned that not long after figuring out who she was. "Is it wise to lead him straight to my place?"

"It is if we're aiming for more damage control. When we get there, we get out. We look like lovers who can't wait to hurry inside and have a go at each other. Get your key ready."

She huffed. "I hate to state the obvious here, but what if he shoots us when we get out?"

"If he'd wanted to shoot us, then he would have done it when we came out of the building. No, I suspect his orders are to follow us and hope that we lead him to whatever information you might have. Or to the baby."

Her heart dropped again. Because as long as someone was following them, she'd never get to see her son.

Kinley got her keys ready, and Jordan stopped his car directly in front of her apartment. It wasn't upscale by anyone's standards. A far cry from the lavish Sentron building and Jordan's palatial estate. But it'd been all she could afford.

"Stay put," he insisted. "I'll get out first and then open your car door."

She glanced back and saw the black car. It'd come to a stop just up the street. Away from the lights but still visible.

Tucking his gun into his holster, Jordan left the car, hurried to her side and helped her out.

He pulled her right into his arms.

And kissed her.

The kiss landed on the side of her mouth. Not a real kiss, of course. But it had a *real* impact, just as the other kiss had done. It made her wonder just what kind of impact a genuine kiss would have.

She didn't have the time or energy to find out, even if her body seemed more than willing to explore the idea.

"See?" he mumbled. "No one's shooting at us."

Yet. She hoped she didn't have to say I told you so.

Jordan kept her pressed to him, and he positioned his right hand next to her breast so he could get his gun. He didn't linger. He kept up the frenzied fake kiss while he maneuvered her to her apartment door. She reached behind her, unlocked it and they practically tumbled inside.

The security system started to beep, and she punched in the code to prevent it from going to a full alarm. Then, Kinley opened her mouth to tell him that she would get the notes, but Jordan put his fingers to her lips. He stayed close. Nose to nose with her.

"Don't say anything," he warned in a whisper.

That spiked her heart rate again. God, did he think someone had broken in? But if so, the person would have triggered the alarm. It was an inexpensive unit, one she'd bought at a discount store a couple of days after she moved in, but unless someone knew the code, she didn't think they could have easily disarmed it.

Jordan reholstered his gun and took out that strange little platinum PDA again. He pressed a few buttons, lifted it into the air.

"Make sex noises," he mouthed.

And with that, he added a manly sounding grunt and

proceeded to walk around the room. After a few steps, he glanced over his shoulder at her and gave her a get-on-with-it bob of his head.

Kinley moaned.

Apparently, it was a good one because he nodded. Grunted. And he flapped his jacket as if mimicking the sound of clothing being removed. While she checked the bedroom and the small bath, Kinley tossed in some deep breathing, though she didn't think it was necessary. No one else was in the apartment.

Then she heard the whisper-soft beep.

She turned and spotted Jordan next to the sole lamp in the living room. It was on a scarred end table. Kinley went closer, and when he leaned down, he pointed to a small dime-size disk stuck to the base.

He made more of those sex noises. "A bug," he mouthed.

She pressed her hand to her lips to stop herself from repeating it, but she couldn't stop the little gasp. Hopefully, whoever was listening would think it was part of the sex that Jordan and she were faking.

He caught on to her arm, and with the PDA device lifted in the air, they made their way through the other rooms.

No more beeps.

But one was more than enough.

Jordan groaned loudly, hit his arm against the bedroom wall, and he maneuvered her into the bathroom. He slammed the door and turned on the shower.

"Any idea how the bug got there?" he whispered.

"No. But it probably happened before I bought the security system." And if so, that meant someone had been eavesdropping on her for over two months.

Anger soon replaced the shock. Kinley felt violated and wanted to catch the idiot who'd done this. But more than that, she wanted to know why.

Even though the water was running, and the door was shut, Jordan put his mouth right against her ear. "While you've been here, have you talked about Gus?"

"No." Her answer was quick because she didn't even have to think about it. "I didn't have anyone to talk to."

He pulled back. Stared at her as if he wasn't sure if he could believe her. "You're positive?"

"Yes." Now it was her turn to put her mouth against his ear. "I did all my research on the Internet, and my laptop is password protected. Never once did I mention my son. When I did searches about the people connected to Shelly, I only used her name, not yours, not Maddox's. If anyone was checking, I wanted to make it look as if I were simply investigating the cold-case murder of an old friend."

During her entire explanation, she kept noticing the close contact.

Correction: she *felt* it.

Jordan was against her again. Body to body. He stared at her, and she stared back. Their breaths mingled, and she could smell the smooth whiskey and sip of champagne he'd had at the party.

They'd been doing a lot of touching for two people who were at odds. And they were at odds, no doubt about it. Kinley couldn't mistake the distrust she saw in him. Maybe other emotions, too.

He wasn't pleased with her arrival.

She wasn't pleased about it, either. If she'd known she would bring this kind of danger to her son, she would have stayed away.

"I'm really sorry," she said.

He continued to stare at her. There was a heat in his eyes. Maybe from the contact. Maybe from his anger. "You should be," he grumbled. He stepped away, turned off the water and threw open the door.

Jordan made a beeline for her kitchen and opened the only cabinet. "Hey, you don't have any scotch," he called out.

"No," Kinley answered tentatively, not sure if this was part of the game they were playing. "I can run out for some if you like."

"I have a better idea. Grab a change of clothes, and we'll go to my place. I have plenty of scotch there."

His place. Where they'd be able to talk without an eavesdropping device. But it would mean going back outside where that black car was likely still parked and waiting.

"What if he follows us?" she mouthed.

"That's what I'm hoping. You've opened Pandora's box, and now I'm going to see if I can close it."

Not understanding, Kinley shook her head. "What does that mean?"

He leaned in again. "I don't want him or anyone else to think I have something to hide." He glanced around. "And besides, this place isn't safe."

Even though he'd whispered that, it rang through her as if he'd shouted it. "But I don't want to lead him to Maddox."

"You won't." And with that, he motioned for her to

pack. "Bring your laptop and your notes, but put them in an overnight bag so they can't be seen."

She didn't question him further. The only reassurance she'd needed was that this wouldn't put her son in any more danger than he already was. Besides, it might help if Jordan looked at her notes. He might find something she'd missed. And if they found it, they might also be able to figure out who was behind Shelly's murder.

Kinley grabbed a small suitcase and hurriedly packed everything she might need for a short stay, including the notes, which she took from inside the lining of a coat she had hanging in the closet. When she came out of the bedroom, Jordan was by the door peeking out the side window.

"Is he still there?" she whispered.

Jordan nodded. He reached out and ran his hand through her hair, messing it up. He did the same to his. No doubt so it'd look as if they'd just had a quick round of sex.

They walked out, their arms hooked around each other, and got into the car. Jordan drove away quickly. So did the other car.

Just as Jordan had predicted, it followed them.

"You're sure this won't make things more dangerous for my son?" she asked.

"I'm sure."

So, that probably meant Maddox wasn't at his house. But then, there'd been no indication that he was. Jordan likely had him tucked away somewhere. But where? And who was caring for him? It broke her heart to think that her little boy might not get enough hugs and kisses.

Because she'd already driven to Jordan's house, she

was familiar with the route. He lived in a subdivision within city limits but still secluded. It had pricy homes on massive lots, some of them several acres. Jordan's was one of the largest in the neighborhood. A true Texas-size estate for a Texas millionaire.

Shelly had certainly made a strange choice when she involved Jordan in this.

"Is it true what you said about Maddox—that Shelly left him on your porch the night she died?" Kinley asked. Right now, she wanted every little detail she could learn about her son and what he'd gone through.

Jordan didn't answer right away. He glanced at her first. "Yes."

It was hard for her to picture that in her mind. Her baby literally left on a doorstep. "God, what did you think when you opened the door and saw a baby?"

"I thought he was my son." He stared straight ahead and repeated that softly under his breath. "Then, with Shelly's murder, it took me a few days to get around to the DNA test. I had Shelly's DNA on file, since she was a former employee, and when I did the comparison, I learned he wasn't Shelly's. Nor mine."

Was it her imagination or did he sound disappointed? Hurt, even?

But she had to be wrong about that.

Jordan was a ruthless businessman, along with being a rich player who enjoyed the company of lots of women. He would have taken care of her son, but she seriously doubted he would ever think of himself as a father.

"Who's taking care of him?" Kinley asked.

She waited.

And waited.

He opened his mouth, and she thought she might finally learn an answer to one of her many questions, but before he could say anything, his phone rang.

Jordan didn't waste any time answering it. "Cody," he said after glancing at the screen. He took the turn toward his neighborhood. The street switched from four lanes to two, and though it was well lit with a line of streetlights, it felt isolated because the lots were so spacious.

She couldn't hear Cody's side of the conversation, but she could see Jordan's reaction. She noticed his grip tighten on the wheel. Saw the muscles flicker in his jaw.

"You're sure?" Jordan asked. Then he paused. "No. I'll take it from here." Another pause. "I need to ask you to keep this between us."

A moment later, Jordan ended the call.

"What happened?" Kinley wanted to know when he didn't offer any information.

"Do you know a guy named Anderson Walker?"

Kinley thought a moment. "No. That name doesn't ring any bells. Why?"

"He's the one following us."

She glanced in the mirror. He was still following them. "What does he want?"

Jordan shrugged, but there was nothing casual about his body language. "He's a P.I. who works for Burke Securities."

Her mouth dropped open. "Burke Securities as in the Burke Dennison who bought your company?"

"The very one."

Kinley shook her head. "Why does Burke have someone following us?"

Another muscle went to work in his jaw. "I don't know, but I intend to find out."

"What do you mean?"

"I mean he's not being very subtle. And he knows we're on to him. If I just keep driving, it might send him the wrong message—that we have something to hide." Jordan took his foot off the accelerator. "Get down now."

Jordan spun the steering wheel around, causing his Porsche to do a hundred-and-eighty-degree turn. It was precise. As if he'd choreographed it, he bumped into the rear side of the black car and sent it into a spin.

Before Kinley could stop him, Jordan drew his gun and threw open the door.

CHAPTER FOUR

THE BLACK CAR screeched to a stop.

Jordan hadn't given the driver much of a choice, since he'd angled his Porsche so that the guy couldn't get around him. That was the plan, anyway.

It was time to confront this bozo.

Jordan didn't get out, but he aimed his gun. And he waited. Since this was Burke's man, Jordan was counting heavily on the fact that the P.I. didn't have orders to kill. His gut told him this was strictly surveillance. Too bad his gut didn't tell him why Burke had put a tail on him.

Thankfully, there were no other vehicles on the street. There probably wouldn't be, either. The street was private, leading only to his neighborhood, and this time of night, there weren't many residents out and about. Jordan wanted that privacy in case this took an ugly turn.

"Should I call the police?" Kinley asked. Her breath was jagged, and she had her purse in a white-knuckle grip.

"No." Not yet anyway. If he phoned anyone, it'd be Burke to find out what the devil was going on. That call would still happen, but first he wanted answers from the guy who'd tailed them.

"Anderson Walker!" Jordan called out, and he made sure it didn't sound like a question.

The man still didn't budge, and Jordan wondered if he'd made a mistake by jumping into this confrontation.

Especially with Kinley in the car.

Maybe he should have waited, but he really just wanted to end this here and now. He didn't want anyone following him, especially when he didn't know their intentions and when they were being so obvious about following Kinley and him.

"Walker!" Jordan shouted.

That did it. The door to the black car opened, and the sandy-haired guy stepped out. Anderson was what Jordan called a muscle man. Bulky shoulders. Young. He looked physically capable of pulverizing someone with his bare hands. Jordan had a few P.I.s like that on the Sentron staff because there were times when a strong arm was needed.

So, why had Burke or Anderson thought he needed some intimidation?

Anderson held his gun in his right hand. Not aimed. He had his index finger through the trigger loop, but the gun dangled upside down in a nonthreatening position.

Jordan went for the threat. He pointed his Sig Sauer right at the man.

"You plan to shoot me?" Anderson challenged. He had *cocky* written all over him.

"That depends on your answer to my question. Why are you following me?"

Anderson started to shift his gun, as if getting ready to aim. Jordan stepped forward and put his Sig Sauer at the guy's head. "Don't," Jordan warned.

Anderson froze. And Jordan said a silent prayer of thanks. He didn't want to start a gunfight, and he didn't want to put Kinley in danger. She apparently had enough danger after her without his adding more.

"Toss your gun into your car," Jordan instructed.

Anderson looked at his gun. At Jordan's. Then at Jordan himself. Jordan put on his best scowl, which he didn't have to fake. There was plenty to scowl about. Anderson finally relented and put the gun inside his car. That didn't mean they were safe because Jordan figured the guy was carrying at least one other backup pistol. Heck, he might even have actual backup in the form of another P.I. or security agent.

"Why are you following me?" Jordan repeated.

"It's not personal."

Jordan arched his left eyebrow and gave him a flat look. "And that's not an answer."

"It's the only answer I can give you. My employer didn't say why he wanted you followed, only that I was to report where you went tonight and who went with you."

That was a lot of info crammed into that brief two-sentence report. "Why didn't Burke just ask me where I was going? I saw him at the party less than an hour ago."

The guy blinked. "Because Burke didn't hire me."

Jordan studied the guy's face, looking for any sign that he was lying, but he seemed darn smug about telling the truth. "Then who did?"

"Dunno. I was contracted freelance through a broker."

A broker. In other words, a middle man who acted as a go-between for P.I.s and clients who didn't want to be identified. That didn't mean the employer couldn't be traced. It just meant Jordan would have to dig through some layers to get to it. Judging from what Anderson had said, Kinley was the reason for this since his employer had wanted to know who went anywhere with Jordan.

"What did your broker-using employer tell you to do?" Jordan questioned.

"Wait outside Sentron." The man paused. "And when you left, I was to follow you and report back."

They were simple instructions, but they could have deadly implications.

Jordan stared at him. "I'm trying to figure out if you're a really lousy P.I. or if you wanted me to know I was being followed."

Anderson lifted his shoulder.

"Well?" Jordan pressed. "Which is it?"

It still took him several moments to answer. "I was told to be obvious."

So, this was for intimidation. "Why?"

"Wasn't told that," Anderson insisted.

Jordan was about to push for more details, but he spotted the headlights of another vehicle. He eased his gun to his side so as not to alarm any of his neighbors who might be coming home late.

But the car stopped.

It stayed idling just up the street. And the driver kept the high beams on so that the blinding light glared through the darkness.

Anderson glanced back at the car. "I'm leaving now. My advice—you do the same."

"Who's your friend in the car?" Jordan demanded.

"Don't have a clue." His cockiness and confidence vanished, and he turned.

Jordan considered stopping him, but it was too risky.

If the guy with the high beams was an enemy, then Jordan would be outnumbered.

Maybe outgunned.

Normally, that wouldn't have bothered him, but he had Kinley in the car. And even though the car and glass were bulletproof, this whole situation was suddenly making him very uncomfortable. Jordan got that uneasy feeling in the pit of his stomach, and that feeling had saved him too many times to start ignoring it now.

"For the record," Jordan said to Anderson, "I'm taking my date to my house, and I'd prefer not to have any interruptions. Understand?"

Anderson held up his hands in mock surrender and looked over his shoulder again. "I'm not the one you should be worried about." And with that, he got into his vehicle, did a doughnut in the road and sped in the direction of the other waiting car. Anderson whipped past it and disappeared into the darkness.

The car didn't budge. It just sat there. Like a predator waiting to attack. Jordan kept his eye on it and walked backward to his Porsche.

"What just happened?" Kinley asked the moment he got inside. She swallowed hard.

"I'm not sure."

He worked fast so that they wouldn't have to sit there any longer than necessary. He opened his glove compartment and extracted a small pair of high-powered binoculars. Through his partially opened door, Jordan looked back at the car.

The high beams were a serious problem, but the binoculars were far from ordinary. His research team had designed them for all-weather, all-terrain surveillance.

He made some adjustments and zoomed in on the Texas plates. The moment he had the number, he fed that into his PDA—which wasn't ordinary, either. He had been able to control most of Sentron, his estate and his training facility with that modified PDA.

Since it might take a while for the data to be retrieved from the Department of Public Safety files, he put the Porsche in gear and started driving.

"What about that other car?" Kinley asked. She turned in the seat and kept watch.

"I'll know details soon." Maybe then he could figure out what was happening and fix the problem. But neither of those things were what troubled him most.

It was Gus.

Jordan prayed he was doing the right thing and wasn't putting the baby right in harm's way. He drove toward his estate.

And the other car followed.

KINLEY FOLLOWED JORDAN through the garage and into the three-story house.

When they'd first pulled into the circular driveway of the estate, Kinley had half expected a chauffeur, a butler or some other servant to come running out to assist Jordan. But no one had come, and with the other vehicle creeping along behind them, Jordan had pulled into the garage, waited for the door to shut and only then had he gotten her out of the car and into the estate.

They entered the house itself through a passageway that led to the kitchen. Massive was an understatement. Like the driveway, it too was circular with floor-to-ceiling windows on the back half of the room. Lights came on as they stepped inside and revealed all gleaming stainless-steel appliances and slick black granite countertops. Not exactly homey, but since there were dishes in the sink, it was obvious that Jordan used the place for mundane things like eating.

"Is it safe to talk?" she asked, looking around. But not at the kitchen decor. Kinley looked for any signs that a child lived here.

She saw none.

"It's safe," he assured her.

Jordan set her overnight bag on the counter, walked ahead of her and made his way through a butler's pantry, a formal dining room and finally into the foyer that was larger than her entire apartment. Again, lights flared on as they entered each new area.

No sign of a child here, either.

Just pristine slate floors, flawless dove-gray walls, a stately, double circular staircase and a twelve-foot-high Christmas tree decorated with silver foil ribbons and delicate Waterford crystal ornaments that seemed to catch every ray of the twinkling lights.

Jordan stopped at a landscape oil painting, one of the few pieces of artwork in the minimally decorated area, and he lifted it to reveal a panel of various buttons and even a small screen. He pressed some of those buttons, probably to activate a security system.

Which they might need.

After a few keystrokes, images popped onto the screen. He obviously had cameras all around the place, and he looked at each frame.

The car was no longer there.

"He must have left." Kinley let out a deep breath.

Jordan didn't respond to that. Instead, he took out his phone, scrolled through the numbers and pressed the call button. He put it on speaker.

Kinley could hear the ringing, but while Jordan waited for someone to answer, he closed the painting and started down the hall that fed off the left side of the foyer.

"Burke, here," the man finally answered. "Jordan?" He obviously saw Jordan's name on his caller ID. "I didn't expect to hear from you tonight."

"Didn't you?" was all Jordan said.

Burke paused. "Hold on a minute and let me take this call in private."

"Yeah. Sure." Jordan zipped past the half dozen or so rooms, went to one at the far end of the hall and put his face close to a small device mounted on the wall. A red vertical thread of light moved over his eyes.

A retinal scan.

This was no ordinary security system.

The door opened, and he walked inside. It was his office, she realized. And as she'd expected, it was well equipped with laptops, various keyboards and plasma screens on the walls that completely encircled the room. With a flick of a switch, all the screens came on to show the different views of the security cameras.

Definitely not ordinary.

"Okay, I'm back," Burke said. "Am I supposed to know what you meant by your last remark? Why would you think I'd expected to hear from you tonight?" His voice was still friendly enough, as if he thought this might be the start of a joke.

Kinley wished it were a joke.

"Anderson Walker," Jordan countered. "Why was he following me?"

"Was he?"

"Yeah." More keystrokes and the largest screen on the center wall changed images. Not the estate any longer. But Sentron headquarters. The party was still going on, and Jordan zoomed in on Burke. The man was walking toward the far corner of the room, away from the others. Probably so this conversation wouldn't be overheard.

Burke's face looked almost the same as it had earlier, except for the slight tightness around his mouth. Hardly any emotion considering the terse discussion. The man certainly had a poker face.

"You think I'd send one of my men to follow you?" Burke questioned. "Why would I do that?"

"You tell me."

"Can't. Because there's nothing to tell. But trust me, I'll check into the matter. You're sure it was Walker?"

"Positive."

Burke walked even farther away from the others, until he was at the edge of the hall that led to the command center where Jordan had taken Kinley earlier. The man glanced around, his nerves showing slightly. "You confronted him?"

"I did. He said he was freelancing. But there was another car. Someone else. Any idea who that would be?"

"None." The assurance was fast and confident. "I'll get back to you when I find out what's going on." He paused. "Why do you distrust me?"

"I distrust everyone," Jordan answered. "And if you don't mind, I'd like to spend a quiet night with my date.

No more P.I.s tailing me." And with that warning still hanging in the air, he hung up.

Jordan kept his attention fastened to Burke and zoomed in even closer when the man pulled back his phone and began to make another call.

But then Burke stopped.

Actually, he froze.

Burke's back was to them so Kinley could no longer see his expression. He waited there just a few seconds before walking down the hall.

Jordan did more keystrokes, and the images on the screen changed. He'd picked up surveillance with Burke now in the command center.

While she knew this was important—they needed to find out why Anderson Walker had followed them—she couldn't get her mind off her son.

Was Maddox possibly at the estate?

It was certainly large enough for the child to be hidden away there. And he would indeed have to be hidden. After the events of the night, Kinley knew for a fact that her son was in danger.

Partly because of her.

And she silently cursed that she'd ever stepped foot in the Bassfield Research Facility. Of course, if she hadn't, she would have never met Maddox's father. It would take time to try to come to terms with that irony. The very man who had put her in such danger had also given her a child she loved more than life itself.

She glanced at Jordan, who had his attention fastened to the screen. Burke made that call, but she didn't think Jordan was able to see the numbers the man had pressed because Burke kept his back to them.

Kinley stepped into the doorway so she could have another look at the hall. She listened. There were no sounds of a child. No sounds except Jordan's keystrokes on one of the laptops. Her heart dropped a little. She'd wanted to see her child, but the evidence wasn't pointing to his being in the house. There were no servants visible and no nanny, either.

She walked up the hall. Still listening. Still hoping that she would get a glimpse of something that belonged to her son. But she didn't make it far. She heard Jordan mumble something, and she hurried back to see what'd caused that.

The center screen was blank.

"Burke just killed the camera feed," Jordan snarled.

Kinley was about to ask why, but the answer was obvious. "He doesn't want us to know what he's doing."

"Either that, or he's just trying to piss me off. Until midnight, I'm still the legal owner of Sentron." He sat down in the desk chair, took out his PDA and connected it to the computer. "I need to figure out who was in that second car, and it might take a while. If you want something to eat, help yourself to anything in the kitchen."

He was giving her free rein of the place. Her heart dropped even further. He likely wouldn't do that if her son was anywhere around.

New images popped onto the center screen. Frame by frame. It was still images of the other car that had followed them, and Jordan began to whittle away at the high-beam lights. He was trying to get a look at who was behind the wheel.

Kinley started to turn to do more snooping around the estate, but something caught her eye. Not the zipping-by images of the car. Or even Jordan's now-frantic keystrokes. But a screen six monitors to the right of the large center one.

She saw a room.

This time, she could indeed describe it as homey. There was a rocking chair. A sofa. But there was also something else in the corner.

She went closer and saw the chest.

Not some antique or high-end piece of furniture. It was white with bunnies painted on it.

A child's toy chest.

That thought had no sooner flashed in her mind when the image disappeared. In that exact moment, Jordan spared her a glance.

"That was a toy box," she said, pointing toward the screen. "Does that mean Maddox is here?"

But he didn't answer. There was a series of sharp beeps, and Jordan cursed.

Kinley frantically looked around at all the monitors, expecting to see some kind of security breach. Maybe the other vehicle had returned. But the screens showed no such threat.

"What's happening?" she asked.

He eased out of his chair and went to her. So close they were practically touching. Kinley stepped back, or rather she tried to, but he caught on to her arm, leaned in and put his mouth against her cheek.

"We have to do more damage control," Jordan told her.

Oh, God. Not again. "Someone's listening?" she whispered.

"No. Worse. Someone's watching."

CHAPTER FIVE

JORDAN COULDN'T BELIEVE what was happening.

Someone was damn insistent, and to compound the problem, whoever was doing this had some high-tech resources. This wasn't an amateur intrusion. The equipment aimed at his estate was expensive, and judging from the signals that his security system had picked up, it was also powerful.

"Someone has a thermal scanner aimed at the house," Jordan explained.

And that meant the thermal scanner was recording their every move. They'd have to pretend to be lovers again, until he could neutralize the threat.

"Can you block the signals?" Kinley asked.

"Not this particular scanner. And not in this part of the estate. It'd possibly disrupt the security equipment. I can't risk that."

Because that might be the point. The scanner was perhaps a ploy to get him to disarm the system so there could be a break-in.

She pulled back, met his gaze and, judging from her expression, Kinley was aware of the dangers of a failed security system. "We need to figure out who's doing this. Is there a way to pinpoint the source?"

Good. She wasn't panicking. She was trying to think

her way through this. Unfortunately, Jordan had already considered that option. "It's a remote signal. In other words, someone likely left a small device near the house, anywhere within a block radius, but it isn't being manned. So, we wouldn't easily be able to find it. Or trace it. The signals are being sent to some other location."

Probably a location at least a mile away. That's the way he would do it if he'd set up this operation.

And that was a big concern.

This person thought like him.

So who was doing this?

He hooked his arm around Kinley's waist and got her moving. First to the kitchen so he could retrieve her overnight bag, and then he started down the corridor on the opposite side of the house. He kept her close, pulled right against him, and hoped they were generating enough body heat to convince their intruder that sex was about to happen.

Jordan figured he would be convincing enough.

For reasons he didn't want to explore, just being near Kinley reminded him that he did indeed want to have sex with her.

"Where are we going?" she asked.

"My bedroom. Not for that," he added when her breath went still. "The thermal scan won't be able to penetrate the walls because I have them lined with thick metal."

Her breath didn't exactly even out. No doubt it was sinking in fast that he did not live a normal life.

On several levels.

He gave her a kiss, his lips landing on her cheek. It

was one last part of the show before he took her into his suite and shut the door.

"Sorry, but you'll have to sleep here tonight," Jordan informed her, his mind already a dozen steps ahead of what they had to do. "I can take the floor. You can take the bed."

She nodded, but her attention wasn't on him. It was on the room. He glanced around as well, trying to see it through her eyes. He wasn't much for decor—he'd left that to the experts—but this was indeed his space.

His sanctuary.

It wasn't palatial like some of the other rooms. It was homey despite the vaulted ceilings and wall of windows that overlooked the gardens. He'd kept the colors in shades of gray and white. Simple. Clean. And with the security features, it wasn't just homey, it was safe.

"Those windows," she questioned, pointing to them, "are they bulletproof?"

Jordan nodded. "And no one can see in."

She nodded as well. "That explains why there aren't any drapes."

"The glass can be darkened when I want to sleep in." Which wouldn't be anytime soon. Too much to do. He put her overnight bag on the corner desk. "I want to go over your notes."

"Of course." But she didn't move. Kinley took another moment to look around the room. Not just at the windows. But at the mantel over the slate fireplace, the custom carved nightstands, the desk.

"There aren't any," he informed her.

Her shoulders went back. "Any what?"

"Pictures of Gus."

"Yes. Because of the risk," she concluded. But there was still disappointment in her eyes.

Soon, very soon, he wouldn't be able to dodge her questions. Or her need to see her child.

But exactly how much and when should he tell her?

Jordan huffed and watched her reach into the dark gray bag and take out her notes. Kinley was literally the only spot of color in the room. Not that he needed her red sparkly dress to remind him that she was there. His body was certainly attentive to her presence.

"The notes are encrypted," she reminded him. "I'll have to interpret them for you."

"Then, start interpreting," he insisted. Jordan tipped his head toward the bed. "And get comfortable. It's going to be a long night."

She eyed the bed as if it were a coiled snake. Then she eyed him the same way.

Man, he hoped she couldn't read his very dirty mind.

"The bed's a lot more comfortable than the desk," Jordan assured her. Better to talk than think the thoughts he was having about stripping that dress off her. "Hit the switch on the side, and it'll adjust to a sitting position."

With the notes gripped in her hand, Kinley approached the bed with caution and sank down onto the mattress. "Oh," she mumbled.

Oh, as in she concurred with the comfortable part. Kinley gave the thick feather mattress a couple of test bounces, and she smiled.

It faded as quickly as it'd come.

Too bad. She was a knockout when she was scowling, but that smile was good enough to taste.

Something he wanted to do—bad.

Thankfully, one of them had the right mind-set because there were no more bounces. No more smiles. Her attention went straight to her notes. "Where should I start?"

He took a moment, focused and made a mental list. "I need names of everyone who might have had anything to do with the research facility." He went to the concealed bar, hit the button, and it opened. He offered her a drink by lifting a glass, but she shook her head, declining. Jordan fixed himself a double shot of his favorite scotch.

Kinley took a deep breath and looked at Jordan instead of her notes. "The lead researcher, Dexter Sheppard, is dead. He died over a year ago when he tried to set explosives that were meant to kill me. The blast killed him instead. Dexter had sold some of his research on the black market, and he didn't want me around because I could have testified against him and ultimately sent him to prison."

"Dexter Sheppard," he repeated. That was a name that'd popped up while he was checking Kinley's background. There had been no mention in her background about a personal relationship with Dexter, but there was something in Kinley's tone that made Jordan suspect that was the case. "He's Gus's father?"

She nodded. Hardly paused. "Grady Duran was his business partner. He's dead, too. Brenna Martel was an investor and Dexter's lab assistant. She's the one in prison. And then there's Howard Sheppard, Dexter's father who also was an investor. He's dead as well."

Yeah. Jordan had already learned that after discovering Kinley's identity. "What about living investors? Any left?"

"Just Martin Strahan," she answered, again without looking at the notes. The names were likely branded in her brain. God knew how many times she'd already gone over this. "He's a businessman from Houston, and he's the person I'm guessing was behind the initial attempts to kidnap me."

Yes, there had been multiple attempts. Attempts that had nearly killed her, too. That's why Kinley had been placed in the witness protection program.

Since Martin Strahan's name seemed uncomfortably familiar, Jordan went to his laptop on the desk, booted it up and ran a flash inquiry. Not using Sentron's equipment. After the stunt Burke had pulled with the surveillance shutdown, it was best if Jordan stuck with his own toys.

Within a couple of seconds, he had a photo and bio on this Martin Strahan.

It was bad news.

Martin was in his late twenties. Born filthy rich, he'd managed to lose nearly half of his trust fund, something that apparently didn't please his father, Martin Strahan, Sr.

"The guy's ruthless," Jordan concluded. "He operates just on the edge of the law." And he was exactly the kind of man who'd try to use Gus to get Kinley to cooperate.

"That's what I figured." Kinley took a deep breath. "He either wants me dead because he's upset about the money he lost on his investment or he wants me to tell him what he thinks I know."

"The latter would be a stronger motive. That way, he might think he can still recoup his money if he can get that missing formula from you." He tossed back some of the scotch and let it slide through him. It soothed a few muscles that needed relaxing. "Any other living investors and researchers?"

"I'm the last researcher," she mumbled. "And the final remaining investor was a silent partner that Dexter referred to only as Simon."

Jordan nearly choked on his scotch. "Simon? You're sure?"

Concern raced through her eyes. "Why? Do you know him?"

"Maybe." Jordan set his drink aside so he could use both hands on the keyboard. "Tell me everything you know about Simon."

"I never met him, but he must have been from the San Antonio area because Dexter would leave the lab about once a month to brief him. Dexter wouldn't be gone long. An hour tops."

Oh, yeah. This was not looking good. "How much did this Simon invest?"

She eased off the bed, walked closer and studied Martin Strahan's picture that was still on the screen. "Once when I was in Dexter's office, I saw a financial report. From what I remember, Simon invested about two million in phase one of the project. When that portion of the project sold, it made a huge profit. Something like two hundred and fifty million. As an investor, Simon would have gotten a nice chunk of that, at least a fourth, maybe more."

And it would have made Simon a very rich man.

"Was the project ever called Phoenix?" Jordan asked.

She sucked in her breath. "Yes. How did you know? That was supposed to be classified."

Jordan groaned. "It was classified. I found it when Burke Dennison approached me with an offer to buy Sentron. I had him thoroughly investigated."

"Burke?" she questioned.

"Yeah. He's Simon. That was the identity that was used on his investment account that was linked to profits from a classified project."

And because he needed it, Jordan finished off that drink. *Hell. Hell. Hell.* This was not a complication he wanted.

Kinley shook her head. "But what does it mean?"

"It means Burke and Strahan both got stinking rich off the phase-one deal. It also means they're the last investors standing. Judging from what I found in Burke's financials, he put about half his profits into phase two of the research."

"So, he'd be out thirty, maybe forty million dollars," she concluded. She no longer looked shocked. Kinley looked worried.

"That's a lot of reasons to find the missing formula, especially since he wouldn't just get back his investment, he'd stand to earn a big chunk of money when the formula finally sold." He looked at her. "How much would a chemical weapons antidote earn?"

She raked her hand through her hair to push it away from her face. "Dexter said the antidote would become a cornerstone for other antidotes and other research. He said it could end up being worth a quarter of a billion."

That's what he was afraid she'd say. And on the black market, it might go for double that.

People had killed, and kidnapped, for much, much less.

"It's my guess that the person who wants you is an investor," Jordan pointed.

"Or someone after the reward money," Kinley added. "The company that insured the project put up a ten-million-dollar reward."

Oh, hell. Yet another reason to come after Kinley. But ten million was a drop in the bucket compared to what a person could make if they got their hands on that formula.

"Okay, let's put aside any reward seekers for now and focus on the big guns in this. With only two living investors, that narrows it down. Added to that, Martin Strahan hasn't surfaced that we know of. Only Burke."

"Oh, God." Kinley repeated it, leaned against the wall and repeated it again. "Does this mean Burke knows you have my son?"

"Maybe. And maybe he's just on a fishing expedition." It might also explain why Burke was following them. And if so, that meant Burke perhaps knew who Kinley really was.

That was a huge problem that fake kissing or simple damage control couldn't fix.

"When did Burke make the offer to buy Sentron?" she asked.

He knew where this was going. "Three days ago."

"That's when I started following you."

Yeah. Did that mean Burke had been watching Kinley all this time? If so, it wouldn't have been hard to connect the dots when Kinley started spying on him.

And those dots led right to Gus.

Kinley groaned, squeezed her eyes shut and, with the wall supporting her back, slid to the floor and sat.

Probably because her legs would not hold her. She stayed there a moment, eyes closed, and then she turned toward him. "Wait. If Burke is behind this, why not just kidnap me? If he knew I was following you, then he also could have taken me at any time."

There was so much hope in her eyes that Jordan hated to burst her bubble. "He might be waiting to see if you lead him to the missing formula."

"That I don't have," she reminded him.

"But if he thinks you do and that you'd be willing to do anything to keep it for yourself or for someone else, he'd look for leverage." That's what Jordan would do anyway.

"Leverage," she said. Her breath shuddered. "You mean my son."

Jordan didn't verify the obvious.

She clumsily tried to get back to her feet, giving him a too-clear view of her thigh when her dress shimmied up. She staggered a bit in the high stilettos, and so that she wouldn't fall, Kinley grabbed on to his shoulder.

She stared at him. There were tears in her eyes, and they shimmered like the sparkles on her dress. "I have to know my son is okay."

"He's okay. Burke can't get to him."

She frantically shook her head. "But I might have led him to you. To Maddox."

"It doesn't matter. Even if he did follow you, that doesn't mean the baby's in danger." Not immediately anyway. And Jordan knew that reassurances weren't going to be nearly enough.

He was right.

"I need to see him," she begged. "Please. I need to see my son."

Hell. There it was again. That punch of empathy. Once, he would have been able to ignore her plea. Her pain. But that was before Gus. Before he realized that there was something more important in life than his precious company.

Hoping he didn't regret this but knowing he would, Jordan used a series of passwords to get into this portion of his security system. Finally, an image appeared on the screen. Not the room with the toy box. Nor any of the other rooms he'd encased with a cyber security shield.

This was the nursery.

Because of the late hour, it was dimly lit, but Jordan zoomed into the crib where Gus was sleeping.

Kinley made a helpless sound. The tears began to stream down her cheeks. And she touched the screen, gently putting her fingers on the image of Gus's face.

"He's so beautiful," she said, her voice broken by her raw breath.

Yes. He was.

"Who's taking care of him? Who's tucking him in at night?"

Jordan debated how much he should tell her. "He has two nannies, both of whom I trust completely." He'd not only handpicked them, Jordan had trained them himself. And he not only paid them extremely well, he did daily checks to make sure neither of them had betrayed him.

"And he's safe?" Kinley asked. "Where?"

He had another debate. One he lost. Because the truth was, Kinley needed to know. "He's here."

Her eyes widened. "Here?" All breath, no sound.

Jordan pointed to the door on the far side of the room. "There."

"So close," she muttered. Kinley smeared away the tears on her cheek and bolted right toward the nursery door.

CHAPTER SIX

SHE WOULD SEE her son.

Kinley wasn't about to compromise on that now. This had to happen.

She threw open the door where Jordan had pointed and came face-to-face with a massive walk-in closet. Certainly not the nursery she'd seen on the computer screen. She looked over her shoulder at Jordan. But instead of an explanation, he calmly closed down the laptop and walked toward her.

"You can't stop me from seeing him," she insisted, though he could. Jordan was in control here. That didn't prevent her from starting a frantic search of the closet. Maybe there was some secret entrance.

Kinley pushed aside some suits and checked the wall. No seams except for the corners. Jordan caught her hand when she reached to move more clothes aside. Maybe it was his touch that drew her back to reality, but it suddenly hit her.

She spun around toward him. "The thermal scanner—"

"Won't work in this area," he interrupted. "It's secured like the bedroom."

Kinley shook her head. "But won't the person scanning notice an entire area of the estate that's not accessible on the equipment?"

"No. The scanner only reads the heat and doesn't register depth. Besides, the estate is over fifteen thousand square feet. The rooms shielded by metal only make up about one sixth of that space, and they're not all clumped together. They feed through the house in a random pattern."

Maybe because her nerves were right at the surface and were making it hard to focus, Kinley had no idea what that meant. "I just want to see my son."

"I know." There was something in his voice. A sadness, maybe? Or maybe it was simply that he was concerned about revealing the hopefully safe haven he'd created.

Jordan reached out and opened the middle drawer of the built-in dresser. He reached to the back of the drawer, pressed in some numbers on a keypad, and a door opened. Not on the wall. But on the floor. She hadn't seen the seam because of the way the slate tiles fit together.

"Go first," Jordan instructed.

Kinley did. In the back of her mind, she considered the danger. That maybe Jordan was leading her here to silence her in some way. But she was surprised to realize that she trusted him.

Maybe that wouldn't turn out to be a fatal mistake.

She went down a flight of stairs that lit up with each step she took. Jordan closed the door behind them and followed her. They were in the basement, and when she reached the bottom, more lights came on. No nursery. No room with a toy box. It was cluttered with large wardrobe boxes. Jordan touched one of those boxes, and it slid to the side to reveal another set of stairs, these leading right back up.

"A security measure," he explained.

And Kinley was thankful for it.

She hurried up the steps to another door where Jordan used another keypad to press in some numbers. They came face-to-face with a gun. And the tall brunette pointing it at them seemed to know how to use the weapon.

"It's okay," Jordan said to the woman. Only then did she lower the gun.

The woman still eyed Kinley with suspicion. "You're sure everything's all right?"

Maybe she thought Kinley was coercing Jordan or something. Part of Kinley was thrilled with the security, and the other part of her hated that her son needed such measures to stay safe.

"Kinley, this is Elsa, one of Gus's nannies."

Kinley nodded a greeting. Elsa nodded back. But she kept that suspicion in her eyes as she stepped aside so they could enter.

"The nannies each have their own room," Jordan explained, pointing to the doors off what appeared to be a playroom. It was filled with toys and painted with bright primary colors, and in the corner was a Christmas tree. "When they need to leave the estate, they dress as maids, and on occasion they help me entertain houseguests. That way, no one will be suspicious if they see them around the place."

Good planning. God knew how long it'd taken him to find, and trust, these women.

Jordan walked to the door straight ahead, took a deep breath and opened it. It was the nursery, the room he'd shown her on the laptop.

And there was her baby.

Finally, she'd found him! The tears came in a flash, filling her eyes, but Kinley quickly blinked them away because she wanted to see her precious baby. She'd never doubted this moment would come because she would have never given up her search to find him. But now that he was here, so close, the emotion and the pain of the past fourteen months flooded through her. God, she had missed him so much.

Kinley couldn't stop herself. She rushed past Jordan and tried to keep her footsteps light so that she wouldn't wake him. He was sleeping so peacefully and was beautiful with his dark brown hair. Like hers. His face was like hers as well. So much of her was in him, and just looking at him broke her heart and filled it all at the same time.

She reached out and brushed her hand over his hair, then his cheek. He stirred, and for a moment she thought he might wake so she could get a better look at him, but his thumb went into his mouth, and he went back to sleep.

"He looks like a Gus," she whispered.

Jordan made a sound of agreement, and that drew her attention to him, so she could see how he was handling this. Even in the dimly lit room, she saw the emotion. Not the emotion of a mere caregiver.

Jordan Taylor loved her son.

"He gets up around seven each morning," Jordan said, checking his watch. "Elsa will call us so you can come and visit with him."

Visit. Yes. That said it all. She couldn't scoop him up and take him away. Not with all the danger and uncertainty lurking out there, but she could visit. For now, that would have to be enough, but it wouldn't be enough for long. One way or another, Kinley intended to reclaim her son.

But how?

Her life was a mess.

Jordan touched her arm, and she knew it was time to leave. She checked her watch as well. It was nearly 11:00 p.m., and that meant she still had eight hours before Gus woke. She'd be counting down the minutes.

She brushed a kiss on the baby's forehead and reluctantly followed Jordan. She had a dozen questions, and it was best if they had some privacy for that anyway. They retraced their steps through the main room, Jordan whispered something to Elsa, and the nanny locked the door behind them when they left.

"How long have you had Gus here?" Kinley asked as they made their way back through the basement. She surprised even herself that she called her son Gus.

"Since Shelly left him on my doorstep. I thought this would be the safest place for him. When I had the estate built, I added the area, thinking I might need it if I ever had to hide away witnesses and such."

In other words, short-term use. "But Gus has been there for fourteen months."

"Yes." That was all he said until they arrived back into the closet of his suite. Jordan closed the door on the floor and reset the security. "That's why I have to move. He needs room to play. He needs a life, and I couldn't give him that if we stayed here."

Jordan stopped and looked away. But Kinley caught on to his arm. "That's why you sold Sentron."

He didn't answer. He didn't have to. In that moment, she realized just how much he'd sacrificed for her son.

And just how much he loved him.

"This is going to be a problem, isn't it?" she heard herself say.

Now Jordan looked at her, with that warning in his eyes. She was getting too close to what he wanted to keep buried beneath.

He tore out of her grip and headed for the bedroom. Kinley went after him and managed to step in front of him before he made it to the desk, where he would no doubt start working so he could avoid this conversation.

But the conversation had to happen.

Their gazes met again. He tossed her another of those warnings, but Kinley didn't move. "You've been a father to him."

But that was as far as she got. Jordan latched on to her arm, pulled her closer.

He kissed her.

Kinley made a sound of surprise. She certainly hadn't seen this coming and she knew it was a ploy to stop the conversation, but much to her disgust, she didn't push him away. She stood there and let it happen.

His mouth moved over hers. Hard. Almost punishing. It was heavy with emotion, and even heartbreak. Maybe it was because Kinley understood those feelings. Heck, she was in the middle of them herself. And maybe she, too, needed to have physical contact with the one person on earth who understood exactly what she was going through.

At least, that's how it was in the beginning.

But then, the kiss softened. So did the grip he had on her arm. Jordan's mouth moved over hers with a clever touch that she hadn't expected. The heat moved from his mouth, generating little fires along the way to her belly. She felt that tug. That need. And Kinley melted, too, against him.

She fought to tear away from his grip, only so she could slide her arms around him. The kiss deepened, and he used his tongue. The heat soared and turned those little fires to much larger ones.

He backed away from her, and the kiss ended just as abruptly as it'd begun. "You were supposed to stop me," he mumbled.

"Sorry." She ran her tongue over her bottom lip and tasted him there. "I was counting on you to do the stopping. And you did." Thank goodness. Because she'd gotten so consumed in the kiss that she'd forgotten the danger.

Amazing that a kiss could do that.

Which meant it was dangerous in its own right.

Jordan put his hands on his hips, and it seemed as if they were going to finish the conversation that the kiss had postponed. But before he could say anything, his cell phone rang. He jerked it from his pocket, glanced at the screen and groaned. When he showed her the screen, she saw the name of the caller.

Burke Dennison.

Jordan put it on speaker. "Burke, what do you want?" He wasn't friendly about it, either.

"I'm outside your place. We need to talk."

Jordan went to the laptop and pulled up the security

screen. Yep, Burke was there, sitting in a high-end black car parked right in front of the estate.

"It's late," Jordan told him. "And I have company."

"Yes. The woman you left the party with. I'm sorry to interrupt, but after our last chat, I think you'll agree we need to sit down and straighten out some things."

Yes. They did. But Kinley wasn't sure they could trust Burke, and she didn't really want him in the house so close to her son.

Jordan glanced at the computer screen again. Then, at her. Kinley shook her head, not knowing what they should do.

"We'll meet tomorrow morning at ten," Jordan countered, and he didn't wait for Burke to disagree. He hung up.

"You think it's safe to meet with him?" Kinley asked.

"No. But that's exactly why I have to." Jordan pointed to the bed. "Get some sleep because you'll need it."

Kinley mumbled an agreement, rummaged through her overnight bag and came up with a white cotton gown. Not provocative, but after that kiss, full armor might not be enough protection.

She started for the bathroom when she heard Jordan mumble something. She turned around and realized he had seen something on the laptop screen.

"Burke isn't still here, is he?" she asked.

"No. It's not that. I just got the identity of the person in that other car."

"The one who was behind Anderson Walker?" she clarified.

"Yes."

She walked closer when he didn't add anything. "Was it another of Burke's men?"

"No. One of mine. It was Cody Guillory."

CHAPTER SEVEN

JORDAN CHECKED HIS WATCH. Within minutes, he'd have to interrupt Kinley's visit with Gus. Judging from the little boy's and her expressions, neither would like it. Both were into the Lego tower they were building.

A skirt-clad Kinley was on the floor with Gus, who was wearing his usual jeans and a top. This one was a bright Christmas-red that one of the nannies had bought for him on their last secret shopping mission.

When Kinley had first come into the room that morning, Gus had looked at her with suspicion. Probably because his entire world had been Jordan and his nannies. Jordan had taken him to pediatric checkups, of course. But those had always happened in secret, with him driving the child to the small town of Fall Creek where Gus had been examined by Jordan's old friend, Dr. Finn Mc-Grath. Finn was a man who knew how to keep secrets.

Gus had had few opportunities to be a normal kid. And that's why Jordan had decided to make some major changes in his life.

Now the question was, what would happen to all his plans?

Kinley's smiles and laughter said it all. She wouldn't just give up Gus. She was here to stay, and Jordan had to figure out how to deal with that while keeping Gus safe. Safety was his top priority.

But then, he rethought that.

It was a priority all right, but so was Gus himself. Watching the boy, Jordan knew he couldn't give him up, either. Even though he'd never allowed himself to say the words aloud, Gus was his son in every way that mattered. Jordan loved him.

He checked his watch again. "It's time," Jordan told Kinley.

Her smile faded, and she reluctantly gave Gus a kiss on the cheek before she got up from the floor. She brushed off her calf-length black skirt, straightened her top but didn't take her eyes off Gus. Gus watched her, too, and then looked at Jordan as if asking for some explanation as to what was going on.

Jordan stooped down to try to give that explanation but got a big hug instead. Gus launched himself at Jordan, and the little boy giggled.

"Jor-dad," Gus called him, and he laughed again because he knew that Jordan would, too. Jordan couldn't help it. He always laughed when Gus babbled the attempt to say Jordan, and it was a game they played nearly every day.

Jordan gave Gus a kiss on the cheek. "Be a good boy, okay?"

Gus babbled his version of "okay" and waved goodbye.

Jordan waited until the daytime nanny, Pamela, came back into the room. It wasn't necessary for him to remind the woman to lock up and stay vigilant. She would. And she'd keep Gus safe while Kinley and he went back into the main living quarters. Not that he wanted Kinley there for the meeting with Burke, but he didn't want Burke getting suspicious as to why she wasn't around.

"Gus is wonderful," Kinley said on their way out. "I had no idea he'd be able to say so many words."

"We all work with him, and Elsa's a former teacher."

"Teacher turned bodyguard," she mumbled.

Jordan heard the disapproval. Not that she disapproved of Gus's safety, but it was the need for safety that'd kept him shut away. That need had also kept Gus from her.

"He calls you dad," she pointed out.

"Jor-dad," he corrected. "He's trying to say Jordan." But he couldn't explain why he hadn't corrected the boy. He wanted to have that dad label.

It was time to change the subject.

"Burke should be here any minute," Jordan reminded her. "Make an appearance. Walk through the foyer when I open the door and then wait in the bedroom."

"But shouldn't I be there in case Burke says something about being Simon, the investor?"

"That's exactly why you shouldn't be there."

Once they worked their way back in through the closet and into his bedroom suite, he went to his laptop and made sure all the security cameras were registering their images on the split screen.

"But maybe I could guide the conversation in a direction where we could learn more info," she pointed out.

Jordan shook his head. "I don't trust Burke, and I'd rather you not be around him."

She blew out a long breath, obviously not happy that she wouldn't be part of this meeting. "What about

Cody? Did you ever find out why he was following us last night?"

"Not yet. He hasn't returned my calls." Which didn't exactly please Jordan. He considered Cody more than a loyal former employee. Of course, it was possible that Cody was simply looking out for him since Jordan had told him that Kinley and he were being followed.

But then, why hadn't Cody let him know that?

It was definitely something he wanted to ask the man. But first, there was Burke to deal with.

Jordan pointed to an image on the top of the screen. "That's the pool house." It was glass encased and sat right in the middle of the garden. "That's where I'll be taking Burke for our chat."

She nodded. "Because you don't want him in the house near Gus."

"Right. Burke's a whiz with developing new equipment, and I can't take the risk that he might have some kind of scanner that can read signals through metal. I know it can't be done at long range, but the technology exits for it to happen at shorter distances."

"Oh," she said, obviously understanding the danger.

Jordan spotted Burke's car the moment it pulled into his driveway. "It's show time," he said to Kinley. And he looked at her to make sure she was steady.

She was.

Steady, and still gorgeous. The clothes didn't help. Her black skirt and silver-gray top clung to her in all the right places. Or the wrong ones, since he probably shouldn't have noticed all those interesting curves.

Jordan had hoped that this attraction would have cooled by now, that the kiss would have been enough for him to realize he couldn't have her. But the kiss had done the opposite. It had reminded him that kissing her wasn't nearly enough. He wanted her in his bed. And not just for sleeping as she'd done the night before when he'd slept on the floor.

He wanted her in his bed with him.

"What?" she said, searching his eyes.

"Nothing."

So that she wouldn't challenge that, Jordan headed toward the front door. "Remember, just make a quick appearance. If you want to listen in on the meeting, you can do that with the laptop."

Kinley agreed, hesitantly, and followed him to the front door. By the time they made it there, Burke had already rung the bell twice. Jordan made sure his gun was positioned for a quick draw in his concealed shoulder holster, and he opened the door to face the man.

"Jordan," Burke greeted, though it was far from friendly.

Jordan stepped aside so he could enter. Right on cue, Kinley made her appearance by walking past them and even managed to look a little mussed and embarrassed, as if she and Jordan had just finished a steamy tryst.

And in his mind, they had.

"This way," Jordan instructed. After he reset the security system, he led Burke past the Christmas tree and through the place. He didn't rush. Didn't want to make it too obvious that he wanted to get him out of the main house. However, he also didn't offer coffee or other refreshments.

"I've spent several hours looking for Anderson

Walker," Burke let him know. "No sign of the man. Did he happen to say where he was going?"

"No." Jordan walked through the glass corridor that led to the pool house. "He wasn't exactly volunteering a lot of details. Did you find out who he was working for?"

"No. Did you?"

Jordan shook his head. Last night while Kinley had been sleeping in his bed, Jordan had tried, but the contract for Anderson's services was buried under layers of dummy corporations. Corporations that Burke could have easily created. It would take time and resources for Jordan to dig through them.

Later, that's exactly what he would do.

The pool house was made of prism glass, circular and with an open top. The outside temp was chilly, but the heated water and floor made the room comfortably warm. It was a room he rarely used anymore. Well, since Gus's arrival. He couldn't risk the boy being seen through the glass, and even though his security system ran the entire perimeter of his property, someone might still be able to see the child.

He and Burke sat across from each other in a pair of cushioned wicker chairs. Neither said anything, but a dozen thoughts passed between them. None good. Burke was now the owner of a company that Jordan had loved. And Jordan didn't trust him. The feeling was obviously mutual.

"You've been digging into my background," Burke tossed out. He didn't wait for Jordan to confirm it, either. "What exactly were you looking for?"

"The obvious. I wanted to know if you had your man following me, and why."

"And did you decide if I'm innocent or guilty?" Burke didn't seem overly alarmed at what the answer might be. Jordan knew the man was cocky, but he hadn't thought Burke would aim that cockiness at him. Of course, their positions were different now that Burke owned Sentron.

"Guilty," Jordan declared.

Still Burke offered no reaction. He calmly reached down and swirled his fingers through the lagoon-blue pool water. "Someone tapped into my investment accounts. Was that you?"

"Yes. And someone tried to tap into mine. The person failed."

They stared at each other again. Jordan decided to wait him out because Burke seemed to be on the verge of giving him some real information instead of just repeating things Jordan already knew.

"I've had some sensitive investments," Burke said as if carefully choosing his words. "You zoomed in on those that I made under the name Simon. Why?"

Ah. Now, this is where he'd lie. Except Jordan didn't get the chance. He saw the movement in the glass corridor that led from the main house, and he stood to draw his weapon.

But it was Kinley.

She stopped in the entryway and motioned for him to come to her. Jordan did. And he hurried. Because only an emergency would have caused her to interrupt this meeting.

"I was watching the security screen," she whispered. "Cody Guillory and another of your former agents just drove up in separate vehicles. They're sitting in their cars, looking at the estate."

Hell. This couldn't be good. Jordan glanced back at Burke. "Did you bring backup with you?"

Burke shrugged. "I don't know what you mean."

Jordan didn't believe him. That wasn't a cocky expression. It was a smug one. Burke was playing some kind of game, and Jordan wanted to know the rules.

And the stakes.

Jordan took out his phone and called Cody. The man answered on the first ring. "Looking for me?" Jordan asked.

"Desmond and I need to talk to you."

Desmond Parisi, Jordan's former communications guru. If a place needed to be bugged or put under surveillance, Desmond was the best at Sentron for that. It made Jordan extremely uncomfortable to have a man like that anywhere around the house. Ironic. Because twenty-four hours earlier he would have trusted these men with his life.

"Why do we need to talk?" Jordan questioned Cody.

"It's about Burke."

Jordan didn't know whether to be surprised or not. "He's here."

"Yes. I saw his car. What we need to say should be said in front of him. In front of both of you."

That was an interesting turn. Had Cody learned something about his new boss? And did it have anything to do with Cody following him the night before?

"We're in the pool house. Come in through the backyard," Jordan instructed. Of course, that left him with a huge problem. Two of them, actually. Kinley and Burke. He didn't trust Burke, and Jordan didn't want Kinley caught in the middle if there was any trouble.

He took out his PDA and routed the security surveillance to it so he could keep an eye on the place while this meeting was going on. Jordan also temporarily disengaged the side gate so the agents could enter.

"Go back inside," Jordan whispered to Kinley.

She nodded, took one step, but then Burke stood. "Kinley Ford."

That stopped her. It stopped Jordan's heart for a second as well. Both Kinley and Jordan turned to face the man who'd called her by her real name and not by the alias she'd used the night before when Cody had introduced them.

Jordan eased his hand over the butt of his weapon that he had concealed beneath his jacket.

Burke laughed and held up his hands. "You're going to shoot me, Jordan?"

"If necessary." Jordan made sure there was nothing joking about his tone or demeanor.

Burke chuckled again and sank back down into the chair. "After our conversation last night where you accused me of having you tailed, I decided to check through some surveillance footage taken at the Christmas party. I ran Ms. Ford's image through the facial-recognition software."

"And?" Jordan prompted when the man didn't say anything else. Because she seemed to be holding her breath, Jordan slipped his left arm around Kinley.

"There's no *and* to this," Burke insisted. "I wasn't pleased with your accusations, and I merely wanted to see what was going on that would make you have that kind of reaction." He paused. "But I have to wonder…

why would a Ph.D. researcher want to worm her way into a party, only to leave mere minutes later with the host?"

"Because the host is extremely hot, and I wanted to be alone with him," Kinley answered before Jordan could tell Burke to mind his own business.

The tension got worse. A lot worse. And that's how Cody and Desmond found them when they crossed the backyard and came into the pool house. That brought Burke to his feet again, and judging from his suddenly tight jaw, he didn't seem pleased with his employees' impromptu visit.

Both agents wore jeans and jackets. They also wore formidable expressions that matched their new boss's. Cody took the lead, walking in first. Tall and lean, his former agent looked like an all-American with his sandy blond hair and blue eyes. Desmond had more of an international look and had often done undercover assignments as someone from the Middle East.

"There's a problem," Cody announced. He tipped his head first to Burke and then to Jordan. "You two are in some kind of surveillance war, and you're putting us in the middle. Now, we want to know what this is all about."

Jordan wanted to know the same thing, and all eyes went to Burke.

Burke shrugged again. "I had Cody follow you last night."

"Yeah. I know. Why?" Jordan demanded.

"I thought there was something suspicious about you leaving with Kinley Ford."

Cody's attention snapped to Jordan, and even though he didn't ask the question, he probably wanted to know why Kinley had used an alias. Jordan didn't intend to give his former employee an explanation. The fewer people who knew about her, the better. Now maybe Cody wouldn't continue to dig when this meeting was over.

"I thought maybe Kinley's arrival at the party was connected to the sale of the company," Burke explained. "I was within hours of taking ownership, and I didn't want anything to go wrong. I also considered that maybe Kinley was blackmailing you, and that her actions would put the sale of Sentron at risk."

Jordan wanted to believe that Burke was telling the truth, but he couldn't. After all, Burke was connected to Kinley and the research facility. Depending on how much involvement he'd had with his investment, he might have recognized her the moment she stepped into the party.

Or even before.

Because if Jordan had noticed she was spying on him from the coffee shop, someone else like Burke could have noticed it as well.

Desmond stepped up to stand side by side with Cody, but he aimed his comment at Burke. "I know you're the owner now, but I don't want to do communications surveillance on my former boss."

"Neither do I," Cody agreed.

And the silence returned. Several snail-crawling moments later, Burke finally nodded. He looked at Jordan. "No more surveillance. Can I have the same assurance from you that you won't spy on me?"

"No." Jordan didn't even have to think about it.

There it was. For just a second. A flash of hot anger in Burke's otherwise cool eyes. Then he chuckled. "Go ahead. Keep me in your sight. Dig into my accounts. You won't find anything illegal."

No. But he might find a motive for Burke to go after Kinley, especially if Burke thought she could provide him with the missing formula for the antidote.

"I'll leave through the yard gate," Burke announced, and without lingering, he headed in the same direction from which Cody and Desmond had entered.

Jordan waited until Burke was out of earshot before he spoke to Cody and Desmond. "I'm sorry you two were put in the middle." But he wasn't sorry they'd ratted out Burke. Jordan intended to make full use of whatever loyalty to him the men had left. "Exactly how deep a surveillance did Burke put on me?"

Desmond tipped his head to Kinley. "It was aimed more at her. When Burke told Cody to follow you, he had me give him a comm pack."

A comm pack—a sensitive device that could be used for long-range eavesdropping. *Hell.* Jordan had developed the device himself and knew it was highly effective. Worse, it could bypass detection with nearly all security systems, including the one Jordan had in the Porsche.

"I only used the comm pack when I followed you in the car," Cody explained. "And I told Burke that I couldn't pick up your conversation."

Which meant he had.

It also meant Cody and Desmond had likely heard all about Gus. Of course, Jordan hadn't mentioned the child was at his estate, not until he was in his secure bedroom, but Cody and Desmond weren't fools. They could fill in the blanks.

"There's more," Cody continued, his voice practically

a whisper. He stared at Jordan. Nope, make that a glare. Cody obviously wasn't happy about this meeting or with Jordan. "Consider this your retirement gift because after today, my allegiance will lie with Burke. Understand?"

"Yeah." Jordan also heard and understood Cody's resentment. It was there and was feeding the glare the man was still aiming at him.

"Desmond and I know who Kinley is," Cody explained. "Burke had us check on her most of last night."

Jordan's stomach tightened. "Did he say why?"

"He gave us the same spiel about being concerned that she could somehow hold up his taking ownership of Sentron," Desmond continued, keeping his voice low as well. "But after a while, Burke changed his tune and told us to dig into her background. It didn't take long for us to learn that she worked at the Bassfield Research Facility." Now it was Desmond's turn to pause. "We know about the research project and the missing formula. And we also know that this morning at six o'clock, Burke met with Martin Strahan."

The investor.

And the person with the most motive to find and hurt Kinley.

Jordan tried not to react. Hard to do, though, because he certainly hadn't expected Burke to do that. "Did you hear their conversation?"

Both Cody and Desmond shook their heads. "He met with him at the Sentron command center."

And that was the one place where Burke's conversation would indeed be private.

What the devil was going on? Since Burke and Strahan were the last remaining investors, maybe they'd teamed up to come after Kinley. If so, this wasn't good. Jordan didn't need the pair trying to sniff out Gus's whereabouts. And eventually that's what they would do.

Cody extended his hand for Jordan to shake. "Good-bye, Jordan. I wish things were different. I wish we could go back to the way things were." And he slipped a piece of paper into Jordan's palm.

Desmond echoed the sentiment, and the men left through the yard gate.

"My God," Kinley mumbled under her breath. "What do we do now?"

Because they both needed the contact, he tightened his grip around her waist. "We go back inside. I'll beef up security to make sure Burke doesn't have free rein of our privacy." He leaned in and put his mouth to her ear. "Don't say anything out here about Gus."

Her eyes widened, and she looked around. Yes, Burke could still be monitoring their conversation. So Jordan decided to play that to his advantage.

"If Burke is after the missing formula for the antidote, then he's going to be disappointed when he realizes you don't know anything about it."

"Yes," she said, obviously playing along. "Maybe he'll quit hounding us once he realizes that."

Jordan added a "yes" of his own. And he kissed her. It was supposed to be all for show, just in case Burke was somehow watching them. But for some reason his body missed the part about this being a pretense. Just like the other kisses, this one fired through him.

Oh, man.

Her mouth was foreplay, and he had to stop and get his mind back on business.

First, he checked his PDA to make sure the house was still safe. It was. Just as he'd expected. If someone had tried to break in, he would have been alerted. Unfortunately, that level of protection didn't extend to the pool house so he got Kinley moving.

He also discreetly looked at the note that Cody had handed him.

"What is it?" Kinley whispered.

"Martin Strahan's phone number." A real gift, since Jordan hadn't had any luck tracking down the man. "Cody must have gotten it when Burke arranged the meeting with Strahan in the command center."

"Will you call Strahan?"

Jordan hoped to do more than that. He hoped to meet with the man to see if he could get to the bottom of this. Of course, he couldn't do that until he had Kinley tucked away in a safe place. He didn't want Martin Strahan within a hundred miles of Gus and her.

He hurried their pace so he could get Kinley out of the glass corridor and into the house. Jordan didn't breathe easier until they were inside and on their way to his suite, where they couldn't be monitored. But they'd barely made it to the corridor next to the kitchen when he heard the sound.

There was no warning. No time to react.

The explosion ripped through the house.

CHAPTER EIGHT

"Gus!" Kinley managed to shout a split second before Jordan shoved her to the floor.

She landed hard on the slate, and Jordan landed on top of her. Shielding her, she realized, from the blast.

The sound was deafening and shook the entire house. Crystal glasses from the open-faced cabinets crashed to the countertops and floor around them, and the stainless-steel pots on the rack overhead clanged and slammed against each other. Everywhere in the house, there were sounds of things falling and crashing.

Kinley fought to get up so she could race to check on Gus, but Jordan held her in place. She braced herself for the roof or walls to collapse, but other than the broken glasses, nothing else fell nearby.

The security system began to pulse through the house. Not nearly as loud as the blast, but it sent her adrenaline up another notch. If that was possible. Her body was already screaming for her to get to her son.

Jordan must have felt the same overwhelming need because he got up and hauled her to her feet. He began to run toward his suite, just as his cell phone rang.

"Pamela," he said, answering it. It was obviously the nanny, and Kinley held her breath, waiting to hear what the woman had to say about Gus.

"They're okay," Jordan relayed a moment later. "She's calling the police and the fire department."

The relief nearly made her legs go limp, but Kinley kept running. She couldn't take the nanny's word that they were safe. She had to see for herself.

But Jordan didn't head toward the closet entrance. He stopped at the laptop on his bedroom desk and started viewing the security cameras. It was a smart thing to do. He could maybe pinpoint the origin of the blast. And, God forbid, maybe he could see if there was another one about to happen.

That thought sent her heart racing even more, but Kinley tried to force herself to stay calm.

Jordan touched the top right corner of the screen where she could see the cloud of gray smoke.

"A fire," she mumbled and tried again to run to the closet and the secret stairs.

Jordan held on to her. "Not a fire. That's just lime-stone and stucco debris from the blast."

That made her breathe a little easier, until she realized where the blast had occurred. On the very side of the house where Burke, Desmond and Cody had made their exit just minutes earlier.

Jordan continued to zoom in on all the areas around the house. The security alarm continued to wail. Her heartbeat continued to pound in her ears.

"The system's detected pieces of a detonator," Jordan informed her.

A detonator. In other words, this had not been an accident. Someone had just tried to kill them by blowing them to smithereens.

He typed in some codes, and the nursery area came

onto the screen. Gus was playing with his rocking horse, and both nannies were in the room with him. Standing guard, though all appeared to be well. Thank God those inner rooms hadn't been damaged.

Jordan obviously felt the relief as well because he let out a long breath and pulled her into his arms for a quick hug. "We can't go in the nursery," he told her. Kinley shook her head, but he caught her chin to stop her. "We *can't*. The police will be here any minute. We'll be questioned, and they'll make sure there's not another explosive device, something that maybe my security system isn't picking up."

"What if there is another one?" Her words rushed out in an unbroken stream. "What if this monster tries to blow up the place again before the cops get here?"

"The house was built to withstand a heavy impact," he let her know. "And Gus's area is reinforced with steel."

That didn't eliminate her fears. "But what about a fire?"

"There's a sprinkler system through the place, even around the exterior." With his hands still gripping her face, Jordan stared at her. "We can't tell the police about Gus, understand?"

Her mind was racing, and it took her a moment to fight through the fear so she could nod. "Yes. I understand." It wouldn't be safe because all it would take was for one cop to say something, and Gus's whereabouts would be known.

"What's wrong?" she asked when she saw the renewed concern on Jordan's face.

"Normally, I'd call Cody at a time like this." He let go of her, took out his phone again and scrolled through the numbers. "But I need to stay away from him and any-one else at Sentron. I'll call a friend. Cal Rico. I know I can trust him."

Kinley hoped that was the case. They certainly needed someone on their side.

While Jordan made that call, he continued to check the surveillance cameras. There were no signs of Burke, Desmond or Cody. Just that billowing dust to indicate how close they'd come to being hurt.

She heard the sirens, and while Jordan finished up his call to his friend, they made their way toward the front of the house. The Christmas tree was still standing, but many of the expensive Waterford ornaments had shat-tered onto the floor.

"Stay back," Jordan warned her when he reached for the doorknob.

Oh, mercy. She hadn't even thought of an attack from something other than an explosive, but the culprit could be waiting outside. Waiting to kill them.

Still, Jordan put himself right in what could be the line of fire when he opened the door. The SAPD were there. Three cruisers and, in the distance, she could hear the sound of a fire engine.

One of the uniformed cops came up the steps and flashed his badge. "Any idea what caused the explo-sion?" he asked.

"My security system indicated fragments of a deto-nator," Jordan answered.

The cop motioned for them to move. "You need to evacuate."

"Evacuate?" Kinley challenged. "No—"

But Jordan cut off the rest of her protest by touching

his fingers to her lips. "It'll be okay. We have to let the police do their job."

She shook her head and tried to tell Jordan that she wanted to stay in the house so she'd be near Gus, but that didn't stop Jordan from latching on to her arm and taking her down the steps. "We'll wait in the cruiser," he told the cop.

And then Jordan froze.

Kinley froze too and followed his gaze. She braced herself to see another explosive. Or something worse.

It was something worse.

Because across the street, standing on the sidewalk, was a man that she recognized from his photos.

The ruthless investor who was likely after her and her son.

Martin Strahan.

JORDAN CURSED. They certainly didn't need this now. But a confrontation was apparently about to happen because Martin Strahan stepped off the sidewalk and started toward them.

Jordan automatically moved in front of Kinley, and he opened his jacket so he could put his hand on the butt of his weapon.

Martin Strahan only held up his palms to indicate he wasn't carrying a weapon. That didn't mean, however, that he wasn't armed. He certainly looked the type to need a weapon. He was around six feet tall and had a solid enough build, but his pale blond hair and milk-white coloring made him look more like an anemic high school computer nerd than a high-stakes investor and businessman.

But he didn't need strength to set explosives.

Jordan figured that's exactly what he'd done. Well, maybe. It did seem stupid to hang around if Strahan had been the culprit. Still, he was there and had the means, motive and opportunity.

So did Burke.

And that meant Jordan had a mystery to solve. Fast. Because until he found the person responsible and put him behind bars, Kinley and Gus were in danger.

"Kinley Ford," Strahan greeted. He stopped right next to the police cruiser and didn't even glance at the chaos in the aftermath of the explosion. He kept his attention fastened to Kinley. "I've been looking for you for a long time. You're a hard person to find."

"I could say the same about you," Jordan countered. The sirens grew louder, and Jordan knew it was only a matter of seconds before the fire department arrived. "Are you responsible for the explosion?"

"Me? Of course not."

Jordan studied his expression but couldn't tell if the man was lying. "Then why are you here?"

"Bad timing on my part. I stepped from my car, and boom! I take it no one was hurt?"

"No one," Jordan assured him. The fire engine and a bomb squad van pulled to a stop in front of the house, and the men began to hurry toward the point of origin.

Now Strahan's ice-blue eyes turned toward Jordan. "I understand you're searching through my background. No need. I'll tell you everything you need to know."

Right. Everything that wouldn't land him in a jail cell. "I'd be very interested in having a conversation with you."

"Yes, I'll bet you would." Strahan turned back to Kinley. "And how about you? Are you finally ready to talk to me?"

"I'll talk to you," Kinley said, stepping out from behind Jordan. "But I know nothing about the missing research information."

"Maybe. Sometimes people know more than they think they know." And with that cryptic response, he turned and walked toward one of the uniformed officers. "Jordan Taylor believes I had something to do with this. How soon can you exclude me as a suspect?"

The officer looked at Strahan as if he'd just sprouted a third eye. Then the cop looked at Jordan, obviously waiting for an explanation.

"I want him questioned," Jordan finally said.

"All right." The officer glanced around and motioned for another uniform to join them. "I'll have him taken down to headquarters."

Strahan started to walk away with the officer but then turned to face Jordan and Kinley. "I'll call you and set up a meeting. It'd be in all of our best interests if that meeting were to happen today."

Jordan wasn't so sure of that. He needed to get things under control here at the estate before he dove into new waters with the likes of Strahan. However, the man might be able to give them answers to put an end to all of this.

"You two need to move farther from the house," one of the firemen shouted to Jordan. "Just in case there's a secondary explosion."

Jordan heard the change in Kinley's breathing and knew she was thinking of Gus. He caught on to her arm and headed not for the cruiser but the guesthouse just inside the high wrought-iron fence that ran the entire perimeter of the backyard. He needed to find a private place where he could monitor security and make sure no one tried to get into the nursery area.

"We'll be in the guesthouse," he told the fireman, and Jordan headed there before anyone could object.

Later, of course, Kinley and he would have to give statements, but that could wait.

"We need to check on Gus," she whispered.

Jordan intended to do that ASAP. They hurried through the side gate and to the guesthouse. It had a keyless entry, and he punched in the code so they could enter the three-room cottage. He shut the door, locked it and immediately put another code into his PDA so he could rearm the estate's internal security system.

If someone went into the house, he'd know about it.

Then he clicked the screen to surveillance so he could take a look at the nursery. He turned the screen toward Kinley so that she could see Gus calmly watching a DVD with cartoon characters.

"Pamela and Elsa will guard Gus with their lives," Jordan reminded her.

She nodded and dropped back so that she was leaning against the door. She was pale. Shaking. And her breath was gusting to the point she was close to hyperventilation.

"I did this," Kinley said. "I brought this danger to Gus."

"No." Jordan couldn't believe he was on her side. But he was. "This has been brewing for a long time, and the only way it can end is for the person to be caught."

Jordan could see that now. He couldn't build a shelter strong enough or hire enough bodyguard-nannies to protect Gus. If they ever hoped to have a normal life, the danger had to stop.

Kinley shook her head. "If I leave—"

"It won't do any good. Burke and Strahan have both already connected you to me. That means they've connected us to Gus."

Tears sprang to her eyes. "God, I'm sorry. I'm so sorry."

Jordan hadn't intended to touch her, but he couldn't just stand there while she fell apart. He pulled her into his arms, and she relaxed as if she belonged there. Not exactly a comforting thought.

"Once we get the all clear," he explained, "I'll add more security measures, and if Strahan doesn't call back, I'll phone him to set up a meeting."

"What about Burke?"

Yeah. Burke had been on his mind, too. "Burke's a problem. Maybe Cody and Desmond as well."

She pulled back, blinked back more tears. "You think Cody or Desmond could be behind this?"

"I can't automatically rule them out. Both were upset that I sold Sentron." But he didn't want to believe his former employees would turn against him.

Of course, there was the issue of money. In addition to the substantial reward being offered by the insurance company, there was a lot of cash to be made if that antidote research resurfaced. Maybe this wasn't personal. But even then, Jordan couldn't quite wrap his mind around such a betrayal.

Since Kinley was staring at him and still looking very

fragile, he showed her the image of Gus again. "See? He's fine, really."

"Why aren't you mad at me?" she asked. "You warned me this could happen. You told me I should have stayed away."

Yeah. He had. But if their situations had been reversed, he would have done the same thing. Nothing could have kept him from seeing Gus.

"We'll get through this," he promised, though he wasn't sure exactly how he could make that happen. He only knew that he had to. No case had ever been this important.

"You love Gus," she said, with those tears still shimmering in her eyes.

This was almost as uncomfortable a topic as the attraction between Kinley and him. "I don't talk about my feelings a lot," he answered. Which was an understatement.

"I understand."

He made a sound that could have meant anything and checked the PDA screen to make sure Gus was still okay. He was.

"I saw the newspaper articles when I was trying to figure out if you might have Gus," she added.

Then, she knew that his entire family—his parents, his brother and his sister—had all been kidnapped and then murdered.

"When you were eight years old, your father was an archeologist in the Middle East working on a sanctioned dig," Kinley continued. "All of you were taken hostage. Only you escaped."

"I didn't escape," he corrected. "The kidnappers released me so I could deliver a message to the American embassy that my family would be killed if other political prisoners were not released. Negotiations failed. My family died. End of story."

But not the end of the emotional baggage it'd created. He'd always have that particular dark passenger lurking in his memory.

She reached up and smoothed the worry lines on his bunched-up forehead. Until she did that, he had not even been aware of his tense expression. She came up on her toes and touched her lips lightly to his. "I'm sorry. I didn't mean to dredge up old memories."

She didn't have to dredge. They were always there. They drove him. They'd made him successful. Because no matter what he did in life, he'd always be trying to save them. An impossible task, and one that had gnawed away at him.

Until Gus came into his life.

Yeah. He loved the little boy. And that scared the hell out of him. Because the last time he'd loved someone, he hadn't been able to save them. They'd all died.

She took his hand, moved them closer to the screen and smiled when she saw Gus. "You've done an amazing job with him. He's happy, very well adjusted."

Kinley brushed her mouth over his again. No doubt a gesture meant to comfort, but his emotions were right there, right at the surface, and he didn't play fair the way she was doing.

He kissed her.

Why, he didn't know.

Yes, he did.

He always wanted to kiss her, and this was an excuse

to do it. The sky-high levels of adrenaline. The fear.
The strange union they'd been forced to form because
of a child. All of that seemed like logical reasons even
if they weren't.

The taste of her soothed him. It seemed to trickle
through him, as if she'd touched him with those delicate fingers. And then she did touch him. She wound
her hands around him and slid her fingers into his hair.

Everything stayed simple. Easy. Just a kiss. But just
as quickly, it changed. Jordan moved closer the same
moment she moved toward him.

Their bodies met.

And the fire blazed.

Oh, man. This was such a bad idea, but he didn't stop.
In fact, he made things worse by sliding his left hand
down her side and to the curve of her hip. Jordan gripped
on to her and dragged her closer until his erection was
right against a part of her that he wanted more of.

Kinley moaned. It was silky and rich. And she moved,
too. Her sex against his caused a multitude of sensations.
All good ones. Except for the dirty thoughts he had about
what he wanted to do to her.

A groan rumbled deep within his chest.

"We can't do this now," Kinley mumbled against his
mouth.

That made him curse. Because she was right. And
because she'd added *now.* That left the door open for
sex at a later time.

Jordan forced himself to pull back, and he met her
gaze. He considered a lecture—meant more as a re-
minder for him than her—to reiterate that they shouldn't
get involved. But he'd be wasting his breath. Sex would

happen. It was inevitable. Now he just had to figure out how to handle the fallout.

The knock at the door caused Kinley to jump, and Jordan moved her to the side and got his weapon ready. However, he soon discovered their visitor was one of the men who'd arrived with the bomb squad.

"Sgt. Hernandez," the man said, identifying himself. "We've made a check of the house exterior, and we found the fragments of the detonator. It set off an I.E.D., an improvised explosive device. It was meant to do some damage, and if anyone had been walking near it at the time of detonation, they would have been seriously hurt or worse. You guys were real lucky."

Jordan had to take a deep breath. Now the question was, had the I.E.D. been left for Burke, or had Burke been the one to leave it?

"We need to know who'd do something like this," the sergeant continued.

"Yes. We want to cooperate, but is it possible to take our statements here at the estate?"

The sergeant stared at them. "Most people want to get away from something like this."

"I understand, but Ms. Ford is shaken up. It'd be easier on both of us if we could stay here."

And that way he'd be close to Gus.

"Okay." The sergeant nodded. "I'll send someone in to take your statements. Stay put, though, until we've finished cleaning up those bomb fragments."

"Will do." Jordan said goodbye, closed the door and relocked it. He looked at Kinley. "We'll have to tell them the truth about everything but Gus."

She didn't get a chance to concur because his cell

phone rang. It was a call he'd been expecting from his friend, Agent Cal Rico. "Cal," Jordan answered, "please tell me you can help."

"Absolutely. I can have security measures in place within the next two hours. I can make your estate a fortress."

"Good. Because we're going to need it. One more thing. I need to arrange a meeting, and it can't be at the estate. I want to have it at my training warehouse. You know the location?"

"The one off Bulverde Road." He didn't wait for Jordan to confirm it. "Why there?"

"Because I can control the security while you keep a watch on things here at the house."

"But if you're going to be at the training facility, then why have me at the estate?"

For the biggest reason of all: Gus. "I'll explain that when you get here. Thanks, Cal."

Jordan ended the call. That was phase one. For phase two, he took out Strahan's number that Cody had given him, and he sent a secure text message to both Strahan and Burke.

Meet me at the training facility. Seven o'clock tonight. Come alone.

Kinley's eyes widened when she saw the message. "You think that's a safe thing to do?"

"No." It was far from safe. But one way or another, Jordan was going to get answers.

CHAPTER NINE

KINLEY STARED AT the building in front of them.

The training facility was indeed a warehouse. A huge one with a dark gray metal exterior that looked exactly like the dozen or so other warehouses that surrounded it. This was not the part of the city that tourists normally saw. It was isolated and downright spooky with the winter mist in the air and lights streaming over the metal.

While he drove into the parking area in front of the building, Jordan entered a code on his PDA, and large doors slid open so he could drive right inside. Another code closed the doors, and while Kinley approved of them not having to walk across the parking lot, the inside of the warehouse was nearly as creepy as the exterior.

Even in the dim light, Kinley could see the center of the building was open from front to end. At least a five-hundred-foot stretch. But the sides were a different matter. Not exactly open space. There were ropes dangling from the ceiling, climbing webbing and what appeared to be bunkers and rooms painted in camouflage.

"I used to train agents here," Jordan explained.

He grabbed two thick legal-size manila envelopes, stepped out, entered something else on that PDA and more lights flared on. She didn't know what was in the envelopes, but Jordan had been working in his office for most of the afternoon while she spent time with Gus.

Even with the lights, the place still seemed just as intimidating. The place loomed over and around her, and Kinley wondered if this had been the safest place to meet Burke and Strahan. While she was wondering, she hoped that Agent Cal Rico was as good as Jordan claimed because the man was essentially responsible for keeping Gus safe. However, if this meeting went well, if she could convince Burke and Strahan that she knew nothing about the missing research, then the danger could possibly end here tonight.

And she'd have a safe Christmas with her son.

Kinley got out of Jordan's Porsche and walked toward where he was now standing. Her footsteps echoed on the concrete floor. "You said Agent Rico would call immediately if there was any sign of trouble back at the estate?" She already knew the answer, but Kinley needed one more reassurance that coming here wasn't the biggest mistake of her life.

"If there's a problem, Cal will call us," Jordan verified. "He has a daughter a little younger than Gus, and he knows what it's like to have a child in danger. Don't worry. He'll protect Gus."

Oh, she'd still worry. Nothing would stop that.

She rubbed her hands up and down her arms. She was wearing a jacket and wasn't especially cold, but she still felt a chill inside her. "Does Burke own this place now?"

"No. He has his own training facility. I decided to keep this for a while in case I ever started another agency."

She nodded, then checked her watch. It was still a

half hour until the meeting was supposed to start. That seemed a lot of time to kill, especially since she was already antsy to get started.

And to get back to the estate.

"Follow me," Jordan instructed. He led her to the right side, through a set of rooms that looked like something from a movie set. They had doors, windows and even some furniture.

There were bullet holes in the walls.

"I had a tunnel built beneath the place," he explained. "And there are all sorts of training tools. Rappelling gear. Rifles that shoot dummy bullets."

"There were real bullet holes in that wall back there," she pointed out.

He nodded. "Sometimes, we train with live ammo."

Good. She hoped his friend, Cal Rico, had as well. That way, if this turned into a worst-case scenario, he would know what to do.

They walked to the midway point of the warehouse where he dropped the two manila envelopes on the floor.

"Are you going to tell me what's in those?" she asked. "The last time I brought them up, you dodged the question."

"They're our freedom, I hope."

And with that cryptic response, he took her up a flight of stairs to a room that was half metal on the bottom and thick glass on top. "This is the observation deck and command center," Jordan explained. "It's bulletproof and has complete communication capabilities. I can control everything from here."

He pointed to the open space in the center below them. "That's where Burke and Strahan will be."

Kinley felt the instant relief and knew then the reason he'd chosen this place. They couldn't have this kind of safety at the estate. This way, Burke and Strahan wouldn't be anywhere near her son, and Jordan and she would be tucked away in that observation area.

"And the envelopes?" she reminded him.

He sank down into one of the two chairs and clicked on some equipment mounted on a console that half circled the deck. "Among other things, I'm giving them copies of your encrypted notes."

Kinley's mouth dropped open. "What?"

"I'm hoping they'll find something to lead them to the person who stole the research. Since I know that wasn't you, it'll get them off your trail."

She tried to work through the logic of that and took the chair next to him. "But one of them might have stolen the info about the project from the lab. One of them could already have way too much information."

Jordan's gaze came to hers. "Good. I hope that's the case. Then, the two of them can fight it out."

Yes. That would be a godsend. Heck, they might even turn their attention to Brenna Martel in prison. Kinley didn't care as long as the men weren't around to endanger Gus. Finally, she could find a happy ending for all of this.

Well, maybe.

"And if they still believe I have the antidote?" she questioned.

"Then, I have a backup plan." He swiveled his chair in her direction. "Do you have any idea what I used to do for a living?"

It seemed an odd question, especially since she'd followed him for days. "Of course. You owned Sentron."

"I've killed people, Kinley," he flatly stated. "I've been ruthless. Cutthroat. All within the parameters of the law. But barely," he added.

She certainly hadn't thought he was a boy scout, but that caused her a moment of uneasiness. Then she reminded herself that she trusted him.

"I can go head-to-head with Burke, Strahan or both, and I can win," Jordan continued. "But what I can't do is put Gus at risk. You understand what I'm saying?"

Afraid of the answer, she shook her head. "What do you mean?"

"If things don't go as planned tonight, if I can't get one hundred percent assurance that these men will back off, then I have to move Gus immediately. I have to send him out of the country."

I'll go with him, was her first thought.

Oh, God, was her second.

Because she couldn't go with Gus. The danger would just follow her, and her son. She'd already done that to him once and couldn't do it again.

"How long would he have to be gone?" But she waved off any response. She knew how this had to play out. As long as the research for the antidote was still missing, then she couldn't be with Gus.

"I'm sorry." Jordan slid his hand over hers. "I've gone over this all day, and I can't figure out another way."

Then, giving Burke and Strahan her encrypted notes would have to work. Because the idea of not seeing her son broke her heart. This had to end soon.

"Kinley?" Jordan said. He leaned over and slipped his arm around her. "I'm not going to let anything bad happen to Gus." And he hugged her.

The hug barely lasted a second because a buzzing sound came from the console. Jordan eased away from her, took a deep breath and pressed a button. On the screen she saw not one car but two approach the warehouse. A moment later, Jordan's cell phone rang.

"Burke," Jordan answered after glancing at the caller ID screen. He zoomed in on the vehicles. "Yes, that's Martin Strahan behind you. I thought it would be beneficial if we all talked face-to-face."

Kinley couldn't hear exactly what Burke was saying, but judging from Jordan's expression, the man wasn't pleased with the additional guest at this meeting. Tough. Kinley wasn't pleased with this entire situation. Well, except for the fact that she had Jordan by her side. As bad as all of this was, she couldn't imagine getting through this without him.

She froze.

Repeated that to herself.

And mentally groaned.

She was falling for him. Not good. The last man she'd gotten involved with had nearly gotten her killed. Besides, she needed to focus on her son and not a relationship. Even if a relationship was exactly what her heart and body thought she needed.

Jordan ended the call and pressed a button that opened the door where they'd driven in. The two cars pulled in and parked behind the Porsche.

"They're alone?" she asked, watching as both men exited their cars.

"They appear to be. I have an infrared monitor, and I'm not picking up any additional heat sources in either of their vehicles."

So, maybe they would play by Jordan's rules.

Burke had stepped from his car first. Then Strahan. Burke spared Strahan a glance—a frosty one—before he looked up at the observation desk. "Jordan," he greeted, obviously able to see them through the glass.

Jordan turned on the speaker function. "Thank you for coming."

Burke tipped his head to Strahan. "You didn't mention that you were inviting him."

"No? Must have slipped my mind. I didn't figure you'd care since you two are old friends."

"Former business associates," Strahan spoke up, his voice much higher pitched than Burke's drawl. "I don't trust him. Even more, I don't like him."

"The feeling's mutual," Burke snarled before he looked up at Jordan and Kinley again. "Do you plan to stay up there in your ivory tower or come down and join us?"

"The ivory tower suits me," Jordan commented. If he was distressed by this meeting, he certainly wasn't showing it. Kinley, on the other hand, was definitely distressed. Her heart was racing, and every muscle in her body had tightened to the point of being painful.

"Well?" Strahan prompted. He impatiently checked his watch. "Care to tell me why you called this meeting?"

"The envelopes on the floor are for you. Your names are on them."

Kinley glanced at Jordan to question why he would label them with their names, since the information inside was supposedly identical, but Jordan had his attention focused on the two men.

Strahan picked up his envelope and tore it open. Burke

waited a moment before reaching down and retrieving his and doing the same. Both began to go through the pages.

"They're copies of Kinley's encrypted research notes. It shouldn't take either of you long to break the code, and when you do, I think you'll find something interesting—that Kinley doesn't know where the missing antidote is."

"So she says," Burke accused.

"No. It's the truth. She made those notes because she was trying to figure out what could have happened to the formula for the antidote before and after the research facility was destroyed in an explosion."

"And what did happen?" Strahan asked.

"I don't know," Kinley volunteered. "But I'm hoping you'll be able to figure it out when you go through those notes and compare them to what you two personally know about the situation."

"I've added copies of the federal investigation," Jordan continued. "There's also a log of everyone who entered the research facility the day it was blown up. Both your names are on the log, by the way."

That caused the men to toss each other a glare. Good. Kinley wanted them pitted against each other. Maybe that would take the focus off Gus, Jordan and her.

Strahan reached inside his jacket, causing Jordan to issue a warning. "The glass is bulletproof."

"And I'm not stupid. I wouldn't risk shooting the one woman who might be able to clear all of this up."

Maybe. Or maybe he wanted her dead for some other reason.

Strahan extracted a thick white envelope from his coat and tossed it on the floor where Jordan's had originally been. "Those are photocopies of Dexter Sheppard's final notes from the research project."

Kinley went still. Dexter's notes. She'd known they existed, of course, but she thought he had taken them with him when he faked their deaths.

She stared at the envelope.

Burke stared at it, too. "How did you get that information?" he demanded.

Strahan shrugged. "I stole Dexter's notes the night of the explosion. But before you accuse me of having the missing antidote formula, rethink that. They're just notes, and I've had men working on them for months, and they haven't been able to make heads or tails of them. I'm figuring that Kinley will be able to help. That's why I've been looking for her."

It made sense. Well, maybe. And maybe this was some kind of trick. "How did you find me?" she asked.

"Through Burke," Strahan calmly provided. "I've been watching him for months—just like he's been watching me—and lo and behold, you walk right into the Sentron Christmas party."

"You hired Anderson Walker to follow us?" Jordan demanded.

"No." Strahan seemed surprised, or something, with the question. "I used my own men. I wouldn't trust one of Burke's lackeys."

Which meant Burke had likely sent Anderson. But why? For intimidation, or was there something else behind that incident?

"Read Dexter's research notes," Strahan told her. "And get back to me. That antidote is worth more than all three of us have in our bank accounts. It's in your benefit to find it because frankly, I'm a bit desperate. I need the money back that I invested."

And desperate men did desperate things. Like trying to use her son to make her cooperate.

What other desperate things had Strahan done?

Kinley thought of Shelly Mackey and how the woman had died to protect Gus. Strahan had been involved with this from the start—including fourteen months ago when Shelly had been killed.

"Are you the one who went after Shelly?" Kinley asked, staring straight at Strahan.

She watched his eyes and saw the flash of recognition. "Shelly who?" he asked.

He was lying. Strahan must have known every little detail about Kinley, and even if he hadn't figured out that Shelly had handed Gus over to Jordan, the man would have at least known that Kinley's P.I. friend had been murdered in the midst of all this. He would have had Shelly investigated to see if she was connected to the missing formula.

Burke tipped his head to the envelope that Strahan had put on the floor. "By giving Kinley and Jordan those, you have no guarantee that if she and Jordan find the truth, they'll tell you. I'm betting they go straight to the Feds."

Strahan smiled. "I think not. Kinley understands the need to have this resolved in such a way that all parties will be, well, content."

"Are you saying we share the profits from the antidote?" Burke questioned.

"I'm saying that when Kinley gives us what we want, she'll be free to go. And you and I can then work out an acceptable compromise that will compensate us for our initial investments and the time and trouble we've gone through since this dog and pony show started."

Burke didn't look like a man on the verge of a compromise, but he also didn't argue. He turned, headed for his car and, a moment later, Strahan did the same. After the men had backed out of the warehouse, Jordan closed the doors.

"I think Strahan hired the person who killed Shelly," Kinley let Jordan know.

"I think you're right." Since Jordan didn't hesitate, he'd likely already come to the same conclusion. "But we have to prove it. A traffic camera recorded Shelly's murder. I'll have someone go through it again and see if they can match Shelly's killer to anyone on Strahan's payroll."

That seemed a long shot, but it was better than no shot at all.

"You think those are really Dexter Sheppard's notes?" Jordan asked.

"If they are, I'll be able to tell. Dexter and I worked closely, and I can recognize his handwriting."

She swallowed hard, remembering her stormy relationship with Dexter. A relationship that had produced Gus. She was thankful for that, but Kinley would never be able to forgive the man for making her life a living hell. If it hadn't been for Dexter, there wouldn't have been a shady research project, and Gus and she wouldn't be in danger now.

Jordan adjusted some of the console instruments and stood so they could leave. Kinley hurried ahead of him on the stairs and reached for the envelope.

"Wait," Jordan practically shouted. He hurried in front of her, stooped down and examined it.

"You think it's some kind of booby trap?"

"With a man like Strahan, you just don't know."

Jordan was right. She'd been so anxious to find a resolution to all of this that she'd temporarily forgotten that she couldn't trust Burke or Strahan.

Jordan used the corner of his PDA to lift the envelope so he could further study it. He must have approved of what he saw, or didn't see, because he picked it up and opened it.

It was indeed notes, and it took Kinley just a glance to realize that was Dexter's handwriting. Or else it was a very good forgery.

Jordan handed them to her, then paused. "You were in love with him?"

The question threw her a moment, because it felt a little strange talking to Jordan about her former lover. "I thought I was." She shook her head. "I didn't really know him. And if he were alive, he'd be the one trying to use Gus to get to me. Dexter wouldn't have protected him the way you have."

A muscle flickered in Jordan's jaw, and he reached out and ran his hand down her arm. It seemed as if he were about to say something. Something personal about this attraction between them. But then he must have changed his mind because he started for the car.

"We have to move Gus tonight," he said from over his shoulder.

"What? Tonight? I thought this plan stood a chance of working?"

"A chance isn't good enough. I know now that neither Burke nor Strahan will back off, not even with a bribe. They're counting on hundreds of millions of dollars from this deal, and they won't stop until they have the antidote. Or until they kill each other." He opened the car door for her. His eyes met hers and in them she saw that he was right.

Still, this would break her heart.

"Then, maybe they'll kill each other," she mumbled, getting inside the Porsche.

"I doubt we'll get that lucky." Jordan got in the car as well. "And even if we use Dexter's notes to learn the formula, we can't just give it to Strahan and Burke. We'll have to turn it over to the authorities."

"Of course." Though she had to admit, the idea of using it to get Burke and Strahan off their backs was tempting.

"They don't trust each other. That's obvious. So, maybe I can push that a little harder, give them a reason for the distrust to erupt." He started the car, opened the warehouse door and backed out. "It wouldn't have to be something to make them literally kill each other. Just enough to incriminate them so they land in jail."

"Jail," she repeated. "You think that would stop them from coming after us?"

Jordan took a deep breath and drove away. Fast. "No."

Kinley tried not to react to that. She'd known in her heart that it was true, that there was only one way this could end.

Someone would die.

The thought had no sooner formed in her head when she heard the sound. Not a blast. More like a swish. At first, Kinley thought it was the noise from the closing warehouse doors, but then the Porsche jerked violently to the right.

"Get down!" Jordan ordered. "Someone just shot out one of the tires."

CHAPTER TEN

JORDAN LATCHED ON to the steering wheel and tried to keep the Porsche steady. It was next to impossible.

Especially after the second shot.

The bullet must have gone straight into the passenger's front tire because his car jerked violently in that direction. He had no control and certainly couldn't speed away from this attack.

"The glass is bulletproof," he reminded Kinley. But that wouldn't be nearly enough to keep her safe.

He had to slow to a crawl, and by doing so, they were sitting ducks.

Jordan grabbed Kinley's hand and put it on the steering wheel. Not that it would help much, but it freed him up to draw his gun and get ready to fire. He looked around, trying to pick through the dimly lit area, but he didn't see the shooter. Then he glanced up at the flat warehouse roof.

There was a man dressed all in black and wearing a dark ski mask. If it hadn't been for the glint of the security lights on the rifle, Jordan might never have seen him.

Jordan didn't want to risk lowering the window so he could return fire. That would create an even more dangerous situation. Instead, he drove forward, creeping along, so he could put some distance between them and the shooter.

There was another shot. The bullet smashed into the back of his car. The body had been modified to be bulletproof, as well, but sparks flew from the impact.

Another shot.

Then another.

"He's not trying to kill us," Jordan mumbled. But the words had no sooner left his mouth when he saw the headlights of another car. It was coming right at them.

Jordan tried to steer to the side of the narrow road, but he had almost no control. And besides, he needed his hands free in case this turned into a full-scale attack. It was a risk—anything he did would be a risk—but he stopped.

So did the other car.

Like the vehicle from the night before, the high beams were on, and they glared right into the Porsche and made it impossible for Jordan to see. He checked the rearview mirror to make sure the rooftop gunman wasn't about to join the fight.

But the man was no longer on the roof.

Hell.

Jordan reached over to the glove compartment and took out another gun and extra magazine clips. "Do you know how to shoot?" he asked Kinley, pressing the gun into her hand.

She shook her head. "But I'll try." Even in the milky light, he could see the terror on her face. "What about Gus?"

"Cal would have called if there'd been an attack." Jordan was sure of that. He was also sure that he couldn't count on Cal to back him up here. Cal needed to stay in place at the estate.

And that meant Kinley and he were on their own.

Well, almost.

"Call nine-one-one." Jordan passed her his phone and kept watch, looking all around them while he shoved the magazine clips into his jacket pocket.

He spotted yet another car. This one was parked on the side of the warehouse with its lights off. But Jordan could clearly see the front license plate, and he recognized it: SNTRN 06.

It was a Sentron vehicle.

He cursed again. This could be a three-prong attack, including one from a former employee who was likely now on Burke's side. Or else after that ten-million-dollar reward for the missing antidote formula. Was Cody or Desmond in that car?

Kinley made the call and told the 9-1-1 dispatcher that someone was shooting at them. She gave them the address and hung up. Jordan estimated it would be at least five minutes before the cops arrived.

During that time, anything could go down.

The adrenaline spiked through him, but he kept his breathing level. Kinley couldn't manage to do the same. Her breath sawed through the small space of the interior, and he knew she was terrified.

There was movement to his right. The rooftop gunman or someone dressed exactly like him was skulking his way across the parking lot toward the Sentron car. The driver's-side door of the car in front of them opened.

And Kinley and he were trapped in the middle.

A man stepped from the car in front of them. Anderson Walker. He had a gun in his right hand and a cell phone in his left. He pressed something on the phone, and a moment later, Jordan's own cell phone rang.

"Jordan," Anderson greeted, when Jordan took the phone from Kinley and answered the call on speaker-phone. "This is how this'll work. You give us Kinley Ford, and I call off the attack that I'm about to launch on your estate."

Kinley gasped.

"Stay put." Jordan grabbed her to stop her from get-ting out.

"Why would I care if you attack my house?" Jordan bluffed.

"Because it's my guess that the kid is there."

Jordan forced himself to stay calm. They knew about Gus, and it didn't matter if they weren't sure if he was there or not. Cal might not be able to stop a full-scale attack with explosives, and Gus could be hurt.

"Who are you working for?" Jordan asked the man. Not exactly a stall tactic. He wanted to know who'd or-chestrated this. But he also wanted to buy some time for the police to arrive. Not that it would do any good, but he might be able to hurry out of this situation and get back to the estate so he could assist Cal. He'd need a car with undamaged tires for that, and a police cruiser would work.

"This isn't time for talking," Anderson answered. "I figure you've already called the cops or one of your G.I. Joe pals and that you're trying to figure out how to get out of this. Well, there's only one way. So, I'm giving you ten seconds to hand over Kinley."

"I have to do as he says." She reached for the door handle, but again Jordan stopped her.

"They'll torture you to get the antidote. Maybe kill you because you won't be able to give them what they want. And with all of that, there's still no guarantee that by sacrificing yourself, you'll be protecting Gus."

The color drained from her face, and her bottom lip trembled. He leaned over, gave her a quick kiss and got mentally ready for what he had to do. Jordan had no plans to die, but it was a distinct possibility.

"I'm getting out," he told her. When Kinley started to shake her head, he caught her chin and forced eye contact. "You stay put. I'll lead them away from the car, but if anyone tries to get in, you shoot them. Understand?"

She was still shaking her head, but he didn't have time to negotiate with her. He knew what he had to do, and that was make himself a decoy and hope that he could dodge enough bullets until the cops arrived.

Jordan opened the door, hit the lock switch and stepped out. He closed the door, locking her inside. She said something to him, something he couldn't understand. Something he shut out. Because right now the only thing he wanted on his mind was keeping them alive.

He crouched down, using his car as cover from the rifleman in black, but there could be others waiting to attack. Including the person in the Sentron vehicle.

"I said I wanted Kinley," Anderson yelled.

"Yeah, I know. You're not going to get her." Jordan turned, aimed his gun at Anderson. And he knew exactly what the man would do.

Anderson aimed back.

And fired.

Jordan ducked, letting the reinforced body of the Porsche take the bullet. Then he returned fire. The shot slammed into Anderson's shoulder and sent the man staggering backward.

There was another shot. From a different weapon, a different angle. It took Jordan a moment to realize the point of origin.

Kinley.

She had her window partly down and had shot at the man with the rifle. *Hell*. That glass was her only protection.

"Kinley, no!" Jordan shouted.

But she fired again.

And missed.

The rifleman dove behind the concrete pylon that held the streetlight in place.

Jordan glanced at Anderson. The man dropped to the ground. Probably not because he was dead. He was merely injured and therefore still dangerous. Kinley and he could still be caught in cross fire.

He heard the siren from a police car. That didn't make Jordan breathe any easier. This was the deadly time, when Anderson and the other man would either try to escape or make a stand.

Jordan didn't have to wait long to find out which.

The rifleman started shooting at them. Not single shots, but a stream of deadly gunfire.

"Put up your window," Jordan told Kinley.

She did. Thank God. But then she reached over and opened his door. "Get in," she insisted.

Since the gaping opening from the door was a bad idea, Jordan fired off several shots at the gunman, added another round in Anderson's direction, and then he dove inside so he could slam the door shut behind him.

The shots continued pelting into Jordan's car. One slammed into the glass, webbing it, but it held in place.

Jordan spotted the flashing blue lights from the police cruiser as it turned onto the road that led to the row of warehouses. The shooter obviously saw it, too, because he stopped firing, and Jordan saw him start to run. He wanted to follow in pursuit, so he could learn the person's identity and apprehend him.

But Jordan couldn't do that.

It would leave Kinley vulnerable and in grave danger.

The Sentron car started to move as well. The driver didn't come in their direction but instead turned around and made an exit behind the warehouse.

Anderson, however, didn't budge.

Which meant the man might be dead after all. Jordan hadn't intended that. He needed answers from Anderson, and a dead man wouldn't be able to tell him who'd hired him to kidnap Kinley.

With the sirens wailing, the cruiser came to a stop just on the other side of Anderson's vehicle. The Hispanic officer who got out had his weapon drawn. So did his partner, a female uniformed cop who couldn't have been much older than twenty-one.

Anderson still didn't move.

Jordan reholstered his gun and handed Kinley his phone. "Call the estate. Speak to Cal and make sure everything is okay."

He got out, raising his hands so that the cops wouldn't think he was the bad guy. "I'm Jordan Taylor," he announced.

"From Sentron," one of the cops added with a confirming nod. "I'm Detective Sanchez." He looked at the man on the ground. "What happened here, Mr. Taylor?"

Jordan took a moment, debating how much he should say and how he should say it. "I'm not sure. When my friend and I came out of my warehouse, someone shot at us, and I returned fire. There's another gunman. Maybe two. They escaped that way." He pointed in the direction in which the Sentron car had gone. "What about the man I shot? Is he dead?"

The second officer stooped down while her partner kept watch. Not just of the area but of Jordan. "He's alive, for now," the woman announced, and Jordan heard her call for an ambulance and backup.

"What about you and your friend?" Sanchez asked, walking closer. But he barely looked at Jordan. He was still keeping an eye on their surroundings. "Are you hurt?"

Jordan looked in at Kinley. She had the cell phone pressed to her ear. She was shaken—and shaking—but they weren't injured. At least not physically. "We're okay."

Sanchez nodded, though he still seemed wary. With good reason. Jordan's Porsche was riddled with pockmarks from the impact of the bullets and a man was lying shot and bleeding on the ground. There'd be reports and an investigation, Jordan knew, but those were things that could wait. First, he had to know if Gus was all right.

"Cal," he finally heard Kinley say.

She didn't have the phone on speaker so he couldn't hear what Cal was saying.

There was a blur of movement from the corner of

his eye, and Jordan automatically ducked down. With his gun aimed and ready, Sanchez turned in the direction of the sound. And Jordan got a glimpse of what was going on.

The gunman dressed all in black leaned out from the side of the warehouse and raised his rifle.

At Jordan.

Sanchez reacted quickly and fired. There was the sound of metal slicing through metal when the detective's bullet slammed into the warehouse. The gunman turned and started to run, following the path that the Sentron car had taken just moments earlier.

Sanchez went in pursuit and disappeared around the side of the building. Jordan was about to provide some assistance, but then he heard the voice. Not Kinley's.

Cal's.

She'd put the call on speaker and was holding it out so that Jordan could hear. Her hand was shaking.

"I was already on the phone to call you. Some men just arrived outside the estate," Cal said. "Three that I can see on the security monitors. They're all wearing ski masks."

Hell.

Jordan jumped back into the car. "What's your immediate status, Cal?"

"The men haven't broken in, and I've already called my brother at SAPD. But I'm in serious need of backup. Get here fast, Jordan."

CHAPTER ELEVEN

KINLEY'S HEART WAS in her throat.

It seemed as if Detective Sanchez was crawling along in the cruiser, but she knew he was going as fast as he possibly could. No speed would have been fast enough.

At first the two cops on the scene at the warehouse hadn't exactly wanted to give Jordan and her permission to go, but as soon as backup and the ambulance had arrived, Jordan had convinced them that this was an emergency. So there was now another cruiser with blaring sirens behind them and others en route. Kinley didn't mind. She wanted every cop in the city at the estate so they could stop her son from being kidnapped.

When Sanchez turned the corner, she spotted the two cruisers already in front of the house. The blue strobe lights sliced through the semidark street, and there was a pair of uniformed officers on the front lawn.

No sign of any gunmen.

Thank God.

Jordan threw open the cruiser door before Sanchez brought his car to a full stop. Kinley was right behind them with Dexter's notes tucked beneath her arm, and they sprinted past the officers to get to the house.

"He's the owner," Sanchez verified to the other officers.

Jordan practically knocked down the front door, and they raced into the foyer. Cal was there, talking to a man in civilian clothes. "This is my brother, Lt. Joe Rico, SAPD."

"Is everything secure?" Kinley asked, choosing her words carefully. She had no idea how much Cal had revealed to his brother. Hopefully nothing about Gus.

"Everything's safe," Cal assured her. "The intruders left when the cops arrived. They didn't get in."

Kinley tried to catch her breath, but it was hard. The adrenaline had already soared through her, preparing her for a fight. She grabbed on to Jordan, and he pulled her into his arms. Gus was safe. The kidnapper hadn't managed to get to him.

Joe Rico studied them with eyes that were a genetic copy of his brother's but with a lot more suspicion. "I got a phone report of what went on at your warehouse. I'm guessing these incidents are related to the explosion that happened earlier?"

"Probably." Jordan eased away from her so he could face the officer. "This is Kinley Ford. She's in the federal witness protection program, and someone obviously wants to get to her."

The brothers exchanged glances. And concerned expressions. "Do you want SAPD to provide protection?" Joe asked.

Jordan seemed to have a debate with himself before he finally nodded. "Maybe they can patrol the immediate area just for tonight. Until I can make other arrangements."

Joe nodded too and gave a heavy sigh. "I'll contact

the FBI and let them know what's going on. There'll be reports to do. And I'll need to get your statements."

"Of course," Jordan agreed. "I've already given Detective Sanchez the weapons we fired."

The lieutenant glanced at her and obviously noted the fear and weariness. "Your statements can wait until later. I'll send a uniform over to take them. Do either of you need to see a medic?"

"No," Jordan and Kinley said in unison, and the responses were loaded with impatience. Even though he was Cal's brother and a likely ally, Kinley wanted him out of there so she could check on Gus.

"Lock down the place," Joe said to his brother. "Call me when you decide what you need me to do. I'll wait out front." And he headed for the door.

None of them said anything until Joe was gone and the security system had been reset. "We have to move Gus immediately," Jordan instructed Cal.

"Yeah. That's what I figured. I have the vehicle and everything ready, just like we discussed. I'll use my brother for backup."

Kinley hadn't been part of that discussion, but she trusted these men, especially Jordan. However, she didn't trust their situation. Jordan had come close to dying tonight, and these arrangements seemed to be happening way too fast.

"Let's get this moving," Jordan insisted. He hurried down the hall to his office. But stopped when his PDA beeped. He cursed. "Someone's monitoring us, probably with a thermal scanner."

"Please, no," Kinley mumbled. It meant someone,

maybe one of those gunmen, had gotten close enough to the house.

Kinley considered going to the basement to see Gus, but she knew this would be the faster way to see her son. Jordan clicked on the surveillance, and on the screen, she saw the nannies waiting in the playroom. Pamela was holding a sleeping Gus in her arms. His head was resting on her shoulder, and she had a blanket draped around him.

"It's time to leave," Jordan said through the intercom that carried his voice into the playroom. "Go into the garage through the basement entrance."

Kinley started for the door. "I want to say goodbye to him."

But Jordan got up and caught on to her. "Sorry. You can't. They're monitoring us, and we can't risk it."

Oh, God. It felt as if someone had clamped a fist around her heart. But Jordan was right. She couldn't put Gus in any more danger.

"How will Cal get him out?" Kinley heard her voice trembling but couldn't stop it.

"We have a plan. The car in the garage is armored and with tinted windows and a thermal blocker for the back area where Gus and one of the nannies will be. It will appear that only Cal is leaving."

"But what if someone follows him?"

"His brother will monitor that. He'll trail behind Cal to a small private airport about twenty miles from here."

She choked back a gasp. "An airport?"

"It'll be safer if he's completely out of the area. Cal's taking him to a place near Houston. For now. If things heat up, we'll move him again."

Kinley had to sit down, but she refused to lose it. She couldn't cry because if she started, she might not stop.

"We need some distractions," Jordan told her. "Find the number to the prison where your research partner, Brenna Martel, is being held. Use the phone in the hall. It isn't secure. Someone will be able to monitor the call."

She shook her head. "Why would you want that?"

"I want them to hear. Burke, Strahan and anyone else involved in this will want to know what Brenna has to say, so ask to speak to her. If the guards won't let you, which they probably won't, then leave her a message asking her about any research notes she made. If they exist, you want a copy. If not, you want to set up a meeting to discuss everything she remembers."

She managed a nod and hoped she could remember all of that. Her head was far from clear, and the only thing she wanted to think about was her baby.

"While you're doing that, I'll find out who was in that Sentron car parked at the warehouse," Jordan continued. "I'll make waves while I'm doing it."

Kinley prayed the waves worked. Anything to give her son a head start.

She went several feet away to the phone on a hall table, and using directory assistance, she got the number of Claridge Prison. Kinley made her way through the automated answering system until she finally got to speak to a person at the guards' desk.

"I need to get an urgent message to an inmate, Brenna Martel." She glanced at Jordan, who was making his own call, while she listened to the man tell her why she wouldn't be able to speak to any of the prisoners tonight. However, he took her message about needing the notes and said he would relay it to Brenna and her attorney. Kinley didn't know when or if Brenna would get back to her, but it was a start and maybe the diversion they needed while moving Gus.

Jordan was still on the phone when she went back into his office, but he had the images of the nursery rooms and basement on the screen. Pamela had Gus still cradled in her arms while she, Cal and Elsa were making their way through the basement. With some keystrokes on the security system, Jordan zoomed in on Gus's sleeping face.

Tears sprang to Kinley's eyes. It was so unfair. Here, she'd finally found her precious baby and had had mere hours with him, and now he was being whisked away. Heaven knew how long it would be before she'd see him again.

Jordan ended the call, stood and watched the images with her. Cal and others entered the garage through stairs that led up from the basement, and without wasting even a second, Cal got Pamela, Gus and himself into a black SUV. Pamela sat in the backseat with Gus. Elsa, however, went to another vehicle in the massive garage. A dark green van. She was obviously going to be a decoy. And from the front security camera, Kinley could see Cal's brother waiting to follow and back them up.

"What about the thermal scanner?" she asked. "Please tell me it couldn't detect them while they were getting into the vehicles."

"It couldn't. The stairs and the garage are protected, and that blanket around Gus will block the scanner. Pamela will keep it over him until they're on the airplane."

So many details, and yet Jordan had seemingly addressed them all despite the distraction of the warehouse attack and the earlier explosion.

"The vehicles will leave at the same time," Jordan let her know. "Once they get on the interstate, Elsa will take the first exit in the opposite direction, toward the San Antonio international airport. If it looks as if no one is following them, an unmarked police car will tail Elsa, to make it look as if Gus is in the van. Cal's brother, Joe, will continue to follow Cal's SUV."

It was a solid plan. As safe as Jordan could possibly make it. But that didn't stop her from being terrified. Because no plan was foolproof, and that meant her son was at risk no matter what they did.

"What about your call?" he asked.

Kinley didn't take her eyes off the screen. "I had to leave a message with the prison guard. What about you, any luck?"

"Not yet. But I'm running a computer search of Sentron's records to find out who was in that car at the warehouse."

Yes. Because that person might not have only had a part in this. He might even be the ringleader.

"Whoever was in that car knew we were in danger," Jordan verified. "He knew someone was either trying to kill us or kidnap us, and yet he sat there and watched it happen."

So, this person could have been Anderson's boss. Or someone else who wanted to use her to try to get that antidote. In other words, definitely not a friend.

Her money was on Burke.

He could have easily switched out vehicles, even though she couldn't imagine why he would do that. If he wanted to watch them, why hadn't he used a car that Jordan wouldn't have easily recognized? Maybe because Burke had wanted them to know he would use Sentron resources against Jordan and her.

Was this part of their game meant to intimidate her?

If so, it was working.

She watched as Cal shut the back door of the SUV, and she could no longer see Gus. A moment later, Cal was behind the wheel and backed out of the garage. He waited until Elsa was right behind him.

And they drove away.

Out of sight.

Kinley forced herself to hold her emotions together, and she was succeeding. Until Jordan slipped his arm around her waist and pulled her to him. Just like that, she shattered. And the tears came in spite of the fight she had put up to stop them.

"He'll be okay," Jordan said, comforting her, though from the slight tremble in his voice, it was obvious he needed some comforting as well.

Gus was his son in every way that mattered, and he'd raised the child even though he could have easily turned that duty over to someone else. But he hadn't. And that's why Kinley had to trust what he was doing now.

Jordan placed his PDA on the counter next to them and showed her the little blips. "That's the car Gus is in," he said, pointing to the green one. "The red blip belongs to Elsa. The blue, to Joe. The yellow one is the unmarked police car tailing Elsa."

Other blips appeared on the screen. Obviously other vehicles on the road. But none stayed close to Cal.

They stood there, watching. Praying. Kinley was saying a lot of prayers. The minutes ticked off with the blips making their way on the GPS-style map. Finally, after what seemed an eternity, Elsa's car and the unmarked police vehicle turned toward the San Antonio airport. Cal went in the other direction.

"No one's following them." The relief was all through Jordan's voice.

Still, they didn't take their attention from the PDA. She wasn't sure how much time passed, but she watched the green blip make its way along the highway that led out of the city limits. The road must have been fairly isolated because the only blips belonged to Cal and his brother.

"They're at the private airport," Jordan finally said.

And they waited again. Kinley held her breath so long that her lungs began to ache.

Then, the phone rang, the sound slicing through the room.

Jordan snatched it up. "Cal," he answered obviously seeing the man's number on the screen.

Kinley couldn't hear the conversation. Nor could she move. She just stood there and said a dozen more prayers.

"They're on the plane," Jordan said, ending the call. "Gus is safe."

He caught her to stop her from staggering. It was in the nick of time. The relief was overwhelming. Jordan had succeeded. Her son was safe.

Kinley looked up at him. His expression was a mixture of joy and relief. But some sadness, too. She understood that completely. Gus was safe, but he wasn't with them.

Since she was already in Jordan's arms, Kinley let

him support her. Yes, it was a risk. The white-hot attraction was always there, but there was something else. Some strange intimacy that perhaps only parents of a young child could have shared. For some reason, that made her emotions run even higher.

It made the attraction even stronger.

She wished for more. That it would consume her. Overwhelm her. That it would make her forget what was going on with Gus.

"Oh, hell," Jordan mumbled.

At first Kinley thought he was saying that in reaction to something he saw on the screen, but he was looking at her. "This is an adrenaline reaction," he said.

A split second before he kissed her.

Yes. It probably *was* an adrenaline reaction. And a human one. Kinley didn't doubt that she needed him in this most basic human way.

This was what she'd asked for. Something to overwhelm her. Jordan was certainly capable of doing that and more.

"We're still being monitored with the thermal scan," he whispered against her mouth.

Kinley tried to think of the consequences of that. Burke, Strahan or someone else might be seeing the heated images of their bodies. The kiss would be easy to detect, even though they'd be just thermal blobs on the scan. This was still an invasion of a very intimate moment.

But Kinley didn't care.

She wasn't going to give this up because someone had them under thermal surveillance.

"Consider it a diversion," Kinley whispered back.

But this was as much a diversion for her as it was for anyone who might be watching. Still, it might be a good idea if it distracted the person responsible for the surveillance.

Soon, though, that thought slid right out of her mind.

That's because Jordan continued to kiss her.

Yes, she was definitely being overwhelmed, and it'd never felt so right.

He slid his hands into her hair, angling her head so he could deepen the kiss. Kinley went right along with it, and even though nothing could have made her forget her son, she needed this moment. She needed Jordan.

She felt her back press against his office door and realized Jordan was leaning into her. Good. She wanted him against her, and Kinley hooked her arm around his waist to drag him even closer. Until closer was as close as two bodies could get. Almost.

His kiss was clever. Not too hard. Not too soft. It was as if he'd found the perfect tempo and pressure to coax every bit of the passion from her. But the kiss also did something else; it revved up the attraction. The need.

The kiss turned from clever to frantic, and he slid his hand down her waist. He found the back of her thigh and lifted her leg so that it was anchored against his. The new position created some interesting pressure, especially when his sex touched hers.

Kinley lost her breath.

And didn't care if she ever found it.

"I can stop," Jordan suggested.

Kinley didn't look at him. Didn't listen. She didn't want to hear the voice of reason. But what did she want?

Full-blown sex?

That certainly wouldn't be wise right now since Gus was on the way to the airport and Jordan was waiting on a computer scan. Oh, and there were cops outside the estate who could come knocking at any minute. They didn't have time for sex.

Or did they?

Jordan moved his mouth to her neck. To the V of her shirt. And he shoved it down so he could kiss the top of her right breast. There went her breath again, and Kinley had no choice but to hang on to him and enjoy this crazy, forbidden moment.

His hand was still gripping her leg, holding it in place, but he also caught the bottom of her skirt.

"Sorry," he said. "This will be way too fast."

She shook her head, not understanding. But then he pushed her skirt up to her waist and just like that his hand went into her panties. And his fingers went into her.

Kinley moaned. Nearly lost her balance. But Jordan hung on to her, anchoring her in place with his body. He worked magic with those fingers but behind his hand was what she really wanted.

She pushed his hand away so she could unzip his pants. But he caught her wrist. "I can't think if we do that."

"It'll be quick," she bargained.

Jordan's jaw muscles stirred. He grimaced. But he didn't stop her when she shook off his grip and reached for his zipper again. He was huge and hard, and that didn't make things easy, but she managed to lower his zipper and take him into her hand.

That was apparently the only foreplay they would

have because he dragged off her panties and hoisted her up, sandwiching her between the door and him.

Since time seemed to matter, Kinley didn't waste any of it. Maybe because if they stopped to think, this wouldn't happen. And her body wanted desperately for it to happen.

She wrapped her legs around him, and he entered her. He didn't stay still, didn't give himself a moment to savor the sensation. He moved once. One long stroke that shot the pleasure straight through her.

But then he stopped.

Just like that, he stopped.

With a groan rumbling deep within his throat, Jordan ground his forehead against hers. "Bad timing," he grumbled. "Really bad."

She shook her head and tried to think of what she could say to make him continue. But before she could speak, he shoved his hand back between their bodies and used his fingers instead of his sex.

"I want you," she clarified.

"I want you. Too much. But I don't have a condom here. They're in the bedroom, and I need to stay here to keep an eye on the monitor. I promise, I'll do better later."

He didn't give her a chance to object. Didn't give her a chance to do anything but go mindless. He touched her in just the right place. With the right pressure. But what caused Kinley to soar was seeing his face. Kissing him.

It was Jordan who sent her over the edge.

Even as the sensations still rippled through her, she instantly regretted it. Not the act itself, not the intimacy, but because she'd been the one to get all the pleasure here. Jordan had remained in control.

He kissed her again. There was control there, too. And he eased her from him so she could stand. He fixed his pants and even located her panties so he could hand them to her.

And the awkwardness settled in around them.

"I'm—" But she didn't know how to finish that.

"Don't think for one minute that I didn't want to have sex with you. I do. I *really* do." He cursed. "I just need to have a clear head right now, understand?"

"Yes." But that didn't stop her from being embarrassed. "And I, uh, need to start going over Dexter's notes." Something she should have started instead of kissing Jordan.

Right.

Who was she kidding? She couldn't have stopped kissing him any more than she could stop worrying about Gus. Jordan had gotten under her skin, and she was afraid he was there to stay. Great. Just what she needed. Another broken heart.

There was a beeping sound, and Kinley forced herself to come back to earth. To focus. Jordan did the same and hurried to one of the many computers.

"Is it about Gus?" she asked, afraid to hear the answer.

"No. I just got back the results of that computer search for the Sentron car that was parked at the warehouse."

So he had the identity of the person who'd sat and watched as they'd nearly been killed. "Was it Burke in the car?"

"No." Jordan scrubbed his hand over his face and groaned. "It was Cody Guillory."

CHAPTER TWELVE

Jordan took a gulp of the strong coffee and hoped the caffeine would kick in soon.

Eventually, Kinley and he would have to sleep. He wanted to keep going. He wanted to find the person creating the danger so he could stop him and bring Gus home. But he was exhausted. Kinley, too, though she wouldn't admit it. The caffeine had to buy them a little more time before they would no doubt collapse.

After an officer from SAPD had taken their statements about the attempted kidnapping and shooting, Kinley had taken a couple of catnaps in his office while still in the process of going over Dexter Sheppard's research notes. Jordan knew this because even though he'd spent most of the night in his bedroom coordinating the new living arrangements for Gus, he'd checked on her and twice he'd found her dozing with her face literally pressed against the notes. The other dozen or so times, she'd been hard at work staring at the pages.

He poured Kinley a cup of coffee as well—it'd be her sixth of the day—and he walked out of the kitchen and through the foyer. The Christmas lights were still on, and with the broken crystal ornaments littering the floor like diamonds, the place managed to look festive. Even if it wasn't.

It wasn't shaping up to be much of a peaceful Christmas Eve.

He'd wanted this to be a special holiday for Gus. For months, Jordan had bought presents and hidden them away. He'd planned on spending the day opening those presents and relaxing with the little boy. A prelude to the move.

A move that'd come early, of course, thanks to the danger.

Jordan had no idea when they'd get around to opening those presents now, and a relaxing day just wasn't in his immediate future.

Looking at the tree, he thought of Kinley. There'd be no real Christmas for her, either, and he wished he'd had the time to buy her some kind of gift. But maybe the best gift he could give her was to distance himself from her. He wasn't doing her any favors by having sex with her. She was an emotional wreck right now, and he needed to give her space so she could sort out her feelings and get the right mind-set for motherhood.

He drew in a weary breath and went to his office. Kinley was still there, seated at the long counter that held monitors, computers and security equipment. She looked up at him and offered a thin smile.

So much for his little pep talk about giving her some space.

Despite her sleep-starved eyes and the impossible situation they were in, he still wanted her.

"I thought you could use this," he said, and set the coffee next to the notes.

"Thanks." She made a sound of pleasure when she took the first sip. "What's the latest from Cal?"

"I called him about fifteen minutes ago. It's all good. Gus is settled in an estate near Houston. I've been there. With all the security modifications Cal has made, it's a safe place. Gus will be fine while we wrap up things here."

"Yes." Definitely not a sound of pleasure but of disappointment and frustration. God knew when they'd actually be able to wrap up things. "And the thermal scanner situation? Are we still being monitored?"

"No. It stopped several hours ago." Which could be a good or bad sign. Maybe the person had given up. Or maybe he was just lying in wait and trying to come up with a new plan as to the best way to kidnap Kinley.

"What about Anderson Walker?" she asked. "I don't suppose he's said anything yet about who his boss is so the police can make an arrest?"

Jordan shook his head. "He's in the hospital, recovering from the gunshot wound. And he lawyered up and isn't saying a word. But maybe if we figure who's behind this, Anderson might be willing to make a deal."

Might being the crucial word.

Anderson almost certainly wouldn't get through this without some serious jail time, but he might not get a good enough deal to force him to cooperate and do the right thing.

Strahan was another matter.

"Cal's brother, Lt. Rico from the San Antonio police, studied the disk of Shelly's murder. He thinks he might have an ID on her killer—a guy named Pete Mendenhall."

Kinley's eyes widened. "Does this guy work for Strahan?"

"We don't know yet. SAPD tried to do a facial recognition match right after Shelly died, but her killer wasn't in any of the databases."

"But he is now?" she clarified.

Jordan nodded. "Not a criminal database, though, but there are a lot more faces and names in the facial recognition system than there were fourteen months ago. Rico got a hit. When he brings in this Pete Mendenhall for questioning, he'll try to link him to Strahan."

And maybe Strahan could be arrested for murder.

"What about Dexter's notes?" Jordan asked.

Her look of frustration went up a notch. "Well, I've solved most of the code but only because I was familiar with it. It's something he used often during his research, even though there are a few entries that don't follow the normal pattern."

"But you're sure they're his notes and not a forgery?"

She nodded. "Oh, they're his. There are some summaries about failed experiments that happened only when Dexter and I were in the lab. No one else would have known about them. That makes them authentic."

That was a start. "Anything about the missing antidote yet?"

"Yes and no. His research for the antidote is here, but he didn't include just one formula but nearly a hundred. I've started to run them on the computer, but the first five took me over eight hours to do."

Jordan wasn't surprised. Dexter wouldn't have plainly stated something like that in notes that could be found. Or stolen.

"I'll keep working," she insisted.

"Maybe after a nap?"

She blinked. And he caught the gist of her surprise. She no doubt wondered if he was inviting her to his bed. As good as that sounded—and it sounded damn good—it couldn't happen right now.

"This morning I called Burke, Cody, Desmond and Strahan. I have a two o'clock video conference set up with them." And that meant he could expect to hear from them any minute.

"Desmond?" she questioned. "I understand why you'd want to talk to the others, but why him?"

Jordan shrugged. "He was here minutes before the explosion."

She took a sip of coffee and peered at him over the rim of the cup. "And his motive?"

"Maybe the same as Cody's? Money that they think they could get from the antidote. Or the reward. Ten million is a lot of cash, and it has to be a serious temptation."

"But these are men you trained. You know them."

"Yeah, I do." That's why he had to at least consider they could do something like this. "There are parts of the job that require some, well, moral flexibility. That character trait that made them good agents might not keep them loyal to me."

She stared at him. Then sighed. "I was stunned when Dexter betrayed me so I understand."

The house phone rang before Jordan could say anything. He glanced at the caller ID. "Raymond Myers?"

Kinley sprang from her seat. "That's Brenna Martel's attorney." She grabbed the phone and answered it. Jordan put it on speaker.

"Ms. Ford, my client wanted me to contact you right away."

"Yes. Thank you. I left a message for her at the prison." Kinley stood soldier straight and stared at the phone.

"She got the message. And she does indeed have notes about the research project you both worked on. I have those notes, and several days ago, Brenna had instructed me to give a copy to Mr. Burke Dennison."

"Burke?" Kinley questioned.

Jordan silently cursed. Now, why hadn't Burke mentioned it? Jordan didn't have to guess why. Burke had likely been on this from the start.

Kinley scowled. "Mr. Myers, those notes are critical. You could say a matter of life and death."

"Yes. Brenna indicated that." He paused. "She instructed me to offer you a deal. She's authorized me to fax you copies if you'll agree to be a character witness at her upcoming trial."

The idea of that turned Jordan's stomach. Brenna had kidnapped Kinley, and he didn't want Kinley to have to endure something like vouching for the woman.

"I'll do it," Kinley told the attorney.

Jordan was certain he was scowling, too, but there was nothing he could do about it. He would have done the same thing because those notes could help them keep Gus safe.

"Good. The notes are in a safety deposit box. I'll leave now and fax them directly from there. You should have them within the hour."

"Thank you." Kinley reached down, clicked the end call button. "Once I have them, I can compare them to Dexter's and mine," she told Jordan.

Yes, and work hours and hours to try to figure out

which formula was real and which were decoys. "Maybe I can help once this video conference is done."

She thanked him for the offer, sipped her coffee and looked a million miles away. Jordan understood that look. Despite all the other things they had to resolve, she was still thinking about Gus.

And that gave Jordan an idea of what he could get her for Christmas.

The phone on the communications console rang, and Jordan knew that was his cue. "Burke and the others are obviously ready."

He turned on the video feed, but he didn't make it two way just yet. He wanted a moment to study the scene. All four men were in the Sentron command center. None looked happy about having their Christmas interrupted like this. Tough. Jordan wanted answers, and he didn't care how much they were inconvenienced. Of course, one of them was no doubt there with the hopes of finding the missing antidote.

But which one?

Or was that the reason they were there?

"You should probably try to take a nap," Jordan suggested to her.

"Right. As if I'd miss this."

He was afraid she would say that. He certainly would have stayed put if she'd been the one telling him to take a nap. This conversation was critical, and Jordan decided it was a good time to place as many cards as he could on the table.

He hit the transmit-feed button so that the four men could see Kinley and him. "Now, which one of you tried to have Kinley kidnapped last night?" Jordan started.

Silence.

Not exactly the reaction he'd hoped for. He'd thought that Cody and Desmond would at least deny it.

"Well?" Jordan prompted.

"I'm insulted you'd ask that of me," Cody finally responded. Desmond echoed the same.

"I didn't," Strahan almost cheerfully volunteered. "I think Anderson Walker was acting alone. I believe he wanted all that reward money for himself. He got greedy."

Maybe. Jordan prayed that were true since it would mean none of these four was a danger. But he couldn't risk thinking that way.

"Burke," Jordan said, looking at the man. "Any reason you didn't tell us that Brenna Martel had given you her research notes?"

Burke shrugged. "That was a private business arrangement and not nearly as helpful as you might think. Without Dexter Sheppard's notes, I'm one-third in the dark." He tossed a stony glance at Strahan, who had those notes but had obviously chosen not to share them with Burke.

So, if Strahan didn't have Brenna's notes and Burke didn't have Dexter's, then that meant they each had two-thirds of the picture. Soon, within the hour maybe, Kinley and he would have all three sets. However, Jordan didn't intend to share that bit of information with anyone just yet.

"There's a lot of distrust in this room," Strahan continued. "I have a suggestion. You tell these two wannabe rich guys to take a hike." He tipped his head first to Cody, then to Desmond. "Burke and I are the wronged investors here."

"But anyone can collect the reward for finding the antidote," Desmond pointed out.

Which, of course, gave him motive.

"You'd risk Kinley's life for a reward?" Jordan asked.

Desmond shrugged. "Her life doesn't have to be risked to find the antidote."

"No, but it sure as hell has been." So had Gus's. "Plus, there's the matter of Shelly's death."

Desmond shrugged again. "I didn't even know about the antidote back then."

Cody still stayed silent.

"As I was saying," Strahan continued, "let's get Cody and Desmond out of here. Other than greed over that reward, they don't have anything to bring to this equation. Then, Burke, the two of you and I will pour through all three sets of notes together. We'll learn the truth, and none of us here are afraid of the truth, are we?"

That put a knot in Jordan's stomach. He turned a notepad so that Kinley could see it, and he wrote, "Did Dexter say anything in those notes about you being pregnant?"

She didn't have much of a reaction, other than a trembling hand when she wrote. "Maybe. I've been working on decrypting the formulas. I haven't tried to figure out the rest of it."

Hell. Jordan should have anticipated this.

"Burke, are you in on this offer?" Jordan asked.

Burke shoved his hands in the pockets of his perfectly tailored suit. "Yes. With one condition. Only Strahan and I will collect the profits from this. Cody and Desmond are nothing more than former employees to me. They've both been given their notice and won't be returning in the new year."

So, Burke had fired them, even though Burke had given his word that he'd keep on all the key staff when he assumed ownership of Sentron. That explained some of the tension he saw on Cody and Desmond's faces.

And maybe something else.

Maybe Burke hadn't fired them after all, and this was merely a ploy to use whatever means necessary to find that antidote.

"You shouldn't have sold Sentron," Cody accused, staring right into the camera and therefore right at Jordan. "Early retirement? You're not the retiring kind, Jordan. And if you wanted a break, you could have temporarily put me in charge." He looked away, cursed. "Instead, you sold me—all of us—to the highest bidder. To a man who cares nothing about Sentron except for how much money it can make him. Now Desmond and I are out of a job."

He'd sold Sentron because of Gus. Because Jordan had wanted every penny in case they had to hide out indefinitely. But he couldn't say that to Cody or Desmond. He couldn't make them understand.

And by doing so, he'd made enemies of them.

"I'm sorry," Jordan said, hoping it conveyed his sincerity.

Judging from the agents' expressions, it didn't.

Later, after this was over, he could do more to make amends. Right now, though, he had enough to deal with, and saying anything could endanger Gus.

"Kinley and I will get back to you with our decision," Jordan announced.

He didn't give them time to object. He cut the feed so they couldn't see or hear Kinley and him. However, Jordan continued to observe the four. Nothing was said, probably because they knew he'd still be watching and listening. But the glances they gave each other were not ones of trust. One by one, the men filed out and Jordan cut the feed completely.

"So, Cody and Desmond do have motive," Kinley commented.

Yeah. All four did, and it came down to money. The worst motive because it was hard to reason with greed.

Still, Jordan couldn't totally surrender to the idea that Cody was pissed off enough at him to go after Kinley. Of course, Cody technically wasn't trying to hurt her if he only wanted to collect the reward.

However, that didn't mean he wasn't endangering her by trying to get to the truth. Desmond, too.

"I need to see about putting some pressure on Anderson Walker to reveal the identity of the person who hired him," Jordan said, more to himself than her. He reached for the phone, but he heard the beep from the fax machine. A moment later, a page started to feed through.

Kinley hurried to the machine. "Brenna's notes," she explained.

Good. So the lawyer and Brenna had come through after all. Now he prayed that Kinley would be able to use them to find out the formula to the antidote.

Kinley gathered the pages as the machine spit them out. "She used the same format as Dexter," she observed. "Different encryption, though."

Which would make things harder.

"I'm pretty sure this encryption is a list of formulas," Kinley continued. "But only about twenty. I can compare these to Dexter's and narrow down which formulas are strong possibilities."

With her attention riveted to the notes, she blindly made her way back to her chair, and rather than take her eyes off the pages, she groped for the seat and then dropped down into it.

He'd leave her to the formula, especially since he had more calls to make. First, about putting some pressure on Anderson to name his boss. Then he needed to do some digging into Cody's and Desmond's latest activities to see exactly how much of a threat they were.

Oh, and he still wanted that Christmas present for Kinley.

Jordan headed for his bedroom so he could get to work.

CHAPTER THIRTEEN

THE CORRECT FORMULA had to be there, somewhere in the combined notes. Kinley was sure of it. But it seemed to be just out of her reach.

What was the problem?

Why couldn't she make any of the formulas work?

She grabbed her mug, because she needed another hit of caffeine, only to realize it was empty again. She'd lost count of how many times Jordan had filled it for her. Lost count of just how much coffee she'd consumed in the past twenty-four hours, but she knew it was enough to make her feel all raw and jittery.

She stood to go into the kitchen and fill it herself, but the phone on the console rang. She glanced at the caller ID screen.

It was Cal Rico.

Just like that, Kinley's heart jumped to her throat, and she grabbed the phone so she could answer it. "Cal, what's wrong?"

"Nothing," he answered just as quickly. "Jordan said I should call you at midnight."

Midnight? Her gaze flew to the clock on the bottom of the laptop screen. It was indeed that late. She had no idea where the time had gone.

"I'm supposed to give you your Christmas present," Cal told her.

"What Christmas present?" But an answer wasn't necessary because the image popped onto one of the screens mounted on the wall.

Gus.

There he was, sleeping peacefully in a crib. Just seeing that precious face made her smile. And yes, her eyes misted up with tears. Her son was safe. He wasn't in the middle of a nightmare.

"This is a preview," Cal explained. "In about eight hours we're opening gifts, and you can watch every minute of it."

"Thank you," she managed to say.

"No. You need to thank Jordan. He's the one who set all of this up."

Of course. Who else?

Jordan knew how much she missed Gus. And that made her remember how much she cared for Jordan. He was indeed a special man to remember something like this with all the craziness going on in their lives.

"Eight hours," Cal reminded her. "All the cameras are already set up. Merry Christmas, Kinley."

She wished Cal the same, thanked him again and clicked off the feed and the call. The emotion hit her almost immediately. Maybe it was the fatigue, her gratitude for the perfect gift or the leftover emotion from her earlier encounter with Jordan. The reasons didn't seem to matter at the moment. She got up and made her way through the house.

And toward Jordan.

She walked through the house, and the corridor, and

she stopped in the doorway, hoping this was a good idea. After all, she was here in Jordan's bedroom, and it was obvious why she was there. She intended to pick up where they'd left off in his office.

Jordan wasn't aware of her sanity check or doubt. He lay in bed. He was facedown, his arms outstretched, as if pure exhaustion had caused him to land that way. The pearl-colored sheet came up to his waist and outlined that lean, muscled body.

He was naked, his clothes discarded on the floor.

She understood the beauty of those massive windows then. The milky moonlight poured through the crystal-clear glass and onto him. He was a picture all right. And she understood something else in that moment.

That she'd never wanted a man the way she wanted him.

Kinley peeled off her skirt and top. She did the same with her underwear. She dropped the items on the floor, and before she could change her mind, she walked across the room toward him. She threw back the covers and slid in next to him.

He was warm. Solid. All man. And his scent went straight through her.

Jordan reached out, hauled her to him, shifting his body so that she was beneath him.

"What took you so long?" he drawled, sounding both sleepy and alert at the same time.

Doubts assaulted her. And fear. Kinley didn't think she could bear another broken heart. But that wasn't what she said to him. "I'm here now."

Jordan looked down at her. He then slipped his hand into her hair and leaned in. His mouth touched hers. So gently. Soft. Lingering. The slow, easy kiss surprised her. She expected him to take her with the same fury that he did everything else in life, but this was a different kind of lovemaking. Even when he deepened the kiss, and his tongue touched hers, everything was unhurried.

Her blood turned to fire.

He controlled the tempo. The angle of the kiss. Everything. And she didn't care. Kinley let herself be swept away.

He kissed his way down her body, his mouth lighting fires along the way. He didn't hurry. Definitely didn't shortchange her with those body kisses. He made his way back up to her face.

Kinley wrapped her legs around him, forced him closer. But Jordan still didn't give in to the crazy frenzy that he'd built inside her.

As if he had all the time in the world, he took a condom from his nightstand and put it on. He returned to her and gave her more of those steamy kisses.

He entered her slowly. Kinley felt every inch of him. And then he stopped. She saw it then. The need in his eyes. The intensity was simmering beneath the surface and ready to break free.

"I shouldn't need you this much," he mumbled.

"I know the feeling," she mumbled back.

He didn't give her a lingering look. Nor any more kisses.

He caught her hands, pinning them to the bed. He moved. Not gently now. He took her because he'd finally lost all control. Because he had to have her now.

Kinley wanted him like this. Wanted him a little crazy. But more than that, she just wanted him *now*.

She lifted her hips, matching those fierce thrusts. She took all of him and let those thrusts take her to the edge.

"Jordan," she said.

He said her name as well, repeating it with each of those frantic strokes.

Kinley came first, and even though the passion completely claimed her for those moments, she still managed to focus and see Jordan's face.

Like her, he lost control.

He gathered her into his arms, drew her close to him and went over the edge.

JORDAN EASED OUT of the bed, careful that he didn't wake Kinley.

It was only 4:00 a.m. Still hours away from the time Gus would be opening his presents. Then, he'd wake her so they could share the moment together.

She was obviously exhausted because she'd fallen asleep almost immediately after they'd had sex. Which meant they hadn't talked.

That was a good thing.

It would give Jordan some time to figure out what the hell he was going to do.

He'd known from the moment he first laid eyes on her that they'd eventually land in bed. He'd also known this couldn't be just casual sex. Kinley wasn't the casual-sex type. Plus, she had feelings for him. He wasn't stupid. He could see that.

And he had feelings for her.

On the surface that didn't seem like much of a problem, and it might not have been if it weren't for all their baggage. It'd been so long since he'd let anyone get close

to him. So long since he'd shared himself with anyone.
Gus had changed that. The little boy had made him see
that love wasn't necessarily a painful commitment. That
the good outweighed any of the bad.

But there was Kinley to consider.

Maybe—just maybe—what she felt for him wasn't
love or a similar emotion but part of her gratitude for
taking care of Gus.

Jordan groaned softly, pulled on a pair of black jeans,
a black long-sleeved shirt and his boots. He shoved his
PDA into his back pocket. The clothes weren't exactly
festive wear for Christmas Day, but they suited his mood.
He'd gotten himself personally involved at a time when
it was imperative that he stay detached and objective.

Personal involvement meant a loss of focus.

It could mean making the situation more dangerous.
And that's why he had to put some emotional distance
between Kinley and himself. Yes, he'd had this pep talk
before, but this time he had to listen.

Really.

He went to the kitchen and started a pot of coffee,
something he'd been doing a lot lately. Kinley's taste
was still in his mouth. Her scent was on his skin.

Hell. He could still feel her.

And hear her. "Jordan." The way she'd said his name
when he was still inside her.

"Jordan?"

That jerked him out of his daydream. Because her
voice wasn't some great memory. It was real. Kinley
had just walked into the kitchen.

She'd dressed. Thank goodness. Well, maybe not. He
could remember what it was like to have her naked de-

spite the dark brown pants and tan top that she wore now. Her hair was still tousled, and her face flushed with color that could only come from a great night of sex.

Okay, so maybe that was his imagination, too.

But it wasn't his imagination that he wanted her all over again. So much for his latest resolution to distance himself from her.

"You're up early," he commented, just so he wasn't standing there gawking at her.

"Yes." She sighed.

Uh-oh. That wasn't the sound of a satisfied woman. It was the sound of a troubled one, and Jordan thought he knew why. "You're having regrets?"

She blinked. "No. Absolutely not." And with that, she went to him and kissed him as if she were about to haul him off to bed. She smiled. "I didn't thank you for my Christmas present." She kissed him again. "Thank you."

Since he liked her way of showing thanks, he kissed her right back. "You're welcome." He eased away from her so he could see her face. "But you could have thanked me later. I was hoping you'd get a few more hours of sleep."

The sighing look returned. "I tried, but I kept thinking about the notes." She shook her head. "There's a problem, but I don't know what's wrong."

"What do you mean?"

She grabbed two cups and began to pour them both some of the fresh brew. "I've tested every single formula that Dexter and Brenna listed in common. None of them could have produced an antidote. Not even close. So, I guess I need to rerun everything—" Her head whipped up, and she looked at him.

Jordan knew what she was thinking. "Maybe that's the point. Maybe none of the formulas could produce an antidote because Dexter never created one."

She set the coffeepot aside, probably because her hand was suddenly too shaky to hold it. "No antidote," Kinley repeated. Then, she groaned. "God, it makes sense. Every time I'd ask Dexter about how the formula was coming, he'd stall me. He locked up his research, and that's the only part of the project that he prevented me from seeing."

Jordan nodded. "And it explains why he wanted to destroy the lab and fake his own death. He'd already taken a fortune in research money, and he couldn't deliver." Unless… "You worked on the project. Could the antidote have even been made?"

"I didn't think so," she readily answered. "In fact, when Dexter took on the project, we argued about it because I knew it would take years just to come up with a workable formula, and by then the investors would already be screaming for results. But I think the idea of all that money was too tempting for him to pass up."

Oh, yeah. Because a man who'd endanger the mother of his child probably wasn't driven by his heart but rather by his wallet.

Kinley bracketed her hands on the granite counter and groaned. "Shelly and heaven knows who else died because of this. Gus, you and I were placed in danger. My son had to live in hiding since the moment he was born, and all of that was because of a lie that Dexter told."

And the worst thing—without an antidote, they didn't have anything to bargain with. Burke and Strahan likely wouldn't believe Kinley if she told them that Dexter had pulled off one big scam before faking his death and then being accidentally killed when he set explosives meant to eliminate her.

No.

As investors, they wanted only their profits.

"So where does this leave us?" she asked.

"First, I'll start with contacting the FBI. We'll give them copies of all the notes so they can run their own independent tests."

"That could take days or weeks," she pointed out. "The only reason I was able to do it so quickly is because I was familiar with the research."

True. It would take the FBI time, but there was no way around that. However, that was just one step. He had to do more, much more, to ensure Gus's and Kinley's safety.

"I have a friend who works at the *San Antonio Express-News*. I'll talk to him about doing some sort of investigative report so he can leak that the antidote was a fraud. Between that and an FBI report, we might be able to convince Burke, Strahan and anyone else that there's no reason to come after you."

He saw something else in her eyes. Something he hadn't seen before. Hope. "You really think that's possible?"

"I do. It might not happen today, or even next week, but it will happen." And that meant soon he'd be able to bring Gus home.

Of course, that posed a whole new set of problems. Kinley would want custody of her son. That was natural. But he wanted custody, too, and somehow, they'd have to work that out.

First, though, he needed to call the FBI.

He grabbed his coffee. Then he grabbed a kiss from Kinley. It made her smile, and he kissed her again just because he liked the way her smile lit her face.

"Work," he reminded himself when the third kiss turned hot and French.

Jordan forced himself away from her and headed for his office. However, he made it only a few steps before his PDA beeped. He took it out, looked at the screen and didn't like what he saw. It was a secure text message from Desmond.

Code Black, the message said.

Jordan stopped, set his coffee back on the counter and raced to his office.

"What's wrong?" Kinley asked, running behind him.

"We might have a problem." He dropped down into the chair and typed in some codes on the computer. The first was to verify that the message was indeed from Desmond.

It was.

Well, it'd come from his private secure line anyway. That didn't mean someone hadn't tapped into it and used it.

Jordan quickly called the man, and Desmond answered on the first ring. "What's happening?" Jordan asked. "Why the Code Black?"

"I came into Sentron to clear out my things and stopped by the command center," Desmond said, his words running together. "I ran a security check on your estate."

"Why?"

"Because I figured something would go wrong. I don't trust Burke, Cody or Strahan."

Then the feeling was mutual. But Jordan didn't trust Desmond, either. He punched in the code to run his own security check of the grounds and house. There were no flags, no indications that anything had been breached.

"I don't see anything," he told Desmond. "And none of the sensors have been triggered."

"Because the breach didn't exactly happen on your property. Jordan, you have to believe me. Look for it. It's just on the other side of the west fence in the greenbelt. If you look, there's no way you can miss it."

The greenbelt was a heavily treed area just about a hundred yards from his bedroom.

"I can't tell how much time you have left," Desmond warned.

Jordan ignored the man's increasingly frantic tone. For the moment, anyway.

With the phone sandwiched between his shoulder and his ear, Jordan gave the security cameras an adjustment. The first was useless. He couldn't see over the high stone privacy fence. But the second camera by the pool house was elevated enough to see down into the thick trees and underbrush. He'd designed it that way for just this type of security risk.

There it was.

A dull silver metal box with a timer on top.

Jordan zoomed in on that timer.

And cursed.

He got up and hit the buttons on the console to clear the codes so that no one could get access to and use the security feed to locate Gus. In the same motion, Jordan grabbed on to Kinley's arm. He started to run toward the garage. There wasn't time to get supplies or grab anything.

They had to get out of there now.

"What does Code Black mean?" Kinley asked, her voice a tangle of nerves and adrenaline.

"It means we have to get out of here. There's a bomb, and it's set to go off in two minutes."

CHAPTER FOURTEEN

TWO MINUTES.

Kinley was afraid that wasn't enough time to escape, though Jordan was obviously going to try to do just that.

He plowed them through the house and into the garage and shoved her into a black Lexus. He made a quick check of his PDA, the screen showing the images from the various security cameras of the estate's surveillance system. Jordan no doubt did that to make sure no one was out there waiting, and he must have seen that it was safe because he pressed the remote control on the dashboard to open the garage door.

The moment the door raised, he barreled out of there.

"What about your neighbors?" Kinley asked, putting on her seat belt.

"They should be far enough away. This bomb was almost certainly set just to damage only my estate. I hope."

Yes, that was her hope as well. It was bad enough that they were in danger. No need to put anyone else smack in the middle of this nightmare that just wouldn't end.

"There's a gun and magazine clips in the glove compartment. Hand them to me," Jordan instructed. His gaze was darting all around, probably looking to see if they were about to be ambushed.

Kinley hadn't said that ambush fear aloud. There was

no need. Both of them knew that this bomb could be just a ruse to draw them out. Maybe the person responsible thought Gus was still inside, and this would pull her baby out into the open, too.

And that infuriated her.

How dare this SOB risk endangering her child all to get a formula that didn't even exist.

She took the gun from the glove compartment and handed it to Jordan. He gripped it in his left hand while he sped away.

"Should I call nine-one-one?" Kinley asked. There were three magazine clips, and one by one, she handed those to him as well.

"No. Not at this point anyway. Besides, I didn't bring a cell with me. The GPS in them makes them easier to track. Don't worry, the neighbors will hear the explosion soon enough and report it."

No doubt. It wouldn't be a peaceful start to their Christmas morning.

It was dark, still several hours from sunrise, but the streetlights helped. What didn't help was the cold, thick pre-morning mist that cast an eerie blanket on the road.

Like Jordan, she looked around and didn't see anyone following them.

"The vehicle's behind us," Jordan told her.

That caused her heart to skip a couple of beats. "What? Where?" Kinley looked again and shook her head, and then she spotted the car. No headlights. That's why she had missed it. But it was there, all right.

Someone was following them.

"Stay low in the seat," Jordan insisted. "The glass is

bulletproof, but I don't want to take any chances." And he hit the accelerator even harder.

There were no other cars out and about. That wasn't a surprise. It was, after all, the wee hours of Christmas morning. Still, with the roads slick with the condensation from the mist, it wasn't safe to be going eighty miles an hour on a residential street. But they had no choice. Which led Kinley to her next thought.

What did this person plan to do?

The bomb had perhaps been set to make them evacuate in a hurry. And they had done exactly that. Maybe the next step was to intercept them and kidnap her.

Or to break into the damaged estate and look for Gus.

She silently cursed. It all went back to that damn formula, and it wouldn't do any good to tell the person that it was a sham. No. That meant she and Jordan were both in grave danger all over again.

Kinley checked the clock on the dashboard. Judging from her calculations, two minutes had already passed, and she'd heard no explosion. Of course, they were far enough away that it still could have happened.

Or not.

"You think Desmond was telling the truth?" she asked, checking the mirror again. The car following them was still there, and the mist cloaked it so that she couldn't see who was in the driver's seat.

"Maybe." Jordan turned the steering wheel and took them into a sharp curve. The tires squealed in protest of the excessive speed. Behind them, the other car did the same.

"I know you said we can't call the police, but is that

where we're going—to police headquarters?" Kinley asked.

"No. If we do that, this person will back off. Then we'll have to go through this again and again. Until I stop him." Jordan glanced at her. "This morning, I'm going to stop him."

She shook her head, not understanding. "But how?"

He didn't answer right away, and that sent an icy chill through her. "This person wants you, and if I try to get in the way, there'll be an attempt to eliminate me."

"Oh, God. You're talking about going head-to-head with this person so you can sacrifice yourself? Jordan, you don't know who he is, or how many hired guns he has with him."

"It doesn't matter. This has to stop. We won't get Gus back until it does, and that's why it ends here. I'm sick and tired of playing games with this fool."

She couldn't exactly argue with the need for this to end, but the question was, how could Jordan make that happen? And better yet, where?

"Where are we going?" she asked.

"The training facility."

Of course. It was the place Jordan had built, and it had excellent security. That was the good news. On the downside, it was also in an isolated area where they might become trapped if things got worse.

She was afraid things would definitely get worse.

Kinley made another check of the rearview mirror. The other car was still there, following them, which meant it would also follow them to the warehouse. Then this head-to-head confrontation would happen.

"I have weapons at the training facility," he explained.

"And I know the place like the back of my hand. I can have you stay in the command center, where you'll be safe, and I can put an end to this."

Yes, by putting himself in a position where he'd be far from safe. "I want to help you," she insisted. Kinley couldn't let him face this alone.

"Good. Because from the command center you'll be able to see what's going on. You can control the lights, the temperature, even the weather. There's an overhead sprinkler system to simulate a hard rain. You can watch what's going on with the monitors and can tell me where anyone is. And you can do all of that while you're safe behind the bulletproof glass."

She didn't approve of the idea of Jordan taking all the physical risks, but at least she could help him.

Maybe, just maybe, it would be enough.

Keeping the same high speed, Jordan ripped through the streets and drove toward the warehouse. With each mile ticking off the odometer, her heartbeat pounded even harder. The only thing that kept her from panicking was the thought of Gus. This would help him. This would make him safe.

It had to work.

Jordan made the final turn to the warehouse. He still didn't slow down, but he looked around. Not just in the rearview mirror but all around them. Probably checking to make sure they weren't about to be ambushed. If there were gunmen positioned nearby, she certainly didn't see them.

Of course, that didn't mean they weren't there.

Jordan used his PDA to open the massive doors to the warehouse. He still didn't slow down. He raced through the opening, and only then did he slam on the brakes. There were the sounds and the smells of the tires burning rubber onto the concrete, and he couldn't bring the vehicle to a full stop until he was about halfway into the training facility.

Kinley looked behind them and saw the other car coming. Oh, mercy. It was headed right into the warehouse as well. If the driver made it inside, there wouldn't be time for Jordan and her to get into place.

Jordan had obviously anticipated that. With his fingers moving fast, he coded in something on his PDA again, and the warehouse doors closed.

The other car slammed into the metal door.

The crash echoed through the warehouse, and with that deafening noise drumming through her head, they got out.

"Get to the command center now!" Jordan shouted.

Kinley hit the concrete running, but she also glanced over her shoulder. The car had indeed crashed into the warehouse, but the wrecked front end of the vehicle had prevented the doors from closing all the way. There was at least a two-foot gap of space.

Plenty of room for a gunman to get inside.

And maybe that was the point. After all, Jordan had wanted a showdown, and he was going to get it.

The cold winter air howled through the opening created by the crash, and coupled with the sound of their footsteps, it made it nearly impossible to hear if anyone was already following them. And she couldn't see much, either. The only illumination came from the headlights on Jordan's car.

"Don't look back," Jordan warned. "Just run." And

to ensure that happened, he pushed her in front of him and guided her toward the stairs that led to the command center.

They only made it a third of the way up when Jordan suddenly shoved her down. She landed hard on the steps. So hard that it temporarily knocked the breath out of her. Kinley tried to look around to see what had caused Jordan to do that.

"Someone's blocked off the command center," Jordan mumbled.

And he cursed.

Kinley looked up but couldn't see anything. "How do you know?"

"The access code to open the door doesn't work. Someone's jammed it so we can't get inside." He shoved his PDA into his pocket and got his gun ready.

That's when it hit her. They were perched on the stairs, literally out in the open. The exterior doors were jammed open with the wrecked car and could easily be breached. And someone had already shut off their access to the command center.

The one place of safety in the entire warehouse.

"We need to make it back to the car," Jordan whispered.

She looked down at the vehicle. Both doors were wide open, but the vehicle was sitting out in the middle of the warehouse with a lot of open space between it and them.

"We can't take the stairs," Jordan said. "We have to jump."

"Jump?"

"It's all right." He tipped his head to the floor. "It's padded below us, to break the fall."

Yes, but it was also a twenty-foot drop. Either of them could break a bone or two. Heck, even a twisted ankle at this point could turn out to be a fatal injury. Then, there was the whole problem of what might be waiting for them at ground level. The driver of that car could be waiting to shoot them. For that matter, so could the person who jammed the entrance of the command center.

Jordan and she could be attacked from both sides.

But that didn't stop Jordan. Probably because it was the only chance they had. "I'm going to slide over the railing and drop. Count to three and you do the same. Unless you hear shots being fired."

That speared the adrenaline through her. "And then what do I do?"

"Stay put. I'll get to you as soon as I can."

Yes, after he dodged bullets and risked getting himself killed. Still, it was obvious she wasn't going to talk him out of this. Besides, she certainly didn't have a better plan. She didn't have a plan at all, other than to do whatever was necessary to survive this.

Jordan brushed a kiss on her cheek and moved so quickly that he was almost a blur. He grabbed on to the metal railing, and with one deft move, he hoisted himself up and launched his body over the side. He'd been right. The floor had some kind of thick, feathery padding because it billowed up around him like a mattress and broke his fall. He bounced right up, aimed his gun and got ready for an attack.

"Now!" he told her.

Kinley got up off the steps. She didn't have the agility that Jordan did, but she still managed to get her leg over the railing. And she prayed. Because she was in a very vulnerable position.

She caught movement out of the corner of her eye and saw someone crawl through the space of the partially opened warehouse doors. Since the headlights weren't aimed in that direction, she couldn't see who it was. And there wasn't time to look farther. Kinley crawled over the railing. Said another prayer.

And dropped.

She landed on her butt and hands and didn't have a chance to get to her feet. That's because Jordan latched on to her arm and pulled her behind one of the wooden partitions draped with netting. The ceiling was low, barely an inch above her head, and Jordan pushed her to the back of the small enclosure. It was dark, cold and quiet.

But it didn't stay that way for long.

A shot rang out.

CHAPTER FIFTEEN

THE SHOT SLAMMED into the wall just inches from where Kinley and Jordan were standing.

So did the second bullet. The third tore through the partition and flew into the ceiling, scattering the acoustic tile into bits over them like little flakes of snow.

This was not how Jordan wanted things to go down. Bullets flying. God knew how many gunmen converging on them for an all-out attack. And with someone else in control. Soon, very soon, he needed to figure out who'd gotten into the warehouse ahead of him and jammed the command center entrance—which should have been next to impossible to do.

But first, he needed to get Kinley safely out of there.

That meant somehow getting her back into the car so he could drive out the back exit. Jordan only hoped his security codes still worked. It was possible they'd been altered as well. If so, Kinley and he were in deeper trouble than just having bullets fired at them.

They'd have no way out.

He could hear her breathing. It was way too hard and fast. And he knew her heart had to be racing out of control. He'd been in too many situations like this, but she didn't have his experience and training. She shouldn't have to be involved in this kind of danger, but she was.

And he could thank himself for that.

The moment she'd walked into the Sentron Christmas party, he should have put her in a safe house and kept her away from all of this. He shouldn't have tried to learn the truth until he had her out of harm's way. Jordan hoped he could undo that mistake and get her to safety.

"It'll be okay," he whispered to her, even though he had no idea if he could deliver on that promise.

Jordan pushed her deeper into the phase-one training room. It wasn't exactly bulletproof, but when he'd designed it, he'd added some metal insulation so a shot wasn't as likely to be deadly.

That didn't mean it couldn't be.

But for now, this was one of the best places for them to be. Soon, though, he'd need extra ammunition. Maybe even extra weapons. Those items were in the warehouse, but to get to them, he'd have to move, and that meant taking Kinley with him.

Perhaps the person who'd accessed the command center didn't know how to operate all the equipment. Jordan prayed that was true anyway. Because he'd personally designed some very realistic training obstacles, and he didn't want to have to go through those, especially with Kinley.

He didn't return fire. Best to save his ammunition for high-percentage shots, and for that to happen he needed to be able to see the target. Jordan used his PDA to enter some codes. And then he held his breath, hoping they hadn't been overridden by the person who'd accessed the command center.

The overhead lights flared on.

Since his eyes had already partly adjusted to the darkness, the lights were nearly blinding. But he forced himself to focus, and using the hole the bullet had made, he looked out to determine the position of the person firing those shots.

There was a ski-masked gunman near the back of his car. That was the only shooter he saw. The guy took aim again at the phase-one room where Kinley and Jordan were.

Jordan took aim, too.

And fired.

The guy dove away at the last second, and he used Jordan's car for cover. Not only was he out of the line of fire, it meant as long as the gunman was hiding there, Jordan couldn't get Kinley into the vehicle. Even more, Jordan didn't want to take too many more shots in that direction and risk shooting out one of the tires.

He needed a diversion.

Jordan used his PDA to see if he could get the overhead sprinklers to turn on, but before he could type in the codes, the place went dark.

Hell.

Someone definitely had tapped into the controls. But what else could the guy do?

Too much, he feared.

Using the backlight on his PDA, Jordan put in the codes to start the sprinkler system. They spewed on immediately, and it began to rain down on the place.

The gunman behind his car didn't move. Not good. Jordan needed the guy to budge, so he cranked up the speed on the sprinklers.

But the water stopped.

"Someone other than you is controlling things, isn't he?" Kinley asked, her voice barely audible.

Jordan considered lying, but a lie wasn't going to make her less afraid. "Yeah."

But the good news was that the person possibly didn't know what kind of power he had or else he would have already unleashed it.

Well, maybe.

Perhaps the culprit was saving those surprises for later. And that meant Jordan had to take some drastic action. If he couldn't immediately get to the vehicle, then he had to get to a phone and call the police. Yes, the officers would essentially be walking into a war zone, but that might be the only way he could get Kinley out of this alive. Still, his first choice was a getaway in the car, and he had to try to make that happen.

"Stay low and follow me," Jordan instructed.

He moved to her side and brushed against her arm. Every muscle was tight and knotted. Something he definitely understood. Every inch of him was primed for the fight, and the adrenaline was urging him on. They couldn't stay put. They needed to move now.

Jordan inched out of the phase-one room. There was only about four feet of space between it and the next area, but those four feet were in the shooter's kill zone. Not the place he wanted to linger.

Keeping himself in front of Kinley, he raced forward. She stayed right with him, and they practically dove into the other room.

The bullets started again.

Not single shots, either, but a barrage of gunfire, and it was all aimed at them.

Jordan pulled her to the floor, amid the dust and straw that covered this particular section. The bullets had no problem eating their way through the partition, which meant the gunman had switched ammo. He was probably using some kind of Teflon-coated bullets.

And that meant they had to move again.

"Let's go," Jordan ordered. He caught her arm with his left hand. With his right, he got his own gun ready.

As he raced forward, he fired. And he just kept on firing until they were in the next room. He repeated the procedure again. And again. Until they were within ten yards of the car.

Moving so close to the gunman was probably scaring Kinley to death, but Jordan figured if he could just get closer, he could take the guy out.

"I'm going to try to draw out the gunman," Jordan whispered to her.

"How?"

She wouldn't like the plan, and he didn't have time to reassure her. "Stay right here, and when I tell you to run, get to the car as fast as you can. I'll be right behind you."

He hoped.

Jordan figured he had six shots left. He'd need them all and then would have to switch magazines. He put away his PDA, took a deep breath and launched himself out of the room. He caught the webbing that covered the adjacent training building, and he hoisted himself up so he could pinpoint the gunman hiding on the other side of his car.

Jordan fired.

The guy stayed down for the first two shots. Then

Jordan went up another rung on the webbing, turned and fired again.

Two more shots.

These tore up chunks of the concrete and spewed the debris right in the man's face. Of course, the ski mask protected his skin, but not his eyes.

The man said something that Jordan couldn't distinguish, and he jumped back away from the flying bits of concrete.

Two more shots got the guy scrambling to the side, and he ducked behind one of the training partitions. Jordan changed his clip.

"Now," he told Kinley.

She was ready. She barreled out of the room and made a beeline for the car.

She didn't get far.

Jordan aimed his gun, but a gun was defenseless against this.

His car exploded in a fireball.

"OH MY GOD," KINLEY MUMBLED. And because she didn't know what else to say or do, she just kept repeating it.

Someone had blown up the car, their means of escape. Now what would they use to get out of there?

She forced herself to move, and she raced toward the cover of the training room. Something hit her hard in the back, and for a moment she thought she'd been shot. But it was just a piece of debris, she realized.

She didn't dare look back. Didn't dare pause to check her injuries. The fiery fragments of Jordan's car were literally raining down on them, and any of those fragments could be deadly.

So could the gunman.

He was no doubt still there on the other side of the warehouse, and if he could manage to see through the cloud of wreckage, he would shoot at them again.

She scrambled back into the room and yelled for Jordan to do the same. He jumped from the webbing and not a second too soon. A piece of the car's leather upholstery had flown against the webbing, setting it on fire.

The smoke was already thick from the explosion itself, but the new fire only added to it. Soon, they wouldn't be able to breathe, and that meant they had to move, maybe closer to the fresh air coming from the gap in the front warehouse door.

Of course, that meant going back through the maze of rooms, and that meant the gunman would once again have clean shots at them.

"Let's go," Jordan instructed.

He didn't waste another moment. With his gun ready and with him positioned at her side so he could shield her, they started to retrace their original path.

Kinley heard heavy footsteps on the concrete. Maybe the gunman was trying to escape, too. Unless he'd brought equipment with him, he wouldn't be able to breathe much longer, either. If he went in the same direction they did, there'd be another gun battle.

That caused her adrenaline to spike even more.

Jordan and Kinley made it through two of the training rooms. Then another. No shots came at them. No one attacked. They were about to race to the area nearest the front door, but the moment they reached it, overhead sprinklers came on again. Cold water began to pour down from the ceiling.

Jordan lowered his gun, putting it barrel down, no doubt to protect it from the water. However, there was nothing they could do to protect themselves. Within seconds, they were drenched. With the winter air rifling through the opening, she began to shiver, and her teeth began to chatter.

"Now," Jordan prompted.

They started to move again toward the front door. Heaven knew what they would do once they were outside. Maybe darkness would shield them long enough for them to take cover.

But then what?

With no cell phone and miles from anyone who might be able to help, getting out of the warehouse was only the first step to what would be a nightmare of obstacles.

They stopped in the first room. And waited. Jordan lifted his head, listening. But with the pounding downpour, they couldn't hear anything. Someone could be sneaking up on them, and they wouldn't know until it was too late.

"Let's move," Jordan finally said.

Just as the water stopped.

That caused him to stop, and she tried to listen again to see what was going on.

She heard a sound as if someone were dragging something heavy. That sound was followed by footsteps. Not one set this time. At least two. And the dragging sound and the footsteps were coming from the front door.

Mere feet away.

Kinley was almost certain someone was moving the wrecked car sandwiched beneath the warehouse door.

Jordan put his left index finger to his mouth in a keep-quiet gesture, and he aimed his gun at the opening to the room. But no one came inside. The footsteps moved quickly past them.

Without making a sound, Jordan leaned his head to the side and peered out the room's opening. Even though there was barely any light, Kinley could still see his expression. His jaw had turned to steel, and he mouthed some profanity.

"What's wrong?" Kinley put her mouth right against his ear so she wouldn't be heard.

Jordan didn't take his eyes off the opening, but he moved closer to her and whispered, "Two Sentron agents just arrived. Both armed."

"Not Cody and Desmond?" She held her breath, praying it wasn't.

He shook his head. "New recruits. I trained them both here just last month."

Now she understood the reason for his reaction. She doubted the men were on Jordan's side. No, they almost certainly had been sent here as hired guns. And they knew the warehouse. They were trained. By Jordan, no less.

The men would know how to kill.

When they joined up with their ski-masked comrade, Jordan and Kinley would be seriously outnumbered. They really had to get out of there now.

Jordan must have come to the same conclusion because he inched his way to the opening. "Stay as quiet as you can," he mouthed.

So, this wouldn't be a mad dash like before. They would need to sneak out without being seen or heard.

Jordan stopped at the room's door. He looked out

again and then crouched down. Kinley did the same, and, following him, they crept toward the warehouse opening. It wasn't hard to find. It was the source of the wind and the only noise in the place.

Well, except for her heartbeat.

It was pounding like war drums in her ears, and she hoped that her breathing wasn't as audible as it sounded to her. She didn't want to give away their position.

Jordan eased out of the room, and, still crouched, he turned in the direction of the still-burning car and command center. He kept watch while they made their way out.

There was a crackle of sound, and Kinley braced herself for another explosion. Or for the overhead sprinklers to spew water onto them. But it wasn't a bomb or water.

The lights flared on.

Not just a few of them. Probably every light in the place. She spotted the still-blazing car.

And the men.

They were a lot closer than she'd anticipated. And both of them had assault rifles trained right on Jordan and her.

"Hold it right there," a heavily muscled, dark-haired man snarled.

Kinley looked at the opening. The wrecked car was indeed gone, giving them a clear path to escape. But the exit was at least ten feet away. Too far for her to even attempt it. The men would gun her down before she could make it another step.

Jordan lifted his hands, and he stood, positioning himself in front of her.

He was surrendering.

Behind them, there was a grinding sound of metal scraping against metal.

And the warehouse door dropped shut.

Jordan and Kinley were trapped.

CHAPTER SIXTEEN

JORDAN HADN'T THOUGHT things could get much worse.

But he'd obviously been wrong.

Here they were, being held at gunpoint by two of his former agents: Chris Sutton and Wally Arceneaux. Jordan had never worked an assignment with either of the men since they'd only been with Sentron a little over a month. But he knew what they were capable of doing.

And what they were capable of doing was killing.

All of his former agents had been trained to do that.

Now the question was, for whom were they willing to kill? Were they getting their orders from Burke, or had Strahan or someone else hired them? Or maybe they were working for Cody or Desmond.

Jordan made a quick check of the warehouse and spotted the ski-masked gunman. He didn't come closer, but he also had his rifle trained on Kinley and him.

Now they were facing three armed men, and with their escape route cut off, that meant he had to find another way to get her out of there.

"Drop your gun," Wally ordered.

Jordan held on to it, but he did ease it down to a position that would hopefully not seem so threatening. "Is this a Sentron-directed mission?" he asked.

"Drop your gun," Wally repeated.

That was standard operating procedure. Don't engage the detainee in conversation. It could be a distraction. It could create an empathetic situation, not that Sentron agents were high on empathy. Jordan had hired them because they had ice water in their veins and weren't easily distracted.

Now that was coming back to haunt him.

"I want to speak to Burke," Jordan tried again. "He needs to know what Kinley found out about the formula for the antidote."

Jordan wouldn't tell them that the antidote didn't exist. That it was a fake. He had to let Burke or whoever believe that it was possible for him to get his hands on it. This way, it would buy Kinley some time and some safety. They wouldn't kill her as long as they believed she could give them what they'd been told to get.

"Drop your weapon," Wally said for the third time, and he lifted his gun, preparing to shoot.

Jordan recognized that look in the man's eyes. This wasn't a bluff. Wally had orders to kill him. And that meant he had to do something fast.

Kinley beat him to it.

She jumped in front of Jordan.

Hell. She was trying to protect him.

"I want to talk to Burke," she insisted. "And Martin Strahan. There are things they need to know."

Wally and Chris exchanged a brief glance. Then Wally nodded. "Come with me. I'll take you to the person you should be talking to."

Wally had chosen his words carefully and hadn't incriminated his boss. That meant Jordan wasn't any closer to learning the identity of the person behind this attack.

But he pushed that aside for now because he had to do something to stop them from taking Kinley.

Even though the agents likely didn't have orders to kill her, they would no doubt torture her to get her to reveal secrets that she didn't even have.

Wally used his rifle to gesture for Kinley to move closer so she could no doubt go with him. She didn't budge, but Wally wouldn't put up with her stance for long. Soon, he'd try to grab her to get her moving. That's when Jordan would have to act, and he only hoped that neither Wally nor Chris would take shots at them.

The seconds crawled by. Each one ticked off in Jordan's head. Each one kicked his heartbeat up another notch. Finally, Wally took a step toward them. He kept his rifle aimed at them. So did Chris.

Wally took another step.

And that was Jordan's cue to spring into action.

Praying that Kinley wouldn't unintentionally do something to get in the way, Jordan threw his arm around her waist, and with her gripped to him, he dove toward the training room. They crashed to the floor, and his shoulder slammed into the concrete. The pain shot through him. Still, he did a quick check to make sure Kinley was okay. She seemed to be. She scrambled to get to her feet when he did.

Jordan fought off the pain and came up ready to fire. But Wally and Chris didn't shoot. What they did do was curse, which confirmed they had orders to keep her alive. Jordan would use those orders to his advantage.

"Move quietly," he mouthed and hitched his shoulder in the direction of the other room. They were going to backtrack, to make their way toward the center of the warehouse. Back to the command center stairs where he could get to the training tunnel he'd had installed.

With the lights on at full glare, Jordan had no trouble seeing Kinley's face. She was drenched from the simulated sprinkler rain, her hair had flecks of ash and debris from his car, and her bottom lip was trembling. Probably a combination of cold and fear. But despite what had to be a terrifying situation for her, she kept moving. When they reached the room exit, they bolted straight into the next area.

Jordan listened, to try to hear what Wally and Chris were doing. Not that he expected differently, but they moved too, following along the outside of the rooms. The men were no doubt waiting for Kinley and him to reach the last training area before the command center.

Then they would grab Kinley.

Or so they thought.

Jordan didn't want the duo to get suspicious and ambush them so he kept watch on the exit and worked as quickly and quietly as he could. He used his foot to kick back some of the soggy straw that covered this particular section of the training area. He grabbed the handle that the straw had concealed and lifted it.

There was a set of steps that led down to a tunnel. A tunnel that Chris and Wally didn't even know existed. This was a route used by the trainers to set up a simulated ambush for advanced training, something that neither of the men had received yet.

When she saw the tunnel, Kinley's eyes widened, and there was just a touch of relief in them. She didn't waste any time. She hurried down the steps and into the dark space. Jordan got in as well, and he pulled the door shut. It wouldn't stop Chris and Wally from finding the escape route, but all Jordan needed was a minute or two head start.

Since it was pitch black, Jordan handed Kinley his PDA so she could use the backlight to illuminate their way. Thankfully, there were no turns to take. They were literally on a direct path to another trapdoor exit near the command center. Too bad the tunnel didn't extend the entire length of the warehouse. That would have been a nice bonus about now, but he had to be satisfied with just making it to the halfway point.

One step at a time.

There was little or no chance for them to get into the command center now, but if they got very lucky, they could quietly make their way out of the tunnel and through the other training rooms at the far end of the warehouse. Then he'd need another dose of good luck that his PDA codes would still work so he could open the exit.

If not, well, he didn't want to go there.

Nor did he want to think of who or what might be waiting for them once they made it out.

This had to work.

Jordan moved ahead of her as they approached another set of stairs that led to the exit. He kept his gun ready in his right hand, and he used his left hand to ease open the hatch door. Just a fraction. Then he waited and listened.

No voices.

No footsteps.

Just the glare of the light bouncing off the water on the floor.

"I should go first," Kinley whispered. "They won't shoot me."

Not on purpose, anyway. But it was possible one of them might have a quick trigger finger. Plus, they had to worry about the ski-masked guy. Jordan had no idea what his intentions were, but he doubted they were good.

"I'll go first," Jordan insisted. "There's about ten feet of space between the tunnel exit and the first training room. Get there as fast as you can."

She nodded, and as he'd done before, she brushed a kiss on his mouth. Jordan wished he had the time to tell her how sorry he was that she was in this predicament. He wished there was time to say a lot of things. But there wasn't. They had to make their move now.

Jordan inched the tunnel door to the side and looked out again. No one. He made his way up the steps, and while staying crouched down, he fired glances all around them. Wally and Chris still had their rifles trained on the room at the other end.

Good.

Two fewer guns to worry about.

Jordan motioned for Kinley to come up the steps as well, and he held his breath. Waiting and praying. She made it to the top, and he motioned for her to move. They needed to get to the cover of the nearest training room and then run like hell.

He reached for her hand and helped her step out onto the concrete floor.

Just as the lights went out again.

Kinley gasped.

Jordan wanted to believe she'd made that sound because of the shock of the darkness, but he knew in his gut that it was much more than that.

There was some shuffling. Footsteps. Since his eyes hadn't adjusted to the darkness, Jordan had no idea what was happening. He couldn't fire and risk shooting Kinley. He could only stand there in the pitchy blackness and wait for what he knew wouldn't be good news.

"Jordan," she said, her voice a tangle of nerves and concern.

"I'm here," Jordan answered and immediately moved to the side.

It wasn't a second too soon because the shot came right at him.

THE SOUND OF THE bullet blasted through the warehouse and echoed off the metal walls.

"Jordan!" Kinley called out.

That bullet could have hit him. He could be hurt, or worse. But there was nothing she could do to get to him because someone had grabbed her and put her in a fierce hold.

Worse, that someone had a gun pointed to her head.

"Move and Jordan dies," the person rasped in her ear.

Kinley couldn't recognize the voice, which was no doubt what he intended, but he obviously didn't intend to stay put. He began to move away from Jordan and to the stairs that led to the command center. If he got her there, Jordan wouldn't be able to get to her.

Even more frightening, Jordan would be a sitting duck.

She had to make a stand and stop this person from getting her up those stairs.

But how?

How could she do that without risking Jordan's life?

Kinley had his PDA still in her hand, and she'd seen him type in various codes to make things happen in the warehouse. She didn't know the codes, but maybe if she could randomly punch in some numbers, she might be able to create some kind of distraction.

Of course, it could be a deadly one.

God knew what kind of training exercises were in place. She hoped she didn't make something explode or cause shots to be fired. Still, she had to try. Her kidnapper was much stronger than she was, and he was using his muscle to get her up the stairs.

Trying not to draw attention to what she was doing, she used her thumb to push some buttons.

Nothing happened.

She pressed more. Then more when the darkness stayed, and still nothing changed. Maybe there was a special sequence of codes. Maybe even fingerprint recognition. If so, the PDA was useless.

The man dragged her up the first step, and when she struggled, he jammed the gun hard against her back. "Think of Jordan," he warned.

She couldn't think of anything else. Jordan was in danger because of her.

Kinley frantically stabbed more buttons.

Everything seemed to happen at once. The lights came back on. So did the overhead sprinklers, and netting dropped from the ceiling landing on the two agents who minutes earlier had held Jordan and her at gunpoint.

She didn't see Jordan.

God, where was he?

She didn't even know if he was alive since that shot could have been a direct hit.

Her kidnapper ripped something from his face. Night goggles, she realized. Now that the lights were on, they were useless. Still, she couldn't get a good look at him because beneath the goggles, he wore a ski mask. This was the man who'd taken cover behind Jordan's car.

But who was he?

He stopped on the stairs, yanked her against him so that her back was to his chest.

And he put the gun to her head.

"Call out Jordan's name," the man growled, his voice still unrecognizable.

She shook her head, but he only jammed the gun harder against her back. "Do it," he insisted. She realized then he was wearing some kind of device to alter his voice. "Or you die here."

"You won't kill me." She dug in her heels to keep him from moving her higher up the steps. "Because if you do, you'll never get the antidote."

"The antidote doesn't exist," he said. It sounded very much like a threat.

And it was.

Kinley didn't say anything. She just stood there, waiting for him to continue while she looked around the warehouse for Jordan. Still no sign of him. But the two agents on the floor were gradually making their way out of the netting. It wouldn't be long, a couple of minutes probably, before they could join forces with the man who had the gun jammed against her.

"I got copies of all the notes, too," he continued. "And

I had people go through them. About two hours ago I was told the formula didn't exist. *Yet*."

"Yet? What do you mean?"

"I mean you're going to create that antidote for me so I can sell it. I already have a buyer."

"Impossible. I can't make it."

"You'll find a way. If not, Jordan will die. And if that doesn't work, I'll track down your son and use him. One way or another, you'll cooperate."

Oh, God. He was talking about holding her hostage while he forced her to make something that probably couldn't even be done. This was just the beginning of the nightmare. Gus was still in danger. And he would stay in danger as long as this man believed she could create that formula.

She would have to die.

That was the only way.

If she were dead, it would stop. Gus wouldn't be in danger any longer and neither would Jordan because he would somehow escape this mess. There'd be no threat that could rear its ugly head years from now when some other person decided to get their hands on a potential gold mine.

A sudden calm came over her. She didn't want to die. She wanted to live and raise her son. Kinley wanted to see if she and Jordan could possibly have a future together, but her past had ruined any chances of that.

She took a deep breath. And got ready to jump. The padded floor would probably save her again, but her kidnapper might shoot. Either way, she'd be away from him.

There was a soft rattling sound that stopped her. It caused her kidnapper to freeze, too. She felt the muscles tighten in his chest and arms. His gaze flew up toward the ceiling.

But it was too late.

Jordan was there, hanging on to a pulley-type rope that was zooming down on them. Her kidnapper lifted his gun and aimed, just as Jordan crashed into him. The collision sent them all plummeting to the floor.

Kinley landed with a thud and quickly rolled to the side so that she wouldn't be crushed beneath them. Jordan's gun went flying, but that didn't stop him. He came up off the padded floor and launched himself at the kidnapper. He landed a quick punch and snatched the ski mask off the man's head.

Kinley got just a glimpse of the man's face before he fired a shot at Jordan.

"Cody," Jordan snarled, and he dove out of the way of the shot.

After the way things had been happening in the warehouse, Jordan figured Kinley's would-be kidnapper was someone with insider knowledge of the training facility, but he'd hoped it wasn't Cody, the agent who'd once been his right-hand man.

Now that right-hand man was trying to kill him.

Jordan would have much preferred to be facing Strahan or Burke. Heck, even Desmond. Because none of them had as much training and experience as Cody.

"Don't!" Cody warned when Kinley went for the gun that had been dislodged from Jordan's hand during the fall. So had his PDA that Kinley had been holding. It was just a couple of inches from Jordan's feet.

Unfortunately, Cody had managed to hang on to his

weapon and had it pointed at Kinley. When she continued to go after the fallen gun, Cody turned his weapon on Jordan.

That stopped her.

Kinley looked at Jordan, and he didn't see fear in her eyes. Just resolve. Which wasn't a good thing right now. He didn't want her taking any risks that could result in her getting hurt. Cody was obviously desperate and greedy enough to do just about anything.

"Cody wants me to create a formula," Kinley explained. She wiped the water from her face.

"I know she can do it," Cody insisted. "I read all about Kinley when I went through Burke's files."

"What were you doing in Burke's files?" Jordan asked. But he wasn't really interested in the answer. He was more interested in how he could get that gun away from Cody.

Cody shrugged. "I was checking up on my new boss. The boss you shoved down my throat when you sold Sentron. Bad move, Jordan. The company was as much mine as it was yours, and you had no right to sell it."

"I didn't have a choice."

"So you say." There was some movement to Cody's left. Chris and Wally were finally making their way out of the webbing that Kinley had dropped down onto them earlier. Once they were free and able to help Cody, Jordan didn't stand a chance of stopping them from taking Kinley.

"Get on the floor, Jordan," Cody demanded.

All in all, it wasn't a bad place to be. Jordan got to his knees, using his leg to hide the PDA. He scooped it into his hand.

"The formula is impossible to make," Jordan informed Cody. "The lab tried for months and couldn't do it." He didn't expect his former employee to believe that. Nor did he care if he did. Jordan needed the sound of his voice to cover the keystrokes he was making into his PDA, and once he was done, he eased the device back onto the floor.

Wally and Chris got to their feet and started to make their way toward Cody. Both turned, however, at the whirring sound. Neither knew what was coming.

"Kinley, get down!" Jordan shouted.

She did, thank God. Kinley dove toward him, just as the dummy bullets sprayed over them. Jordan had turned the training rifles toward them and had coded the signal for all to fire. It wasn't a training exercise he used often, but he was damn glad it was in place now.

The shock and the piercing pain from the rubber pellets caused Wally and Chris to run for cover. Cody automatically turned as well, to shelter his face.

Big mistake.

Jordan grabbed his gun from the floor.

Cody whirled back around and aimed his own weapon at Jordan and fired. But he was a split second too late. Jordan fired first, a double tap of the trigger.

Shots meant to kill.

And that's exactly what they did.

Jordan saw the startled look go through Cody's eyes. It was probably wishful thinking, but he thought he saw remorse and regret as well.

Then Cody dropped dead to the floor.

The rubber bullets continued to slam into them. Kinley yelped in pain. She was obviously getting hit. Jordan was, too, but he had something else to do before he could stop the training exercise.

He turned, pointing his hand in Wally and Chris's direction. "Drop your weapons and get on the floor," Jordan yelled.

There was hesitation, and for one sickening moment, Jordan thought he was going to have to kill again tonight. But both men finally complied. Their weapons fell, they kicked them toward Jordan, and they got to the ground.

"Code in six-seven-three on the PDA," Jordan instructed Kinley.

She did, and the assault from the dummy bullets stopped.

Jordan made his way to Cody and checked for a pulse. He found none. He then rifled through Cody's pocket and located a cell phone. Without taking his eyes off Wally and Chris, Jordan tossed the phone to Kinley.

"Call nine-one-one," he told her.

He heard her press in the numbers, and because the warehouse was almost deadly silent, he heard the ring. And he also heard the emergency dispatcher say, "What's your emergency?"

What Jordan didn't hear was Kinley respond to that critical question.

He glanced at her to see what was wrong.

And his heart dropped to his knees.

She had the cell phone cradled next to her ear, but her eyes were closed. She was ash pale.

Lifeless.

And there was a pool of blood around her.

CHAPTER SEVENTEEN

THE SOUND OF voices woke Kinley. Jordan's voice and several others that she didn't recognize.

She forced open her eyes. Everything was blurry and she was woozy, but she could tell she was in a hospital. Specifically, she was in a bed surrounded by white walls, white floors and white bedding.

Kinley started to get up but came to an abrupt halt when she felt the jab of pain in her shoulder. And then she remembered.

She'd been shot.

The bullet that Cody had fired had ricocheted off something in the warehouse and had slammed into her shoulder.

"You're awake," Jordan said. He practically ran across the room to get to her. Behind him, she saw the massive Christmas tree that several orderlies were decorating.

Jordan leaned down and kissed her. Not some lusty foreplay kiss. But one so soft that it barely touched her lips. He was gentle, and judging from those lines on his forehead he was worried about her.

"Where's Gus?" she asked.

"On the way. He should be here any minute."

Good. That would be the best medicine for her. She put Jordan in that category, too. He could certainly cure a variety of ills, though he didn't seem certain of that. That's because he didn't know how she felt about him.

He didn't know that she loved him.

And that meant it was time to tell him.

Kinley tested her shoulder again. The pain was still there, but it was manageable so she tried to ease herself into a sitting position so they could talk.

Jordan stopped her.

With that same gentleness, he took hold of her arms and had her lie back down.

"I'm okay, really," Kinley assured him.

"No, you're not. You had to have surgery to remove a bullet lodged in your shoulder." He paused, put his hands on his hips. "Why didn't you tell me you'd been shot? Here I was ordering you to make calls, and I didn't even look at you to make sure you were okay."

Kinley knew where this was going.

Or rather where it'd already been.

While the doctors had been removing the bullet, Jordan had no doubt beaten himself up because he hadn't been able to stop her from being injured.

She reached out and pulled on his hand to draw him closer. Much closer. She dragged him down so that he was sitting on the bed next to her. "You saved my life a dozen times in that warehouse," she reminded him. "If it weren't for you, I'd be dead."

"But I didn't stop you from being shot."

She smiled. It was probably a weary one and God knew how bad she looked, but it was heartfelt. "Jordan, you have some amazing qualities, but even you can't stop a bullet from ricocheting and hitting my shoulder."

He shook his head. "I wasn't careful enough with you."

To stop him from continuing his guiltfest, she pulled him down to her for a real kiss. No whisper-soft one. Kinley kissed him as if he were the man she loved. Because he was.

"Women in hospital beds shouldn't kiss like that," he drawled with his mouth still hovering over hers.

She smiled. Though she wanted to continue this lighter banter, she heard a crash in the corner and automatically jumped and braced herself for the worst.

But there was no worst.

One of the orderlies who was decorating the tree had dropped an ornament, and it hadn't even broken. Amazingly, the delicate-looking glass had hit the floor and rolled a few feet away.

"The tree was no doubt your idea?" she asked.

He eased back just a bit. "Since you have to stay here for a day or two and since it is Christmas, I thought you and Gus would like the tree."

That brought tears to her eyes and reminded her that Jordan was a very thoughtful man. "Thank you. It's beautiful."

Her gaze left the tree and came back to Jordan at the same moment that he looked at her. "Cody's dead," he told her.

Yes. She remembered that. "You did what you had to do."

He shrugged. "Cody used his remote control to get into the facility. That's how he was able to set up those obstacles for us. If I'd figured out beforehand that he was responsible—"

Kinley grabbed him harder this time. Kissed him harder, too.

"I guess that means you don't want to talk about Cody," he remarked.

"Or maybe it means I just want to kiss you," she joked. But he was right. She didn't want to talk about the nightmare that had come to life in the warehouse. Unfortunately, though, she needed to know if it was safe for her son to come home.

"Is the danger over?" Kinley stilled, trying not to cry. But she was afraid she'd do just that if they had to go on the run again.

"It's over," Jordan assured her.

Because he said it so calmly, it took her a moment for that to sink in. "Really?"

"Really." He scrubbed his hand over his face and groaned softly in a where-do-I-start kind of way. "Martin Strahan has been arrested for Shelly's murder."

"How did that happen?" she asked, surprised.

"Lt. Rico brought in Pete Mendenhall, Shelly's killer, and the guy made a deal. He'll testify that Strahan hired him, and the D.A. will take the death penalty off the table. Don't worry, though. Pete will spend the rest of his life behind bars."

And Strahan wouldn't be able to terrorize them anymore. "What about Cody?"

"Anderson Walker, Chris and Wally have all confirmed that Cody put this plot together and hired them to help him. First, he wanted to get the formula just to collect the reward because he was riled with me for what he considered a betrayal for selling Sentron. But when he realized the formula didn't exist and that he could potentially earn a fortune if it did, he decided to kidnap you so you'd make it for him."

And now that Cody was dead, he could no longer threaten her. But someone else could.

Someone else who might believe she could create the formula.

Jordan reached out and smoothed his fingers over her bunched up forehead. "The FBI has put out the word that the formula was a sham, that it can't be developed."

The breath rushed out of her. "So, there'll be no more attacks, no more attempts to use Gus to make me co-operate?"

"No more," he promised.

She believed him. Besides, Jordan wouldn't be bringing Gus home unless he was positive that her son would be safe. After all, he'd devoted the last fourteen months of his life to the child.

"What about your company?" she asked. "Will you be able to buy Sentron back from Burke?"

"I don't want it back. To run it right, it would mean more eighty-hour workweeks. I'm thinking I'd like to create something smaller where I can hire some of the agents that Burke fired. Something more specialized. And less dangerous."

Well, that certainly sounded good to her. They'd had enough danger to last them several lifetimes.

"All done," one of the orderlies announced. The men gathered up the now empty boxes that'd held the decorations and went out the door.

Kinley spotted the gifts under the tree. At least a dozen beautifully wrapped boxes.

"For Gus," Jordan volunteered. "I had to do something

while you were in surgery, so I ordered a few things and had them delivered. I also had some presents brought from the estate."

He'd done that so Gus would have a Christmas. Yes, Jordan was indeed thoughtful.

And much more.

She touched his face again so he would turn and make eye contact with her. "You gave up so much to keep Gus safe."

"Yeah. But I got a lot more in return. I wouldn't have you if it weren't for Gus." He paused and kissed her. "Do I have you, Kinley?"

Even with the pain meds making her a little woozy and the dizzying effects of that kiss, she didn't even have to think about her answer. "You have me, Jordan. Any way you want, you have me."

But then she stopped. Rethought that. And considered why he was asking. "Does this have anything to do with me getting shot?"

"In a way."

So this was a pity reaction? She didn't want his pity. She wanted *him*.

"When I came so close to losing you," he explained, "that's when I realized just how important you are to me."

Important? Well, he was more than important to her. "I'm in love with you, Jordan."

Yes, it was a risk. To a confirmed bachelor, an I'm-in-love-with-you confession might send him running, but Kinley didn't want to go through another minute without telling him. That nightmare in the warehouse had taught her that every minute was precious and that life was too short to hold anything back.

He took a deep breath. But didn't run. "You're in love with me," he flatly stated.

Kinley silently groaned and tried to brace herself for a rejection.

"Will you marry me?" Jordan asked.

Because she wasn't expecting to hear that, Kinley had to repeat his question. Several times. However, once the proposal sank in, she didn't have to think about the answer.

"Yes," she said.

Still no reaction from Jordan. But then, she wasn't reacting, either. They were both sitting there, holding their breaths.

Then he shouted, "Yes!" And he pumped his arm in a gesture of victory.

Kinley laughed, partly at seeing him so emotional and partly because she was overwhelmed with joy. "You really want to marry me?" she clarified.

He answered that with a kiss. It was long, hot and so Jordan. It was also the best way to answer because it left no doubt that he had marriage on his mind.

But what else did he have on his mind?

Maybe it was everything she'd recently been through that gave her doubts, but she had to wonder: Was this proposal for Gus's sake?

In part she loved Jordan for everything he'd done for her son, but she didn't want a marriage based on convenience for the sake of a child. She wanted a real marriage.

"Uh-oh," Jordan grumbled. "You're having doubts already."

Unfortunately, yes. But she didn't get a chance to voice them. That's because there was a knock at the door and a split second later, it opened. Kinley heard Gus before she even saw him in the doorway with Elsa.

Nothing would have stopped Kinley from sitting up then and there. She wanted to give Gus a huge Christmas hug.

Elsa stood the boy on the floor, and with a big grin on his face, Gus began to toddle his way toward Jordan, who got off the bed and onto his feet.

"Jor-dad," Gus squealed. But the little boy stopped when he spotted the Christmas tree. His soft brown eyes lit up. "Tris-mas." And he clapped his hands, nearly throwing himself off-balance in the process.

Gus would have made it to those presents, too, if Jordan hadn't scooped him up in his arms. "Those are for later, buddy." And Jordan kissed him on the cheek. "For now, why don't you say hello to your mom."

"I'll give you guys some alone time," Elsa insisted. She stepped back into the hall and shut the door.

Jordan brought Gus to her, and even though those presents were still obviously distracting her son, Gus gave her a sloppy kiss on the forehead. But he got a concerned, curious look on his face when he saw the bandage on her shoulder.

"Boo-boo?" he asked.

"Just a little one," Kinley assured him, smiling.

"Boo-boo," Gus confirmed, and he leaned down and gently kissed the bandage.

Kinley's smile turned to a few tears of joy. Both Jordan and Gus had magical powers when it came to her pain and her mood. Just being there with them made her feel as if everything was right with the world.

Well, almost everything.

There was still that issue of why Jordan had proposed.

Apparently no longer concerned with her boo-boo, Gus pointed to the tree again, and Jordan walked with the boy in that direction. Jordan picked up one of the smaller boxes, carried it and Gus back to her.

"This one is for you," he told Kinley, and he placed the box on the bed beside her.

Surprised, she stared at him. "You found the time to get me a present?"

"I made the time." Jordan stared at her, too.

Gus, however, sprang into action. He yanked off the lid and looked inside. "Ohhhh," he said. "Pretty." He grabbed whatever was inside and brought it out for her to see.

It wasn't just *pretty*. It was beautiful.

Her son dropped the sparkly diamond engagement ring onto her lap and squirmed to get down, probably so he could head back toward the tree and the rest of the presents. Jordan let the child go, and while keeping an eye on him, he slipped the ring onto her finger.

"Well?" Jordan asked. "What about those doubts now?"

Kinley blinked back the tears, and not all of them were of the happy variety. "The ring is perfect," she started. "Gus is perfect. So are you." She shook her head and reached to take off the ring. "But I don't want a marriage of convenience—"

"Good." He caught her hand to stop her from removing the ring. "Because I wouldn't ask you to marry me for Gus's sake."

"You wouldn't?"

"No way. I have an even better reason. I asked you to marry me because I'm in love with you, and I want to spend the rest of my life with you."

Her breath caught, and she hadn't realized just how much she'd wanted to hear him say that. Kinley went into his arms and melted against them. "Then, everything is perfect because I want forever with you, too."

No broken breath for Jordan. But there was a sigh of relief, right before he kissed her blind.

The man definitely had a clever mouth.

Jordan was smiling when he finally eased away from her, and they both automatically checked on Gus. He was ripping the paper from one of the packages. When he got through all the ribbon and paper, he struggled and finally pulled out a red plastic fire engine that was large enough for him to sit on and ride. That's exactly what he did. With him in the driver's seat, he scooted it across the tile floor.

"I think he likes it," Kinley said, knowing that was an understatement. Gus was laughing and obviously enjoying his gift.

Kinley looked up at Jordan. "But I didn't get you anything. There aren't any presents under the tree for you."

He made a show of looking disappointed and then tapped his chin as if in deep thought. "Well, let's see. What can you get me? Not that," he joked and gave her a naughty grin. "Well, not at this moment. You have to heal first. Then we'll get married. And maybe next year, you can give me what I want for Christmas."

"And what would that be?" she asked, moving in for another kiss.

Jordan tightened the hold he had on her and tipped his head to Gus. "You can give me a baby. A brother or sister for Gus."

"A baby?" she questioned.

He nodded and seemed to hold his breath.

She nodded as well. "Jordan, I'd love to have your baby."

And that earned her the best kiss of all.

Kinley had thought the moment was perfect, but she realized it hadn't been. That had made it perfect. Jordan and she weren't just in love and headed for the altar. They were a family—a soon to be growing one—and Kinley couldn't wait for them to begin their lives together.

* * * * *

Get 3 FREE REWARDS!

We'll send you 2 FREE Books plus a FREE Mystery Gift.

FREE Value Over $20

Both the **Romance** and **Suspense** collections feature compelling novels written by many of today's bestselling authors.

YES! Please send me 2 FREE novels from the Essential Romance or Essential Suspense Collection and my FREE gift (gift is worth about $10 retail). After receiving them, if I don't wish to receive any more books, I can return the shipping statement marked "cancel." If I don't cancel, I will receive 4 brand-new novels every month and be billed just $7.49 each in the U.S. or $7.74 each in Canada. That's a savings of at least 17% off the cover price. It's quite a bargain! Shipping and handling is just 50¢ per book in the U.S. and $1.25 per book in Canada.* I understand that accepting the 2 free books and gift places me under no obligation to buy anything. I can always return a shipment and cancel at any time by calling the number below. The free books and gift are mine to keep no matter what I decide.

Choose one: ☐ **Essential Romance**
(194/394 BPA GRNM)

☐ **Essential Suspense**
(191/391 BPA GRNM)

☐ **Or Try Both!**
(194/394 & 191/391 BPA GRQZ)

Name (please print)

Address   Apt. #

City   State/Province   Zip/Postal Code

Email: Please check this box ☐ if you would like to receive newsletters and promotional emails from Harlequin Enterprises ULC and its affiliates. You can unsubscribe anytime.

Mail to the Harlequin Reader Service:
IN U.S.A.: P.O. Box 1341, Buffalo, NY 14240-8531
IN CANADA: P.O. Box 603, Fort Erie, Ontario L2A 5X3

Want to try 2 free books from another series! Call 1-800-873-8635 or visit www.ReaderService.com.

---

*Terms and prices subject to change without notice. Prices do not include sales taxes, which will be charged (if applicable) based on your state or country of residence. Canadian residents will be charged applicable taxes. Offer not valid in Quebec. This offer is limited to one order per household. Books received may not be as shown. Not valid for current subscribers to the Essential Romance or Essential Suspense Collection. All orders subject to approval. Credit or debit balances in a customer's account(s) may be offset by any other outstanding balance owed by or to the customer. Please allow 4 to 6 weeks for delivery. Offer available while quantities last.

Your Privacy—Your information is being collected by Harlequin Enterprises ULC, operating as Harlequin Reader Service. For a complete summary of the information we collect, how we use this information and to whom it is disclosed, please visit our privacy notice located at corporate.harlequin.com/privacy-notice. From time to time we may also exchange your personal information with reputable third parties. If you wish to opt out of this sharing of your personal information, please visit readerservice.com/consumerschoice or call 1-800-873-8635. **Notice to California Residents**—Under California law, you have specific rights to control and access your data. For more information on these rights and how to exercise them, visit corporate.harlequin.com/california-privacy

STRS23

HARLEQUIN
PLUS

Try the best multimedia subscription service for romance readers like you!

Read, Watch and Play.

Experience the easiest way to get the romance content you crave.

Start your **FREE TRIAL** at
<u>www.harlequinplus.com/freetrial</u>.